DEAD HEAT

CAROLINE CARVER

NEW YORK   BOSTON

Warner Books Edition
Copyright © 2003 by Caroline Carver

This Warner Books edition is published by arrangement with Orion, an imprint of the Orion Publishing Group Ltd., Orion House, 5 Upper Saint Martin's Lane, London, England WC2H 9EA.

Mysterious Press
Warner Books

Time Warner Book Group
1271 Avenue of the Americas, New York, NY 10020.
Visit our Web site at www.twbookmark.com.

Printed in the United States of America

First Warner Books Printing: March 2004

10 9 8 7 6 5 4 3 2 1

Library of Congress Cataloging-in-Publication Data

Carver, Caroline.
    Dead heat / Caroline Carver—Warner Books ed.
        p. cm.
    ISBN 0-89296-778-1
        1. Women detectives—Australia—Queensland—Fiction. 2. Survival after airplane accidents, shipwrecks, etc.—Fiction. 3. Wilderness areas—Fiction. 4. Queensland—Fiction. 5. Sabotage—Fiction. I. Title.

PR6103. A78D43 2004
823'.914—dc22   2003065005

In memory of my father

Acknowledgments

My agent is Elizabeth Wright at Darley Andersons; my editor is Jane Wood. Huge thanks to them both; they worked way beyond the call of duty.

Also thanks to my New York agent, Liza Dawson, and my editor at Time Warner, Sara Ann Freed. This Brit author couldn't ask for a better team across the pond.

Special thanks are due to a number of people who helped me as technical advisers: Francis Holborne, Ferretti guru; Micky, Ferretti captain; Colin Heathcote, A21 chum at CabAir; Derek Edwards, also at CabAir; Gary Goodban, rainforest expert; Moley Mitchell and Paul Greensmith, life raft survival pros; Rachel and Simon Walker, medical aces; Dr. Michael Seed, whiz on weapons and all things scientific; Beatrice Law for her expertise on Chinese references. Any errors of fact will be mine.

Grateful thanks to those who acted as critical readers: Tania Harper; George Loizou; Rachel Leyshon; Emma Stamper; Sophie Hutton-Squire; and my anonymous proofreader.

To my mother, as always, for her love, encouragement, and support.

To my friends who inspire, comfort and console, and help answer some strange questions: Meg Gardiner, Sarah Cunich, Bob Child, Tessa Bamford, Ian O'Hearsey, Steve and Amanda Morris, Ali Price, Dominic Cole.

Lastly, mention must be made to my best buddy and co-driver, Caroline Readings, who told me to stop thinking about car rallies and get on with the book.

DEAD HEAT

ONE

The cassowary had died instantly.

A single whack from the hood of the Suzuki broke its neck. One moment the largest and most spectacular animal of the rainforest was crossing the road, the next it was a corpse, a seven-foot hump of sodden black feathers with blood seeping from one open brown eye.

Georgia Parish couldn't believe she had just killed one of the rarest birds in the Wet Tropics. Sure, she'd been driving fast, trying to make it to the aerodrome on time, but in the torrential downpour she hadn't expected to meet any wildlife. She'd assumed all possums, bandicoots, rat-kangaroos, and the like would be tucked up immobile in their dens and nests, sheltering from the secondary storms of Cyclone Tania.

Not this guy, though. Wiping her face of rain, she glanced behind her at the outskirts of the town, the handful of ramshackle weatherboard cottages slumped beneath palm and fig trees, but nobody was about. She wasn't sure whether to be glad of this or not. On the one hand she wanted to apologize; on the other she knew that any resident of Nulgarra would be tempted to knock her flat, especially since she'd just driven past a huge yellow-and-black sign cautioning motorists that cassowaries sometimes cross roads.

Her stomach hollow with guilt, Georgia surveyed the dent above the bull bar, where the bird's head had thumped the hood. I'm sorry, she told the dead cassowary, but I'm very glad of the bull bar or you'd have come straight through the windshield and probably killed me. Not that I'm happy you're dead, but better just one of us than two, don't you think?

She turned her mind to Evie, who had loaned her the Suzuki. Even if Georgia paid for the damage, it would be Evie who would have the hassle of taking it to a body shop, maybe even getting the thing resprayed. Talk about a favor backfiring in her friend's face.

She said a brief prayer for the dead bird. The heavy smell of the rainforest, a place of wet moss and mud and mangroves, coated the back of her tongue. When the sun came out, she knew the temperature would soar, as though the atmosphere had been ignited by a giant gas burner. The air was like a simmering stew and she was glad of the cloud cover.

Back inside her small four-wheel drive, Georgia eased around the carcass. No way was she strong enough to haul the corpse clear of the road. The young male had to weigh at least as much as she did, around 130 pounds, if not more. She set a more sedate pace down the dirt road, her wipers thumping, her senses alert for another encounter with a forest creature.

Two deaths in one day. Not that her grandfather had died today, but he'd been cremated four hours ago. A shiver of foreboding made the hairs stand up on her forearms and she was suddenly glad her mother, Linette, wasn't with her. She would have been clutching the crystal around her neck and pronouncing all sorts of grim portents and fateful connections between the two dead males while Georgia rolled her eyes and tried to change the subject.

Skirting a broken palm on her side of the road, she pondered on her mother's almost unnatural composure at the funeral, until she remembered the huge joint she had rolled in the car on the way to the crematorium.

"Sweet, you've had your brandy," she had said serenely in answer to Georgia's raised eyebrows, "and since you know I don't drink . . ."

Georgia wondered how many mourners had caught the scent of marijuana on their clothes and decided she didn't care. Everyone knew that they'd once lived at the Free Spirit Commune just outside of Nulgarra, and had probably been surprised, maybe even a little disappointed, that the chocolate sponge at the wake was not some colossal hash cookie.

Holding the steering wheel tight as the little four-wheel drive dipped and shuddered over water-filled potholes, she squinted through the rain for the first sign she might be nearing the creek. Just about everyone had told her she'd never make it through, and despite the fact that her mate Bri hadn't been able to guarantee her a seat on his plane to Cairns, she had to try. No way did she want to stay with Mrs. Scutchings another night. Thanks to her mother, she'd been bunked up with her old headmistress over the last few days and, boy, had her patience been tested to the limit. The old bag was about as liberal as a barracuda and went as far as believing that the American tourist killed by a crocodile last season had done it on purpose, to keep potential tourists in Sydney.

"You lot down south," Mrs. Scutchings had said over a breakfast of rubbery fried eggs, "twist all the facts to make Far Northern Queensland look remote as heck and twice as dangerous."

Georgia had remained silent and forced down her solid egg. So far as she was concerned, the newspaper reports were right on the nail. The nearest major city up here wasn't Queensland's capital, Brisbane, 1,200 miles south, but Port Moresby in Papua New Guinea, 450 miles across the water. Driving to Sydney would be the equivalent of driving from New York to Miami. London to Gibraltar. Remote was exactly the right word. And not only were there estuarine "saltie" crocodiles to contend with, but there were sharks, stinging trees, and poisonous spiders. There was even a deadly jellyfish that, with a single sting, could kill an adult within five minutes.

Some days she could hardly believe that her mother had dragged her and her sister, Dawn, out here from Somerset just to be near their grandfather. Yet Georgia could also see she hadn't had much choice. When their father died, killed in a hiking accident in Wales, it fell to their mother to run the New Age shop in Glastonbury. Within weeks they were overdue on their rent and being threatened with eviction, and then the bailiffs began to appear. Hightailing it to the other side of the world must have held enormous appeal.

She could feel the shock of arriving in Nulgarra, aged eight, as if it were yesterday, straight from a frostbitten winter into the sticky heat, where clouds of mosquitoes seemed bent on draining the last drop of blood from her. She recalled those first bewildering twenty-four hours, trying not to cry, missing the snug comfort of their little flat above the shop, the smell of burning incense, the sounds of wind chimes tinkling above the Glastonbury traffic.

She wondered if Glastonbury had changed much since she'd left, because Nulgarra hadn't. The town looked exactly the same as it had ten years ago, along with its residents. God, even Bridie hadn't changed. Her old schoolmate had bounced up to her outside the chapel. "George! I can't believe you haven't cut your hair! Heavens, don't you find it awfully hot? It's so long! And you're still wearing trousers! You always were such a tomboy. You haven't changed a bit!"

Maybe, if she hadn't felt so tired, she could have embraced Bridie and told her she hadn't changed a bit either. As it was, Bridie had managed to make Georgia feel bad-tempered and disagreeable, as always. She possessed that endless cheerfulness Georgia found exhausting, the kind of girl mothers asked to help bake birthday cakes or decorate the tree at Christmas, because she was so pretty and enthusiastic. Georgia didn't get approached to do any of that stuff. She was the kind of girl who got asked to nail the chicken shed back together, or change the oil in the ute.

"Are you married yet?" Bridie asked. "Anyone special in your life? Go on, spill the beans, I won't tell a soul!"

She had made a noncommital gesture and Bridie looked at her pityingly, then added in a more sympathetic tone, "Mr. Right will be along soon, don't you worry. And get some rest, will you, George? You look like you need it."

Which wasn't surprising, since she was tired to the bone—tired from organizing the funeral, tired of the fact her sister wasn't there to help, and most of all tired of being asked if she was married yet. It had been a struggle to find her usual good humor each time she was asked where her other half was. Why in the world did everyone assume she didn't have a life unless she had a man?

Briefly wiping her face—the four-wheel drive Suzuki soft-top leaked like a sieve—Georgia swung the car around the next corner and caught a flash of white through the torrents of rain. Immediately, she slowed. "Cassowary Creek," the sign said, and after an initial jerk of regret at the bird she had killed, Georgia halted the car and gazed glumly at the boiling, soil-capped torrent.

Hell, she thought. It wasn't a creek, it was a goddamn *river*.

How on earth was she going to get out of here? The inland road south, to Cairns, was closed, and the coast route hopeless since the ferry across the Daintree River was shut. The road north led nowhere but to tiny Cooktown, with nothing but storm-tossed ocean to the east and impassable jungle to the west. If she didn't fly, she was well and truly trapped.

Please, God, she prayed, let me get through, let there be a spare seat on Bri's plane. Please get me back to normality. I can't stay with Mrs. Scutchings another night, and if I stay with someone else I know she'll be hurt, and even if she is mad as a cut snake, I wouldn't want that. She's been kind.

A log the width of the Suzuki churned past, creaming the water a muddy brown, and she watched it slam briefly into the opposite bank before the tide snatched it free and hurled it downriver. Should she risk crossing? Or should she return to Nulgarra and spend the next few days sitting in the pub drinking beer and watching geckos climb the walls?

Wearily she replaited her hair, retying it with the black felt scrunchy she'd worn at the funeral. Bridie was right. It was too long, too shaggy. She wondered if cutting it would thin it down or thicken it to a mop. She'd always had long hair. Maybe it was time to chop off her bell-rope, as her boss called it, and risk going short, even change the color.

She wiped the rearview mirror clean of condensation and tried to imagine her too-large jaw and gray eyes topped with a cap of red or black instead of the usual muddy blonde. No chance. It would make her freckles stand out even more. Not for the first time she glared furiously at her reflection, wishing she'd been blessed with a little sprinkle of the things across the saddle of her nose, which might have been attractive, rather than spread all over her face.

Georgia became aware that, way in the distance, a bright blue fissure had cracked the leaden clouds. The break in the weather had arrived as predicted, and she knew that Bri's SunAir flight would be leaving as planned at 2 PM. She had forty-five minutes. The sooner she got to the airfield, the better, in case others were doing the same and turning up in the hope of a ride out of the storm-thrashed area.

With a critical eye, Georgia studied the churning torrent ahead, wishing her grandfather was with her; he would have tackled the creek no problem.

"Georgie," she fancied she could hear him, "you really oughta wade it before you cross. And where you going to aim?" Tom's voice seemed to grow louder the more she stared at the foaming water. "Does the water come above the axles? The engine fan? The body floor?"

"Yes, yes, and yes," she replied. The water looked dangerously deep and the current was quite fast, so she'd have to aim well upstream to go straight across. And she would bet the bottom was sandy, giving her less grip than large, heavy stones, and pitted with bottomless holes made by other vehicles getting stuck. She swallowed, aware her palms had dampened.

Evie had loaned her the four-wheel drive specifically for Cassowary Creek. She'd told Georgia the water level was bound to be high, and not to worry if she flooded the car, it was used to that. She and her trusty Suzuki had crossed the creek loads of times, even when it appeared impassable, so Georgia had better not be a wuss.

She could hear Evie's voice start to override Tom's caution.

"Why'd you think I bought a bloody four-wheel drive in the first place? To sit outside my van and look pretty? Stop buggering about and go, girl!"

Two

Engaging low-ratio, Georgia inched the Suzuki down the muddy slope to the creek. She held her breath as the bank steepened, waiting for the car to slip, but she had full traction right to the bottom and her confidence soared. Evie's little car might not look like much, but it seemed to be up to the job.

Go, girl!

When the Suzuki hit the water it gave an initial jerk, almost in surprise, then the wheels dug in. Her hands tight on the steering wheel, Georgia headed the car upstream, for a point just above the distinctive circular shape of a fan palm the size of a trash can lid. She concentrated on keeping the engine speed high to avoid the back pressure of water drowning the exhaust pipe and stalling the engine.

Despite the battering of water against the car, the shaking and juddering from the current, the Suzuki's wheels were gripping nicely and, amazingly, they were moving steadily forward.

"Always keep your eyes on where you want to go," she heard Tom say. "You look at the trees, you hit the trees. You look at the precipice on the side of the road, you fall into it. *Look at where you want to go.*"

So Georgia fixed her gaze past the clacking wipers and onto the fan palm and the muddy, stone-pecked slide on the opposite bank and kept her foot on the accelerator, her thumbs free of the steering wheel to avoid a sudden twist breaking them. Her shoulders were hunched forward, every inch of her body willing the Suzuki toward the opposite bank.

Now they were in the middle of the creek, at the deepest point, and she was aware that the vehicle was struggling, teetering against the current, its tires slipping. A muddy wave broke over the hood. *The electrics.* Water gushed past. Georgia felt a sudden ghastly pause from the car.

Get a grip, dammit! *Get a grip!*

The Suzuki's hood began to swing downriver. Gritting her teeth, Georgia yanked the steering wheel from side to side, seeking a fresh bite. Water poured through the doors.

She felt the off-side front tire suddenly dig in, then the near-side, and inch by inch, the little four-wheel drive crawled through the swollen, battered creek. The bank was getting closer, and then the front tires were churning on the soft, muddy bank, gripping the stones beneath and hauling the Suzuki out of the river. Georgia let the car scramble up the slope. She purposely didn't change gear in order to avoid breaking traction and spinning the wheels. When she reached the top and was on hard dirt road, she pulled over.

Her hands were trembling as she released low-ratio and pushed the stick back to its normal driving position. The road ahead was littered with potholes, dead leaves, and branches. Tangles of vines, soaked with humidity, hung motionless from the trees, and the air smelled peculiarly bitter and pungent, like freshly dug earth.

More out of habit than in expectation of seeing anything, she checked her side mirror. To her astonishment, she saw a white Ford sedan on the road behind her, heading straight for the creek.

You've got to be kidding, she thought. They'll never make it in that.

Heedless of the rain, Georgia sprang out of the car and belted to the riverbank, waving her arms and shouting, "No! Go back! It's too deep!" But it was too late. The Ford was already a third of the way across.

When it reached the middle of the creek, the sedan paused, much like the Suzuki had. She could see the driver was turning the steering wheel and searching for some grip, but the car was already beginning to float. Slowly, the vehicle's hood swung downriver and within five yards had jammed itself against something underwater. The engine stalled and water rushed through the open windows.

Georgia raced to her car to look for a tow rope, but all the Suzuki had was a standard jack and spare tire. No ropes, no straps, no winch, no high-lift jack.

She turned to see the driver, a tall guy in jeans and sweatshirt, slide quickly through the car window and drop into the creek. The water came up to his thighs. He waded around the sedan and helped his woman passenger open her door against the current and climb out. The woman had to cling on to her companion to avoid being swept away. When she glanced up, even though she was yards away, Georgia could see the relief on her face. Relief she hadn't been swept four miles downriver and into the Coral Sea.

It didn't take the couple long to grab their belongings from the trunk. The man had only a small bag, one of those standard black ones that carry laptop computers, the woman a pint-size backpack and a sodden, new-looking leather fanny pack on her hips.

Georgia slid down the bank and reached out to the woman, who put her hand in hers and let herself be hauled out of the river. Her fingers felt fragile and tiny as mouse bones in Georgia's clasp, her body light as a child's. She was spattered with mud and soaked to the waist, but she was grinning when Georgia swung her clear of the bank and onto firm ground. The man came up behind her.

"You're brilliant," the woman said, wiping rain from her cheeks. She was Chinese, and her face had the delicate prettiness of a young girl, but Georgia reckoned she was more her own age, late twenties. "Thanks so much for helping us."

The man stepped forward. Water streamed from his thick black hair and down his face but he made no attempt to brush it away. "We've a flight to catch," he said, voice curt. No thank-you from him or attempt at small talk. "You okay to take us to SunAir? Nulgarra's aerodrome?"

Oh hell, she thought, I hope they're not on Bri's flight or there may not be room for me. Glumly, she said, "That's where I'm going."

"Thank you, God," said the woman, looking into the sky and exhaling hard. "You're doing great so far. Keep it up."

They introduced themselves. The man, Lee Denham, took the front seat while Suzie Wilson squeezed into the back. Lee must have been thirty, at most. His skin was the color of cashew nuts, and close up she was sure he was mixed-race Chinese. He had a pale scar running up through one eyebrow, another on the edge of his jaw, and she could see the puckered ridge of a larger scar running up the side of his neck into the hair behind his ear. More scars on his knuckles. Wounds like a fighting dog might have, she thought warily. Strong jaw, narrow nose, and a wide mouth she couldn't imagine ever smiling. His features resembled a rock face. His body looked like rock too, broad shoulders and a narrow waist; the build of a triathlete.

If Bridie had been there she'd have been matchmaking like mad, asking him what he did, how much he earned, if he wanted children, but all Georgia said was, "Where are you flying to?"

"Cairns," Lee said, and Georgia's spirits sank. She just had to hope the third person who'd been booked to fly south with Bri couldn't make it.

"And from there?" she asked, wondering if they were on the same connecting flight to Sydney, but Lee just shrugged. Not much of a talker, old Scar Face.

Suzie leaned between them, voice bright with curiosity. "Are you English?" she asked Georgia.

"I'm Australian," she said on a sigh. "Have been for twenty years."

"You sound English."

"So I'm told." Georgia turned to Lee. "What about your car?"

Another shrug. "It's a rental."

"Do you want to borrow my mobile? Tell them what's happened?"

"Nope."

"But you can't just leave it there."

He turned his head to give her a direct stare. He had eyes the color of fresh tar, glistening black, devoid of expression.

Georgia fired up the engine. Just my luck, she thought, to rescue the least friendly man on the planet. Looking in her rearview mirror, she saw Suzie was going through the contents of her damp leather fanny pack.

"Everything okay?" she asked her.

"Yes," Suzie said breathlessly, "you've been great and I—"

She broke off when Lee snapped at her in what sounded like Chinese. Georgia saw Suzie blink rapidly as though she might cry.

So much for a lighthearted journey filled with jokes about submersible cars, Georgia thought, and pulled out. Driving a little way with her left foot on the brakes to dry them out, she set a brisk pace for the aerodrome. With only two miles to go it shouldn't take long, she thought, unless there were any trees across the road.

"You came from Nulgarra?" she asked.

Lee shrugged.

"Suzie? Do you live up here, or were you just visiting?"

In her rearview mirror she saw Suzie glance at Lee before fixing her gaze outside.

"I was here for a funeral," Georgia offered. If that didn't elicit a response she might as well give up. "My grandfather died last week."

"I'm sorry to hear that," said Lee.

She might as well have told him she'd put a blue sock in her white wash and everything had come out gray for all the sympathy in his voice. Next time, she thought mutinously, I won't stop to help you. I'll leave you to bloody walk.

THREE

The one thing about having lived in a small town, where everybody knows everybody, is that no matter how long you've been away, nobody forgets you. Change is slow, and chances are the boy you had a crush on at school is still around, maybe taking tourists big-game fishing or reef-diving, and your best girlfriend is now his wife with three kids and a pool out the back with two utes in the driveway.

So Georgia wasn't surprised that Bri Hutchison was still piloting the SunAir planes, or that his wife, Becky, continued to handle the bookings and office administration and, when the sky got busy during the tourists season, the radio. Seven hundred feet from the airstrip, the SunAir office was surrounded by ginkgos, ferns, and club mosses. Built of unpainted timber, it had a tin-roofed veranda, a dirt parking lot, a single open hangar, and a patch of lawn with a brick barbecue by the edge of the forest.

After giving her a hug, Becky said, "Sorry about Tom, love. We'll miss the old bugger."

"Me too."

"Anyhow, looks like we'll get you out. Some bloke ain't turned up, so you can have his seat. Go for it, love."

Lugging her backpack to the Piper plane, which was parked well back from the rain-puddled runway, she stowed it inside before taking the seat behind the pilot's. Bri greeted her briefly with a smacking kiss on the cheek, then turned back to study the map spread on his lap.

Like Mrs. Scutchings, Bri hadn't changed much in the ten years she'd been away. A few more wrinkles maybe, but he was just as short and square and solid as brick, and still missing his left upper incisor, where the boom of his yacht had hit him all those years ago, when he'd been teaching her and Dawn to sail. Georgia had been eleven and unself-conscious enough to ask why he didn't get a false tooth, to which he'd replied, "You think I ought?"

She'd put her head on one side. "Not unless you mind looking like a pirate."

"Nope."

She had always had a soft spot for Bri. They'd first met in her second term at school, when he'd been dropping off his nephew. She and Dawn had arrived at the school gates, miserably soaked through after a rainstorm. They had forgotten to bring an umbrella, and their satchels and schoolbooks were sodden.

"You walk to school every day?" Bri had asked, frowning.

Dawn and Georgia nodded.

"On your own?"

The sisters nodded again.

"What about your grandfather?"

"He's helping at the bait shop," said Dawn. "They open at—"

"Eight," said Bri. "Yeah. I know."

He had chewed his lower lip, then said, "How about if I pick you up each morning? You're at the commune, right? It'll be no trouble for me, so long as your mum won't mind, and I'll make the airfield in time for the first trips. Joey here could do with the company."

Joey didn't say anything, but the sisters knew he was appalled. His peers in town had been locked in battle with the children from the commune since anyone could remember, and now Joey was going to have to share a car with the enemy! All term Dawn and Georgia teased him mercilessly from the back of Bri's ute, which culminated in Joey leading the townies down the lumpy dirt track into the heart of the commune and its timber cabins and chicken yards and pelting them with mud, destroying their treehouse, and finally dragging the commune kids into the stream and dunking them.

A week later Georgia led an ambush with Dawn and six others, throwing sticky balls of flour mixed with water at the townies, who were on their way to a party. The townies' parents had gone berserk, calling Georgia an uncontrollable little savage, but her mother had never been great on discipline and merely said in that calm tone of hers, "Playing is healthy behavior for children. You'd rather they sat indoors watching TV?"

Georgia had been delighted that the enmity between townies and commune kids had deepened to another level. She loved the freedom of the commune and she had loved fighting for it. The day it closed, three days after her seventeenth birthday, sold to a guy from Brisbane who wanted to develop it into a rainforest health center, was the day her childhood ended.

Bri turned around in the pilot's seat and looked at her critically. "Don't they feed you in the big city?"

"They feed me just fine, Bri."

"You're too bloody skinny," he grumbled. Then, "Getting married soon?"

"Bri, get serious, will you? We've got better things to do than sit and talk about my private life. Like getting me to Cairns for a connecting flight."

"Are you?"

She made an exaggerated groaning sound and banged her head in the palm of her hand in a parody of agony. "Even my mother doesn't give me such a hard time."

"Yeah, well." Bri grinned and shook his head, chuckling. "Someone's got to, young lady, or you'll run wild the rest of your life."

"I don't run wild! I'm very responsible, I'll have you know. I've a full-time job with a very reputable publishing company and a rented house in a very nice part of the city. I have a company car and an expense account." Her chin lifted. "I've even been offered a promotion. National marketing manager. What do you think of that, then?"

He snorted. "Full-time nothing. It's not for you, all that soft city stuff. You need something to get your teeth stuck into. Something you're proud of, that you care about and want to fight for. Like the commune."

Momentarily she was shocked into silence, then she said, voice small, "I tried."

She could feel Lee's and Suzie's gazes on her, but she ignored them.

"You did good," said Bri, voice softening. "Your mum too. You both did real good, but it wasn't to be, was it?"

"No."

Bri reached a hand around the back of his seat and waggled his stubby fingers at her. She gripped his hand briefly. He squeezed back, giving their clasped hands a little shake like he used to, and she could feel the back of her throat close with tears.

"You find something worth fighting for, you call me." He dropped his hand and peered at her over his shoulder. "I'd like to sling a handful of flour patties at some blokes, believe me."

While Bri radioed Becky at Control, she leaned across to Suzie and murmured, "Sorry about that, but we haven't seen each other in a while."

"I think it's nice," she said. "Especially now I know you are *the* Georgia."

"What do you mean, *the*?"

As Suzie's face softened into a smile, Georgia realized she'd done the woman a disservice. She wasn't pretty. She was stunning. Glossy, shoulder-length blue-black hair, slanting almond eyes below fine arched wings of eyebrows, a perfectly formed tiny nose, and a heart-shaped mouth. Her cheekbones could have cut Parmesan.

"I've been flying with Bri the past few years," Suzie said. "Cairns, some days all the way to Brizzy. Long flights, just me and him for hours. I know all about Joey and your battles. Bri never quite knew who to root for, you know. He was torn between family loyalty to his nephew, and admiration for your indomitability."

"I don't know about that," said Georgia ruefully. "I got pasted regularly."

Suzie was laughing. "So I gather."

Georgia sensed Lee watching them from the copilot's seat, but before she could say a word, Bri was offering a headset to Lee. "You fly?"

"Yup."

"Wow. Two pilots," Georgia remarked. "Does this mean we get inflight service?"

Lee leaned around to give her one of his scary stares, but she refused to back down. The more unfriendly he was, the more he got under her skin and the more she wanted to irritate him. She took a good long look at his watch, a Tag Heuer chronograph with a copper dial and fine-brushed steel bracelet, and was reminded of her exboyfriend, Charlie, hankering after a Tag just like it in David Jones's window. Even if she took the promotion she'd never be able to afford a watch like that. She knew it was worth over four thousand bucks.

From the look on Lee's face, suspicious, guarded, she reckoned he was daring her to remark on it.

"Nice watch," she said cheerfully. "Can I get one like that duty free?"

"I doubt your annual expense account would stretch that far," he responded coolly.

Incensed, she was going to tell him about her upcoming Easter bonus, but Bri interrupted, wanting to know what airplanes Lee had flown—pilot bonding, she supposed—and then he started the engine. No chance of sensible talk through the clattering roar that followed. As Bri ran through the pre-takeoff checklist he tapped each instrument with a forefinger, and Georgia settled back, putting Lee's unfriendliness aside and hoping the flight wouldn't be too bumpy.

Through the window she could see Evie's little Suzuki, slumped beneath a dripping African oil palm. She wondered what Evie would say about the fresh dent in her car. She must ring her as soon as she arrived home in Sydney and offer to pay for the damage. Not that Evie would take her money. Local etiquette dictated that if a neighbor or mate was in need, you loaned your chainsaw or mower, your boat, your car, no worries about insurance or getting paid back if you destroyed their property. In fact, all the better if you wrecked what you'd been loaned; it made a good tale to tell down the pub, and you owed them. Big-time.

Finally, Bri taxied the little airplane to the far end of the puddle-dotted dirt runway. Way in the distance Georgia saw a tall figure standing on the SunAir office steps, looking their way. For some reason he looked familiar, but she couldn't think why. Probably another local she'd known as a kid.

"All buckled up?" Bri asked.

Nobody said anything, so Georgia said dutifully, "All buckled up."

The engine note rose as Bri pushed the throttle forward a fraction, then again, and they were buzzing and bouncing and shaking and rattling along the runway. A strip of rubber from the window seal wriggled loose and fell onto Georgia's lap. She tried to push it back into place but it fell off again, so she gave up and put it in the seat pocket, hopping the airplane would stay together for the rough ride south.

As they swooped into the sky, a vision of the dead cassowary filled her mind, the vivid blue of his face spattered by grit from the road, the sturdy legs and great spread toes with their elongated spikes upturned and lifeless, his rudimentary wings of glossy hairlike feathers, reduced to a few long, bare quills, marred and smeared with mud.

If her mother had been there, they would never have flown. She would have taken the death of the great bird as an omen, a sinister and fateful promise.

The cassowary is, after all, flightless.

Four

Georgia was staring at Lee's tattoo when the Piper's engine gave a splutter, but she didn't take any notice. Bri's aircraft always spluttered.

They had been flying about half an hour when Lee took off his sweatshirt, revealing a tight-fitting gray T-shirt with the sleeves stripped off. Smooth-skinned and muscular as he was, the tattoo suited him. A blue Chinese dragon twisted up his biceps, wings unfurled, its tongue forked with flames. It reminded her that she had wanted a tattoo, just after her first organized raid on the townies. Her mother had given her permission to have a tattoo of a rose or a heart, but flatly refused the request for a snake entwined around a dagger.

Miles away, still staring at the snarling dragon, she barely looked up when Lee leaned forward and tapped a dial, checking with Bri. "Fuel pressure," he said.

"Switch fuel tanks," Bri said on a half-yawn. "That'll sort it."

Turning her gaze outside, Georgia could see a river snaking through the carpet of trees, winding east for the Coral Sea, and guessed it might be the Bloomfield. Apparently there was an exquisite luxury hotel nestled in there somewhere, with lagoon pools and swim-up bars, and she peered down, wishing she'd come to Queensland for a pampering holiday with massages and five-star service rather than Tom's funeral.

She was going to miss her grandfather. Not that they'd spent much

time together since she moved to Sydney, but he'd been a rock, someone she could always turn to, and despite her protests, every month
on the dot, he'd sent her a check to help her out with the rent.

Without Tom, she'd probably still be stuck in Nulgarra, working
in the supermarket or on one of the deep-sea fishing boats, but he had
urged her to get away from small-town thinking and taken her to
Sydney, found her a shared rental house, and only when she had a
full-time job did he fly back to his happy retirement in the rainforest.
Mentally, she blew him a kiss. Love you, Tom, she told him. And
thanks.

A little while later Lee said, "Pressure still dropping off."

"What the hell . . ."

The Piper's engine suddenly started to choke.

"I don't believe it . . ." Bri was tapping and scanning dials, and so
was Lee.

The engine gave a single great cough, and died.

Georgia's heart just about leaped into her throat. "Jesus," she said.

With a shuddering bellow the engine started again, but it was running so roughly that she expected it to give out any second. God, oh
God, she thought. Please, make it run smoothly.

Convulsing to catch properly, the engine gave another huge
cough, and at the same time the aircraft lurched violently sideways.
Georgia heard herself let out a ragged gasp. She was gripping the arm-
rests so hard that her knuckles stood out white. Bri's and Lee's voices
were low and urgent.

"Anywhere to land round here?" asked Lee.

"Start looking. We've ten minutes max."

Georgia jerked her head to stare down at the ceaseless canopy of
green way below, broken only by great jagged peaks of rock jutting
through the trees. She couldn't see anything they could land on, not
a road, not even a forest track.

The engine gave two more coughs, then silence. All she could hear
was wind against the fuselage, the whine of the starter. Lee pointed at
a thin streak of what could have been fuel on the windscreen at the
same time as Georgia smelled the faintest trace of smoke.

"Something's burning," she said, astonished by her calm tone. She wanted to scream.

Lee said something in Chinese to Suzie, but Suzie didn't respond. The woman's face was chalk-white and frozen with terror. Much like her own, Georgia guessed. She was already drenched in cold sweat, and when she tried to swallow there was no saliva.

"Over there." Lee was craning his head high as he pointed through the windscreen. "Clearing."

Bri sat up tall and took a look. "Christ, it's small."

"Check wind direction."

"North-northwest."

"Yup. Let's go for it."

Bri swung the airplane to the left and the Piper began to lose height.

"Mayday Mayday Mayday. VH Charlie-Alpha-Tango, Piper PA28, declaring an emergency." Bri sounded remarkably unruffled. "VH Charlie-Alpha-Tango. Seems we're out of juice. We're at four thousand feet, and intend to land . . ." He rattled off the coordinates fast.

Lee swiveled around in his copilot's seat. Voice calm and steady, he said, "We've less than ten minutes before we make an emergency landing. First, I want you to tighten your seat belts, hard as they can go."

Georgia's fingers felt stiff and numb as she did as he said. Adrenaline was pouring through her and she was amazed she wasn't yelling. She didn't want to die. But she was about to. She'd never read a newspaper report that said, "A light aircraft crash-landed in the rainforest yesterday, but everyone survived because they were wearing their seat belts."

Lee swiveled around for a second to check the instruments, then turned back, telling them to remove pens and any sharp objects from their pockets. "As we go down, I'm going to unlock my door, and once we've landed, I'm going to help Suzie out first, then you, Georgia, and lastly Bri. Keep your feet flat on the floor and when I say 'brace,' brace this." He calmly took them through the emergency procedures. "We'll be fine," he added. "I've done loads of these land-ings."

"Crikey," said Bri. "We talking tens or dozens here?"

"Over a hundred."

"Sure glad to have you aboard, mate. You know where the fire ex-tinguisher is?"

Lee bent double and reached under his seat. "Here."

"I'd say we'll make a—"

Bri never finished his sentence because the plane suddenly hit an air pocket. Or that's what Georgia assumed, but she gave a startled yelp when the plane slid violently to the right, its nose dropping dra-matically, making her stomach lurch and her handbag slide across the floor.

"Okay, okay, let's go wide. Use flaps," Lee instructed.

"Use flaps."

The smell of smoke intensified.

"Better get her down fast," said Lee.

"Too right."

Georgia was streaming with sweat. She glanced at Suzie, who im-mediately took her hand in hers and gripped it hard. Georgia's re-sponding grasp was stronger than she could remember gripping anybody. She wondered if she wasn't breaking the fragile mouse bones of Suzie's fingers. They stared at each other. Neither spoke.

"Control?" said Bri. "We've an engine fire . . . We're heading for a clearing just east of Brahmin Point."

The plane's nose continued to drop.

Georgia thought about death. She hoped she would die quickly. Then she thought, What will it feel like to have my head and arms ripped off? She pictured the plane smashing through the trees and metal crashing around her. *Will I feel anything? Will I die straight away?*

She heard Lee alerting the emergency services. Then he turned in his seat and told her and Suzie a rescue chopper was in the air and on its way.

Georgia found she couldn't speak. Her tongue was stiff, her

mouth as dry as tissue paper. She looked at her hand clasping Suzie's. Suzie's skin was pale, almost paper-white; her own was lightly tanned. She saw Suzie was staring at them too, strangers gripping each other in desperate fear.

"We'll get through this okay," Lee said firmly. "Remember, stay down, and only get out when we've come to a complete stop."

Suzie suddenly gave Georgia's hand a hard shake, forcing her to look at her. Her expression revealed her terror. Suzie worked her mouth, then leaned across and said unsteadily, "If I don't make it . . ." She touched the fanny pack settled on her hips. "Please, give this to my brother. It is very important. Please."

Georgia managed a nod.

"Nobody else," Suzie added, eyes pleading before they flickered to Lee, then back. "Please. Promise me."

Georgia nodded again and glanced at her own handbag on the floor. She couldn't think who she could ask Suzie to give it to if she didn't make it herself.

She became aware that the plane had leveled out a little, and that its sickening angle to the right had lessened. Or perhaps it was just wishful thinking. She didn't know. She felt as though her brain was shutting down. Nothing seemed real. Suzie was crying silently, tears streaming down her face.

The plane pitched and lurched violently. She didn't dare look outside. She was breathing fast, smoke in her mouth.

She could hear Bri talking to Control. Talking to Lee. Both men's voices calm. She could feel the plane vibrating, hear the sound of wind on the wings and fuselage, air whistling through a tiny crack in the window.

She had no concept of time, whether seconds were passing, or minutes. She tried to think of her mother, but her mind was blank. She turned her thoughts to Tom, to no better effect. All she could think, as the plane plunged downward, was, Please God, don't let me die. Please, don't let me die.

"Control," said Bri. "Okay, we've passed Rattlesnake Rock. Coming over Timbarra River."

Brief silence.

"Bri? Throttle?"

"Closed."

"Fuel?"

"Off."

"Fuel pump."

"Off."

"Magnetos."

"Off."

"Door . . . unlocked. Battery master, alternator?"

"Off."

She risked a quick glance outside, seeing stands of kauri pines separated by sharp outcrops of rock, feeling the plane trembling, then hearing Lee's yell: "Brace position!"

Petrified, Georgia's gaze was fixed on the solid mass of dense foliage approaching fast.

"Stay down!" shouted Lee.

She ducked her head to her knees and put her arms over her head, hearing Bri's sudden pleading; "Help me make it, help me, help me."

"Stay down! Brace! Brace! This is going to be rough!"

She squeezed her eyes shut.

FIVE

Georgia heard metal tearing, a horrific sound, like tons of rocks crashing onto an industrial-strength aluminum roof, a noise louder than she'd ever heard before. Branches, ferns, dirt clods, and rocks crashed against the windscreen. She felt the ground stripping the plane's underbelly. *My feet might be torn off.* She hurriedly raised her legs.

The plane tumbled and then rolled onto its left side. Objects flew at her: headsets, rocks and sticks, fragments of metal she couldn't identify.

As the left wing gouged branches and ferns, from the front of the plane came a man's scream. Gradually the plane slowed its endless skid against the rocks and earth and came to rest in front of a giant strangler fig tree. Dust and debris settled over the aircraft.

Georgia lay there, blinking slowly and feeling as though she had just awoken. She must have briefly lost consciousness. Her ears were buzzing. She couldn't hear a thing. Nothing at all. The frogs and insects and birds had been shocked into silence.

She became aware she was breathing. In. Out. Slowly and calmly, she was breathing. Georgia continued to breathe for what felt like hours. A tiny trickle of fear seeped into her brain, which deepened as her senses awakened. She could smell smoke, the cloying scent of engine oil. Her brain kick-started as if somebody had turned an ignition key.

I think I'm alive.

She raised her head, and a shock of intense pain rocketed from the fingers in her left hand and up her arm into her shoulder. She looked at her hand in amazement. Blood was pouring from a huge gash across her palm and dripping from her fingers. She wanted to wrap something around her hand, a bandage to stem the bleeding. She looked up and saw the shattered shell of the plane, wires and cables poking out at odd angles, metal mangled and torn. She could see Bri's form slumped in front. Suzie was nowhere to be seen. Nor Lee.

Gray-black smoke swirled all around. Where the starboard wing had been was now a gaping hole, and through it she could see feathery grasses and a broken ribbonwood plant. The daylight outside seemed incongruous and unreal. Somehow she'd expected it to be black.

She was coughing against the bitter stench of burning plastic and fumbled at her seat belt, snapped it free, and pushed herself upright, but something held her back. Her hair. Her plait was caught. She tried to twist around, to tug it clear, but it held her fast.

The smell of burning intensified and a cloud of black smoke belched through the fuselage. The next instant there was a dull *whump,* like a gas fire being lit, but louder. A burst of flame shot from the engine cowling. *Whump.*

A chunk of fractured metal crashed past and a great tongue of flame licked through the shattered windscreen. She struggled furiously to release herself, the awful realization that she was about to be burned to death filling her mind.

With all her strength she yanked against the fuselage pinning her hair. Suddenly Lee appeared, and she was yelling, "Help me! Help me!" but he didn't seem to hear. The tongue of flame had turned into a crackling, roaring column that drowned out her voice. He ducked down to his right and then she saw that he was holding a black, wickedly curved knife. He began yanking her hair, pulling and tugging, and all at once, miraculously, she was free.

"Go, go *go*!" he yelled.

He had her by the scruff of her T-shirt, her right elbow, and was hauling her with him toward the fire. Flames licked at her skin as she scrambled after him, and suddenly they were outside. She nearly wept in relief. Lee dragged her clear of the flames. He dropped his hands from her and she fell to her knees. She saw he was turning, spinning back for the plane. "I'll get Bri!" he shouted over his shoulder. He had a cut above his left eye and his left ear was pouring blood. "You go to Suzie!"

Shaking, disoriented, Georgia looked around. Over piles of shattered metal she saw they were in a long, granite-topped clearing surrounded by tall trees covered in vines and lichens. She looked back to the airplane. The cockpit was belching fire. Grasses and dead leaves were burning around the plane. Distantly she took in the way the plane rested on its belly, and realized the undercarriage had been torn away. A deep groove was behind the plane, where it had plowed through the rainforest floor. There were scratches in the rocks, and a dead crow lying beside part of a propeller blade. Unable to comprehend what had happened, she knelt in the chaos, panic mixed with incredulity.

She heard a woman's plea. It came from the treeline to her right. Suzie's voice shook her to her feet and she made her way across the forest floor to where Suzie lay on her back.

Trembling and bleeding, Georgia folded to her knees. "Hi." Her voice was scratchy from smoke.

Suzie turned her head to look at Georgia. Her face was streaked with blood and tears. "Where's Lee?" she whispered.

"He's getting Bri," she said. "But until he comes, I'll look after you."

Using her good hand, she gently brushed the woman's hair off her face. Suzie had a deep gash above her right eye, which was bleeding heavily, but what worried Georgia was the quantity of blood soaking her shirt. Never having done a first aid course, she was unsure what to do and settled for holding Suzie's hand. It was cold. Not a good sign. She looked around for something to cover her, but all she could see were ferns and palms, shredded, snapped, and crushed, and a mangled mass of metal spilling black into the sky.

Whump.

A wall of flame was now roaring through the shattered wreckage of the Piper. The flames were so fierce that she could feel the heat where she knelt. She could see Lee hauling Bri away from the plane, staggering slightly . . .

To her horror, she realized Bri was on fire. Engulfed in flames from the waist down, he was tearing at his clothes. Lee pushed Bri to the ground, yelling. He picked up handfuls of wet mud and slapped them against Bri's burning trousers.

Georgia rushed for them.

"Roll to the ground!" Lee yelled. "Roll! Roll!"

Georgia made to slap at the flames but Lee pushed her aside, flinging himself across Bri and rolling with him, smothering the flames with his body and the damp mulch of the forest floor. Georgia thought, He's fine, the fire's out, Bri will be fine. Then she took in his feet. His boots had melted into his skin. The backs of his legs were a strange white color, like the dead flesh of a swordfish steak.

For a second she thought he couldn't have survived, but then he croaked, "Am I dead yet?"

"Just a little sunburned," Lee said.

"Sunburned?" Bri said. "You mean I forgot the factor five thousand?"

Georgia didn't know then that a victim may suffer severe burns yet be able to talk and walk, albeit only for a short while, because when the nerve endings were burned, the pain died. She thought that if Bri was coherent, he'd be okay, even if his legs were a mess.

Lee rose to his knees. His shirt was charred and his hands bleeding. "I'll take care of Bri," he said. He didn't look at her. "You go to Suzie. Talk to her."

She walked unsteadily back to Suzie and knelt at her side. The woman gave a shuddering cough, then another. Blood dribbled from the corners of her mouth. Fear crawling through her, Georgia called out to Lee, and he held a hand over his shoulder with two fingers extended, which she assumed meant: Wait two minutes.

"I'm cold, Georgia," Suzie murmured. "Really cold."

"It's the shock. It makes you feel cold. I'm not exactly warm myself. I'm still shaking."

"I think I'm dying."

George looked into Suzie's eyes. They were deeply frightened.

"I don't want to die. Not yet."

"You're not dying," said Georgia firmly, forcing down her own fright and concentrating on making her voice steady. "You're in shock, that's all. Before you know it, helicopters and paramedics will be here and flying you out. You are *not dying*."

Suzie began to shiver. "I'm sorry. Oh, Dutch. Please. I'm so *cold*."

Georgia yelled to Lee. This time he looked around, and she could see the regret on his face. He shook his head, mouthing, "Sorry."

Her skin tightened. Oh my God. He knows Suzie is dying. That's why he asked me to talk to her. So she wouldn't be alone. Georgia looked into the elfin face and felt her throat close up. She was so pretty, so *young*.

"Georgia," Suzie whispered. "Help me."

"Sure, anything I can—"

"My . . . bag? Promise?"

"To give it to your brother, should anything—"

"Now." Her voice was choked. "Take. Now."

"No, Suzie, I'll do it later."

With a monumental effort, Suzie made to lift herself up and free the fanny pack from her hips, but she fell back with a long, agonized groan and closed her eyes. Horrified, Georgia saw that the curd of blood on her shirt had thickened and turned the color of tar.

When Suzie struggled to raise herself again, Georgia relented quickly. "Okay, okay. I'll get it. Don't move, I'll get it now."

Fingers trembling, she snapped open the plastic buckle and, as gently as she could, eased the strap free. The pack's stiff new leather was sticky with blood, but Georgia turned her mind from that as she lengthened the strap before clipping it around her own waist.

"I'm wearing it, okay? I'll give it back to you soon as you're in the hospital. I swear I'll look after it."

Suzie gave another groan, a sound of agony so deep that Georgia started sweating and longed for her to lose consciousness.

"Cold," Suzie moaned. "Dutch, I'm cold."

Swiveling the fanny pack to her right hip, Georgia lay beside Suzie on the wet mire of decaying leaves and carefully nestled against her, hoping her meager body warmth might help. She could feel Suzie's blood seeping into her own clothes, warm and viscous, and through the pervasive smell of smoke she detected the faint perfume of fresh, bright jasmine on her skin.

"Wish I was warmer," Georgia murmured. "Or had a hot water bottle for you."

Suzie gave a soft hiccup, then her breathing became more labored. Blood bubbled through her nostrils. Georgia felt her heart constrict. Please, no, she prayed. Not this pretty young woman, please God, no.

"Dutch." It was a gasp more than a word.

"Hang in there, Suzie . . ."

Suzie trembled in her arms. "Want. Dutch."

"He's coming. Dutch is coming right now. You'll be fine, Suzie, I promise . . ."

The slender body gave a shudder.

"Suzie, you are *not dying*. You're so pretty, so lovely, don't give up, *please*, Suzie . . ."

The shuddering increased. Georgia held her breath, willing the young woman to keep breathing, wanting to lessen the tension in Suzie's body, fill her with warmth, life . . .

Suzie's feet suddenly drummed on the ground, then stopped. Her body softened against Georgia's, went limp.

Lying on the swamp of rainforest floor, with Suzie's fragile body warm against her, Georgia wept.

————

She was still crying when Lee came to her. He gently extracted her embrace from Suzie's and helped her to her feet. Only then was she aware of the drone of light aircraft and the distinctive clatter of a helicopter. Lee glanced into the sky, then between Suzie and Georgia. A question stood in his face.

"She asked for you," Georgia said. "And someone called Dutch. I didn't know who Dutch was so I just held her. Tried to comfort her."

He glanced at the blood-soaked fanny pack around her waist and frowned. "That's Suzie's?"

"She asked me to give it to her brother."

The distinctive buzz of rotor blades was loud now, but when she glanced up all she could see were towering trees and gray sky.

"Georgia," he said, "let me have the bag. I'll give it to her brother."

She took a step back. "I'll do it. She asked me."

He rubbed his face and left a smear of blood on his cheek. "That's kind of you, but there's no need."

"Sorry," she said. Her tone wasn't apologetic.

Lee briefly studied her face and seemed to come to a decision. "Okay, but can I just check—"

His words were drowned by a helicopter swooping over them, and he had to shout to make himself heard above the rotors.

"You know where her brother lives?"

Squinting against the downdraft and the swirling debris of twigs, leaves, and charcoal, Georgia shook her head. He gestured at the fanny pack, indicating that she would have to check inside for Suzie's brother's address, so why not do it now, while he was there?

Before she could change her mind, she unclipped the pack from her waist, unzipped it, and peeled back the hard leather lid, sheltering it from the helicopter's blast. Air tickets. What looked to be a Chinese passport. Purse. Two lipsticks, house keys, car keys, two pens, a credit card receipt for petrol.

The helicopter was thundering downward and Georgia narrowed her eyes into slits to prevent them filling with lumps of ash.

Lee was squinting too as he stepped close and lifted the lipsticks and pens to peer at the bottom of the bag, which Georgia held. He opened the inside zipper and pulled out a handkerchief and what looked like a car parking card before stuffing them back. He checked the purse and flicked through Suzie's passport. Out of the corner of her eye she could see a man in fluorescent yellow charging for the prone figure that was Bri, but Lee's focus remained on the fanny pack.

At last he stepped back, rubbing an ash-darkened arm across his face, frowning. Perplexed, Georgia turned away from him and zipped the pack closed. Then she was staring at the helicopter.

Oh my God, she thought, to get out of here I'm going to have to fly again.

Six

"My name's Greg," said the paramedic in the helicopter.

Another man said, "Georgia, we're going to give you a shot of morphine now to help the pain in your hand."

She registered the tiny prick of a needle in her upper arm, and then they were airborne, roaring into the sky, and Greg was talking to her, holding her good hand, while the other man bent over Bri. Suzie's body lay on the metal floor of the chopper in a body bag. Lee sat opposite, holding a giant pad of cotton wool to his torn ear, staring blankly past her shoulder, blood running from the cotton pad and down his neck, onto his shoulder, and she wanted to ask him if he was okay, but she felt disconnected, peculiar, and found herself toppling sideways. Greg's arms caught and held her, and he was telling her she was fine, she was okay. He felt so solid and warm and safe, like Tom, but Tom wasn't here anymore, never would be. Then they were landing—they were here already?—and the ambulance was wailing and Greg was still holding her hand and Lee was still opposite. Then suddenly they were at a hospital and at last it was quiet.

Georgia sat on a worn beige plastic-covered chair in hospital reception, waiting her turn with the doctor. The receptionist, an overweight, red-faced nurse with a badge saying her name was Jill Hodges, had sat with her for a while, talking quietly about everyday things, fetching her a glass of water when she asked, but now she was alone. The little hospital needed every qualified medic to help with Bri.

The door was open to the street and she could see it was raining. The dirt out front was pulverized into mud. Water dripped steadily into the two tin buckets in front of the reception counter. It felt weird being back in Nulgarra, having left just this morning. She had expected to be hurtled to Cairns, but the air-rescue services had taken one look at Bri and brought them to the nearest medical help, which had turned out to be the Douglas Mason Hospital on the corner of Upolu and Ocean Roads, Nulgarra.

She'd been twelve the last time she was in this hospital. Cyclone Nicola. A sheet of galvanized iron had come loose on the chicken shed and was beating and hammering in the wind like a mad thing, the iron tearing slowly apart. Up a ladder, she'd been trying to nail it back into place when it ripped upward and sliced her arm open. The drive to the hospital had been scary. A massive branch had missed their ancient ute by inches, and all three of them had ended up staying in town for the night. When they returned, the sheet of iron was lying on top of a bunch of ferns and the chickens were huddled miserably on their soaked bedding.

Fingering the small white ridge of scar tissue on her right forearm, Georgia heard a crash of thunder. She glanced up and pulled the blanket closer around her shoulders. It was muggy, the temperature around the low nineties or so, but Georgia wanted the sensation of comfort. She wondered if Lee was okay. After Bri had been rushed in, a doctor had given Georgia and Lee a quick once-over, and given immediate priority to Lee.

Funny how she'd initially thought Lee unfriendly and cold. Talk about getting the man completely wrong. He'd been incredibly brave, talking to them calmly as they went down, then helping them all out of the burning aircraft, using his body to smother Bri's flames. He'd certainly come good when the chips were down.

She heard the fly screen crash shut beside her, then a female voice said, "Georgia Parish?"

A tall woman with tangled black hair, frizzy in the humidity, was holding her hand out. "God, sorry," the woman said, snatching her hand back, even though it was Georgia's left hand that was injured. "You're hurt. I'm India Kane."

Georgia frowned. The name was familiar.

"From the *Sydney Morning Herald*."

Surprised, Georgia stared at her. India Kane was well-known for her national and international exposés. What she was doing here was anyone's guess, but somehow Georgia didn't think it would be to investigate the famously flexible drinking hours at Nulgarra's National Hotel.

"Thought I'd better be up-front about it." India Kane smiled, and her deep brown eyes grew warm. "You've got a problem talking to a journo?"

Georgia shook her head more out of politeness than honesty.

"I heard what happened. About your plane. And Bri Hutchison." The reporter grimaced. "Jesus. Tough call being injured like that."

Georgia watched the rain in the street, picturing Bri and his sturdy brick shape striding for the harbor and his yacht. A truck splashed past. She watched it swing right into Ocean Road and disappear. Opposite, two Aboriginal women in baggy cotton dresses were sharing an umbrella. They were barefoot, spattered with mud and rain up to their knees.

India pulled a crumpled pack of Marlboros from her jeans pocket and offered them. Shaking her head, Georgia watched the reporter go to stand by the open door and light up. "Do you live here?"

Georgia shook her head again.

India looked at the lightly falling rain as she exhaled a stream of smoke outside. "Not enchanted with our rainforested north?"

"Visiting from Sydney," she managed. "Funeral."

"Shit," the reporter said. "I'm sorry."

Georgia bent her head, not wanting to talk. Her body was aching and she felt nauseous.

"Georgia, do you know anything about the flight plan?" India Kane asked.

She didn't bother responding. She couldn't think of any sort of reply. Didn't care to.

"Georgia?" the reporter said again, and at the woman's insistent tone, Georgia looked up. India was studying her. "Your name wasn't on it. The flight plan. I was just wondering if you knew why, that's all."

"A bloke didn't turn up," she said. "I took his place."

"Hmm. I see. A man called Ronnie Chen was down to fly . . . And it's a strange thing, but his body has just been found washed up on Kee Beach. They reckon he's been dead a couple of days. Murdered. He had a bullet hole in the back of his head."

Blankly, Georgia repeated, "Murdered?"

"Yeah. And you took his seat on Bri's plane."

"What does that have to do with me?"

"I'm just checking things out. It's what I do for a living."

Unable to make sense of it through the throbbing of her body, Georgia gazed at a laminated poster of the lymphatic system pinned up behind the reception counter.

"You okay for money?" India suddenly asked, then added, "Oh, you've got your fanny pack. Good on you."

Georgia touched Suzie's bag. The blood on it had now dried, and if she didn't know it was a fanny pack, she'd think she had a plank of wood at her waist, it was so stiff. She hadn't given any thought to money. Hell. Her handbag had been incinerated along with all her credit cards. Was Annie around to help her out? Or had her housemate left for her Hong Kong holiday already?

"If you need somewhere to stay," India said, "I've got a spare bed up here. As well as the best view in town."

"I'll manage, thanks," Georgia said. Her mind was now taken up with the problem of finding some money. Her mother was staying with friends out of town and she couldn't for the life of her remember their name. Her boss would loan her some cash, though. She'd ring Maggie.

"You're worried I'll extract my pound of flesh later." India sighed audibly along with a stream of cigarette smoke. "How about if my paper pays? Say if we did a story on how you overcame your phobia of flying again, or—"

"It's okay, honestly," Georgia said. "I'm going to ring a friend. I only need enough for the odd sandwich and a couple of taxis. My air tickets are still valid, or so I've been told."

India blinked. "You lost your money?"

Georgia gave a nod.

"Look, don't worry about hassling your friend. Why don't we travel down to Sydney together. You really want to fly? Or shall we drive?"

Georgia jerked her head to stare at the reporter. "You'd drive with me all the way to Sydney?"

India grinned. "It's only fifteen hundred miles or so, and since I don't mind a bit of open road . . ."

Both of them flinched when the door banged open and a man said, "Georgia. I'm Dr. Ophir. Sorry for the wait, we've been trying to stabilize Bri, but if you wouldn't mind . . ."

The man wore a white coat and his face was anxious, his hands spread wide. He took in India Kane, then halted. His expression turned hard.

"Miz Kane. I thought I already—"

India Kane flicked her cigarette stub behind her and onto the rain-drenched concrete path. "I was just going." Delving into her bag, she pulled out a card, gave it to Georgia.

"Call me on my mobile," she said. "I've got to be elsewhere tonight, but let's meet tomorrow."

"Mobiles work up here?"

"Yeah, I was surprised too. Some new mast went up around Butchers Hill."

Turning India's card in her hand, Georgia wondered if the new mast meant Far Northern Queensland was at last catching up with the rest of the world.

"Anyway, ring me, Georgia. I'll give you a lift to the airfield tomorrow, if you like, and we'll decide then whether we'll fly or just keep heading south until we hit Sydney. And if you change your mind, let's share a bottle of wine sometime anyway."

––––––––––

Dr. Ophir checked Georgia over minutely, pausing at a circular white scar on her right arm. "What happened there?"

"Tropical ulcer."

"Went mighty deep."

The ulcer had smelled like flyblown meat, she recalled, and her mother had turned white as milk when she'd removed the bandage.

"Whatever is this stuff?" Linette had asked as she gently bathed away a mass of brown-gray fibers from the pus-fouled wound.

"A poultice," Georgia had admitted.

Linette had given the nurse a lecture that made her flush bright red with a combination of anger and remorse. "But you told us to use natural remedies—"

"Not for a streptococcus infection," Linette was horrified. "Put her on antibiotics immediately!"

Dr. Ophir gave Georgia some lidocaine, ringing a block of local anesthetic around her wrist, then carefully washing the gash in her left palm with a saline solution before stitching. She didn't watch, concentrated instead on looking through the little window overlooking the town's main drag. Nulgarra, sleepy ocean-rimmed backwater, where tourists didn't stay long. By the time they'd gotten this far north they'd already visited Cape Tribulation and the Daintree, the largest surviving tract of tropical lowland forest in Australia, and even in the peak season, from May to November, when a lot of Aussies headed here to escape their winter down south, the town wasn't exactly a hive of activity.

It was March now, seriously low season. Through the sprawling fig trees splitting the sidewalks she could see that the bait shop where Tom used to work was shut, along with the dive store and the office that sold tickets to Port Douglas and the reef, but Price's Supermarket was open, along with Mick's Café, famous for its all-day brekky and deep-fried oysters. She'd seen Mick shut up shop only once, and even then it had only been for two days when his mum had died, because the second the news got out, the town rallied around. Sheryl, the local attorney's wife, had donned Mick's huge grease-stained pinafore, her brother the vats of oil, and between them they'd kept the café going. Sure, the sausages were underdone, the oysters burned into circular cinders like lumps of coal, but nobody cared. They were doing their bit. Doing what neighbors were supposed to do.

As Dr. Ophir stitched, Georgia couldn't feel anything through the anesthetic, just the sensation of pulling and tugging. She watched a bare-chested man the color of tea walking down Ocean Street. He had a fishing box and rod in one hand, a big cooler in the other, and her breath caught. She knew he was heading for the mouth of the Parunga River, where Tom used to love fishing for flathead and trevally just after a storm. This time of year was the best angling, when the streams were full and fish movement at its greatest. If Tom were alive, he'd be out there fishing too.

Distantly she wondered what would happen to her grandfather's little fibro house now that he was dead. Her mother would probably sell it and take the proceeds back to Byron Bay with her. At least now her mum would have some money in her bank account, so long as she didn't give it away to one of her charity cases, that was. Not for the first time, Georgia wondered at her mother's astonishingly care-free attitude to life. At fifty-one, her mother had no pension, no su-perannuation, no savings. She lived in a rented caravan at the far end of a huge caravan park in Byron Bay, just south of Brisbane, where she drew up astrological charts for sixty bucks a throw, and read for-tunes for twenty. She sold the odd crystal at the local market and col-lected her monthly state benefit check, but some days she had no money, not even a dollar-twenty for a liter of milk. It never seemed to bother her. Inheriting Tom's house wouldn't change her mother's life, but it would help stop Georgia worrying.

The doctor finished stitching. "There's no need for you to be in overnight. Are you okay to stay with someone in town? It's all arranged, and if you have any difficulty, they can bring you straight back here." He paused and gave her a smile. "But I doubt that'll be necessary. You're in excellent shape, considering."

"Where's Lee?"

"He left after I'd sorted him." Before she could say anything, he added, "He didn't leave an address, if that's what you're asking."

"Is he okay?"

Dr. Ophir nodded.

"Can I see Bri?"

He shook his head. "Why don't you come tomorrow?"

"Do you know who I'll be staying with?"

"Mrs. Scutchings is waiting outside. She said she'd put Lee up as well, if he needs a bed."

Georgia gazed at her mud-caked deck shoes, too drained to protest.

SEVEN

Armed with a roll of gauze bandage and a tube of antiseptic cream, Georgia watched Mrs. Scutchings march into the hospital, sweep her arctic gaze over the rapidly filling buckets, and bark, "The roof should have been fixed before the wet."

Irritated, Nurse Hodges tucked the phone beneath her plump chin and glanced up, but Mrs. Scutchings already had hold of Georgia's elbow and was marching her down the muddy path toward an ancient, rusting white Honda, which was double-parked beside an ambulance.

With a ghastly rattle, the Honda started, its wipers making screeching sounds on each downward arc. Mrs. Scutchings jammed the stick into gear and drove down Ocean Road, past Price's Supermarket, the National Hotel, Mick's Café, and a Bendigo Community Bank.

There was a new sign outside the park and adventure playground: "Welcome to Nulgarra. Population 1,800. Enjoy Your Stay."

As if anyone would bother staying in Nulgarra with Port Douglas on the other side of the Daintree. Port Douglas had boutique hotels, motels, countless pubs and cocktail bars, a yacht club, a marina filled with millions of dollars' worth of oceangoing yachts, and supermarkets that never closed their doors. If their mother had taken them to Port Douglas instead of Nulgarra, Georgia wondered whether her sister would have stayed instead of hightailing it to Vancouver, away from the relentless humidity and hordes of insects. Maybe, she thought. Maybe not.

Mrs. Scutchings jabbed the brakes as they approached the harbor, preparing for the sharp, right-hand bend at the end of Ocean Road, and Georgia looked left, hoping to catch a glimpse of Three Mile Beach through the mangroves, but instead her gaze was riveted to the mega-yacht moored in deep water at the end of the southern pontoon.

Instantly she was back at Tom's funeral, looking at the vines creeping across the roof of Nulgarra's crematorium and listening to heated gossip all around her. She felt a debt of gratitude to the boat, which had enabled her to distract those who pressed her about her marital status.

"You hitched yet?" asked some guy in his fifties, wearing an ill-fitting suit and an aggressive expression.

She'd said, "You seen that boat in the harbor?"

"It belongs to some gangster," the man said in an authoritative tone, knowing exactly which boat she meant.

"A Triad," another man added firmly, as though he'd met the Triad personally.

Then Bridie piped up, almost breathless with excitement. "I've heard it's got gold fittings in the bathrooms and bidets in every one!"

Considering some folk in Nulgarra didn't even have an inside toilet, just the dunny out the back of the house, Georgia had bet Bridie's rose-dotted knickers that the bidets on the boat would be the only ones in town.

As Mrs. Scutchings rocketed past the Shipshape Chandlery, Georgia gazed at the gleaming white monster dwarfing its neighbors. Who owned the thing? How much had it cost? Squillions, no doubt. Just filling the fuel tanks had to cost over five thousand bucks, and she guessed the mooring fees were three times her annual rent.

She studied the large saloon window shaped like an almond and reckoned she could probably fit her whole house inside the one room. No doubt it would be equipped with all modern conveniences, full air-conditioning, a bridge with an array of dials and dozens of satellite phones. Global Positioning System, radar, compass, depth monitor, perimeter monitor, and probably a video to oversee the engines. It was seriously over the top, and seriously out of place.

"Unreal," murmured Georgia.

Mrs. Scutchings swung her head around. "Oh, that. Hideous. Just hideous. The sooner we get rid of it the better. Word going round town says it belongs to some Chinese gangster, but nobody really knows as such and it's racking up mooring costs like you wouldn't believe. The harbormaster, Pete Dunning—he'll be new to you—has his lip well and truly buttoned, believe you me."

"Surely somebody must have seen it being moored and the crew disembark?"

"It turned up during the night a couple of days back, before the storm hit. Whole town was asleep."

With a little lurch Georgia recalled India Kane and her questions about the man whose body had been found on nearby Kee Beach, with a bullet in the back of his head, who should have been on the plane. What was his name? Chen. Ronnie Chen.

"What's with the police boats?" she asked. "Are they anything to do with it?"

"Oh, no. They'll be dealing with illegal immigrants trying to sneak in by boat. The police are trying to intercept them before they land but they're having the very devil of a job. They've missed two lots this month, boats *heaving* with Afghans, Iraqis, the whole Middle East from the sound of it. How they managed to miss the last lot is anyone's guess, but believe you me, our boys in blue are not happy bunnies. There's talk of someone tipping the immigrants off. If I could get my hands on whoever it is . . ." Mrs. Scutchings gave a gusting sigh. "You'd think they'd learn they're not wanted, wouldn't you, but no, they just keep on coming. Greedy bunch of freeloaders, the lot of them."

Georgia studied the side of Mrs. Scutchings's face. The woman had a mole the size of a dung-beetle on her chin and Georgia wondered why she'd never had it removed. "But you're an immigrant."

"I didn't turn up expecting red-carpet treatment, free food and lodging."

"Er, with all due respect," Georgia said, casual tone belying the tiny prickles of defensiveness brushing over her skin, "you weren't a refugee."

"They shouldn't come here." Mrs. Scutchings's nostrils flared wide. "Most of them don't even speak *English,* for goodness' sake. I'll have you know I'm behind the government one hundred percent. Three billion dollars to keep out asylum seekers? Good on them. We don't want any more. The instant they plant their grubby little feet on our land they should be sent packing to where they came from."

Bloody hell, was the woman rabid or what? If she went on like that in Sydney she'd be lynched. Just about everyone Georgia knew lived in fear of being sexist or ageist, and after their ancestors' appalling treatment of the Aborigines, the average Australian's greatest horror was being racist.

Aside from Mrs. Scutchings, obviously.

"But what about the Mighty Chopstick?" Georgia flapped a feeble hand behind her. She didn't have the energy for a full-blown argument, but she couldn't not defend half the population of Australia. "Without Timothy Wu, we wouldn't have a Chinese restaurant anywhere in the area, and I'll bet a hundred bucks Dr. Ophir at the hospital is an immigrant too. This country is built by immigrants."

They passed a rusting sign advertising fishing rods for hire. Just after the school's pedestrian crossing, Mrs. Scutchings swung the Honda right and accelerated along Jacaranda Road.

Georgia's old headmistress said darkly, "We're being overrun with the dregs of the world; you name it, they're all turning up for a free feed. We don't want spongers. Not here."

———————

Three blocks from the seafront, Mrs. Scutchings's red-brick house was on the corner of Julian and Church Streets, set in a half acre of neat garden with the usual Hills hoist clothesline in the backyard.

Each window had a fly screen. The trees still dripped water and the light was dull, shading everything with a coppery-gray sheen.

On the opposite side of the street was the cemetery. Georgia looked through the rain pattering on the windshield, wishing Tom's grave was there, and felt sad that he was a clump of gray ash in a jar instead of a sturdy corpse in an eco-aware cardboard box covered with a mound of freshly dug earth. That was Mum for you. Much more romantic to scatter ashes on a beach than imagine her father's body decomposing underground.

"Well, here we are!" Mrs. Scutchings announced. The instant she switched off the engine, several elderly citizens emerged from various houses in the street to gather around and gawk. As Georgia climbed out of the car, they sheltered her with their umbrellas, eyes bright with curiosity.

"You remember Georgia Parish?" Mrs. Scutchings said. Georgia recognized Angie Jeffrey, whose husband ran the Road House Café just out of town, and Liz Daniels, the local GP's wife. Both had come to Tom's funeral, but she didn't know the others.

Mrs. Scutchings ushered Georgia toward the house, still talking. "Bri Hutchison's in a bad way, he's been burned terribly badly, and some poor woman called Suzie Wilson didn't make it. But here's Georgia, and we're grateful for that, at least."

"Becky's already alerted the insurance company," someone said. "They'll be sending a man up from Brizzy to sort it out."

"Wonder how much it was worth?"

"About sixty grand."

"Sixty grand for one of Bri's rattletraps? You're joking."

"She's closed the airfield. Matt's well fed up. He was hoping he'd take Bri's flights tomorrow, make some extra cash."

"I wouldn't fly with *him* if you paid me a million bucks. All that beer he gets through. Aren't pilots supposed not to drink?"

If India Kane worked up here she'd soon be out of a job, Georgia thought dimly. In Nulgarra, where word traveled at the speed of light, there wasn't much point having a newspaper.

She felt so drained that she had to concentrate on putting one foot after the other as she followed everyone up the concrete path. The conversation had turned to what they'd cook for Becky and her kids, and who would make the next lot of sandwiches and cake for the helicopter paramedics and the hospital staff.

Nulgarra may be claustrophobic, she thought, but at least it's got community spirit.

———————

Dressed in a thick toweling bathrobe she found hanging on the back of the bedroom door, Georgia did as she was told and gave Mrs. Scutchings her clothes to be washed. Then she headed for the bathroom, which needed a major makeover. Tired, olive-colored tiles were in need of regrouting, and the paint was peeling in the corners. The carpet had lost its pile and was hard as burlap under her bare feet.

The shower looked as old as the rest of the room, and Georgia turned it on cautiously. A small clanking sound started up, and then a torrent of hot water gushed from the massive showerhead. Normally she'd have reveled in the deluge, but having to wash one-handed in an attempt to keep her bandage dry was more difficult than she'd anticipated, and she managed to get shampoo in her eyes. She hadn't done that since she was a kid and had forgotten how much it hurt.

Using Mrs. Scutchings's phone in the hall, she called India and arranged for the reporter to collect her at nine the following morning. India agreed to take her back to the aerodrome, and when they were there, to decide whether to fly or not.

Still in the robe, Georgia crawled into bed. It was daylight, but she didn't care. She turned on the bedside light, hoping to cheer up the room with its yellowing lace and faded dried flowers and a carpet the color of porridge. The windows were tiny, barely any light leaked through, and the room smelled of mulch and damp. Georgia knew if she opened the cupboard in the corner that anything inside would be covered in mold.

That was the trouble with living in the tropics. Everything got damp, then it went moldy.

She turned off the light, longing to sleep, not to think. She wanted it all to be a bad dream. She could hear rain rattling against the window and women talking and the whir of a kitchen mixer. She imagined cakes being baked, lemon sponge drizzled with syrup, carrot cake smothered in butter icing.

Her mother baked great cakes, but it didn't always mean that children could eat them. Georgia remembered reaching for a slice of what she thought was a chocolate brownie and having the plate whipped from beneath her fingers at the last second.

"Mum!"

"Darling, sorry." She had looked genuinely regretful.

"But I love brownies!"

"They're not brownies. They're for adults."

Georgia had looked at her mother, who sighed. "Sweet, it's not the end of the world. If I promise you brownies tomorrow, will you promise to stop scowling at me?"

Burrowing deep into the narrow single bed, she pulled the toweling robe close around her neck. She heard the distinctive sound of an oven door banging shut and imagined a perfectly luscious banana cake emerging. It would have creamy icing, she decided, and walnuts in its center.

Georgia slept restlessly, shivering a little against the damp bedclothes, sore and aching and aware of protecting her hand, her bruises. Despite her best efforts, her mind filled with flashbacks of the crash; the smell of smoke, the sound of tearing metal around them.

A crack of thunder woke her in an instant, her heart pounding until she realized where she was. It was pitch-dark outside and rain lashed against the window. Her heart sank. The secondary storms after Cyclone Tania had set in. Great. It looked as though she and India might not leave tomorrow after all.

She rolled onto her back and gave an involuntary groan. She hurt about a thousand times more than she had before she fell asleep. What she needed was a handful of painkillers. Pushing the bedcovers back, she turned to the door where Suzie's fanny pack hung on the hook. Then she thought she saw the door handle move.

Her breathing stopped as she stared. For a second she reckoned she must have imagined it, but then it shifted again, just half an inch or so, but it definitely moved.

Gut instinct told her it wouldn't be Mrs. Scutchings.

EIGHT

Georgia gazed rigidly at the door handle as she considered the alternatives: screaming for hep at the top of her voice, or lying in bed, pretending to be asleep.

Click.

Christ, the door was going to open any second.

There was no room beneath the bed to hide. No wardrobe to scurry inside, no open window to flee through. The corner cupboard could have sheltered a family of white-tailed rats, but not much else.

She made a snap decision against playing doggo and pretending to be asleep—she'd be a sitting target—and slipped from under the covers. She tiptoed hastily across the room to hide behind the door. Back flat against the wall, she saw the door open a crack, then a little more. Her breathing was shallow, her heart galloping.

A dark shape stepped inside. A man. He was holding a pistol in his right hand. Holding her breath, she watched him approach the bed. He moved cautiously, gun in readiness.

She had to get out. She had to get out *now*.

Quietly as she could, she started to creep around the door, heading for the corridor, when he spun around and came for her.

She leaped backwards, opened her mouth and screamed, loud as she could, *"Help!"*

The man clamped his hand over her mouth and she wriggled,

jerking to break free, but he was too strong. Suddenly the light snapped on and a voice said, "Georgia, what in the world—"

The man twisted away from Georgia and rushed for Mrs. Scutchings in the doorway, pushing her so hard that she smacked into the opposite corridor wall.

"Stop!" Mrs. Scutchings shouted. "Just stop right there!"

But the man wasn't stopping for anyone, least of all Mrs. Scutchings, resplendent in a cream robe of polyester that reached to her ankles, shouting loud as a foghorn.

Without stopping to think, Georgia ran after the man, but by the time she had flung back the front-door fly screen and raced down the concrete path to the street, all she could see was rain slanting against a single orange streetlight and palms bowed low.

"He was Chinese. Clean-shaven. Black hair, longish." Georgia took a gulp of her coffee and grimaced. Not only had she neglected to add sugar, but it was almost cold. "He wore jeans and a sweatshirt. Sneakers."

She stepped to the sink and poured her coffee down the drain before turning to face the cops. "That's it, I'm afraid. I can't really help any more. I only saw him for a second."

Glancing at her wrist, she realized for the first time that she had lost her watch. Not that she was going to have a spasm over it; it hadn't been a swanky Tag Heuer chronograph, just a Swatch she'd been given by her housemate last Christmas. Annie would buy her another, she knew, and enjoy teasing her for losing the thing in such a spectacular fashion.

Looking around, she saw a plastic green-and-gold clock above the door. It was 6 AM. Pale gray light filtered through the windows and she doubted they'd see the sun rising. Heavy, black-bottomed clouds filled the sky.

"Tell us a bit more about our hero," said the cop called Sergeant Riggs. He loaded the last word with sarcasm. "Where can we find him?"

"I've already told you, I don't know. The last time I saw him was at the hospital. And as I've said before, the intruder wasn't Lee Denham."

"You didn't see him leave the hospital?"

Sergeant Riggs's voice was as hard and uncompromising as his appearance. Early thirties, large and raw-boned, with a roll of fat spilling over his belt, he had buzz-cut red hair and a pair of small, watery blue eyes that never seemed to blink.

Riggs and his sidekick had turned up thirty minutes after Mrs. Scutchings had called triple zero and had been grilling her for over an hour. Despite her exhaustion, Georgia held her chin up and tried to ignore the fact that not only did she have the remnants of blue nail polish on her toenails, which Sergeant Riggs seemed to find fascinating, but she looked a fright. To free her from the plane Lee had sawn her hair into varying lengths that hung limply from her scalp. To make things worse, her clothes were still damp from being washed and her T-shirt kept sticking to her skin. Riggs was torn between staring at her toes or her breasts.

She folded her arms across her chest. "No," she said.

"You sure about that? The man saved your life, didn't he? You sure you're not feeling obligated, wanting to protect him?"

"I told you, it wasn't Lee."

She tried not to show her apprehension at his interest in Lee. Did it have anything to do with Lee wanting to take Suzie's fanny pack, his frown after he had searched it?

Wanting to change the subject, she looked pointedly at the door. "Where's Mrs. Scutchings? The poor woman must be wondering what on earth's going on with you interrogating me before she's had her cornflakes."

"Watching breakfast TV," said Riggs.

Small pause.

"So, Miz Parish," said Riggs heavily. "You're saying quite definitely that you don't know where Lee Denham is?"

"Yes. *Yes.* I have no idea."

"So who was the intruder."

"It wasn't Lee," she repeated. "He was too short, for a start. Lee must be six foot and this bloke was smaller than me, maybe five six or so."

How she wished she could walk outside and jump into a taxi and drive away. Riggs seemed to think that if he asked the same questions over and over, she'd suddenly come up with a different answer. An overweight bully, that's all he was, and she knew how to deal with bullies. If you couldn't settle it with a fistfight, the only option was to ignore them and hold your head high until they tired of you.

"I'm thinking there's more going on here than you're telling. You sure you're being straight?"

Her body was pulsing with pain, but she didn't sit down. She stood tall and kept her voice firm. "I cannot tell you something I don't know. Now, please, I've helped you all I can. May I go now?"

She made for the door, but the sidekick sprang into position right in front, forcing her to spin around. Feeling like a sheep nipped at its heels by a keen collie, she paced back to the stove. Mrs. Scutchings's kitchen was stale with age, with small windows, brown linoleum worn in its center, and an ancient Kelvinator fridge the size of a sedan car. Perhaps twenty years ago the walls and cupboards had been a cheerful green, but the color was now flat and dull as pondweed.

"Miz Parish." Riggs's voice was a low growl. "Maybe we can start again. Do you know—"

The door thumped open. A whippet-lean man in black boots, black jeans, and T-shirt walked in. "Sorry I'm running so late, guys."

She thought, I don't believe it! It's Daniel Carter. The boy I had a monumental crush on at school, the boy three years ahead of me who never knew I existed. It was surreal.

Daniel's dark blond hair was sticking up as though he'd been running his hands repeatedly through it, and although deep lines at the corners of his mouth indicated stress, he still looked good. How bloody typical, she thought, that ten years after I leave town he gets to see me looking a complete mess.

Daniel nodded at Riggs, who nodded back. "I'll take it from here."

Riggs stretched his arms to the ceiling, looking relieved. "Great. Give me a chance to grab a shower. Start the day over on a decent note."

"I'll join you when I'm done."

"Sally G's? Or you going straight to the station?"

"Sally's."

The other cop piped up. "I'll drop Riggs off, sir. Grab some breakfast at home."

So the other cop was local, but Riggs and Daniel were from out of town. Sally G's was one of the larger, more amenity-appointed guesthouses in Nulgarra, well-known for putting up the odd businessman and traveling salesman. And now a couple of cops.

Riggs and his sidekick left, discussing whether Sally would be awake yet and able to rustle up some eggs. She could hear their voices as they walked down the side of the house.

Daniel crossed the kitchen and stuck out a hand. "Sergeant Carter," he said.

The man had a grip like a mangle, and she tried not to flinch. "Georgia Parish," she said. "I was at school with you."

"I know."

"You remember me?" She doubted it.

He shook his head. "I heard all about you at the station before I came, and remembered the name."

She raised her eyebrows and suddenly he grinned, losing ten years and looking like the boy she'd known at school, the crooked smile, the penetrating, almost indecently blue eyes. He used to wear a black bandanna, she remembered, and practiced kung fu. His fascination with China had briefly become her own, and she had even read Sun Tzu's *Art of War* back to front, because he had.

"And I mean, *all.*" He was still grinning. "You were the leader of the pack that used to give the town kids such a hard time. Everyone remembers you as a major mischief maker."

"Nuisance, more like," she agreed ruefully, and gestured at what had to be a forty-year-old jug in the corner. Jugs were an Aussie type of kettle, and she'd never seen anything like them until she arrived out here. "Coffee?"

"Love one."

The grin vanished and she saw that his brilliant eyes were very bloodshot. He looked exhausted.

"You look done in," she told him with her customary honesty. "Sit."

"No. Your hand. I'll do it. You take a seat and give me directions."

As he moved to the jug, she felt the energy rush out of her and had to grab the back of a chair to steady herself.

"You're okay?" he said over his shoulder. It was a statement more than a question.

"Yup." She made her voice strong but didn't think she could pick up a teaspoon, she felt so weak. She sank hurriedly into a chair before she fell. The chair cushion matched the linoleum covering the aluminum table. Both were covered with little yellow teddy bears.

She watched Daniel—she couldn't think of him as Sergeant Carter—make coffee, pour milk, add sugar, and stir, with a sense of weird amazement. Her schoolgirl crush was making her coffee. If she was fourteen years old, she'd be pinching herself.

Sitting opposite, he pushed her coffee toward her, took a steady sip of his own, and sighed.

When he looked up, his face had smoothed into a neutral expression. His cop face, she assumed.

"So, you had an intruder last night."

"More like early this morning." She took a gulp of strong, dark coffee and added, "But your colleagues seemed more interested in Lee Denham than the prowler."

There was a short pause, and then he asked the same questions Riggs had asked, but faster and without any repetitions. Then he topped up the jug and plugged it in again. Immediately it started to make its usual hideous crackling, popping noise as the twin electric filaments heated up. Georgia decided to buy Mrs. Scutchings a jug from the twenty-first century before the woman either electrocuted herself or blew up the house. She'd find something at Price's, she was certain.

She'd just registered a smell of smoke when Daniel jumped up and said, "Jesus." He unplugged the jug, flipped back the lid, and peered inside. "Ah." She watched as he pulled a Swiss Army knife attached to a piece of string from his jeans pocket, opened a blade, and poked it inside the kettle. "That'll do it."

Jug now churning away, he said, "I'd like to talk to Lee."

Georgia frowned, wondering why he was interviewing her when Riggs had already done a pretty good job. "You think he had something to do with the intruder?"

Ignoring her question, Daniel leaned his hips against the countertop and folded his arms. "Ronnie Chen's name was on the flight plan. So were Lee's and Suzie Wilson's." He gave her a long look. "How come yours wasn't?"

It was the same question India had asked, but this time, restored by the coffee, she had the energy to give a longer reply. "Probably because nobody knew I was flying until the last minute. SunAir's a bit like a taxi, sometimes you get a ride, sometimes you don't. You can book, but you're not always guaranteed to get on board. Especially if someone has an emergency, like needing to get to a wedding because their car's broken down, say."

The kelvinator emitted a loud rumbling noise, making the plastic salad bowl on top rattle.

"Bri told me his flight was fully booked, but with the weather being so bad, he wasn't sure if anyone would turn up, so he told me to come anyway."

"So, Ronnie Chen didn't arrive, and you took his place."

"It looks that way."

"Hmm."

He refilled their cups and brought them over. She took a sip and attempted to hide her grimace. The man sure liked his caffeine. This cup was even stronger than the first.

"If Lee gets in touch with you, could you call me direct?" He withdrew a card from his jeans pocket and pushed it across the table. It showed his name and rank and a mobile number. "Would you do that for me?"

Ten years ago she would have walked over burning coals for him, but today all she said was, "Sure."

He seemed to relax at that, and smiled. She smiled back. "God," she said impulsively, "it's been so *long* since Nulgarra High."

He flinched, and for a second she wondered if it was the mention of their old school, but he was pulling out a mobile phone the size of a cigarette packet from his front pocket and snapping it open.

"Carter," he barked, then his face softened. "Well, hello to you too, pussycat . . . Oh, you've been drawing, have you? A princess? And she's got black hair?" Daniel got to his feet and went and leaned against the fridge, expression absorbed. "Yes, I'm sure she's very beautiful, but is she as beautiful as you? No, I thought not . . . Oh, hi, Gran. Yes, sounds like you've everything under control . . . Yes, I'll be back for Wednesday, Riggs is covering for me . . . Yes, I'll pick up the cake . . . A pink-frosted Barbie cake, right . . . I'd better go. I'll call you usual time, before Tabby goes to bed. Yeah . . . Bye."

Clicking the phone together, he came and sat back down again. He was smiling.

"Tabby?" Georgia asked.

"Tabitha. My daughter. She's four this Wednesday, and we're having a party with all her friends. Twelve of them! God, I hope the cake's big enough. And that the clown turns up on time."

He hadn't mentioned a wife or girlfriend. Georgia threw caution to the winds. "And Tabby's mother?"

The smile immediately vanished and she saw a flash of grief cross his face.

"I'm sorry," she said hastily. "I shouldn't have asked."

Head bowed, Daniel rubbed the bridge of his nose. "Lucy died three years ago. My wife . . . she was only twenty-eight."

Horrified, Georgia filled in the awkward silence. "I'm sorry, it must have been awful." She didn't dare ask how his wife had died. She racked her brains to think whether there'd been a Lucy at Nulgarra High but couldn't remember one. He'd obviously met Lucy later.

"Tabby and Gran live with me in Canberra, which works fine at the moment, but . . ." He sighed, ran a finger around his coffee cup.

Georgia changed the subject. "So what are you doing all the way up here if you live in Canberra?"

Leaning back in his chair, he said, "We travel wherever required. Gathering intelligence, conducting investigations. I'm on the PST. The People Smuggling Strike Team. We decided to drop an 'S' to avoid being nicknamed *psst*." He gave a wry smile. "We work from the federal office in Canberra, trying to bust illegal immigration."

She'd never heard of the PST and said so.

"We've only been going a couple of years. The penalties for people-smuggling used to carry a maximum of two years in jail, but now they get twenty years or fined a quarter of a million bucks. The stakes have been upped so much that the amateurs have dropped out and now it's run by professional criminal enterprises. Lots of bribery and official corruption. Hence the creation of PST."

"Why Nulgarra?"

"I got intelligence from our Chinese counterparts that the head honchos of a particular gang we're after, the RBG, Red Bamboo Gang, might be up here. The RBG were responsible for the container ship that disembarked three hundred illegals in Cairns a couple of years back."

She remembered reading about that in the newspaper. The police had managed to catch only forty of them. The rest had been smartly trucked off to urban centers around Australia to melt into the general population.

"It's big business for the RBG," he added. "Twenty grand or so a person."

She did the sums. Six million dollars for a single shipment of people. Not bad.

"I've been working with the Brisbane police and we flew here this morning, hoping to track them down. Make some arrests. Your intruder, we thought, might be connected. We'll see."

She recalled the figure she thought she had recognized as they taxied for takeoff. "I saw you," she said, her voice surprised. "I saw you on the SunAir steps."

He looked startled. "You did?"

"I didn't know it was you," she added. "Until now."

"Wish I'd had a crystal ball. I could have stopped the flight before disaster struck." Small pause. "Are you planning to stay long?"

"I'm leaving today." She glanced at the clock. "After I've seen Bri."

"You'll be lucky. Becky's closed the aerodrome and the roads are still impassable. I checked on my way here."

"Then I'll leave tomorrow, or the day after that. Soon as I can, actually." She turned her cup around in her hands. "How long are you up here for?"

He didn't answer, just drained his coffee and pushed the cup away. Then he stretched, and stood up. "I'll file the report about your intruder. Thanks for the coffee."

She followed him to the front door.

"Why don't you wear a uniform?"

He turned and smiled at her. "My kind of cop doesn't wear one."

"Why not?"

"We're supposed to be invisible."

NINE

Georgia watched Daniel's black-clad figure lope down the narrow concrete path, wondering how he'd come to be a policeman, and then she remembered Mathew Larkins. Everyone in Nulgarra knew the story. Mathew Larkins had fleeced Daniel's father of all his savings in a get-rich-quick scheme, something to do with prawn farms.

Daniel's father had died of a heart attack soon after he heard he'd lost all his money, and Daniel, aged sixteen, now head of his poverty-stricken family, had blamed Larkins for his father's death. When Larkins got off scot-free, Daniel had pestered the courts and the police, and when he had no luck, swore retribution. Four years later, when her mother had visited her in Sydney, she'd asked for news about old school friends and, eyes twinkling, Linette had said, "Daniel Carter, you mean?"

Embarrassed that her mother knew about her crush, she'd shrugged.

"He firebombed poor Mathew Larkins's house," her mother told her. "They didn't find any evidence it was him, but I heard from Angie at the Road House Café that his mother is sure her son did it." Linette sighed. "I don't understand him. Waiting all that time, planning Mathew's destruction. So unforgiving."

Now, as Georgia caught a glimpse of a police car sweeping down Church Street and vanishing from sight, she thought it was little wonder Daniel had joined the police. The boy may have exacted vengeance, but at least the man had a badge.

Still thinking about Daniel, she flinched when the phone rang. Since Mrs. Scutchings had gone to buy a newspaper—she was itching to get the gossip on the murdered man, Ronnie Chen, at the beach—and there was a little pad of daisy-decorated paper beside the phone, along with a pen, she decided she'd better do the right thing and take a message.

"Hello?"

"Georgia?"

"Mum?"

"Sweet, I heard from Katie at the general store this morning." Her words were hurried, breathless. "How awful for you. And poor old Bri. I'm bringing some hypericum. It's meant to help injuries where the nerves are affected. Do you have some arnica? And what about rescue remedy? You really should have a drop or two every hour or so. Jeremy and I were planning on heading south this afternoon, stopping over with the Arlies in Lakeland, but we've already rung them . . ."

Georgia tuned out as soon as her mother mentioned Jeremy, her latest earring-toting, ponytailed boyfriend. They'd met for the first time at Tom's funeral, and just as she knew he wouldn't want to see her again, she didn't particularly wish to see him either.

"Mum, I'm fine. You head on home."

From the window by the phone she could see the top of an ornate crypt in the near corner of the cemetery. A stone angel stood with its wings furled, hands clasped in front of its chest, head bowed. Rivulets of rain were running down its face. Oh, Tom, she thought, her tears rising. That angel. He's crying for you.

"Sweet, you shouldn't be alone."

Georgia swallowed her tears. "I've barely a scratch on me, I swear it. You go to Lakeland. I'm fine."

"No, Georgia."

Startled, Georgia started at the phone as if it had levitated. The only time she'd heard her mother use that tone of voice was when, just outside their cabin, she had gone to pick up a centipede the size of a Havana cigar, which she hadn't known was poisonous.

"Jeremy's going to make his own way south, so it'll just be me. I'll be leaving for Nulgarra the second I've put the phone down." Linette's tone hadn't changed. Hard, determined. "I want to see you. Make sure you're really all right."

"I'm *fine*."

"The more you say you're fine, the more I want to make sure. I'll be there in a couple of hours."

Click.

Georgia stood gazing at a straggly spider plant on the window sill. Mum to the rescue. Amazing. She didn't think she had it in her. But then she remembered the time not long after Dad had died, when a burglar had seen their unlatched windows in Glastonbury and crept into their house. Her mother hadn't hidden beneath the bedclothes; she'd ripped her bedside light free of its socket and charged for the man. Then she'd chased him outside and along the street dressed in nothing but her flimsy nightie.

Back then she and Dawn hadn't been astounded as much as impressed, and now she was going through the same emotions. Georgia gave a small smile, and shook her head. Her mother could certainly pull a surprise when she wanted. Turning her mind to practicalities, she decided to get some lunch in, rather than rely on Mrs. Scutchings cooking for them. She'd get some snapper or maybe some bream. Her mum loved fish.

Promising to leave Mrs. Scutchings some money to cover her calls, Georgia rang India Kane. It was barely eight o'clock and India was, she said sleepily, still in bed. Georgia told the reporter that the aerodrome was shut and some roads still impassable, and they arranged to meet at the National Hotel for a drink in the evening. Then Georgia rang her housemate, Annie, and filled her in.

"You mean your plane got trashed into a million pieces and I still don't get to inherit your estate?"

Georgia laughed. "Better luck next time."

After reassuring Annie she was okay, that she'd be back soon,

Georgia hung up and redialed. The line was terrible, but she could just make out Maggie's voice shouting anxiously, "G? G, is that you?"

Now was definitely not the time to remind her boss not to call her G, which made her sound like a goddamn horse.

"Yes, it's me!" she yelled back, and suddenly the line went crystal clear.

"Ah, that's better." Maggie sighed. "Bloody Harbour Bridge always interferes with reception. So, how was the funeral?"

"More's happened since then," she said, and quickly filled her in on the crash.

"Shouldn't you be in the hospital?" Maggie sounded shocked and upset.

She reassured Maggie as she had her housemate, and was reminded of the run-up to Tom's funeral, where she had spent an inordinate amount of time reassuring everyone she was okay when all she wanted was to be left alone. Heavens, reassuring people was just so *exhausting.*

Eventually Maggie began to sound relieved, and resumed her normal brisk tone rather than sounding as though she was speaking to someone lamebrained and on their deathbed.

"Well, obviously you won't be back in time for the conference. We'll miss you and, dammit, you'll miss Alan McGary! I'll get him to sign one of his books for you, I know what a fan you are."

"Only because he's gorgeous!"

"And what would Charlie say about that?"

"It's none of Charlie's business."

She heard Maggie's sigh down the line. "Don't tell me you two split up."

"That's right."

"He proposed again?"

"For the last time, apparently."

"And what's wrong with being proposed to?"

"Why do we have to get *married*? What's wrong with things as they are?" Georgia picked at a desiccated leaf on the spider plant.

"Some people like a bit of commitment. That's all."

"You sound like Charlie."

"It's not all balls and chains. You might even get to like it. Having someone to depend on, to help out when things get tough."

"Now you're definitely sounding like Charlie."

She heard Maggie clear her throat. "Can I announce your promotion at the conference?"

"No" she said hurriedly. "Sorry, Maggie, but no, you can't, not yet. I'm still thinking about it."

Another sigh. "But what else will you do if you don't take it? You've got to move on, Georgia. You can't be a rep the rest of your life."

"But is a promotion the only option? Move up the publishing ladder like a good employee until I drop dead of exhaustion? I don't think I want that."

"So what do you want?"

Georgia picked the dead leaf free and rolled it between her fingers. "I just want something to matter."

Maggie gave an impatient snort.

"Maybe I should go into the desert and eat locusts and find God."

This time Maggie laughed. "You'd be bored in two seconds, and if you weren't, I'd send in the men in white coats. Look, let's discuss this over a meal when you get back. You need anything, call me."

"Thanks."

"And don't rush back, Georgia, for God's sake. There's absolutely nothing that can't wait. Take all the time you need. And what about your poor friend? Will he be all right?"

"I'm going to see him in a minute, after I've found some breakfast. I'm starving."

Small silence, then, "Well, if you've an appetite . . ." She could almost see Maggie nodding in satisfaction.

Hanging up, Georgia flicked the dead leaf into the pot. She wished she *wanted* the promotion—it would make life so much easier. All her friends were firmly on their chosen career paths, knowing exactly where they were going, but she hadn't a clue. Having to give up her usual day-wear of jeans and sneakers for some sort of managerial outfit didn't help. Nor did the thought of keeping office hours and attending countless meetings in frigid, air-conditioned offices. And there was no way she'd still be able to fit in a quick surf at the end of her working day.

Besides, what was wrong with being a book rep? The salary wasn't great, but she had a company car, could organize her days as she liked, and so long as the figures came in on target she had total autonomy, with nobody looking over her shoulder. Why did everyone want to *change* things? Why didn't she *care* about being promoted? And what about Charlie? Why didn't she want to marry him?

"Not everyone is like your mother," Charlie had said.

"Thank heavens for that," she'd replied, her tone heavy with sarcasm.

"Just because Linette never got married doesn't mean you have to follow suit."

"I'm not!"

"I won't abandon you, Georgia." His expression was earnest. "I'm not one of your mother's boyfriends who'll vanish just when you start to get to like them. Trust me, won't you? I'm sticking around. For good."

Except he hadn't stuck around. He'd given her an ultimatum: marry me, live with me, have my children, or I walk. Children? It was the first time he'd mentioned children. Oh God, she thought, if I marry him, of course I'd be expected to have his babies. I'll have to give up my company car, my lovely booksellers, my surfing, to be at home breast-feeding. I'm not even thirty. No, I'm not ready for all that.

———

Before she headed into town, Georgia upended Suzie's fanny pack on her bed, looking for an address for Suzie or her brother, but found nothing. Riggs had told her that the police had informed Suzie's employer of her death, but he hadn't said who they were, or mentioned Suzie's family.

Suzie's purse had to be the neatest Georgia had ever seen. No cash register receipts, no video store cards, library cards, or dry-cleaning slips. Just a single twenty-dollar note and a handful of change.

Her passport had been issued in Wuhan, China, and showed a girl ten years younger who barley looked like Suzie and went by the name of Wang Mingshu. She had no work permit for Australia, not even a tourist visa, and the address given was in Xian, China. For a second Georgia considered mailing the bag there, then remembered Suzie knew Bri, and must have lived locally. Would anyone still know her in Xian?

Opening the internal zipper, she took out a folded cotton handkerchief with a hand-stitched lily in one corner, and an electronic key with the words "Tempo Car Park" above the magnetic strip. As she pushed the card and hanky back, she saw that the inside lining had been restitched. Pressing her fingers against the leather, she frowned. She could feel something inside. Something hard and flat and square. Peering harder, she realized Suzie had sewn whatever it was into the lining.

Her stomach gave a jump. It had to be what Lee had been looking for after the plane crash. Was it connected to her intruder too? Deciding to open the lining and see what was inside, hoping it contained an address, Georgia trotted to the kitchen and, using a fine, sharp knife, picked the threads free.

No address, just an unmarked floppy disk.

Georgia turned the disk over and over in her hands, wondering how she hadn't felt it before, and how Lee had missed it, but when she considered the fanny pack again, holding it against her waist with one hand and rummaging inside with the other, the leather still felt like a block of wood even without the disk. And it wasn't as if Lee had been rough when he'd searched the thing. He'd picked through Suzie's lipsticks and pens delicately, like a cat.

She decided to see if she could find out who Suzie's employer was, and if she had no luck, she'd write a letter to Xian. She could send Suzie's stuff on when she'd received an affirmative response. Pushing everything back inside, she paused at the twenty-dollar note. She hadn't had breakfast and she was ravenous. Would Suzie mind? She'd replace it later . . . Hurriedly, Georgia shoved the note in her jeans pocket and zipped up the fanny pack.

She was heading back to her bedroom, intending to put the bag on the bedside table, then thought better of it. Computer disk in hand, she looked around the room. She decided to wedge it in a loose section of baseboard behind the bed. Then, carefully, she propped Suzie's fanny pack between the chest of drawers and the wall. Just in case.

Ten

The sky was overcast, the air close and humid. Sweat trickled down Georgia's chest and back as she walked down Church Street before turning right into Jacaranda Road and zigzagging her way toward Ocean Road and the Coral Sea. She passed the Bendigo Bank and the little brass war memorial, in remembrance of the three men from Nulgarra who'd died in the Second World War. Two bulky, sun-wrinkled men in boots and shorts, drinking coffee out of the back of their van, tried not to stare as she walked by. I must get a haircut, she thought, but not at Sheryl's Bib and Cut or I'll come out looking like a poodle. I'll wait till I get to Sydney.

Crossing Ocean Road, she went into Mick's Café and ordered a dozen deep-fried oysters. It might be only nine-fifteen, but after her session with the cops, then Daniel, it felt like lunchtime and way past the time for eggs and bacon. Mick wasn't there and she chatted to the man mixing a fresh batch of batter, comparing oysters from around the world, why the ones from Dublin were so fat and creamy while others were half the size and flat as pancakes. She was inordinately glad she didn't have to answer a single question about her marital status.

Ten minutes later, the bag of oysters greasy and warm in her hand, she headed for the beach, wanting to fill her soul with space before seeing Bri. She followed the hard-packed sandy track between the town hall and adventure playground, picking out an oyster and eating it as she walked. Through the mangroves to the right, she could just see a dark glimmer of the Parunga River, oozing slowly to its ocean mouth, and hear the distant burble of a powerful inboard motor. One of the cop boats maybe, going for a recon.

Salty juice trickled down her chin and she wiped it away with the back of her hand, wondering how many dozens of oysters she'd eaten since she was a kid. Hundreds? More like thousands. She loved them, always had. She paused on the edge of the beach and took in the brand-new sign stuck in the sand. Etched out of wood were letters painted red and white: "Warning, Estuarine Crocodiles Inhabit This River System."

Her spirits sank. For estuarine, read "saltie," she thought, and automatically began scanning the area. Did this mean she couldn't walk on the beach? For a second she empathized with Mrs. Scutchings. If the American tourist hadn't been attacked last season, the sign would never have been erected. Or would it? Maybe someone had seen an old, displaced crocodile entering the river system, and erected the sign accordingly.

"Whatever's in that bag smells good." The man spoke right behind her, almost in her ear, making her spin around.

"Jesus!"

Lee Denham stood there, studying her. He wore blue jeans tucked into boots and a gray sweatshirt with the sleeves cut off. "Windsurfers Do It Standing Up" was stitched in red across the chest.

He said, "Sorry about your hair. Talk about making a mess of it."

"Where *have* you been?" she said, adrenaline making her tone aggressive. "Everyone's been looking for you!"

"Are you eating crab sticks?" He leaned over, trying to peer into the bag. He wore a large Band-Aid above his left eye and his ear was bandaged. Despite his wounds he bristled with energy.

"Oysters." She offered the bag to him.

He took two, popped one in his mouth. "Nice," he said, muffled. "Haven't had them done this way before."

"Where have you been since the hospital? You just vanished."

He ate the second oyster and ignored the question.

"It's beautiful up here. Really beautiful. I had no idea. You see the crabs in the mud? Size of my thumbnail but fantastic colors. Like jewels."

He was right. Even though the sun wasn't out, the crab shells gleamed bright as sapphires.

"Look at this." He made to bend over to pick up a shell the color of freshwater pearls.

"Don't!"

He looked up at her. "What?"

"It might be a coneshell."

Lee straightened and stared at the shell. "A what?"

"It's a poisonous creature that lives inside shells."

"Venomous seashells?" he said. "I don't believe it."

"Along with box jellyfish, stingrays, blue-ringed octopi, and stone-fish. They're the worst because they're so well camouflaged. When you tread on one, its spines go straight through your shoe, injecting you with venom."

"Then what?"

"You die."

He blinked. "Jesus. I had no idea . . ."

"How beautiful it is up here," she added with a smile.

She picked out an oyster and offered him another. Both of them turned their heads at the small movement at the edge of the beach. Georgia spotted the whimbrel first. Small and brown and unassuming, the bird was feeding on shrimps between the mangroves.

"Is that venomous too?"

"Not that I've heard."

"Glad to hear it." In the same tone, he said, "You've had a busy morning. All those visitors?"

How did he know? Disconcerted, she said, "Do you mean the police?"

"Cassell and Riggs. And Sergeant Carter." His expression was unreadable. "Quite a turn-up for the books."

She felt a small swoop in her belly. "You've been *watching* me?"

He smiled briefly. "You're my responsibility after what happened."

Ignoring the sensation of sea lice scurrying down her spine, she said, "Am I? Well. I haven't thanked you, have I? I mean, thanks."

"I'd prefer it if you didn't tell anyone you've seen me," he said. "Especially Carter."

"Why not?"

He fixed his gaze on something past her shoulder. "I'd just rather he didn't track me down, that's all."

"But he asked me to call him if I saw you. What am I supposed to tell him when . . ."

The look he gave her made her fall silent.

"You owe me."

"Yes, and don't think I'm not grateful, but as far as I'm concerned, when the police ask . . ." She trailed off when she realized she was getting to the point of telling him she was a law-abiding citizen and would do anything the police told her to. Which was absolutely right, wasn't it? But she didn't feel right saying it to this granitelike man, especially since he'd saved her life. She could almost feel Daniel's card burning a hole in her pocket.

"You know our aircraft was sabotaged?"

It took her a second to take in what he'd said; he sounded like he was discussing the weather.

"*What?*"

"When I went to try to put out the engine fire I saw the fuel pipe had been loosened, where it fits onto the electrical fuel pump. It had to have been deliberate, because it's normally wire-locked. That's why we ran out of fuel. And the whole time we flew, fuel leaked into the engine bay, and with that engine so hot . . . It's a miracle the plane didn't explode before we landed."

There was a silence, then Lee took a long breath. "You know anyone who wants you dead?"

She was speechless with disbelief.

"Obviously not," said Lee drily. "Wonder who they wanted to kill? Me, perhaps. Suzie. Bri."

Unable to make sense of it, she said, "Are you *sure?*"

"Oh yes. I'm sure, all right."

"Have you reported it?"

He looked amused. "I like that. Me going into the local cop shop to report my plane was sabotaged. Yeah. Right."

"But if it was, surely shouldn't you—"

"No. *You* should. They won't listen to me."

"I didn't see anything, let alone the . . . wire thingy."

"Wire-lock."

"I don't see how I can report something I know nothing about."

"You've no interest in who nearly wiped you out?"

"Of course I have! It's just that . . . well, it'll be difficult."

"Just call the insurance company. And the AAI. The Air Accident Investigators. They'll find their evidence."

"I still think you should report it. And how can I not tell Daniel I've seen you after you've told me—"

"So, it's Daniel, is it?" He raised an eyebrow mockingly.

"We were at school together."

"Ah."

Absently she offered him another oyster. When he'd finished it he said, "Tell Carter I told you about the sabotage at the crash site. But that you'd forgotten, with the shock and all of the incident."

She looked away from him at the whimbrel. It had inched its way out of the mangroves and was now pecking for crabs in the mud.

"Did you find out where Suzie's brother lives?" he asked.

"No. Apparently the police have notified her employer, but I don't know who it is. Do you?"

Again, he ignored her question. "You're saying you don't know how to find her brother?"

"Well, no. But if her employer can't help, I'm going to send a letter to the address in her passport."

"Xian."

"Yes." She took a breath and added, "The police asked me loads of questions about you. About why my name wasn't on the flight plan, but someone else called Ronnie Chen was. Did you know he's dead? His body was found washed up on Kee Beach." She couldn't bring herself to mention that the man had been murdered.

"I heard." He turned to stare at the steely flat sea.

"Why are the police so interested in you?"

He glanced down and withdrew a beeper from his front pocket, studied it. "Sorry," he said. "I'd better go." His expression had closed. Instinct told her that the interview, if that's what it had been, was over.

"I'll go and see Bri, then."

"You do that. And be sure to tell him I said thanks. He did a good job there."

"I will."

As she walked away, greasy paper bag clutched in her hand, she could feel his eyes follow her along the beach. She felt them as she stepped over a handful of smooth pebbles the color of ash, her footsteps making no sound on the soft combination of mud and sand. All she could hear was the whine of a mosquito and the occasional splash of tires from the road. Nobody was on the beach today.

She knew she was out of sight of Lee Denham when she turned onto the track that led to the rear of the National Hotel, and she felt the muscles in her back relax.

ELEVEN

Bri had tubes up his nose, down his throat, in his arms, and was surrounded with machines that hissed, wheezed, and thumped. His legs and feet were covered in saline sheets and his head had been shaved; he had a black-clotted gash as thick as a worm across his scalp, which was studded with stitches like barbed wire. He seemed to have shrunk, become half his normal size, and Georgia stood there for a moment, trying to maintain a calm expression and hide her shock and alarm.

"Will he be okay?"

"They can do amazing things with burns nowadays," said Jill Hodges. Her tone was gentle.

Georgia stood over Bri in silence. Here was the man who, eighteen hours ago, had held the stricken Piper, and managed to get them down. He had unerringly flown them over gorges and ravines for the safest landing he could find, and had made it. Suzie may have died, but Lee hadn't, and nor had she. She wanted to press a kiss against Bri's cheek to let him know how much she owed him, but didn't dare in case she hurt him.

"Is he in pain?"

"We're giving him morphine. We want to transfer him to the burns unit in Brisbane, but don't want to move him . . . just yet."

Georgia was staring at Bri, unable to think of anything else to ask.

She was sure thousands of intelligent questions would come to her later, but right now she couldn't think of one.

"I'd better be getting on. Please, call in anytime you want." Jill Hodges touched her shoulder briefly, then left.

Georgia's hands clenched and unclenched at her sides. "Jesus, Bri."

"Georgia." Bri's voice was faint and slightly slurred, barely discernible.

"Bri?"

She bent close and smelled the stench of sickness on his breath, but she didn't draw away. She watched his eyelids fluttering. They opened. She tried not to look appalled. There was no white in his eyes at all. They were filled with blood.

"Fuck 'em," he said.

Not knowing how to respond, she settled for a firm, "Right."

"They fucked with my plane. The fucks."

A frisson ran through her, as though someone had dropped a skink down the back of her T-shirt.

"What do you mean?"

"Fucked my plane," he repeated.

Georgia saw that his blood-clotted eyes were engorged with rage.

"Are you saying it was sabotaged?"

"Damn right. Find 'em for me." Bri made a gasping noise, then, "Bloody well kill 'em."

"I'm not sure about that, Bri. Not my sort of—"

"I'll kill 'em."

"I don't know if—"

"Georgia!" It was a hiss and Georgia knew that if he could, Bri would be shouting at the top of his voice. "Promise!"

"Okay, okay." Her hands were raised and she realized she was drenched in sweat. "I promise."

Bri closed his eyes briefly and for a second Georgia thought the effort had made him pass out, but then they opened again. "Swear it, Georgia. For me. And for Suzie."

She barely hesitated. "I swear it, Bri. Okay?"

"Okay."

The silence was filled with the rattle of a passing trolley outside. She gave him a minute or so, then said softly, "You did a great job getting us down. Lee says so too. I just saw him. He said thanks."

Bri didn't respond. His breathing was loud and rasping. Quietly she told him that she'd had her hand stitched, but otherwise she was okay, that she'd talked with the police that morning, how juicy her oysters had been, and how Lee hadn't a clue about the wildlife up here. After a while she fell silent.

The minutes ticked past. Bri didn't move.

"I'll come back later. This afternoon. Keep checking up on you."

She waited a few more seconds. Bri remained motionless. As she walked through the door and down the corridor toward reception, her legs felt unsteady, her mind filled with the vision of the diminished figure in his hospital bed. Head down, chest tight with repressed tears, she nearly collided with two Chinese men coming around the corner.

She was opening her mouth to apologize, then stopped. She thought she recognized one of them. The stocky figure, the flat black hair. But when she looked again, it wasn't her intruder after all, just a man with his friend, visiting a patient.

"Sorry," she muttered.

The bigger man ignored her, but the smaller one in a leather jacket spat on the ground as he passed.

Jesus, she thought, turning to stare after them. Talk about unhygienic. Revolting.

———————

Back on the main street outside the hospital, Georgia paused. The sky was still a heavy gray, filled with towering cumulonimbus, the atmosphere stifling. Brushing sweat from her temple, she reckoned her mother would have arrived by now and decided to head back to Mrs. Scutchings's house. She hadn't bought any fish, but since her mother loved oysters too, they wouldn't starve so long as Mick's was open. She watched a ute splash past, laden with cartons of soft drinks, and saw the Fanta logo, and a drink she hadn't heard of before, Twango, which she took to be a combination of mango and . . . What? God, she'd be no good at marketing, she couldn't even work out what new soft drink it was.

She heard footsteps behind her, and a male voice said, "Are you okay?"

Daniel Carter caught her up.

"I'm fine." She gave him the bright smile of reassurance she had perfected over the days preceding Tom's funeral.

"You saw Bri?"

"Yes."

"He's not doing so well, I hear."

"No."

Fighting against the knot of emotion inside her, she concentrated on a bunch of Aboriginal boys walking down Ocean Street, laughing as they ducked one another's mock blows. Two emaciated mongrels were tagging along beside them. Despite their mangy appearance, their tails were high and their steps springy.

"I'm sorry."

As Daniel turned to track the boys' progress, she felt his shoulder touch hers. He moved away at the same time she did. She heard him clear his throat.

Shoving her hands into her pockets, she said, "You ought to know. Lee told me our airplane was sabotaged."

Daniel stiffened. "Sabotaged?"

"Bri reminded me"—she couldn't look at him while she lied—"that Lee said something after the crash. When we were up there. I mean, I forgot, with everything going on, you know, Lee dragging Bri from the aircraft, his legs on fire, then Suzie dying . . . did I tell you she smelled of jasmine? I wasn't sure if it was perfume or just the way she smelled, maybe her soap, but it was so pretty, so sweet, and when Bri—"

"Hey, slow down." Daniel was holding his hands up, looking stricken. "Take a breath."

She did as she was told. Tried not to think about the fact that she was lying to the police.

"Just before the paramedics arrived, Lee told me he saw something had been tampered with when he went to put the engine fire out. A wire-lock."

"I thought the airplane ran out of fuel." Daniel was frowning. "That's what the initial report says, anyway. That you'd run out of juice and had a fire in the engine bay."

"That's what Bri said when we went down," she agreed, "but it was Lee who saw something once we'd crashed."

"Jesus." He ran a hand through his hair. "Who, apart from Lee, thinks it was sabotage?"

"Bri. He told me just now."

"Right." Daniel glanced past her as a Nissan ute trundled past, two blue heelers hanging over the tailgate, thick fur ruffled and tongues lolling.

A bead of sweat worked its way down his cheek and he wiped it away. "It's the first I've heard of a possible sabotage. If it's true, I'd better alert the Air Accident Investigators. Get them to pick the wreckage over." He turned to her. "I really need to talk to Lee. Get it from the horse's mouth, so to speak, to know exactly what he saw."

Georgia remained silent, praying he wouldn't ask her if she'd seen Lee. She was sure he'd see the barefaced lie lit like neon on her face.

"You fancy a coffee?" he asked suddenly, a definite sparkle in his vivid blue eyes. "The National does a great Irish. I think you might need one after the past twenty-four hours. I certainly do."

Her teenage self nearly fell over. Daniel Carter, inviting her for coffee! But the adult took over, and cautioned her to say no, in case he pressed her about Lee. Besides, her mother would be waiting for her at Mrs. Scutchings's.

Georgia looked at his hair sticking up as though he'd just gotten out of bed. "Sounds great," she said. She'd ring her mother from the National.

———

They were halfway down the street, discussing why Nulgarra hadn't invested in a new community center since the decrepit old one was home to three families of fruit bats as well as having half the rainforest growing across its roof, when a black Mercedes cruised past and stopped fifty yards ahead of them in a cul-de-sac. Three Asian men climbed out.

Two of them leaned against the flank of their car, smoking. The third walked past them without looking their way. All wore reflective sunglasses despite the fact that it was overcast. Georgia glanced up and down the street and saw it was empty. No young kids or their dogs, nor a single car driving along. She felt the hairs at the back of her neck rise.

As they approached, the two men pushed themselves from the Merc and walked toward them. They were smiling. Daniel stopped short. "Do you know these blokes?"

She thought the larger one might be the man she'd nearly collided with in the hospital, but wasn't sure.

"No."

"Me neither." His hands hung loosely at his sides. "Start walking, Georgia. The other way."

Georgia didn't hesitate. She spun on her heel and set a brisk pace. Her heart was hammering. She glanced over her shoulder and saw, to her horror, the two men lunge at Daniel. Daniel threw a punch at one and caught him on the chin, which made him fly backwards, but before he could attack again, the second had drawn back his leg and kicked him hard in the groin. Daniel staggered and fell to his knees.

"Daniel!" she yelled, and sprinted for him.

He was groaning, trying to get up, when the first man kicked him in the head. Daniel went down like a stone. She was yelling his name when someone grabbed her and punched her just below her diaphragm.

She doubled up and collapsed on the pavement. Another blow landed deep in her ribs, another in her midriff. She groaned and vomited. She tried to get her face out of the vomit but her head was pressed against cement. She was gasping, struggling for air, sucking in vomit through her nose and mouth.

She thought she heard her name being yelled. Oddly, she thought it was Lee, but the next instant her ear exploded, erupted into a single giant bloom of pain. It blossomed into crimson, then black.

TWELVE

Georgia's consciousness crawled awake. She was lying in the corner of a dimly lit room. Vaguely she registered dusty floorboards, bare walls with cracked and peeling paint, a handful of chairs behind a big wooden table.

She saw a Chinese man sitting behind the table. Her eyes latched onto him. She wanted to speak to him, but as she lifted her head, he rose and left the room. She could smell cooking, and hear a television blaring, along with the chatter of Thai or Chinese, she couldn't tell, and the clanging of a metal pot.

Cautiously, she struggled to her knees, holding her bandaged hand protectively across her waist. A stab of pain sliced through her ribs and she bent double, retching drily. She wiped the trickle of spittle from her mouth with the back of her right hand. She made it to her feet and started to shuffle for the door. She stopped when it opened.

Four men entered the room. One placed a small black backpack on the table and sat down. He wore a black leather jacket over a white T-shirt. She recognized him as the man who had spat on the floor at the hospital. Another sat beside him, older, dressed in a suit. The others, large, bulky men in jeans and shirts, stood side by side against the wall, their arms folded. With the window behind them, she couldn't make out any of their features, only their silhouettes.

In what she took to be Chinese, the Suit said something to the one in the leather jacket. His voice carried the deep tones of a heavy smoker.

Leather Jacket finally looked at her. "Where is Lee Denham?"

Her breathing was jerky, her mind spinning.

"*Where is he?*"

"I d-don't know."

He looked at the Suit, then back at her. The Suit lit a cigarette, barked a question. Dimly she took in the broad gap between his two front teeth, stained brown with nicotine.

"And Mingshu?"

"Who?"

"Suzie Wilson."

"She died in a plane accident."

Leather Jacket strode forward, and that was when she saw the letters stitched on the T-shirt beneath his jacket: "Windsurfers Do It Standing Up."

The same as Lee's. She didn't know what it meant, didn't want to know.

"Where is Mingjun?"

"Ming who?"

"Mingshu's brother."

"I've no idea. Sorry."

As he approached he stretched a hand wide and she took in the hideous fingernail on his left pinky finger. Roughly two inches long, it was gnarled the color of old ivory dipped in ash.

"Why are you lying?"

Raising her head, Georgia met his eyes squarely, determined not to cringe as he stood before her. "I am not lying."

Leather Jacket's hand moved so fast that she had no time to avoid it and took the slap full on the side of her face.

"Where is Lee?"

She was holding her throbbing cheek, her mouth stinging, but she managed to keep her tone steady as she said, "I saw him on the beach this morning. Three Mile Beach."

"Where is he staying?"

"I don't know."

He slapped her other cheek, but this time she was ready for it and rolled with the blow to lessen its impact.

"Don't lie."

She was about to say she wasn't lying when the Suit interjected and pushed a small bag onto the table. It was, she saw with a little shock, Suzie's fanny pack. He unzipped it and emptied the contents on the table. Then he held up the floppy disk for her to see.

"Where is the rest?" asked Leather Jacket.

If you can't use your fists, don't let bullies see your confusion or your fear. It only makes them worse. Tom's voice.

"What do you mean, the rest?"

Another stinging slap, this one against her left cheek.

"If you continue to lie, you will be sorry."

Ignoring her burning cheeks, holding her fear tight inside her, Georgia said steadily, "I don't understand what you mean. I'm not being obtuse, and I'm not lying. I simply do not understand."

Leather Jacket looked at her, expression unmoved.

"Please believe me," she said in the same calm tone, "when I say I don't know anything about Suzie Wilson, or Lee Denham. I was just a passenger on the same plane as them, that's all."

Leather Jacket walked back to the table, indicating Suzie's fanny pack. "I repeat. Where is the rest? Where is her brother, Mingjun? Where's Lee Denham?"

"I'm s-sorry . . ." She paused and took several breaths until she knew her pulse had calmed a little. "Until now, I'd never heard of Mingjun. And I don't know where Lee Denham is. It's the truth." She gestured at the chairs. "May I sit down? I'm not feeling very well."

Leather Jacket clicked his fingers and flicked a hand at a chair, then at Georgia. One of the men brought the chair over. She sat down, her right hand gripping her wrist above her bandage, trying to ensure they couldn't see her trembling.

Leather Jacket folded his hands on the table. "You have many police friends."

"No, I don't. I know only one policeman. Someone I was at school with. Daniel Carter."

"You are also a police officer?"

"No, I'm not. I'm a book rep. For a publishing firm."

"You work undercover," he said decidedly.

She rose from her chair, alarmed. "No, I don't! I don't work with the police at all. *At all.* I've never worked with them, never wanted to. Just because my school friend is a cop doesn't mean I'm one." Her breathing was coming really fast now; she was terrified they might not believe her.

"You drove Mingshu and Lee Denham to the airfield." Once more Leather Jacket indicated Suzie's fanny pack. "You had Mingshu's personal bag, hidden in your room. Yet you continue to lie."

"I'm not lying! Lee and Suzie got their car stuck in a creek and I helped them out. It was a coincidence, that's all! I'd never seen either of them before."

"What creek?"

"Cassowary. It's on the road two and a half miles southwest of Nulgarra. En route to the airfield. You can't miss it."

"The make of car?"

"A rental Ford. White sedan."

He pulled a mobile from his back pocket and punched in some numbers. A stream of Chinese followed, then he disconnected and put his mobile on the table. "Tell us about the air crash."

"Could I have some water, please?" she asked. "I'm very thirsty."

Another finger click, followed by a guttural command, and one of the heavies left. Nobody spoke until he'd returned and handed her a chipped mug. Her hand trembled as she took a sip, rinsed the stale vomit in her mouth, and, although she wanted to eject it, swallowed.

"The air crash," Leather Jacket prompted.

The Suit was tapping a fingernail on the table, so Georgia started talking. Her voice wobbled occasionally, but as she went on and the heavies remained at their posts, it gained strength. From time to time the Suit would ask Leather Jacket a question, which he would then put to her, dragging out the process.

She told them about the intruder, but they showed little interest, which she took as confirmation that he had been one of their own men, although not one of those in the room; he'd been much smaller.

"You were at the hospital," Leather Jacket stated, indicating she move on, so she told them about Bri, the state he was in. Finally, when she got around to Daniel and their last conversation, the Suit leaned forward, elbows on the table, and let out another torrent of Chinese.

"You talked to this policeman, Daniel Carter, outside the hospital for quite a while. What did you talk about?"

"The plane's sabotage."

"It was sabotaged?" Leather Jacket sounded startled.

"It hasn't been confirmed. I don't think it's even been reported yet."

The sudden image of Daniel sprawled on the pavement, face ashen, filled her mind. Jesus, she hoped he was all right. Did they have him too?

A lengthy consultation followed between her two interrogators. She sipped at her water, never taking her attention from the backlit figures in front of her. Leather Jacket reached for the backpack on the table, pulled out a white object she couldn't identify, and slid it onto the table. The next item he extracted she could identify. It was a pistol. He calmly laid it in front of her, next to the white object.

"You and Lee Denham stole Suzie Wilson from us," Leather Jacket said firmly. "You wanted her for yourselves."

"Stole her? What do you mean, I stole her? For God's sake, she was just on the same plane as me!" she insisted, trying to fight her panic and retain some sort of calm. "It's a coincidence, can't you see? It's got nothing to do with me."

The Suit interjected briefly, then Leather Jacket said, "We are finding it hard to understand."

"Me too! One minute I'm at a funeral of someone I love, then I'm in an air crash and the next thing I'm being interrogated by the police, then kidnapped by you and I've got *nothing to do with anything*!"

Silence.

The Suit clicked his fingers. Leather Jacket nodded at the heavies, who left the room.

Everything was quiet.

Then the door slammed open and the heavies returned, dragging a barefoot figure across the room, tied to a chair, head covered with a black trash bag. The instant she recognized the floral cotton trousers and flowing Indian shirt, she felt her spirit being broken into tiny pieces.

"Mum," she choked.

Her mother's head swung her way and she made an urgent mumbling noise. Georgia couldn't make out what she said and realized she had been gagged.

"Mum, are you okay? Please. God, I'm sorry . . ."

Leather Jacket came and stood next to her. The two heavies stood on either side of her mother on her chair.

"Where is Lee Denham?"

Her mother made a mewling sound. Then a soft plea that sounded like, "Sweet. Run."

Black rage overcame her.

Blacker than she'd ever known.

It swept through her like a tidal wave, blotting out everything. It could have been night. Her vision went completely dark.

Georgia launched herself at Leather Jacket. Both hands punching, gouging, nails tearing for his face. He wasn't ready for her and stumbled backwards, losing his balance, crashing to the floor.

She swarmed on top of him, teeth bared, hooking her fingers to tear at his face, but suddenly there were bands of iron around her chest, pulling her away, and she knew the heavies had her and she ducked her head and caught the only flesh she could find between her teeth. Leather Jacket's wrist. She bit as hard as she could, shaking her head from side to side like a dog killing a rat, enraged and engorged with hatred, out of control.

Leather Jacket was hollering as she bit down hard, the heavies trying to drag her away, but she had his wrist and no way was she going to let go. She was a pit bull terrier and she was growling, chewing, and biting . . .

A blow to the side of her head made her mouth go numb, but she simply bit harder, growled louder.

Another blow, and her mouth went slack. Leather Jacket's wrist slid free from her bite. She felt herself folding to the floor, but Leather Jacket was still yelling fit to burst.

Good.

She hoped it bloody hurt.

Her *mum.* How dare they.

THIRTEEN

Georgia lay panting on the floor, the heavies surrounding her. Leather Jacket came over, cupping his wrist to his mouth, and as he brought his foot back, she rolled to protect her kidneys. When the blow came, it wasn't as bad as she thought it might be, but she groaned a lot and saw his look of satisfaction.

She rolled a little bit farther for the next blow, which glanced off her ribs and still hurt like hell, but the damage would be minimal. Just a bunch of bruises. She yelled to make him feel big, and as he was going to kick her again, she heard the Suit bark an order and Leather Jacket paused, looked across at the Suit then down at her. He made a guttural sound deep in his throat, then spat a gob of mucus at her. To her delight, it missed, landing on the floor beside her head, rather than in her face as he'd intended.

Pulling her lips back from her teeth, she snarled at him and he glared back.

The Suit barked another order. Leather Jacket marched stiffly to stand by him at the table.

Her breathing seemed to fill the room. She raised herself to see her mother on the chair, body shuddering, indecipherable sounds jerking from beneath her gag.

"Mum," she said. "I'm fine—"

Leather Jacket spun around and clicked his fingers, and to her horror one of the heavies strode back to the table and brought a baseball bat into view, raised it away from his body, and swung it straight toward her mother's face.

"Mum!" she yelled, and her mother swung her face toward her but it wasn't enough and the baseball bat smacked into the side of Linette's head with a hollow slapping sound, like an armload of wet towels dropping onto tiles. Her chair flew sideways and her mother plummeted to the floor still tied to it, elbows angled awkwardly, head rolled to one side. Georgia stared at her mother's still form and then she leaned over and retched and retched until her ribs ached.

"Where is Lee Denham?" Leather Jacket insisted. "Where is Mingshu's brother?"

The heavy was swinging the baseball bat casually in his right hand, tapping it against her mother's bare foot. Georgia saw she had magenta nail polish on her toes. Her feet were brown and beautifully pedicured. No doubt done by a mate who wanted an astrological reading in return. That was the way Mum's life worked. You baked a bunch of hash brownies and people fixed your roof, gave you tax advice, introduced you to a plumber who could sort your leaking cistern.

Ignoring Leather Jacket, she concentrated on her mother. Georgia could just make out that she was breathing. She was alive, but as Georgia watched, a trickle of blood seeped from beneath the black trash bag and onto the floor. Gazing at the blood, she felt a black ice creep into her veins. From her fingertips to her chipped, blue-painted toenails, it crawled malevolently to her heart. She would see them dead for this, she thought. Dead.

"We can break every bone in your mother's body. We *will* break every bone in her body if you don't tell us what you know."

Georgia barely felt the pain in her ribs with the new ice-cold, numbing black stream running through her, and her voice was strong when she spoke. "You've got the wrong people, don't you get it? Do some checking. You'll soon find out you've messed up big-time. And I mean big-time." She rolled onto her front and pushed herself steadily upright until she was standing. With the windows behind him, she couldn't see Leather Jacket's eyes, but she settled her gaze where she thought they might be. "I'll be there when you realize it."

"Are you trying to scare me?" he sneered.

"I'm a Scorpio," she said. "If that isn't a warning, then I don't know what is."

"I was born in the Year of the Dragon."

"What a surprise. Arrogant, intolerant, and discontented. Sounds just like you. In case you didn't already know, Dragons are also capable of spectacular failure." She took a long pause. "I was born in the Year of the Tiger."

The way he stilled told her he knew that in Chinese lore, the tiger was instinctively protective and once involved in battle, invariably won. When the mobile on the table chirped, Leather Jacket started as though he'd touched a live wire. Excellent. She had rattled him.

Snatching up the phone, he listened briefly, then disconnected.

Leather Jacket said something to the Suit, who didn't seem to react, but when he slowly reached out and picked up Suzie's parking card, she saw the heavies shift uneasily. Talking in a low undertone, the Suit slowly ripped the card into tiny pieces.

Everybody remained silent. Absolutely motionless.

Suddenly the Suit slammed his open palm down on the table, and the pieces of parking card scattered across the table. Every person in the room flinched, except her mother, who lay as if dead. The Suit spoke to Leather Jacket, who looked at Georgia.

"At last we have part of the truth," he said. "Ronnie Chen rented a white Ford three days ago, but the rental company is still awaiting its return. We are wondering where it is now."

So they knew Ronnie Chen, she thought. She said, "I've told you, Lee left it in the creek."

"There is no car in Cassowary Creek."

She stared at him blankly. "What?"

He gave a long-drawn-out and exaggerated sigh, as though he was bored. "So, where is the car, and where is Lee Denham?"

A sense of dread descended upon her, but she made her tone as firm and strong as possible. "I don't know. It's the truth. It was there yesterday, I swear."

Leather Jacket picked up the metal object off the desk. The two men peeled themselves off the wall and came and stood on either side of her.

She swallowed reflexively. Her mouth and throat felt balled with blotting paper.

Another click of the fingers.

The two men gripped her upper arms and hauled her bodily across the room. She struggled instinctively, bucking and kicking like a captured rabbit, as they carried her to the table and forced her face down so her cheek was pressed hard against the wood. Her right hand was forced high behind her back until she screamed, "Don't, please don't!"

Infinitesimal pause.

The pressure eased a fraction.

Then her left arm was stretched out flat on the table. Her bandage removed. Her hand was spread wide, pulling the stitches and making her bite her lip against the pain.

Leather Jacket leaned over to peer into her face. So close she could count the acne scars on his cheekbones. "You had Mingshu's bag," he said. "You hid the disk. You were taking it to Mingshu's brother, weren't you? We want to know where Mingjun is. We want the truth."

"I wasn't taking it anywhere," she moaned. "Suzie gave it to me."

"Stop lying!"

She felt his spittle on her face and smelled cigarettes on his breath.

"I'm not lying, I swear I don't know anything."

"If you know nothing, tell me why you hid the disk!"

"Because of the intruder."

"Liar!"

"I'm not—"

"See this?"

Leather Jacket brought the metal object into view. She felt her bowels soften. It was a pair of pruning shears. They had a white plastic handle and a small black button on the side. Slowly, he pressed the small button so the blades sprang free.

A child was screaming, an endless shriek of terror. She realized distantly it was her.

Leather Jacket gripped the third finger of her left hand. Her wedding ring finger. He said, "I ask you for the last time . . ."

She was yelling and fighting, trying to break free, but there were lead weights on her back, her shoulders and arms. She was pinned to the table like a live rat to a dissecting table.

He positioned the blades around the second knuckle. She felt the keen steel brush against her finger.

"Where is Lee Denham?"

She could smell her own rank smell of fear. Bitter sweat and vomit and urine. She wanted to cry and scream and plead with him, but knew it would make no difference. Voice trembling, she said, "If I knew, I would tell you. But I don't."

The shears brushed her skin. In that moment, with sudden clarity, Georgia knew this was it. She was going to die. An endless, painful death. A death of blood and screaming and no dignity, her corpse chopped into pieces and flung into a darkened alley. There was nothing she could do about it. Nothing.

She'd seen her mother breathing, and knew she was alive. Would they kill her too?

She saw Leather Jacket's hand squeeze the shears, felt the pressure of the blades. Blood blossomed on her finger.

This is it, she thought. *This really is it. And I've no idea why.*

FOURTEEN

The shears cut straight through the flesh of Georgia's wedding ring finger and through the knuckle and bone with a small crunching sound.

For a split second the shock was so big, she thought it didn't hurt. Then the pain hit.

Screaming black howling shrieking red, it raced from her finger into her hand and up her arm and into her heart, white-hot as a poker, and she was screaming so hard her voice cracked.

"Where is Mingjun?"

Scalding pain licked at her, scorching her skin, her blood and veins, and she was shuddering and shaking against the weights pressed on top of her, and as the pain thundered and roared and pulsed, her screams faded into choking gasps.

"If you do not tell us, we will continue until you have no fingers and no toes."

"Please," she managed, "help me . . ."

"Where is Lee Denham?" Leather Jacket demanded.

Her voice came out as a whimper. "I don't know."

Leather Jacket positioned the shears around her thumb knuckle and she was begging him, pleading with him, but he didn't seem to hear.

"One more time," Leather Jacket said. "Where is he?"

She opened her mouth and yelled and yelled, waiting for more pain, more agony, worse pain . . .

Please God, she prayed, let me faint. Let me die. *Please.*

Gradually, she became aware that nothing had happened. Gulping convulsively, she saw Leather Jacket had put the shears down. *He had put them down.*

The seconds ticked past. Leather Jacket was saying something to the Suit. The Suit sounded angry. Leather Jacket sounded insistent, and nobody moved or spoke except Georgia, who couldn't stop the involuntary whimpering sounds jerking from her throat.

Finally, the Suit spoke. Quietly, almost a murmur.

Leather Jacket picked up her bandage and clicked his fingers at the heavies. They held up her hand. She was saying, no, no, no as she saw the top third of her finger lying on the table, the bloody mess of her stump showing a splinter of white bone through the pulp of red, the slightly yellow sheen of cartilage in what used to be her finger pumping, *pouring* blood . . .

"If you tell anyone of this," Leather Jacket said, "we will find you and we will kill you."

Leather Jacket reached for her bleeding hand.

"And no police."

He made to bind her finger with the bandage.

"We have friends in the police. We will hear."

As the gauze touched her gaping, pulsing stump, the pain rocketed into her head, her brain, and she was shouting again, longing to faint, praying for oblivion, but it never lessened, and then one of the heavies produced a length of black cloth and blindfolded her and, gripping her upper arms, they carted her out of the room and down some stairs. She smelled garlic. Then they were outside, and rain was on her mouth and chin. In a car. She lost track of time as she sat there, unable to see, pain crashing in her finger, her hand. Eventually the car halted, engine still running. There came the sound of someone getting out of the car, her door opening.

She was shaking convulsively, unable to believe they were going to let her go. She couldn't make sense of it. The same thought went around and around her head: *Please don't kill me, please don't kill me.*

Someone gripped her arm from outside and pulled her, scrambling and bewildered, into the rain. She stood cupping her left hand, protecting her damaged finger, which throbbed in a single, sickening black ache. As soon as the men left her, she lurched violently and fell to her knees. The engine was still running.

She flinched when Leather Jacket spoke close to her right ear.

"I only bound your hand to stop you bleeding all over my car."

His shoes scrunched as he shifted closer. She felt him push something into her rear jeans pocket.

"So you know how to find us."

She knelt there, trembling.

"Meantime, we will keep your mother. But only for a week. You have seven days to find Lee Denham and Mingjun before we chop off all your mother's fingers and toes and leave her to bleed to death. Then we will come and kill you. Slowly. One knuckle at a time. Do you understand?"

She gave a jerky nod.

"We will find you wherever you are. You cannot hide from us."

Another nod, then she heard footsteps crunching lightly on asphalt and two doors slam shut. The automatic transmission kicked in. With a wet swoosh of tires, the car drove away.

Georgia didn't dare move. Was it a trap? Was one of the men still there?

The engine hummed into the distance and gradually disappeared. Cradling her throbbing, pounding hand against her chest, she tilted her head to one side, checking for any sound, but otherwise didn't move. She didn't want them to think she might have seen which way they went and come back to kill her. She tried to ignore the pain pulsing through her and listened some more. Nothing. Just the patter of rain on leaves. Cautiously, she raised her right hand and pushed the blindfold up and over her head.

She blinked a few times to clear her vision. Glistening asphalt and rainforest. The air was thick and warm and wet, and she breathed in deeply. A great choking sob of relief caught her lungs and her head dropped almost to her knees. She wanted to pray, to thank God for her life, but her mind wasn't functioning properly. She sprawled there numbly in the rain, shuddering convulsively.

———————

She wasn't sure how long it took before any sort of rational thought began, but it had to have been well over ten minutes, because she realized she was soaked to the skin.

Checking the bandage on her finger, she saw it was already seeping blood and that it needed rebinding. Leather Jacket had done a sloppy job, but she thought she might either pass out or throw up if she unwound the sodden gauze and saw her stump right now.

She knew the pain throbbing in her finger was tolerable, but only if she didn't think about what had happened. It wasn't the pain as much as what it *meant*.

Resolutely, she turned her mind away from her finger and concentrated on getting to her feet. It took her two tries, but then she was upright, swaying slightly, and looking up and down the dark, rain-puddled road. In her pain she didn't recognize it. Were they near Nulgarra?

Instinct told her the thugs would have driven toward a town, wherever they were, so she started walking in the direction they'd driven. She felt so weak and drained that it was more of a shamble than a walk, but at least she was moving.

———————

It was still raining when she heard an engine in the distance. Turning, she saw a pair of headlights cutting through the darkness behind. Her legs were desperately tired and it wasn't because she'd been walking for that long, maybe half an hour or so, but her body was reacting to the shock and stress and simply wanted to rest.

She stood in the middle of the road and waved. Immediately the car slowed as the revs were cut, then it lurched to a rocking stop and a man leaped out and ran for her, his face a pale white shape in the headlights. He wore a long white robe and sandals. For a second she thought she was hallucinating. He looked like Lawrence of Arabia.

"Are you all right? What happened? What are you doing all the way out here?"

"I'm just a bit wet, that's all. Thanks for stopping." Her voice was surprisingly calm through her chattering teeth.

The man made to touch her arm and Georgia flinched.

"You're hurt," he said, expression mortified. "You've blood everywhere. Do you want me to call the police?"

"No!" Georgia could feel her features stiffen in horror. "No police!"

The man paused, then said cautiously, "How about a doctor?"

Georgia shook her head and headed for his car. She heard his footsteps behind her. Following her.

"You need a hospital, there's so much blood. Your jeans . . ."

He sounded tense and anxious. Georgia ignored him and clambered inside the car, pulling the door shut and buckling up. She covered her bandaged finger with her right hand. She was shivering and aching all over. Her head was thundering. She felt like she might be sick.

A click, then the sounds of the man climbing inside the car, slamming shut his door. The sound of a seat belt being buckled.

Small silence.

"My name's Yumuru."

"Georgia."

"Georgia, let me take you to a hospital. Please."

She gritted her teeth against his gentle tone.

He started the engine. "Okay. How about the Lotus Healing Center? It has a wonderful clinic. Mind you, I would say that, since I run the place. And I won't report anything to the police if you don't want."

She couldn't think where else to go, so she gave a small nod.

"I'll check you over when we get there. Then you can rest up for as long as you like."

FIFTEEN

They weren't far from Nulgarra after all, and when Yumuru slowed down before a driveway on the edge of town, Georgia could hardly believe it. The headlights lit a familiar bend in the road and an ancient fig tree she recognized, but instead of a small notice hammered into the tree saying "Free Spirits Welcome," there was a large new wooden sign—"Lotus Healing Center."

"This is it?" she asked incredulously, as he turned the car down the drive.

"Yup."

It was where the commune used to be. She'd lived here for nine years with her mother and sister and, it seemed, dozens of other free spirits. When the land had been sold and they'd been forced to leave, none of them returned. They couldn't bear to see what the developer had done to their home.

"The road's been graded," she said. "It must have cost a fortune."

"Two hundred grand. It's worth it, though. I get patients from all over the country, some from overseas too. Not all of them appreciate being shaken, rattled, and rolled down the drive."

She saw that the rickety phone pylons had gone and assumed the lines were now underground. Not that the commune had had phones in every cabin, just the one in the cookhouse, left by the previous owner, who had abandoned his run-down property. Her mother's boyfriend at the time hadn't wanted it reconnected when they moved in, but Linette had insisted, for emergencies.

Yumuru looked across at her, then back at the headlights cutting across the forest-lined road. She couldn't make out much of him in the gloom of the car, except that he had a well-defined profile and curly black hair flowing in luxuriant waves from a high forehead and caught in a ponytail at his nape.

"You've been here before?"

"I used to live here." Georgia's tone was faint.

"Not the commune?"

She nodded.

"You'll find things have changed a bit since then."

She glanced over at him. The light bounced off his little round, gold-rimmed glasses. She wanted to ask him why he'd chosen such a remote location, but didn't have the energy against the pain of her finger.

"I've been healing for over fifteen years now. I used to be in the army, if you can imagine it. It's good for marketing. The last headline was 'Killer Turned Healer.' I quite liked that."

His voice was calm and steady, and she realized he was trying to build her confidence in him and inject a sense of normality into her pain and her silence.

"It's the center's tenth birthday soon. Some days I can't believe we've been going that long. I healed a very ill, very rich woman in Melbourne once and she helped get me started. She even named the place, the lotus being her favorite flower. Without her, I'd never have helped as many people as I have, and being half-Aboriginal—half-psychic, my mum used to say—it's not entirely surprising I changed careers so dramatically. The army indeed." He snorted. "Thanks, Dad."

He braked, and the automatic transmission clicked as it changed down a gear. The headlights swept over an immaculate parking lot dotted with baby African oil palms.

"You need a wheelchair or anything?" Yumuru's tone was light, but Georgia could feel his anxiety.

"No, thanks."

He stopped the car in front of a broad set of slate-and-wood steps and tripped off the floodlights. Georgia clambered dizzily outside, barely able to recognize the place. There were no tin-roofed cabins, no vegetable plots, no chickens and bantams scratching between flowering shrubs. The forest had swallowed all evidence of the commune, and in its stead was a large, thatched Balinese-style building. Its roof was draped in bougainvillea, its wraparound veranda adorned with elaborate wicker chairs and glossy ferns. A large sign, "Seminar Building," pointed left to a low-slung building made with the same materials. The place was tasteful and elegant, and dripped with exclusivity.

A man in shorts and a jersey came across the parking lot and spoke with Yumuru before Georgia was shepherded into a reception area. Lots of deeply polished wood, bamboo chairs, and scattered rugs. The smell of hay. In the light Yumuru was older than she'd thought, probably in his early forties. She noticed his hands, long and delicate, the color of nutmeg. They were surgeon's hands, smooth as a girl's, the nails lightly shaped and buffed to a high sheen.

Glancing at the man in shorts, Yumuru said, "Frank tells me the police are searching for someone matching your description who was kidnapped earlier today. Can we at least let them know you're okay? We don't, er . . . have to tell them where you are."

Georgia ignored the longing to fall into a heap and straightened her spine. "That would be great. And you're right, they ought to know . . . It might help if you spoke with a Sergeant Carter, if he's around. Tell him it was a case of mistaken identity. As soon as they realized they'd got the wrong person, they ditched me."

"Right." Yumuru spun around and ordered Frank to call the police, but not to tell them where she was. Frank obediently trotted off.

"Now." He turned back to Georgia, puffing a stray strand of hair from his lips. "Let's get you to the examination room."

———

Georgia hadn't a clue what time it was when she woke with a start, an excruciating pain pulsing furiously from her finger and up her arm. Groaning under her breath, she reached for the pack of co-dydramol painkillers Yumuru had left on her bedside table. He'd told her one or two would be enough and not to take any more, even if the pain was bad, as they'd make her queasy. She downed two and settled back, waiting for them to kick in. After a while the pain settled to a dull throb and her breathing leveled. She opened her eyes.

Sunshine poured into her room, and she could hear the raucous screech and chatter of parrots through her open window. A blowfly droned above her head. She could see three more flies on the outside of her mosquito net, and she lay there for a while, listening to the sound of the bush awakening, trying to ignore the throbbing in her wedding ring finger. The pain was a fraction of what it had been, and she thanked the heavens for Yumuru and his surgeon friend from the Douglas Mason Hospital in Nulgarra, who had clambered out of bed to arrive just before midnight.

Because they didn't have a qualified anesthetist on hand, the surgeon was only able to give her a local anesthetic. He gave her some midazolam, and she'd floated in and out of consciousness while he injected her around the wrist and trimmed and pulled and stitched her finger, chatting to Yumuru about mutual friends—who'd gotten married, who was having an affair with whom—which gave her a peculiar but comforting sense of normality and security.

The surgeon had asked her what the implement had been and she'd told him, saying it had been a gardening accident. Yumuru looked at her with his sharp brown eyes but didn't say a word. He reminded her of Tom, with his intelligent face and kind nature, so much that her throat ached.

Georgia raised her hand and studied it. A fresh bandage protected the wound in the pad of her hand and incorporated more bandage on her finger. It almost didn't look as though the top third was missing.

Taking her time, she rose and showered, then went back to bed. She fell asleep again, finally waking when the sun was high in the sky. Her body was sore and aching from Leather Jacket's kicking, and she downed another painkiller, not caring if she got queasy. Anything rather than the constant agony of her body trying to heal. Slowly, she got dressed, her stomach lurching every time she thought she might knock her finger.

Her clothes were clean and ironed, thanks to Yumuru, and he'd put her handful of change and two business cards carefully on top of her underwear, where she couldn't miss them. One was Daniel's, the other Leather Jacket's. She tucked the latter into her front jeans pocket without looking at it.

Finally she was standing at her window. Warm morning air drifted around her, and birds fluttered after insects in thick grass the height of her thighs.

She thought of her mother, bound and gagged and bleeding from her head, and her legs immediately began to tremble, her lungs unable to grab any air. She wanted to howl and cry and lash out at something, but it wouldn't do any good. She had to remain strong, and not let her grief and rage take control.

"Sorry, Mum," she said. "I can't think about what you're going through. I'm going to have to pretend you're okay, or I won't be able to function and I'll be no use to you."

Georgia turned her mind to Leather Jacket and the Suit.

We will keep your mother. But only for a week. You have seven days to find Lee Denham and Mingjun before we chop off all your mother's fingers and toes and leave her to bleed to death. Then we will come and kill you. Slowly. One knuckle at a time.

She pictured Leather Jacket's sneer, the Suit's nicotine-stained teeth, and felt the rush of black ice return.

She had seven days.

Seven days to save her mother, to save herself.

She had better get started.

Sixteen

Intending to find Yumuru, Georgia was about to open her bedroom door when someone knocked sharply on the other side.

Stepping back, she called, "Who is it?"

"Dominic."

"Who?"

"Are you decent? I hope so, because I'm coming in." The door opened and a slender man in blue linen trousers and matching shirt marched inside. "I've been told you might not want to see me but, well, here I am, and you'd better know I can be extremely determined."

He had a pink holdall in one hand, which he put on the end of her bed, then he looked at her, expression appalled. "I've come to cut your hair. Immediately."

She found herself smiling at him, and as she moved to close the door she saw that a tray of fresh fruit, coffee, raisin toast, and butter had been left outside her room. With her good hand she brought it in. The coffee was in a pot, the fruit sliced mango and papaya, and the butter came in a little pack, marked unsalted. Yumuru had to be a mind reader. Her favorite breakfast.

"Let's go short, shall we?" Dominic said briskly. "Very gamine, very chic."

Georgia let him sit her on the edge of the bed, fluff a blue-spotted robe around her neck, and damp her hair down with a handheld spray. While he cut her hair, she ate her breakfast, and when he'd finished, she looked in the mirror he held for her. She blinked.

"You don't like it?" he asked anxiously over her shoulder.

Spikes and a chin the size of the Great Australian Bight gazed back. She ran a hand over the spiky creation, amazed at the feel of silk against the vision of aggression. She looked like an echidna, spines erect and ready to defend its life, but it was so *soft*.

"No, it's not that I don't like it," she said. "It's just that it's not who I used to be."

He cocked an eyebrow at her. "So who are you now?"

"I don't know." Impulsively she turned and kissed his cheek. "I felt so *ugly*. How much do I owe you?"

"You don't have to worry, it's paid up."

"By who?"

"This was a personal request from the guy who runs this place. A gift."

"Yumuru?"

"Is that a problem?"

Georgia studied her reflection again.

"No," she said faintly. "No problem. It's a lovely gift."

Dominic was replaced by a huge, barefoot Aboriginal woman who introduced herself as Joanie. "'Muru asked me to show you round," she said. "Tells me you used to live here."

Georgia looked outside at the sun streaming through the grass. In her day the grass would have been shorn, thanks to the goats. "It was a long time ago," she said on half a sigh, "when it used to be a commune."

"Not anymore, but 'Muru's turned it right round." Joanie pulled her too-tight yellow-and-red dress down over her hips, looking proud. "He gets patients from all over. Even had a bloke from Perth last month. Real sick he was, but 'Muru fixed him up."

"Perth's a long way to come," Georgia agreed, but despite her friendly tone, Joanie gave her a narrowed look.

"Don't know what you've heard in town about 'Muru, but whatever they've said, take it with a bucket of salt. He's all right, 'Muru, okay? Goes a bit troppo from time to time, but most of us do anyway up here. Especially in the bloody wet."

"I remember."

Joanie grinned, showing purple gums and broad teeth. "That why you leave? Fed up with the wet?"

Not wanting to go into the fight they'd had trying to keep the commune, she shrugged and said, "I guess so."

The commune had been a swamp in the wet. Just getting from their cabin to the cookhouse was a struggle, and she and Dawn invariably arrived at breakfast muddy and bedraggled and feeling like creatures from the deep lagoon. Dawn hadn't taken to living in the rainforest as well as Georgia. She missed town life and loathed the long-drop loos with their plethora of creepy-crawlies. It wasn't the fact that a spider might bite her rear end as much as the smell. No wonder she'd fled to Canada and all that clean, pure air.

For a brief moment, Georgia considered calling Dawn and immediately rejected the idea. Dawn would drop everything and come over, the thugs might snatch *her,* and then she'd have two people to worry about, not one.

"You okay to follow me?" said Joanie. "Then you'll know where everything's at. 'Muru said you can stay long as you like."

"Joanie, I'm sorry, but there's no point in showing me round. I won't be staying."

Joanie looked shocked. " 'Muru will kill me if I haven't done the full tour. He's proud as hell with what he's done since you lot were here."

"I have to be going, honestly—"

"We'll do the shortened version, then," Joanie said firmly and ushered her out of her room and down a long corridor for a door at the far end, which Georgia hoped was the exit. However, it was just a very small room, and as she reluctantly followed Joanie inside, Georgia put a hand against the wall, suddenly unsteady. The air was filled with the scents of sandalwood, lavender, and burned juniper. If she closed her eyes she could be at the commune, but the commune had never been this silent. Too many chickens and parrots, laughter, the odd argument, pots and pans being bashed about, children playing, someone singing.

"You okay?" Joanie was peering at her, big brow creased.

Georgia straightened. "Fine. Thanks."

"This is where he prays. Well, anyone's welcome. But it's mostly 'Muru's place."

The room was tiny, and against the opposite wall was an altar. Made out of simple whitewashed boards, it had three small steps flanked by vases of flowers and little bowls of sand stuck with incense sticks.

There were two photographs on the altar. One was of the Dalai Lama, but the second made her breathing falter.

"You okay?" Joanie asked again.

Wordlessly, she pointed at the photograph.

"She used to work here." Joanie rubbed her forehead and looked at the floor. "She was on the plane that went down. She didn't make it."

Georgia touched the photograph with a finger.

It was Suzie Wilson.

———————

Joanie took Georgia's sudden enthusiasm to take the full tour in her stride and showed her a communal living area, where there was a kitchen as well as a small library and a balcony overlooking a fig tree, which was being slowly strangled by the biggest vine Georgia had ever seen. Her mind in overdrive about Suzie, she asked Joanie if she knew Suzie's family.

"She didn't have none," Joanie said. "Well, not here, anyway. They're all in China."

"Where did she live?"

Joanie frowned and Georgia hurriedly added, "Sorry. I heard about the crash. I was just curious."

Joanie didn't reply and, seemingly unperturbed by Georgia's nosiness, proceeded to lead her along a long corridor of polished boards covered with tatami mats and into reception. Georgia glanced into the parking lot to see nine cars, two of which were brand-new, white, top-of-the-range Land Cruisers. Each had a bright purple emblem of a lotus on its front doors.

"Who finances all this?" Georgia asked.

Joanie spoke over her shoulder as she walked, her huge buttocks bunching and wobbling. " 'Muru charges a bloody fortune. Five hundred bucks for a one-on-one healing session. Eleven hundred for a weekend seminar." She leaned over and picked a tiny shred of tatami from between her bare toes. "Mind you, if you're broke, he'll do it for nothing, but don't spread it around or we'll have the whole bloody world on our doorstep."

"How many people attend his seminars?"

"Anything between twenty and fifty. Depends."

Which made Yumuru anything between $A22,000 and $A55,000 in a single weekend.

"How often does he hold them?"

"Every three months or so."

Georgia did a couple of calculations. Not bad. Maybe her mother should have charged people for the pleasure of staying at the commune. They might have been able to afford electricity instead of having to rely on two hours of power from the generator.

A little bubble of distress popped in her chest and she forced it quickly back down. It's fine to think of Mum, she assured herself. Just don't think about where she is right now.

A woman in a white uniform, sitting behind a reception desk, said hello, and Joanie introduced Georgia. "Just going to check on Tilly now," Joanie said to the receptionist. "How's she doin'?"

"Not so good today," the woman replied. "But you know how it is."

"You can join me, if you like," Joanie told Georgia. "Do Tilly good to see someone new. She's getting sick of the sight of us."

Hoping she'd find out more about Suzie, Georgia said, "Sure."

The instant they entered Tilly's room, Georgia wanted to turn around and bolt outside, away from the thick, warm smell of suppurating flesh. Thick as custard, it coated her tongue, and it was so revolting, like rotting, maggot-infested flesh, that she tried not to clamp a hand over her face, but she couldn't help it, it was *disgusting*.

Head turned to the wall, Tilly's face was gray and drawn with exhaustion and pain. Georgia fought to breathe as shallowly as she could, but she still gagged.

"Hey you," Joanie said, apparently oblivious to the stench.

In torturous slow motion, Tilly managed to roll her head their way. Georgia dropped her hand and tried to breathe without contorting her face.

"How are they?" Tilly whispered.

"A bloody pain in the backside," said Joanie, scowling. "Chasing bloody piglets all over the place. The sooner you can take them off me, the bloody better."

"Piglets," Tilly whispered.

"Too bloody right. Don't suppose they give pigs such a hard time in Pitman? Guess not, being your mum and all, but they do me. Get your ass into gear and take 'em off me, will ya? Had enough of babysitting your brood."

Sweat beaded on Tilly's face. The gray hue to her skin had deepened. She was, Georgia realized with a shock, close to death.

Yumuru entered the room, scraping tendrils of hair off his face. He wore a white coat and held a small aluminum bowl and a syringe. "Hi, Joanie. Tilly." His expression brightened when he saw Georgia. "How are you today?"

"Pretty good, considering. And thanks for my haircut. It's possibly the best present I've ever had."

He flashed her a smile, his teeth almost luminous white against the dusty brown of his skin. "I thought it would help you feel better." Small pause, then he said gently, "I just want to administer Tilly's vitamins. Then we're going to have a healing session. You can come back in an hour, if you like."

"No worries," said Joanie. "We're all done here now as we know Tilly's gonna sort out her bloody kids for us."

They left Yumuru and Tilly and as they walked down the corridor, Georgia said, "What'll happen to her kids?"

"Nothing. She'll be right soon."

"But she's *dying*."

Joanie stopped and looked at Georgia. "Not for long, she isn't. She only got brought in a coupla days back, so she's still crook, but she'll be sitting up and watching telly in a few days. She's not got no cancer or anything, just a sickness."

"What sort of sickness?"

"Got chewed by a croc a while back. Silly cow slipped up doin' a show with Jimmy. Jimmy's her dad, right? They've a croc farm over Pitman way. Opened it up as a tourist attraction. They know crocs real well, but even they get caught out, time to time. She was waving her bucket of croc feed to the right, expecting the croc to go for it, but she slipped and the bucket ended up between her legs."

Georgia felt her eyes round in horror.

"Got it in one. Crocs took the bucket and half Tilly's groin too."

"Christ."

"That's not it, though. Doesn't matter how you get chewed by a croc, it's not the bloody bite that gets you, but the water you fall into or the crap on their teeth. Pure poison. You get a croc bite and it's likely to fester and eat at your body until you die."

"Like Tilly?"

Joanie pushed open a door. "No, she'll be all right. Yumuru can't cure cancer, but he's sure got a talent for croc bites."

SEVENTEEN

They made their way back to Georgia's room. On the way
they passed a steel door with a punch-key lock.

"What's in there?" Georgia asked.

"Pharmacy."

"Why the lock?"

"They had two hundred dollars' worth of Chinese herbs nicked
one time. Not that the lock stopped the next lot, mind, they just
smashed in the window. Happened a couple of days back. We found
blood everywhere, silly buggers."

Georgia paused outside the ladies' room. "Joanie, I'm sorry. I'm
feeling tired. I'll just use the loo here and go to my room afterwards,
so please don't wait for me."

Joanie nodded. "You know to turn right at the waterfall? Otherwise you'll come round full circle."

"Thanks."

Joanie raised a hand as she turned aside. "No worries."

Georgia slipped inside the ladies' and waited half a minute or so.
Then she crept to the door and checked the corridor. Empty. Slipping
outside, she headed straight for the pharmacy door. Tried the handle
anyway. Locked, of course. Walking a little way down the corridor,
she stood there, senses alert, waiting for someone to go in or come
out. Without a watch she had no idea how fast or slow time was pass-

ing. She counted sixty seconds away. Waited some more. Counted another three minutes.

Part of her couldn't believe she was planning on seeing what was behind the locked door, but her finger pulsed and hardened her resolve. Suzie had worked here, and the day after she'd died the clinic had been broken into. She could see the Suit holding the floppy disk up for her to see, and hear Leather Jacket's voice.

Where is the rest?

She couldn't sit around waiting for answers. She had to take action.

Straightening at the sound of a small clunk inside the door, she took a deep breath, drew her shoulders back, and walked toward the pharmacy. As it opened, she kept going, nearly colliding with a girl exiting. "Sorry," the girl said, looking startled.

"That's okay," Georgia said, and brushed past the girl. She didn't pause, or look around, simply strode inside like she knew where she was going.

Posters of the Canadian Rockies on one wall. Two chrome laboratory benches running the length of the room. The aroma of coffee and a spicy medicinal scent that reminded her of tiger balm. Piles of computer printouts on the floor. Files, folders, charts, and journals all jumbled together with aspidistra and rubber plants. There was a window on the left, presumably the one used for the break-in. Refrigerators and freezers against the wall on the right were covered in more debris. Five large stand-up bins overflowed with paper. There was a door at the far end of the room.

A young Asian man was sitting at one of the benches in front of an electronic balance, carefully scooping soft white powder from a weighing boat into a small clear plastic bag. He looked up, and Georgia gave him a nod and marched forward. Sweat trickled down the inside of her arms.

Okay, so what can they do me for? Breaking and entering? I'll get a caution, that's all, so keep going. And don't think about Yumuru's kindness. You've got to concentrate on Mum.

"Excuse me . . ."

She turned to see the young Asian man standing behind her. At the far end of the pharmacy a florid-faced man stopped leafing through the mess and glanced up, gave her a narrowed look, then started sorting again.

"Are you Terry?" the young man said.

"Er . . ."

"The guy to fix our computer." He looked abashed. "Sorry. I mean *person* to fix our computer."

She took a step forward and shook his hand. "Yeah. I'm Terri . . . Deewell. That's right."

"Robert. Robert Curtis." He looked at her bandage. "What happened to your hand?"

"Gardening accident," she said. "A handful of stitches. It won't hold me up work-wise, if that's what concerns you."

She followed him to a workstation in the corner. Photographs and magazine clippings were pinned on the partition walls, and piles of computer printouts spilled from the table and onto the chair.

"Sorry it's such a mess." Robert picked up the printouts and put them on the floor. He scooped a pile of files from the desk and put them beside the printouts. "Got burgled yesterday."

"They find who did it?"

"Nah. One of the patients saw a couple of Chinese-looking guys prowling in the grounds, that's all."

Her skin tightened. She knew it. Her kidnappers had broken into the clinic. What were they searching for?

"Anything taken?"

"We're not sure yet. Dave's missing his computer disks, me too, and they got two of our computers. Otherwise not much. They were disturbed before they could strip the place. We've a security guy, he scared them off."

While he cleared the work space, Georgia looked at the photographs. Three were enlarged photographs of tropical rainforest, another of a broad river with long, sluglike shapes on the sandy banks. "Are those crocodiles?" she asked Robert.

He glanced around. "Yeah. Monsters, aren't they?"

Georgia paused at a photograph of a bound crocodile beside a tin boat on a riverbank. Its snout was tied with rope and a small figure sat astride its shoulders, holding what looked like a giant syringe.

Georgia peered closer.

"She's not hurting them or anything," said Robert. "Just collecting wild croc blood. Farmed crocs have too much fat in their systems for her to work with. Suzie was doing some private research in her free time. Something about their serum."

"Good Lord," she murmured, amazed. Tiny, fragile-looking Suzie Wilson, collecting wild croc blood. Who would have thought it?

He gestured to the far corner of the room, at a worktable covered in an array of shiny, new-looking equipment. "She came to an agreement with 'Muru so she could work after hours. Use our fridges and freezers and stuff. She was our head of pharmacy." He swallowed audibly, then cleared his throat. "She's not here anymore," he added. "She got killed in an airplane accident a couple of days back. It's awfully quiet without her."

Georgia clamped down the empathetic wave of grief threatening to rise. "I heard on my way in, Robert. I'm really sorry."

He surreptitiously brushed at his eyes, then turned on the computer and showed Georgia the problem, a corrupted file allocation table, otherwise known as a FAT.

"Hmm," she said. "It's trickier than I thought. If you leave me for twenty minutes or so, I'll see what I can do." She paused. "Is this Suzie's computer?"

"Yeah. She had a laptop too, but she always took it home." He glanced at the photographs. "I haven't had the heart to take anything down yet. Can I get you a coffee?"

She shook her head. "I had some before I came out, but thanks."

As soon as Robert left, she scrolled through the computer's directory, which, thank God, seemed to be working fine.

What shall I look for? References to Chinese things? Lee Denham? Mingjun, Suzie's brother?

After ten minutes, she hadn't found anything she considered relevant, so she turned to the filing cabinet placed on her left, glad she was well tucked out of sight behind the partition walls. She checked the plastic tags and pulled out the one marked "Personal." A handful of household bills in Suzie's name confirmed the cabinet was hers. She found a checkbook, and more photographs of crocodiles along with a thickset man squinting in the sun and wearing nothing but shorts and a pair of battered heavy boots. Pocketing a house-rental contract with Suzie's address, she looked around at the door on her right. It had an identical punch-key lock to the main pharmacy door.

Georgia got to her feet and checked the room. Florid-Face was on the phone, and Robert was absorbed in counting tablets and checking long strips of computer-generated labels.

She quickly walked to the door and tried it. Locked. The worktable was next to it, and she took a hurried glance: a microscope, something with a sticker declaring itself a centrifuge, a laminar-flow cabinet, incubator, autoclave. Under the table stood cardboard boxes bulging with notebooks and papers and more equipment.

Now what? Take the bull by the horns.

She walked away from the worktable and over to Robert. "Big problem," she said. "It's more than a FAT. I'm going to have to bring in backup."

He sighed. "Yumuru won't be best pleased. But you'd better go ahead."

She looked around. "Nice place to work."

"Yeah. I like it."

Gesturing at the door at the far end of the room, she said casually, "How come that door needs a lock if you've already got one on the other door?"

"It's where we keep the more expensive stuff. The boss's special vitamins cost a fortune."

"You've the code?"

He looked surprised, as if he hadn't thought about it before. "No, I don't. Not that I need it, I guess, since 'Muru administers them."

She was about to ask him more about Yumuru's expensive vitamins when a man barked, "Get this woman out!"

Georgia jumped and spun around. Florid-Face was standing right behind her.

"Wow. You gave me a fright," she said, and stretched out her hand. "I'm Terri Deewell. Here to fix your computer problem."

He didn't shake. "BCP Computers don't employ a Terri Deewell. I just checked."

She assumed surprise. "You're kidding me, right?"

"I'd like you to leave right this minute. Before I call the police."

"But I was just—"

He came and gripped her upper arm. "Out."

Robert stepped back. He was scratching his cheek.

Georgia snatched her arm free. "Okay, okay, I'm going . . ."

"You lot make me sick. Pack of hyenas is all you are."

Florid-Face picked up a phone and punched some numbers.

"Steve? We've another journo here. Come and see her out, would you?"

Steve the security guard didn't seem to care that he was three times her size and that she had a bandage on her left hand. She pleaded with him to be careful, that she'd only just had an operation, but he ignored her and hauled her unceremoniously down the corridor, gripping the collar of her T-shirt tightly in his fist. It made her feel as though she was a disobedient puppy being thrown out for lack of bladder control.

They entered reception, Steve striding, Georgia scrabbling to keep up.

"What's going on?" It was Yumuru, looking surprised.

"She's a reporter. Hassling the guys in the pharmacy about Suzie."

Yumuru's eyebrows remained high. "Really?"

"You want me to drive her into town? Get rid of her?"

Long pause while Yumuru studied Georgia. He had said she could stay in the clinic as long as she liked, but now that she'd been caught nosing around his pharmacy, she wondered if the invitation would stay open.

"No," said Yumuru. "I've got to go into town myself. I'll take her."

EIGHTEEN

Y ou're not a reporter," Yumuru said.

They were walking down the slate-and-wood steps to the parking lot. The atmosphere was stifling and she could smell the soft earthy mulch of the rainforest simmering in the midday sun and hear the screech of sulphur-crested cockatoos.

"No," she agreed. "I'm a book rep. Venus Publishers."

"I've heard of them."

"They're one of the larger companies in Sydney."

He gave a couple of nods and said, "You've somewhere to stay in town?"

Rather than stay with Mrs. Scutchings, she wondered if Evie would put her up. "Yes, thanks."

"Come back tomorrow and we'll change your bandage. It really should be changed daily for a couple of weeks or so, until the wound has granulated, then we'll remove the sutures."

"Thank you."

He didn't say any more, just walked for one of the massive Land Cruisers, hopped inside, and started the engine. She was about to walk for the passenger side when he held up a hand and said, "Just a sec," and popped the hood before jumping back out.

Yumuru peered at the V-8 engine, then cocked his head and appeared to be listening hard.

"Something wrong?" she asked. It sounded fine to her.

He reached past her and pushed the accelerator cable, making the big engine roar. Without looking up, he said, "What were you doing in the pharmacy?"

Georgia decided on the direct approach.

"I was on the plane that went down," she said. "With Suzie."

"Yes. I recognized your name from the papers."

"Oh. Well. I didn't realize Suzie worked here until this morning," she added cautiously, watching the side of his face. "I thought maybe seeing her office, I might . . . I don't know, come to terms with her death. She died in my arms, you see."

He glanced up at that, and she recognized her own pain of recent grief reflected in his face. "She was lucky to have you with her," he said quietly. "Dying alone, especially after such a violent event, would have been terrible."

Clearing his throat, Yumuru bent back over the engine, fiddling with a dirty hose. He then unclipped the air-filter lid and had a look. She watched him pull the big circular filter out of its casing and bash it against his leg, dust flying in a cloud. "Filthy," he muttered.

"You seem to know your way around an engine," she remarked.

"That's the army for you." He pushed the filter back into place before looking up. "Train you to fix cars, build bombs, lay a minefield."

"Healing suits you," she said.

He unhooked the strut and let the hood slam shut. He smiled into her eyes. "I think it does too."

––––––––––

As they cruised down the drive, a whip bird flashed past. Above the engine she heard the musical thrum of insects and was glad Yumuru didn't believe in driving in an iced cocoon of air-conditioning. She liked having the windows open somewhere so lovely, even if it was hot enough to broil a steak on the hood.

She rolled her head on the headrest to look at him.

"Do you mind if I ask you about Suzie?"

"No, I don't mind. Talking about her might . . . ease how I feel.

She was a good friend. A very good friend." His voice thickened. "I loved her very much."

Georgia let some time pass, allowing him to regain his composure. When they reached the end of the drive, Yumuru halted the car.

"Where would you like to be dropped?"

"The Newview Caravan Park on Kee Beach. It's where a friend of mine, Evie, lives. If it's not too much trouble."

"No trouble."

He swung the car left.

"Did Suzie work for you for long?"

"She turned up on the doorstep five years ago, applying for a job in the pharmacy. Not many people want to work somewhere so remote, so I grabbed her with both hands." He sighed. "She had a wicked sense of humor."

They talked about Suzie's liking for practical jokes, the hours she kept, how good she was with the patients, and then they reached a T-junction. He swung the Land Cruiser left and accelerated hard to pass a sedan towing a small tin boat.

"Do you know what sort of private research Suzie was doing?" she asked. "Robert said something about wild crocodile serum."

His knuckles glowed white as his fingers tightened on the steering wheel. She'd touched a nerve, she knew it, but when he spoke his voice didn't betray anything, and his knuckles had relaxed.

"She never said. I let her use some of our equipment, that's all."

"But didn't she come to an agreement with you? Surely you must have had some idea what she was working on." Georgia wanted to add, "Especially if she was such a good friend," but decided not to push it.

"It might have been something to do with arthritis. Her grandmother suffered terribly. Suzie used to send packets of glucosamine to her in China. A lot of them never got there, but she kept sending them. I reckon half her salary went on those pills. They're horribly expensive."

Braking smoothly before a sharp bend in the road, Yumuru eased the car into the corner and pressured the power after the apex. Her body barely moved.

"Suzie was Chinese, wasn't she? With a Chinese passport. Did she have a work permit? A visa of some sort?"

Yumuru flicked her a mock alarmed look. "Please don't tell me your publishing job is a cover and you're actually working for the immigration department."

She laughed. "No. I promise."

He shot her a quick smile. "In all honesty, I never checked. I was only too grateful having someone so well qualified. I paid Suzie cash every month, and it suited us both fine."

So, she thought, Suzie could well have been an illegal immigrant. She wondered if that had a bearing on the thugs' motive, their questions. Leather Jacket had said Lee had *stolen* Suzie. Why?

"I gather the pharmacy got broken into yesterday?"

"Yes. Not that they got much. A couple of computers. We can replace them with the insurance money. It's the hassle more than the actual theft. The place is such a mess."

"I don't suppose any of the people at the clinic had their houses broken into as well?"

He jerked his head around, obviously startled. "Not that I'm aware of. Why?"

"Just a thought," she said vaguely.

Yumuru signaled right and joined the main road heading north. After a long, sweeping bend, Kee Beach appeared. With bright white sand, glossy palm trees, and ocean the color of turquoise, they could have been driving into a holiday brochure.

"Do you know anything about Ronnie Chen?" she asked. "The man whose body was washed up here?"

"Only what I read in the papers."

As he drove under the timber post of the caravan park, Yumuru peered around at the deserted vans and the half-full swimming pool, its surface littered with branches and leaves from the storm.

"Is Evie open?" he asked. "It's not exactly the holiday season."

Confidently, she said, "She will be."

"Have you known her long?"

"All my childhood."

He pulled up outside the park's white-painted office but didn't turn off the engine. Georgia climbed out, shut the door, and looked at him through the open window.

"Thanks, Yumuru. You've been great."

He leaned toward her. All friendliness vanished. She took a step back. She wasn't looking at a healer anymore.

"If you go poking about my clinic again," he said, "I'll have you prosecuted. Do you understand me?"

Georgia swallowed. "Yes."

Without another word he gunned his Land Cruiser away.

NINETEEN

To Georgia's relief, Evie was there, and welcomed her with open arms. Engulfed against her huge bosom, the bitter smell of the Aborigine's sweat mingling with the aroma of spices and barbecued meat, Georgia felt like she was a kid again. Evie had always given the best hugs on the planet.

Before Linette had set up the commune, they'd stayed at Evie's caravan park, which had been a quarter of its current size back then. When they eventually moved into the rainforest, Evie became a regular visitor, bringing crates of cold beer and boxes of wine, sometimes some vegetables or fresh fish, but even if she came empty-handed she was always welcomed. Evie was the best gossip in town. When they got thrown off the commune, her mother didn't have to ask Georgia or Dawn where they wanted to go. Evie's park was their second home, Evie like a second mother.

"What the hell you do to your hand?"

"Slammed my finger in a car door."

Evie looked shocked. "You poor bugger. You break it?"

"Not quite."

Evie pulled her into another, but more gentle embrace, patting her back rhythmically as if she was a baby that needed burping. "That's to help it get better."

"Sorry I dinged your car."

Pulling back, Evie said, "One of Becky's pilots brought it back from the airfield. I thought Matt had whacked a tree."

"I hit a cassowary. Killed it."

"You barbecue it, or bush-roast it? Meant to taste good, those things. Like emu or some such." Evie was chuckling, seemingly indifferent that Georgia had depleted the tenuous population of cassowaries from 1,500 to 1,499.

"I left it in the road."

"Wish I'd known. I'd have had it chopped up and in my freezer in no time." Evie fetched a handful of keys, and Georgia followed her to the storeroom at the back of the office. "Always fancied a drumstick the size of a barrel."

Arms laden with fresh sheets and towels, they headed through the park and toward the beach, Evie waddling like a gigantic goose in front of Georgia along the concrete path. The way her bottom wobbled beneath her tight green dress was very familiar.

"Evie, do you know Joanie, at the healing center?"

"Sure I know her. We're cousins."

"Ah."

"Best van here's already taken," said Evie. "You can have the second-best, but then you'd be neighbors, and since I seem to recall you like a bit of space round you, you can always take number seventeen, right the other end of the place."

Scampering to keep up with Evie's giant stride, Georgia wiped her cheeks of sweat. The temperature had to be in the high nineties, the humidity level somewhere around ninety percent. The tumultuous clouds that had been skulking above had been swept aside by boiling winds and had left the sky clean and clear as polished crystal. Sweat leaked out of her hairline, and her T-shirt was sticking to her chest and back like a second skin. On a day like today she could hardly believe she'd lived up here for so long. Nine years without air-conditioning. Bloody hell.

"Who's staying?" she asked Evie.

"That reporter. India Kane."

"Then the second-best van would be fine. I don't mind being next to her."

"You met?"

"At the hospital."

She asked Evie what she knew about the murdered man, Ronnie Chen. After all, the man's body had washed up on her beach.

"Shot in the back of the head, I've been told. Jonesy—he's one of our local constables—told me the bloke was a right piece of work. Into everything bad you can think of. Blackmail, prostitution, kidnapping, murder, drugs, you name it, he made money out of it."

"You're kidding."

"Good riddance, if you ask me."

Evie unlocked the door to a huge deluxe caravan overlooking Kee Beach and the Coral Sea. Each van stood on blocks between close-cropped lawns, surrounded by cluster fig trees and varieties of ferns. As well as the swimming pool, there was a tennis court, a crazy golf course, and a giant shower block with hibiscus climbing its walls.

India had the prime van, right on the edge of the sand and facing the mile-long northern stretch of beach, but Georgia's was barely second-rate. Her van merely faced south, with a half-mile view, and not the full mile. Both vans had their own electronic fly-killers, brick-built BBQ, and private, open-air freshwater shower for rinsing off after your swim. She could see India's laundry baking in the sun. Loose cotton shirts and shorts, and a row of raspberry-colored G-strings.

"Bit stuffy," said Evie as they stepped inside. "It's been locked up a while. Here's your key. Why don't you leave me to it for a bit? I'll shake the sheets out, dust down, and get it ready for you when you get back."

Georgia was staring at the green-blue water, wishing she could take a swim and ease her throbbing, aching muscles before sprawling under a palm tree and sleeping the rest of the day away, but she had more important things to do. Like see if Suzie's house had been burgled, and if so, whether there was a connection to the pharmacy break in, not to mention the intruder and the thugs who had mutilated her.

She heard a car pull up outside. Which reminded her.

"Evie, I forget, is there a bus I can take into town?"

Dumping the sheets on the double bed at the far end of the van, Evie said, "Stop being so bloody English. Just come straight out and ask. Yes, you can use my Suzuki. Keys are hanging up in the office."

"Are you sure?"

Evie gave her a reproving look and Georgia hastily said, "Thanks heaps," and made a hasty exit.

––––––––––

India was at the back of her ute, heaving a case of beer, and when she saw Georgia, she dropped the beer and raced across.

"Jesus, Georgia. I heard you were kidnapped. Are you okay?"

"They picked up the wrong person," Georgia said.

"Thank God for that." Scraping hair from her face, India added, "Who were they after?"

Georgia shrugged.

The reporter frowned. "What happened to your finger? I thought it was only your palm that had to be stitched."

"Er . . . well, the guys who snatched me were in such a hurry they slammed it in their car door."

"Jesus," the reporter said again. "They were Chinese, weren't they? The guys who grabbed you?"

"Um . . ." Georgia looked away. "I suppose they could have been."

"I'm wondering if they weren't something to do with Ronnie Chen," India mused. "The RBG. The Red Bamboo Gang. Did you hear Ronnie's name? Or hear of anyone called Chen Xiaoqiang, Gap-tooth Chen?"

Despite the simmering heat Georgia's skin went cold. The Suit had a space between his nicotine-stained front teeth. Was he Gap-tooth Chen? Licking her lips, she said, "Who?" as blankly as she could.

"Gap-tooth Chen runs the RBG. Ronnie was his elder son. Jason

Chen's his younger. I've heard Jason always wears a leather jacket, even in this heat."

When Georgia didn't say anything, India sighed. "Bugger it. I'm having no luck discovering who murdered Ronnie. Not from lack of trying, though."

Trying to push the image of the Chens aside—the father smoking his cigarettes, the son in his leather jacket—Georgia ventured, "You came up here to find out who killed Ronnie Chen?"

"No, that happened after I'd arrived. I came up to see Suzie Wilson."

Startled, Georgia said, "Suzie?"

"Yeah. She rang me with a story she thought I might be interested in. About how healing centers could be exploited. We were going to meet on Saturday, for lunch, but . . . well, you know what happened."

"Suzie thought the Lotus Healing Center was exploiting people?"

"She didn't say exactly, but I've checked it out and can't see anything but a lot of happy patients." India indicated the case on the back of her ute. "You fancy a cold beer?"

Pulling her damp T-shirt from her chest, Georgia said, "Maybe later. I need to go to the bank and see if I can get some money."

India brightened. "How about if I come with you? Vouch for you to save some time? Banks are notoriously difficult when you've no ID." When Georgia hesitated, she added, "You need a ride?"

"I've Evie's car, and it's very kind of you but—"

"Let's meet at the Bendigo in half an hour, okay?" India didn't wait for her to respond and hopped into her car.

———————

After filling the Suzuki's tank, Georgia found India at the bank, already in full flow on her behalf.

"I've known her yonks," the reporter was saying to a pretty girl with a stud in her nose. "I'll be her guarantor, no worries. She'll need at least a thousand bucks cash, and a credit card. Like in ten minutes."

The counter was awash with India's ID, driver's license, bank cards, passport, press card. A quick meet with the Bendigo's manager, who made a single call to Georgia's bank in Sydney, and she was issued eight hundred dollars along with a Visa card.

"Thanks," Georgia said to India on the street. It would have taken hours longer without her.

"Anything else I can help with?"

"No, but thanks. I'm just going shopping. Clothes and stuff."

"See you later for that bottle of wine?"

"Sure."

Georgia held her Visa card in her good hand as she left India and walked down the street, amazed at the sensation of comfort a small plastic square could give her, that she could walk into any rental car office or airport and go pretty much wherever she wanted. Not that she intended to head anywhere without her mother, but it was the principle of freedom that caught at her at that moment.

Ducking into Price's, she grabbed a shopping cart. Feeling a strange sense of cheerful normality as she trundled along the air-conditioned aisles, she instantly felt guilty. She was shopping, while her mother was in the clutches of the Chen family, the RBG . . .

She could see her mother tied to the chair on the floor, elbows angled awkwardly, head rolled to one side, her bare feet and beautiful pedicure.

Hurriedly she pushed the image out of her mind and concentrated on buying basic items, from a pack of cheap cotton undies to raisin toast and shampoo and deodorant, double-strength acetaminophen for when Yumuru's supply of co-dydramol ran out, then a pair of half-decent shorts, a couple of T-shirts the color of daffodils, canvas shoes, a small denim handbag, and a plastic, ten-dollar watch with a bunch of fruit on its face.

With the shopping in the back of the Suzuki, Georgia drove south, all the windows open and fanning scalding air inside. She was drenched with sweat and her T-shirt was stuck against her spine, her jeans glued to the backs of her thighs. Since the car was a stickshift, she had to use the fleshy base of her left palm to change gears, but she could barely feel the stitched wound through Yumuru's painkillers, just the continual throb of her finger.

Nick Clarke, the postmaster-cum-travel agent, had told her how to find the address on Suzie's contract. Since he'd been known to do mail deliveries himself some days, Nick knew where everybody in the area lived, even the ferals, who had opted out to hide in the rainforest and only came into town to collect their security benefit.

"At the end of Ocean Road," Nick had said, "don't turn into town but head straight ahead. It's a bit rough, but you're a local, you should be okay."

Passing the harbor and its Shipshape Chandlery, Georgia did as Nick said and took the bumpy, mud-slicked track that ran parallel to the river. She just had time to jab the brakes before the car's hood rose over the first hump and slid down the other side with a splash that threw muddy water over the windshield.

Flicking on the wipers, she doused the windshield with washer fluid, wondering why the council hadn't graded the track. From memory there were at least five houses down here, and it must have been impassable a few days back, even with a four-wheel drive. She guessed the residents probably liked it, or were resigned to being flooded for one or two months every year.

Suzie's single-story house was right at the end of the track, and although it had taken Georgia only ten minutes to get here from the center of Nulgarra, it felt remote, as though she'd traveled much farther. Flanked by the Parunga River on one side, rainforest on the other, it had mosquito netting on every window and a big tub of cheerful daisies beside the front steps.

You couldn't see any neighbors—unless you drove back along the track six hundred yards and peered through the foliage away from the river. Georgia reckoned people in this neighborhood weren't particularly neighborly, but she could be wrong.

As she shut the car door she took in the sound of cawing behind the house, toward the forest. Crows, she thought. Lots of them. Something had probably drowned in there during the storms, like a big lizard, or someone's cat.

The contract in Georgia's back pack stated that Suzie rented her house for a hundred dollars a week, which seemed reasonable considering it needed a new roof, a coat of paint, and new shutters on the windows. Trotting up the steps and across the veranda to the front door, she halted at a doormat that said, "Beyond Therapy," and felt an urge to knock even though she knew no one was home. She peered through the window to her left.

"Jesus," she murmured.

The room was a mess. Each drawer had been upended. Potted plants and CDs, books and cushions were intermingled in careless heaps. She bet the Chens had been here. Glancing around to check that she was still alone, she pulled her T-shirt out of her jeans and covered her hand with it before trying the front door. Her heartbeat picked up when it opened.

Cautiously, she stepped over the debris. There was an overpowering stench of decay, which she soon discovered came from the kitchen, where the doors of both fridge and freezer had been left wide open, their contents dumped on the linoleum. An army of cockroaches bolted for cover at her arrival, but the carpet of ants continued their feeding, seemingly oblivious.

As Georgia stared at the ants, a sudden realization hit her. It had only been two days since the air crash. Just two days. It felt as though she'd experienced two years of hideous pain and fear.

She moved around the house without touching anything. Lots of posters on the walls. Vistas of Katherine Gorge, the Great Wall of China, views of rainforests and Australian beaches.

Two bedrooms, only one used.

One bathroom and one living room. A dining room, which was used as a study. There was a space on the dining table where a computer would have sat. The filing cabinet was empty and the files strewn all over the floor. Carefully, she shifted a few about with her elbow.

Electricity. Health. Receipts. House Management.

No computer disks. She wondered if the Chens had trashed the house before or after they'd snatched her, and decided probably before. That's why they were so angry. They hadn't found what they wanted.

Where is the rest?

The rest of what?

T-shirt back over her hand, she opened a fat beige file filled with an assortment of handwritten papers. They were all in Chinese. Great. Some were pieces of paper torn from what looked like school notebooks and A4 pads, while others were on stiff quality paper and typed. As she rose, something caught her eye. Something urgent. She looked around but couldn't see anything. Just the mess of a house that had been well and truly ransacked.

Georgia crouched back down. Trained herself to recall exactly where she had been. She relaxed and went back to the files. Shifted a few about. Rose a little.

Blink, blink.

A tiny red light was flashing at the corner of her eye.

She looked up at the Panasonic fax-phone machine.

Georgia leaped to her feet.

New Message. Blink, blink.

T-shirt over the button, she pressed it.

"Yo, Suzie. Me here. Where the sod are you? It's bloody Saturday night and I can't believe you've stood me up. Hope you've a good excuse because even old Nail-tooth's pining. Bloody call me, you rotten cow. I've been missing your skinny, bony ass."

Click.

Silence.

Georgia looked at the little red light, still flashing. Should she leave the message for others to listen to? Before she could change her mind, she pressed erase. A single beep, then the center panel flashed "ICM Erase OK?" She hit a big green button and was told "Erase Completed."

She quickly pressed speakerphone, followed by the star button, the number ten, then the pound key.

A woman's monotone filled the silence. "Your last unanswered call was . . ."

Georgia scrabbled inside her pocket for Jason Chen's card and, lunging for a pen on the floor, scribbled the number on the back. Her writing was uneven and shaky from the adrenaline ticking through her. Getting to her feet, she pocketed both the pen and the card.

Everything was still and silent. No sound of wind in the trees, or an outboard motor, a neighbor's car. Just the distant sound of the crows.

Okay, she thought, trying to ignore the sweat trickling down her flanks and drenching her waistband. What else?

"What else" led her to the small handful of mail by the front door. A couple of bills. A letter addressed to a Marc Wheeler, which invited the man to upgrade his platinum American Express card for a black one. Perhaps Marc Wheeler used to live here. An old tenant maybe?

Georgia spent the next fifteen minutes wandering around the house, trying to get a sense of Suzie and her life. There were no postcards or photographs or diaries. It was as though Suzie had lived in a timeless vacuum. No past, no present, no future. Aside from the one phone message, she'd have thought the woman lived like a nun on a religious retreat. There was no evidence that she had contact with anybody.

———

Eventually Georgia stepped outside and walked down the side of the house and into the backyard. The cawing and flapping increased. To the left, the trees were studded with crows and magpies, and she could see maybe half a dozen or so black kites wheeling low in the sky.

Something had definitely died out there. And not something small either, or it wouldn't have attracted so many scavengers. It couldn't be a cow or sheep, because there wasn't any livestock around. A tree kangaroo?

Cautiously, Georgia approached the fence surrounding the yard and peered into the forest. Nothing. She looked up and a crow flapped heavily into the air, its belly so full it could barely clear the ground.

It must be a roo, she thought, but as she turned to head back to her car, a faint breeze sprang up and trailed across her face.

Christ almighty! She spun around, a hand across her nose and mouth, but the forest was the same. Dark and impenetrable. She took a tiny experimental breath and retched. Holding her breath, Georgia jogged to the front of the house, glancing over her shoulder as she went.

Inside the house, using Suzie's phone, she resisted calling triple zero and rang Daniel Carter instead.

"Hi. It's Georgia here. Georgia Parish—"

"Christ, as if I don't know who you are . . . What the hell's going on? I got an anonymous call from some bloke saying you were okay, but what the hell happened?"

"I've no idea. They picked me up, realized they'd got the wrong person, and dumped me out of town."

"So the anonymous caller said. Where are you now?"

"Suzie Wilson's house. I want to call the police, well, I know I am, but I'm worried it might be nothing."

"What is it?"

"Well, there's all these crows and kites gathered in the forest. And an awful smell. I'm talking a really, really awful smell."

"And you don't think it's a dead rat."

"No."

"I'll be there in twenty. Sit tight."

TWENTY

Daniel arrived looking cool and crisp in chino shorts and a loose blue shirt. Nice legs, she thought. Long and muscular and tanned, and not overly hairy. He even had nice knees, lucky man.

"What on earth happened to your hand?"

"Looks like hell, doesn't it?" she said. "It is hell, actually, because in their hurry to get away, those damned thugs managed to slam it in their car door."

"Will it be okay?"

"Oh, sure. In a little while."

Like never, she thought. If I ever get married, I'll have to wear my wedding ring on my right hand. Or on my index finger. Or just not get married, and keep life and all its little complexities of chopped-off fingers out of sight.

"Who were they?" he demanded.

"I don't know."

"You didn't pick up any names?"

"They didn't introduce themselves, if that's what you mean."

"Shit. Why *you*?" He held up his hand before she could reply. "I know, it was a mistake. But who the hell *were* they after? And who was your anonymous caller? The guy who told me you were okay?"

Realizing she was backed into a corner, she hastily said, "What I called you about? Shall I show you?"

Without waiting for him to agree, she headed to the backyard and to the fence at the far end. He took one breath of the stench and said quietly, "Shit." He looked into the forest, expression unreadable, then with a single fluid movement he vaulted the fence and paused, head cocked to one side, listening. Unholstering his Glock pistol, he started moving soundlessly into the undergrowth, and within seconds he'd vanished.

She was filled with dread at what he might find. What if, she thought suddenly, the Chens had decided not to keep her mother and had dumped her body here? A wave of sheer panic washed over her. She could hear the baseball bat smacking into the side of her mother's head with a hollow slapping sound and see the trickle of blood seeping from beneath the black trash bag onto the floor. What state was her mother in now? Bleeding slowly to death from her shattered head? She had to hurry. Try harder to save her.

She started at the sound of a twig snapping, but it was only Daniel, Glock holstered. He sprang over the fence and walked toward her. He was shaking his head.

"What was it?"

"Pig. A record-breaker too, around three hundred pounds. Got shot maybe two days ago."

"A *pig*?"

"Feral," Daniel added. "They're a pest up here."

Georgia looked toward the dripping rainforest, the tendrils of creepers against the fence. "Are you sure it's just a pig? Nothing more?"

"If you don't believe me, look for yourself. He's fifteen yards in, five yards to the right. Watch out for the maggots."

"No thanks." She felt her tension ebb away. She was so grateful it was just a pig. Thank God.

They both looked up at a sudden noise. Three crows were dive-bombing a kite.

He said, "Did you know Mrs. Scutchings's place was turned over yesterday morning? She came back from buying her morning newspaper to find it ransacked. They even ripped out her baseboards."

The Chens. That's when they'd found Suzie's fanny pack and the disk, which had led them directly to her. Georgia was glad Daniel was studying the flurried aerobatic display and not her face, which had gone rigid. "Poor Mrs. Scutchings," she managed.

"Have you heard from Lee Denham?"

"No. Sorry." At least not today, she added to herself.

He gestured at the house. "What are you doing here?"

To buy herself some time, she began to walk back along the yard to the front of the house. Daniel followed. She desperately wanted to tell him everything, have someone strong and professional to lead on and take charge, but she daren't breathe a word about the Chens or her mother.

We have friends in the police, we will find out.

It wasn't that she didn't trust Daniel, but he might mention something to another cop, and they'd tell another, and it would get back to Jason Chen and his father and they'd kill her mother without a second's thought and then come after her. *One knuckle at a time.*

"Georgia?"

"I hoped it might help me come to terms with her death. Seeing where she lived. What type of person she was . . ."

He gave her a look that told her he was finding that hard to believe, so she hung her head, finding it no difficulty to look shamefaced since she was lying through her teeth. "Okay, so I'm nosy. Is that such a crime?"

"Not in itself, but—"

"Her house has been ransacked too," she said, wanting to avoid the lecture she reckoned was coming.

"Vandals," he said. "I'll bet they were here the second they read about her death in the newspapers."

For a moment she was filled with doubt about the Chens trashing Suzie's place, but then she remembered the break-in at the healing center.

They were at the front of the house, and since it felt like the sun was trying to cook her brain, she moved into the feathery shade of a bunch of black palms. Brushing the sweat from her forehead, she then busied herself in inspecting the bandage, already filthy, while Daniel stood close to her, studying his fingernails. He had strong, lean hands that were lightly freckled, and his knuckles were bruised. She hoped the thugs were suffering from the punches he'd thrown at them.

"Did you speak to the Air Accident Investigators?"

He let his hand fall to his side. "I've been wanting to talk to you about that."

Looking up she saw that the kite was now high in the sky, wings spread into peerless blue, and the crows had dispersed, leaving it alone to soar the thermals.

Daniel said, "The report says the plane ran out of fuel, which means it was pilot error."

"Doesn't the aerodrome have records of who refueled which aircraft and when? Then we could prove Bri filled up."

"No record. No need. They've their own tank." He sighed. "They reckon Bri was in such a hurry to take advantage of the brief break in the storms he miscalculated, believing he had enough fuel to make it to Cairns, when he hadn't."

Shocked, she said, "But he'd never do that!"

"It's not the first time it's happened. A bloke had to ditch his Cessna in the Tasman Sea last year because he was in too much of a rush to beat the southerly coming in to fill up. The insurance company came good, though. Pilot error is okay, like reversing your car into a lamppost. Insurance covers those glitches. That's what it's there for."

Hell. She hadn't considered the insurance before. Would the insurance company pay Becky if the plane had been sabotaged? After September eleventh, she doubted insurance companies covered malicious damage or terrorist acts. Maybe she should leave the sabotage well alone and protect Becky and her vulnerable family against a bunch of suits who would leap at the chance not to pay out.

Find 'em for me. Swear it, Georgia. For me. And for Suzie.

What next? Bri wouldn't want Becky and their kids to suffer, but she couldn't repress the vision of saline sheets draped across Bri's legs and feet, the way his boots had melted into his skin, the fury in his blood-filled eyes. She had promised him.

She'd have to see Becky, she realized. Sit down and talk it through. See what Becky wanted. And talk to Bri again too, if he was up to it.

"How's Bri doing?" she asked.

"Not so good. Sorry." Daniel ran a hand over his head. "I think Lee's trying to distract us. By getting us to look for a phantom saboteur, we're not looking for him. Lee can continue, business as usual. We can't be in two places at once."

"Why do you want him?"

"He's a member of the RBG. The Red Bamboo Gang."

A little shock beneath her breastbone. Lee's and Jason Chen's T-shirts. *Windsurfers Do It Standing Up.*

"He's quite near the top of the people-smuggling pile. Helps a guy called Chen Xiaoqiang oversee the gang here and in Fuzhou, China. Bribes the right officials. Disposes of those who don't fall in line. Launders money through various companies around the world. Hong Kong, L.A., Rio, you name it, Lee's got a finger in it. Take Lee out, and we'd stand a chance at nailing the bastards, but he's too clever. I get within spitting distance of him, and he vanishes like a puff of bloody smoke."

His jaw rippled with tension, but she could see he was making an effort to relax when he took a couple of deep breaths and gave her a rueful smile. "I feel I know the man inside out I've been after him for so long, and I'll bet my last dollar he knows I'm in the area, trying to track him down. Lee's fabricating the sabotage story, interfering with my efforts to run him to earth. Cunning bastard."

Sweating helplessly in the stagnant mangrove air, she remembered Lee reproaching her on Three Mile Beach. *You owe me.* Daniel was right—Lee had known Daniel was in the area, and now she knew why Lee hadn't wanted her to tell anyone she'd seen him. He was a member of the RBG, working with the Chens, who were holding her mother.

There was a long silence while she reviewed Lee's involvement with her mother's kidnappers against his saving her life. She still couldn't tell Daniel about Lee, she realized. It came back to the same old thing. *We have friends in the police. We will hear.*

"So." Daniel cleared his throat. "When are you heading back to Sydney?"

"Soon," she said vaguely.

"Route eighty-one was given the all-clear this morning. Would you like a lift to Cairns later? I've got someone to see down there, it'll be no trouble."

"Er . . . that's kind of you, but I've a few things to do. I'll, um, maybe head there in a couple of days or so."

"Oh. Well. I thought perhaps"—he looked almost embarrassed—"you might have dinner with me."

A tingle ran down her spine. "Daniel, I'd love to, but . . ." She trailed off, desperately trying to think of an excuse that would make him see it wasn't that she didn't want to have dinner with him, but had a genuine reason not to.

He gave her a smile, one of those that lit his face and made her feel fourteen all over again. "Come on, you'll love it. I know this great place overlooking the sea. They've one of the best wine lists around, and have a selection of oysters from all over the place."

Small swoop of delight, astonishment. He knew she loved oysters? Or just a guess? Was Daniel Carter *interested* in her? The thought made her flush, and his smile broadened to a grin.

"You're on?"

God, she was tempted, but the sudden thought that she couldn't call her mum to say she'd be late, that she was having dinner with her old school crush, extinguished the feeling.

She'd been twelve when she'd gone to her first evening barbecue on the beach. Unchaperoned, she'd felt proud and grown-up and slightly smug that her friends from the commune hadn't been invited. Around ten o'clock someone's father said it was time to take her home or she'd be late. She had refused his offer. Wouldn't her mother be worried? he asked. No, Georgia cheerfully told him. My mum isn't like other mums, she's chilled.

But when Georgia turned up past midnight, she discovered her mother wasn't chilled at all.

"How dare you be late!" she had yelled. "The next time you're enjoying yourself and want to stay longer, *call me,* or you'll never be allowed out again!"

She couldn't remember her mother ever shouting at her or Dawn before. Georgia had been so shocked that she spent her teens constantly ringing home, which all her peers found odd considering she had the coolest mum around.

"Daniel, I'd love to," she said, "I really would, but—"

He shuffled his feet and looked aside. "It's okay. Next time maybe."

"Yes, please."

Flapping aside a mozzie droning by her ear, she gazed at the thin film of what looked like dust on the surface of the Parunga. It wasn't dust, she knew, but nutrients stirred up by the crabs feeding on the bottom of the river. Jesus, she'd almost forgotten why she was here. Suzie and her private research. Mingshu and her brother. One ransacked clinic, two ransacked houses.

"Daniel, am I right in thinking you speak Chinese?"

"Holy heck, however did you know that?"

"Oh, something I heard at school probably," she said. She remembered the hours she'd spent poring over Sun Tzu's two-thousand-year-old text and could even remember some now.

"Disorder arises from order," she said, thinking of her previously calm and ordered life, now blasted apart.

His eyebrows lifted. "Cowardice arises from courage."

"And weakness from strength."

"You are a bundle of surprises," he said. "How do you know Sun Tzu? It's not exactly required reading in Australia, although I believe it's used in America for courses about management leadership."

"I was planning on being an ascetic nun."

The eyebrows practically disappeared into his hairline. "Really?"

"I thought it would complement a warrior who was deeply entrenched in the politics and psychology of conflict."

For a moment he appeared completely nonplussed.

"Sorry," she said hurriedly. "We got sidetracked. You speak Chinese?"

"Cantonese."

"Can you read Cantonese?"

"Why?"

She led him into Suzie's house and picked up the fat beige folder. "I was just curious. She hasn't anything personal here, aside from these."

He looked at her askance. "You've been through her things?"

"I thought, er . . . that maybe I'd write to her family. I was with Suzie when she died. I mean she came from China, and they might like to know . . ." Georgia trailed off at Daniel's incredulity.

"Nosy is right." He gave a snort. "Along with interfering, prying, and snooping."

Her face grew hot. "That's me."

But to her surprise, he reached for the beige folder and flicked through the pages. Eventually he murmured, "They're letters to Suzie."

"What do they say? Are they from her family?"

"No. They're begging letters. From people who knew her in China and who want to come to Australia. They're asking her to sponsor them, help them get visas, emigrate out here."

If Suzie was an illegal immigrant, she thought, there was no way she could help them. Suzie would get deported the instant the authorities heard from her.

"This one's from . . . I don't believe it."

"Who?" she demanded. "Who is it from?"

"It's not who they're from so much as who they mention." He suddenly looked up and she saw a gleam in his eye, a spark of something dangerous, something dark.

"Lee Denham," he said. He bit his lips and looked suddenly focused, cold.

"What does it say? About Lee?"

The coldness disappeared as he shrugged. "Not much. It just refers to him as 'our friend.'"

"Is there anything else?"

His expression turned distant, thoughtful.

"The man who mentions Lee is in a detention camp. Right here in sunny Queensland. An illegal immigrant called Paul Zhong." He flicked through the rest of the letters, then pushed the papers back to Georgia.

"Which detention camp?" asked Georgia.

"Why the interest?"

"Maybe Suzie has a relative there?"

Another snort of disbelief. "Do you *like* doing this stuff? Do you really want to share the details of how she died?"

She didn't reply, and guessed he'd now be relieved that she'd said no to dinner. Could Paul Zhong be the link between Suzie and the Chens? Or was Lee, near the top of the RBG and mentioned in the letter, the connection? He'd been flying with Suzie, after all, and if she saw Paul Zhong maybe she'd find a clue to propel her on the road to rescuing her mother. But how to get Daniel to help her?

Turning the letters over in her hands, she said, "I thought you wanted to catch Lee. If I can get a clue from this Paul Zhong, maybe it will help you find him."

"The thought had crossed my mind." His tone was dry.

"Maybe we could go together."

"I don't think so."

"Come on, Daniel, you owe me! If I hadn't rung and got you out here, you wouldn't have a lead to Lee. Where's the camp? Is it far?"

A lengthy debate with himself, then he relented. "Restwood. It's way west. Towards Palmerville."

She was about to suggest she go there now when he added, "They're as tight as ticks, you'll never get in."

"But they'll let you in. A policeman. I can map-read, if you like."

Another pause. "Okay."

She followed him back outside and watched him go to his car, reach through the open window, and pull a radio off the dash. She could just hear his voice above the crows' cawing, but not what he said. Ten minutes later he returned, looking annoyed.

"Appointment's all set. Midday Wednesday. They're refusing to make any other time. Talk about inflexible."

"But Wednesday's great! It's only two days away!"

He was scowling. "I've a birthday party I can't miss."

"Oh."

"So they're expecting you."

"Daniel . . . thank you."

"One condition."

"No problem."

"That any information you get on Lee, you give to me immediately. Immediately, do you hear? Ring from the camp if necessary."

He was staring at her so intently, his expression so fierce, that she wasn't sure if he was actually seeing her. He seemed to be looking beyond her and at something else, something dreadful, and the way he looked reminded her of an emotion she had felt, but couldn't remember what it was.

"Okay," she said, slightly unnerved.

"You've a mobile?"

"No."

"I'll drop one off to you. Where are you staying?"

"The Newview Caravan Park."

He gave a couple of nods. "Right. I'd better be getting on, then."

They walked to their cars. His was a white police Holden ute with a big blue number twenty-two painted on its hood. She wouldn't like to get on his wrong side, she thought. He had one hell of a temper. Out of nowhere, Mathew Larkins sprang into her mind, the man Daniel blamed for his father's death, whose house he had firebombed. Slow-burning embers had nothing on Sergeant Carter.

But of course. Daniel was a Scorpio, like herself. In her besotted school days she'd recorded his birthday—November 15—in her diary and surrounded it with hearts. Scorpios possessed a sting in their tails and an inordinate ability to remember every grudge and to exact vengeance whenever the opportunity arose, no matter how much time had passed.

She let Daniel back his ute out before she climbed into the Suzuki, which she knew would be like an oven inside. As she watched him pick the Holden carefully over the ridges in the track, keeping one tire on firmer ground all the time, she was reminded of her mother, who had never gotten used to driving in the wet and regularly got stuck on the commune's track and had to get a tow out.

A shock of recognition ran through her.

The way Daniel had looked reminded her of the black ice she had felt running in her veins when she saw her mother gagged and bound to the chair. The emotion, she recalled, was hatred.

TWENTY-ONE

By the time Georgia got to the hospital it was late afternoon, but the heat, amazingly, had increased. Roofs, bricks, and pavement had absorbed the sun's rays all day and were reflecting the heat back into the air. It was like walking through a sauna fully dressed and her body cooling system appeared to have broken down. The moisture on her skin couldn't evaporate in the excess humidity, and her clothes were saturated with sweat.

The hospital wasn't much cooler, and as Georgia headed for the reception desk, she wondered if the air-conditioning had packed up. Jill Hodges, the nurse who had held her hand after the air crash, looked up and said, "You just missed him." Her brow was creased and her mouth set tight. "I'm so sorry."

"He's gone to the Brisbane burns unit?"

Jill Hodges studied her face a second, then she rose and came around the counter. "Perhaps you'd better take a seat."

A jet of alarm shot through Georgia. "Why? What's wrong?"

"Please."

It was obvious the woman wasn't going to say another word until she was seated, so Georgia sat. When the nurse sat next to her, Georgia focused on a poster of the lymphatic system. She said, "He died, didn't he?"

"I'm so sorry."

Dimly Georgia realized she was sitting on the same chair she'd used after she'd been airlifted to the hospital. Instinct? Or habit?

"He was strong, but his age . . . He had terrible burns. Becky was with him. His wife. Just an hour ago. We tried our best, but we lost him."

Tears spilled down Georgia's cheeks and she wanted to run to her mother and burrow in her embrace and cry and cry and cry. Too much death. Tom, then Suzie, and now Bri.

"Will you be all right?" asked the nurse. "I can call a friend for you, if you like. We wouldn't charge you. Nor for a taxi either."

"Thanks, but I'll be okay. I'm going to see a friend right now."

———————

Georgia parked beside a clump of flowering ginger the height of her waist and, taking her shopping from the back of the Suzuki, went inside the caravan to unpack. She found a note from Evie, in her large, loopy handwriting, propped by the kettle telling Georgia to help herself to the milk, juice, and water in the fridge, no charge, and to keep the Suzuki since she didn't need it for the next few days.

Besides Evie's note was a mobile phone with a fluorescent green Post-it attached. Daniel's slanting black handwriting.

"All charged up and ready to go. Speak to you tomorrow."

He must have grown wings to get it to her so quickly. Talk about an action man.

After a shower and changing into her new shorts and one of the daffodil-colored T-shirts, she downed the last of Yumuru's painkillers—her finger was pounding like a piston engine—then picked up Daniel's mobile.

For the first time since he'd given it to her, Georgia was able to look at Jason Chen's card. *The Xian Restaurant. Authentic Sichuan Cooking.* Under the Cairns address was a color photograph of a table laden with dishes of shrimp, chili beef, vegetables, a whole fish, and crispy roast duck. It looked delicious, but there was no way she'd be eating there, not even if you paid her a million dollars, not *ever*.

Georgia turned the card over and dialed the number she'd scribbled down in Suzie's house.

"Yo," a man's voice answered.

Georgia introduced herself and told the man that she'd been to Suzie's house and picked up his number.

"Miss her bony ass," the man said on a sigh. "Can't believe she got wiped out like that. Damn shame."

She said, "Would you mind if I came and talked with you?"

"Where you coming from?"

"Nulgarra."

"It's a bit of a hike," he said. "I'm way north of where you're at."

"I don't mind."

"Tomorrow okay?"

She said tomorrow was fine, and he gave her directions before adding, "Make sure you're covered head to toe in insect repellent. Can't stand a girl all bitten up by the little peckers."

She promised and then said, "Who's Nail-tooth?"

He chuckled. "A mate of Suzie's. We can always see if he's about, if you like."

They ran over the arrangements again, and hung up.

Going to the fridge, she pulled out a bottle of water and went and sat with her back to an African oil palm, watching the sun set. It didn't take long, maybe twenty minutes or so, and then it was dark, the air filled with the whine of mosquitoes and the occasional spit and crackle as an insect got zapped by the electronic fly-killer. She could hear waves lapping gently against the shore. No surf up here, not with the Great Barrier Reef just over the horizon.

It was a tranquil, tropical paradise, but Georgia couldn't appreciate the beauty of the place; her mind was filled with chaotic images of Bri and Suzie, of Tom and her mother, and she just about leaped a foot in the air when a voice said, "Hey, Georgia."

It was India, dressed in a short skirt that showed off her long brown legs. "I brought the wine," the reporter added.

Georgia patted the sand beside her. "Have a seat."

India settled beside her, propping her back to share the trunk of the broad oil palm, and poured the wine, handed her a glass. Georgia took a long slug, then another, suddenly wanting the alcohol to hit her veins, take the edge off her tension and dull the constant pulsing pain in her finger.

"Nice night," India said.

Georgia held her glass out for a refill and India didn't say a word, simply topped it up to the brim.

"Here's to paradise," said Georgia and took another long pull of wine.

Small silence.

India lit a cigarette, then said quietly, "Paradise is all very well, but not if you've got troubles. Then you barely see it."

A small wave rushed against the sand. There was a faint pause, then the hiss as it started to recede.

Georgia said, "Bri died today."

"I heard."

She felt India's hand close over her forearm and squeeze it tight, give it a small shake of compassion, then fall away. It was a far more powerful gesture than words, and Georgia was grateful she didn't have to say anything. No exhausting words of reassurance.

"He used to pick us up from school," Georgia said. "With his nephew Joey."

"Tell me," said India.

So Georgia told her about the war against the townies, Bri teaching her and Dawn how to sail, how his tooth got knocked out, the day he had arrived at the commune with his ute covered in balloons for her thirteenth birthday, the handful of photographs he'd given her when she'd left for Sydney, half of them out of focus, but each one showing a view of Nulgarra, so she wouldn't forget the place.

When she fell silent, India said quietly, "He was a good man."

"The best."

A sliver of black ice settled in Georgia's heart.

She could hear the sea rustling over the sand and the crackle of dry palm fronds in the light breeze and smell the smoke from India's cigarette, but all she could think of was the oath she had made to Bri.

She had promised him retribution. Someday, somehow, someone would feel the sting in her tail.

"Georgia." India's voice was hesitant. "Can I ask you a question?"

"Sure."

"Would you mind me asking you about Lee Denham? I know he saved your life, but there's a whole bunch of issues surrounding him. Did you know he's a member of the Red Bamboo Gang?"

"Daniel Carter told me."

"Right. Well, I'm still trying to find out what happened to Ronnie Chen." India took a long drag of her cigarette. "Anything you could tell me about Lee might help."

Georgia carefully checked what she knew against what she might learn from the reporter, and decided a little honesty might go a long way.

"He's an enigma," she eventually said. "On one hand, he's a hero, pulling us all out of the burning plane, cool as a cucumber, but on the other the police want his guts for garters."

India pushed her cigarette in the sand. "What else?"

"Lots of things. Not just his saving our lives, but little things too. Like he'd done hundreds of emergency landings. He told Bri so when the plane ran out of fuel. He really knew the drill too. He wasn't bullshitting. He was yelling, 'Stay down, brace!' Right until the last minute. Some sort of training there, don't you think? And where did he learn his first aid? At the international school for criminals?"

"So what are you saying?"

"I'm not sure," she said, feeling defensive. "But he doesn't add up. That's all."

"Okay, here's what I've learned."

India lit another cigarette and exhaled into the soft evening air.

"Lee owns the big boat in the harbor. You know the one?"

Georgia felt her jaw slacken. "Not the monstrous yacht?"

"The one and the same. I've dug around a fair bit, and I discovered Lee and Ronnie Chen sailed here from Cairns just before Cyclone Tania hit. I reckon Ronnie was killed on the boat and dumped overboard." She flicked a speck of ask from her cigarette. "Lee's in the shit with the RBG, and not just because of Ronnie. He wiped out two prime guys from a rival gang in a teahouse in Fuzhou last month. This rival gang, the Dragon Syndicate, were about to join hands with the RBG and have been screaming for revenge ever since."

Georgia licked her lips. Despite the wine, her mouth felt dry, and she couldn't work out whether it was because she couldn't talk about Lee openly to India, or because she was hearing that the man who'd saved her life was a killer.

"Needless to say," India continued, "the Dragon Syndicate haven't joined the RBG, and the RBG are furious. They were hoping to increase their power base and take over the whole of the criminal world from southeast China right through the Philippines and Indonesia to Australia."

Sudden flash. Was it the Dragon Syndicate who sabotaged the Piper in order to eliminate Lee? Or maybe it was Gap-tooth Chen, supremely annoyed at Lee for messing up his plans? But then she remembered Jason Chen's surprise at the sabotage and Daniel's words: *Lee's fabricating the sabotage story, interfering with my efforts to run him to earth.*

"Why did Lee kill the two men in the teahouse?" asked Georgia.

"I'm not sure. I've heard various reasons. A gambling debt gone wrong. Something about a drug deal. There was even talk of some woman dishonored. It's like nobody really knows. Weird."

"Weird, like Lee," Georgia said with a sigh.

India poured the last of the wine into their glasses, raised hers, and clinked it with Georgia's. "Nothing wrong with that. So long as weird is on your side, that is."

They drank to the sound of insects buzzing and chirruping, listening to the soft slide of water on sand, the air a damp, warm blanket against their skin.

Then India uncoiled from the trunk of the oil palm and stretched, arms to the sky then down, and said she had to get some sleep. They said goodnight between the vans. It was still incredibly humid, and she could see India's skin glistening in the light seeping from her van window. Georgia thanked her for the wine and India said it was fine and for her to take care.

Georgia undressed with difficulty. Doing everything one-handed was extraordinarily awkward, but eventually she slid between Evie's fresh clean sheets dressed in a T-shirt and knickers, and switched out the bedside light. At least if the Chens appeared in the dead of night, she wouldn't have to face them naked.

Lying on her bed under a single sheet, she felt no cooler at night than during the day. She didn't expect to sleep in the heat, with visions of Bri and Suzie and Lee dancing across her eyelids, and settled onto her back, her bandaged hand on her stomach. Her finger was aching dully, and she closed her eyes to the sound of India playing some bluesy music next door. She thought it might be Norah Jones, but couldn't be sure, and when a mosquito began to drone around her face, she didn't bother turning on the light to look for it. The last thing she heard was a chirrup from what sounded like a frog in the bathroom.

Twenty-two

Just after dawn Georgia was woken by the raucous screeches of a sea eagle. Go away, she thought. I'm knackered, you rotten bird. Can't you keep the noise down?

Until 3 AM she had slept like the dead, but then she'd woken, sweat soaking her sleeping sheet, trickling down her chest and between her thighs. It was like she had a fever, with her skin so hot and wet, her brain buzzing at a trillion miles an hour, picturing Jason Chen in his leather jacket telling her what he'd do to her mother. She tried to think how to give herself an advantage. God, she didn't even know how to handle a gun. Sure, anyone could pull a trigger, but what about reloading the thing?

She had fallen into an uneasy doze about ten minutes before the sea eagle had started screeching, and now she felt tired and edgy. Crawling out of bed, she stumbled for the bathroom. A family of green tree frogs was ensconced inside, and Georgia spent the first few minutes removing one from the door handle, two from the basin, and four from the shower. One the size of a duck egg sat firmly on the shower faucet, almost daring her to move it.

The lid on the toilet seat had a notice pasted across: "Please Close Lid After Use to Keep Frogs Out."

She showered one-handed, then struggled to get dressed without banging her finger. Eventually, she made it to the kitchen, and it was the weight of her dreams pressing on her, Jason Chen's violence, that made her pick up the mobile phone and ring Daniel.

"Carter," he said, sounding awake and alert.

"Hi, it's—"

"Georgia. What's up?"

"I need a favor."

"Must be important," he said, sounding amused, "since you're ringing so early. In my experience women aren't so good in the mornings."

"Are you telling me you don't sleep?"

"Only during the day," he said on a bark of laughter, "and in a coffin."

"How cozy."

His voice turned serious. "What's the favor?"

"Teach me to shoot?"

Small pause.

"Shoot what? Quail?"

"Just to shoot, okay?"

Short silence.

"What's the need to know?"

She took a breath, exhaled. "Daniel, I need this favor. Just teach me, will you?"

"No. I'm busy."

"But . . ."

"Okay, tell me why you've a sudden interest in firearms, and I'll see what I can do."

"I've always wanted to learn to shoot," she said lamely.

"And I've always wanted to learn to wax my legs," he responded. "The answer is no. N. O."

"Please?"

"Ring me when you hear from Lee, not before."

Without another word, he hung up.

———

After comforting herself with a tall glass of mango juice, a big bowl of Special K, and two pieces of thick-cut raisin toast drenched in honey, Georgia drove the Suzuki to Harbour Road and parked in front of the letterbox of number forty-three, trotted up the concrete path, and pressed the bell of a suburban house that was identical to all the others in the street, with the same tin roof, bleached weatherboard, and square of toughened buffalo grass with a concrete path down the middle.

The fly screen was open, and after the bell emitted a rude buzz she heard a boy yelling inside. A few seconds later a small girl came to the door. Crinkly mouse-colored hair, bright brown eyes, mottled T-shirt hanging to her knees and tie-dyed the color of autumn leaves.

"Yeah?" she asked.

"Is your mum in? Tell her it's Georgia."

"I'll get her." She scampered away.

Becky came to the door. She was in her blue overalls with her usual bun on the back of her head, but her skin was mottled and gray and her posture slumped. Georgia's heart squeezed. Since losing Bri, Becky had aged ten years.

"Georgia?" Her voice was small, but she stepped onto the veranda. "You heard?"

"Yes." She touched Becky's shoulder tentatively, wary of encroaching on the woman's grief, but Becky turned into her raised arm and then Georgia was holding her, hugging her tight, feeling the cloudlike softness of Becky's body, the sobs wrenching from her core.

"I'm so sorry," she whispered against Becky's hair, rocking her, cradling and comforting her as best she could. "He was the best, you know. The best."

With her face buried in Georgia's shoulder, Becky's words were muffled. "Mutual admiration, love. Old Bri loved you to bits and back."

"You too."

"I know. I know he did. Loved all of us. To bits. The bugger. How the hell . . ."

Becky pulled out of Georgia's embrace and wiped her eyes. Took several breaths. Gave a sob, then took a few more breaths. Another sob escaped, and Georgia saw Becky was fighting against her grief, trying to shovel it to one side, and she made to touch her, pull her into another embrace, but Becky pushed her away, scrubbing her face with both hands, mouth working, tears incessant.

"You were there," she choked, "when the plane went down."

Hands helpless at her sides, Georgia said, "Yes."

"Tell me," Becky begged. "Tell me everything. Please. I have to know."

So Georgia told her. How Bri had brought them down safely. His pleas, *Help me make it, help me, help me.* Lee flinging himself at Bri and dousing the flames, engulfing him in the rainforest mulch. The airlift. Seeing Bri in the hospital.

She could hear Bri's voice. *They fucked with my plane. The fucks.* But she couldn't say the words.

"They're saying it was pilot error," said Becky. "That he messed up and didn't have enough fuel to reach Cairns, but he wouldn't do that. The only time he flew close to the edge was when the Doyle boy out at Blackdown got real sick two years ago or so, he got bit by a snake and would have died if Bri had taken time out to fuel up. Bri took a chance that night, risked his own skin to pick that boy up and get him to hospital."

Hands shaking, Becky twisted her wedding ring around and around. Around and around. Georgia felt her own finger responding to Becky's compulsive movement, aching in sympathy.

"No reason for him to fly without filling up," Becky insisted. "He had loads of time. He *wouldn't.*"

Behind them, Georgia heard a car start up with a rattle, pull away. As its engine dwindled into the distance, she offered the only positive thought she had. "What about the insurance company? Pilot error's covered, isn't it? And if Bri ran out—"

She swallowed her words when Becky rounded on her, shoulders suddenly bunched, her lips drawn back like a cornered she-wolf.

"He was sabotaged," she hissed. "He told me in hospital. He *knew* it."

"Becks, the insurance company won't pay out if—"

"You think I don't know about that?" Becky's aggressive stance drained. "It's down as an accident at the moment, but having our kids think Bri messed up when he didn't, well, it's not right. It's not on for them to think their dad did something he didn't."

The street was silent, but Georgia could hear a TV inside the house, what sounded like a cartoon, and a boy laughing.

She took a breath. "I'm not sure Bri's plane was sabotaged, but if I could prove it was, would you be okay with it? Even if the insurers don't pay?"

Becky pushed a filament of gray hair from her forehead. "You find who killed my Bri, and I'll shoot them myself."

––––––––––

Georgia left Becky and headed for the Lotus Healing Center where she asked Yumuru to check her finger. She hadn't been able to think of anyone else to go to, and decided to face him head-on. She couldn't blame him for being annoyed when he'd dropped her off at Evie's. After he had taken her into his healing center and been unbelievably caring toward her, she'd repaid him by prying through his property. And since he hadn't reported her injury to anyone, it would be nice to make amends after his kindness.

"I promise I won't snoop," she said. "And I'm sorry. Really I am."

He gave a sigh. "You're forgiven, okay? But honestly, Georgia, if you wanted to know something, why didn't you come to me?"

"You weren't around."

"Next time, *ask.* I've nothing to hide."

She remembered the white of his knuckles on the steering wheel and thought, if he had nothing to hide, then she was a fluorescent orange kangaroo, but let it lie for now.

Gently he peeled off the bandage and layers of padding and inspected the wound.

"Excellent," he pronounced.

Teeth clenched, she forced herself to look at it.

A tiny row of bristling stitches edged with red. Thick crusty scabs that resembled the backs of beetles. A little shock of amazement. She'd expected a little moisture seeping from the wound, maybe some oozing blood, but there was nothing. Her stump was clean and dry and healthy. She was astonished at how fast it had healed in just forty-odd hours, and felt absurdly pleased until she saw how much shorter it was then her other fingers. Suddenly it was hateful, *hideous,* and a vision of her mother's beautifully painted magenta toenails flashed into her mind. She abruptly pushed the picture away, but she couldn't stop the scurry of cold sweat prickling over her skin.

Oblivious to her discomfort, Yumuru passed her half a dozen packs of new bandages. "Remember, a fresh bandage daily for ten days or so, then start feeding it oxygen. Oxygen is the greatest healer."

She felt better once it was bandaged again and she was unable to see its ugliness, and after thanking him, she said, "How's Tilly?"

"Why don't you visit her? She's terribly bored."

Bored of what? she wondered. Dying?

"Is Joanie around?"

Yumuru thought for a moment. "She's probably with Tilly."

When she got up to go, Yumuru came and gave her a hug. It was what Tom would have called a full hug, firm yet gentle, where his right arm went around her shoulder, the other her waist, so his heart met hers.

"Hug therapy," he said. "Not only does a hug make you feel good all day, but stimulation by touch is absolutely essential for healing."

She felt a surge of affection for him and hugged him back.

He was smiling when he released her. "I couldn't do that in the army, no matter how much a soldier needed it. They'd have tarred and feathered me."

She laughed.

"Now, you keep changing the bandage, okay?" His expression turned serious. "And take care of yourself. I don't want to find you in the pouring rain bleeding all over the road again."

"Um . . . about that night," she said hesitantly.

"I haven't told anyone, if you're worried." He was returning to his desk.

"No, it's not that. It's just I have a rather odd request . . . I, er, wondered if you could teach me how to shoot."

Yumuru slowly turned around. There was a long silence while he studied her, but she couldn't read his expression thanks to a sprinkle of sunlight trembling on his little gold-rimmed glasses. Eventually he said quietly, "You're serious."

She nodded.

"Why?"

Georgia ran over various replies and ended up saying simply, "Instinct."

"You think whoever did that to your hand is going to come after you?"

She nodded again.

Another long silence. "I thought I'd never have to go near a gun again . . . But if you're in fear of your life, which you obviously are . . . I know a gun club the locals use. Outside Helenvale. It's well signposted. How about if you meet me there first thing tomorrow? Say, eight o'clock?"

"Oh, Yumuru, thank you so—"

"Save your thanks." His voice was curt. "You might come to regret it. I know I did."

———

Wanting to speak with Joanie about Suzie, Georgia hastened to the west wing. She took a deep breath before she entered Tilly's room, already dreading the filthy stench that would greet her. She tapped on the door, more out of politeness than in expectation of Tilly responding.

She started when a voice called, "Come in."

Georgia pushed open the door and walked inside. There was nobody in the room aside from a woman in her early twenties lying in bed, watching morning television.

"Tilly?" she said uncertainly, wondering if she hadn't got the wrong room.

"Yeah." Using the remote, the woman turned off the TV and

rolled her head around to study Georgia. "Sorry, do I know you?" Her voice was faint, and although her pale skin hung loosely across the bones in her face from weight loss, her eyes were bright.

"But . . . you were . . ."

Tilly gave a tiny smile. "Yeah, I know. I turned the corner last night, apparently."

Georgia crossed the room. She was shaking her head in amazement. "Well done, you."

"Well done, 'Muru, you mean. After all those doctors . . . Tried every known antibiotic, but none of them worked. If the croc had taken my leg, they would've amputated, you know, and I'd never have come here and remained in one piece."

Remembering that Suzie had mentioned exploitation at the healing center to India, she said, "Why did you choose to come here? Why didn't you stay in hospital?"

Tilly looked away. "What with Joanie looking after the kids, a nice environment, and all . . ." Her voice was quiet as she admitted, "I came here to die."

"But you didn't."

" 'Muru wouldn't let me. Gave me healing twice a day, sometimes hours on end."

Georgia approached the bed, recalling the locked door in the pharmacy and Yumuru's injections the last time she was in this room. "And vitamins."

Tilly looked away. "Yeah. Vitamins. I couldn't eat. Didn't want to eat. I guess I needed them."

"Isn't it unusual they're administered by injection?"

"No idea." Tilly plucked at the blanket. "All I know is 'Muru says I'll need a jab every day. Until I'm really strong."

For a brief moment, Georgia wondered whether Yumuru really was the quintessential healer, or if the vitamins had something to do with Tilly's spectacular recovery. And what, her mind zigzagged, did Suzie Wilson, head of pharmacy here, have to do with the Chens?

"How are the kids?"

Tilly's face lit up, and they talked a little more until Tilly told her

Joanie had gone into town. Georgia then excused herself and headed for Evie's Suzuki. As she headed down the drive, the buzz of insects was so loud that it made her think of strips of Velcro being ripped apart inside a metal bin.

———————

It took her three hours before she came to a junction she reckoned fitted her scrawled notes. For the last twelve miles she had worried that she'd misunderstood Suzie's friend's instructions, but here it was, with a big notice: "Cape Archer National Park."

Turning right as instructed, she wondered if he lived in the park or worked there. She couldn't think he had anything to do with the healing center or even Suzie's research, not all the way out here.

She spent the next half hour bouncing about on a dirt track with potholes big as washing machines that had Evie's little Suzuki scooting from one side of the road to the other, and when she arrived she was disheveled. She had great patches of damp between her shoulder blades and beneath her arms, and her hair was flat against her skull, swimming in sweat.

She crawled out of the car. Her neck popped as she stood up straight, and she heard a soft click somewhere in her lumbar region.

The house ahead was low-slung and roofed with tin. There were two outsheds, and an aluminum boat slumped in the shallows of a broad, slow-moving river the color of dull copper. The air was filled with the unceasing chatter and trilling of insects. What on earth did Suzie's answerphone friend do out here?

She'd barely reached the house when she felt a sting on her calf. Georgia slapped it. Her hand came away bloody. Another sting on her ankle, then one on her forearm. Dammit. She'd forgotten the man's advice.

She was practically dancing on the doorstep when the fly screen banged open.

"I warned you."

A bare-chested man in shorts pulled her inside.

"Deet," he said. "It's the only stuff that works against the bug-gers."

He marched down a dark hall. Georgia stood there, trying to ad-just to the sudden gloom.

"Come on in then, don't stand there like a spare part!"

Georgia hurried after him and into what appeared to be a laundry. He thrust a plastic liter bottle at her. "Douse yourself, or get eaten alive."

Then he took in her bandage. "Hold your hand out. I'll pour."

Breathing shallowly, she applied the repellent. Feet, ankles, legs, arms, face. It reeked of bitter chemicals and felt as though it was burning her lips. Georgia reached for the tap, to rinse her hand.

"Leave it," he said. "They love that thin skin over your knuckles. They love any skin that isn't doused, period."

"Thanks," she said.

"No worries." He pushed out a paw. "We haven't been introduced. I'm Huub Zwartendijk. Park ranger. My mates call me Dutch. Can't get their tongues around my real name."

Oh, Dutch. Please. I'm so cold.

At last it was beginning to make sense. Dutch was, she realized, the guy with the battered boots in Suzie's photographs. And Nail-tooth had to be one of the crocodiles.

"Georgia Parish."

"Yeah, so you said." He looked at his big bare feet, then away. "Come on outside. Let's visit old Nail-tooth. We can talk on the way."

She scurried after him and into the kitchen, where he picked up a large blue cooler, a shotgun, and a box of shells before striding into the wet blanket of humidity and whining, whirring insects. Dutch marched to the aluminum boat on the muddy bank of the river and dumped the cooler and shotgun beside a huge gaff and a box bulging with fishing gear.

"Hop in," he said.

"You don't have to push me. I don't mind getting wet," she said.

"Just get in, will you?"

Georgia jumped inside and made to sit on the central strut.

"Hold it there!"

She hovered uncertainly while she watched Dutch gallop back into the house. He returned with a towel and an umbrella. The towel was to protect her behind from the scalding aluminum, he told her as he unfolded it across the bow strut.

"Sit," he said.

She sat and watched him lay the umbrella next to the shotgun in the belly of the boat. She didn't dare ask what it was for and make herself look even more stupid than he already thought she was.

Pushing the boat into the river, Dutch jumped aboard and fired up the twin-stroke. Sitting in the stern, he held the tiller in his right hand, engine buzzing, while Georgia sat up front, warm sultry air whipping against her face.

The river had low, wide banks owing to the floods bringing down so much soil. In the dense growth on either side were thousands of mangroves with tangles of roots, boughs, and branches. Creepers hung from trees and white egrets stalked through the low rushes in shallow water, long necks undulating. The sky was a dusty blue, the sun an ashen blur overhead.

Briefly she glanced at the creamy wake behind them, then turned her face forward. She had no idea where they were going, or what Dutch had planned, and she didn't care. She was on the water again. She spent all her spare time in Sydney crewing or swiping a free ride on someone's motorboat, and although it had only been a fortnight since she'd been on the water, it felt like months. For the first time since the Piper's crash, she was smiling.

They hadn't gone far when Dutch cut the revs and the twin-stroke eased into a low chuckle. Their sudden drop in speed, to around four knots, she reckoned, made it feel as though the temperature had increased a thousandfold. Georgia looked at the water gliding beneath the hull and longed to dive in and rinse the Deet and sweat from her skin.

"You're a water baby," he said.

Georgia turned and looked at him. "I like the water, yes."

"Not like Suzie, then."

"She didn't like water?"

He grunted at the same time as he blew air from his nose. He sounded like a horse snorting. "Couldn't swim. Shit scared, she was, but she came out here, time after time. Admired the pants off her for that."

They cruised slowly around a long bend in the river, and after a minute or so he slowed the boat further and said, "See that slide? That's Nail-tooth's front driveway. To the left of the elephant grass."

The slide, as Dutch called it, was a broad, churned-up section of mud that looked as though somebody had dragged several oversized sacks of cement into the river.

Georgia indicated the embankment. "How on earth does he get back up again?" she asked. "It's quite steep."

Dutch grinned. "He doesn't. He waits for the tide to come in. Then he walks it."

Clever croc, she thought, impressed.

"Let's potter around a bit and see if he's about." Pointing the bow upriver again, he reached down and snapped the cooler lid open. He passed her a beer dripping with condensation. "Might take a while. May as well enjoy ourselves."

Georgia popped the tab and tipped the lager down her throat. She felt the chill flow into her stomach. Wiping her mouth with the back of her hand, she couldn't help the small belch that followed.

"Why the interest in Nail-tooth?"

"He's a big bugger, is all. Around twenty-three feet, maybe a bit more. Suzie had a kind of affection for him. Be nice of you two to meet, seeing how you were with Suze at the end."

Twenty-three feet? The croc had to weigh over a ton. Georgia hastily took another swig of her beer. Jesus. She wasn't certain she wanted to meet a croc the size of one of Yumuru's Land Cruisers.

"How did he get his name?"

Dutch gave her a look like Mrs. Scutchings used to whenever she'd given a wrong answer to an obvious question at school.

"Because of his nail tooth, right? Got knocked about during a fight or some such and one of his incisors split in half. Crocs regrow their teeth, so you can't see it anymore, but his nickname stuck." Dutch shook his head. "Never seen a croc do that before. Poor bugger. Must've hurt like hell."

They'd coasted for about five minutes when Dutch said, "See that log?" He was pointing at what looked like a felled tree trunk lying on a sandbank.

Georgia nodded.

"Croc."

As soon as he said the word "croc" it was no longer a piece of wood but a prehistoric creature with a ridge of scales reaching along its spine to the tip of its powerful tail. Its snout faced the river. She looked ahead and saw another unmoving shape on the riverbank that wasn't a log. Then what appeared to be a broken branch, flattening tufts of dried grasses, poking out of the rainforest.

"Heavens," she said.

"Croc city. That's where we are."

Dutch pointed out three more crocodiles lurking in the mangroves. If he hadn't drawn them to her attention, she'd never have spotted them. They were well camouflaged, their skin mottling into the darkness of the rainforest.

"Why was Suzie so interested in crocodiles?"

"Not just any crocs," he corrected her. "Wild crocs. The farmed ones are too fat. You know they farm crocs for leather? Crocodile handbags and shit? Some bloke's even using croc leather for sex toys. Can you believe it?"

Georgia swallowed some beer the wrong way and had to cough to clear her throat.

"Anyhow, farmed crocs were useless for the work she was doing. She needed blood samples from the wild blokes out here, all skinny and lean and pure from living the way they do. Not fed with the shit farmed crocs are."

"What work was she doing?"

He fiddled with the outboard for a moment, adjusting the mixture of fuel and two-stroke oil. "She wanted it kept quiet. I respected that."

Georgia took a breath of air. After the iced beer, it was like inhaling a quart of warm grease.

"She's dead, Dutch," she reminded him.

The engine note was running sweetly, but he was still fiddling with the fuel mixture.

"She was in my arms when she died. The last thing she said was your name. Dutch. And then she was gone."

He stopped fiddling with the fuel and studied his broad brown feet. When he spoke, it was a choking growl. "Silly cow."

She gave him a minute or so, then said, "What she was working on could have a bearing on the plane crash."

Small pause. "Yeah. So you said."

"Could you tell me? Please?"

He gave his horse's snort and shifted his hips, resettling at the stern. The boat continued to trickle, inch by inch, upriver.

Eventually he gave another snort, and said, "She was ashamed of something her dad had done a couple of years back. One time she told me about it, and I'm talking something really bad. She was bloody crucified. Turned into a bony-assed, uptight, and freaked-out creature overnight. Say boo and she'd nearly die of fright."

"What did her father do that was so bad?"

For the first time, they truly looked at each other. His skin was worn and creased and his nose skewed to one side. He had a puckered scar running from his right eye to the corner of his mouth as though he'd been clawed by a big cat.

"That's between me and her. Promised her that. Ask me another."

She glanced away at the sandy riverbank and slumped torpedoes of ancient creatures.

"Okay," she said. "So how come she ended up here? With you and crocodiles?"

"Because she wanted to do good." He looked past Georgia to the horizon. "It was like she took responsibility for what her father had done. She tried to explain to me how it worked in China, and how her father had dishonored her family, big-time. Didn't matter what I said to reassure her, she was convinced she had to make amends, get it together to come back with something so bloody good it would outweigh the bad he did. Rebalance the family's scales, so to speak."

Georgia thought of Jason Chen and his gap-toothed father and wondered if they'd be ashamed if either were dishonored.

After a while, she said. "Dutch, can you tell me about the good? What Suzie was working on? Please?"

He thought about that for a bit, then said slowly, "Well, she never told me not to say anything about it. Just to keep it quiet for a bit."

Georgia glanced ahead to see a sludge-green torpedo with a middle the size of a household trash can lying on the bank, mouth agape. "Wow," she said, distracted. "Is that Nail-tooth?"

"Nah. Too small."

Holy moley, she thought.

"Our Suzie wanted to cure the world." He pushed the tiller out a little to follow the curve of the river. "She'd heard about some bloke coming out here who was interested in finding a new antibiotic. You get torn up by a croc and you can end up shite, full of gangrene and the like, and you'll be lucky if you live out a fortnight."

Georgia's nerves leaped. Tilly. Gray-faced and smelling of corrupted, decomposing flesh.

"Suzie was working with the crocs to find out why a croc can get a leg chewed off by another croc and not die in a week, as we do. Their immune system is heaps better than ours. She was convinced the crocs offered a miracle cure."

Tilly, forty-two hours later, practically *healed*.

"Suze reckoned she found it a couple of years back. She was doing final tests with her brother. He's a big shot with access to a high-powered laboratory. She reckoned on presenting this antibiotic to the medical authorities any day now." He looked glum. "Shame she died."

Heart jumping, she said, "Her brother? Do you mean Mingjun?"

"Jon," he said. "Jon Ming. Like me, he found it easier to change his name a little."

"Where does Jon live, do you know?"

"Brizzy. In a place called . . ." He scowled, then said, "Tallawoo? Talla-something, I remember that. It's a real fine suburb, she said. I wasn't supposed to tell anyone that either," he added.

"You don't have a contact number for him, do you? An address or something?"

"Nah. Sorry."

"If you remember the name of the suburb . . ."

"Yeah, I'll let you know." He suddenly scowled. "Hope Suze left her research for someone else to decode, 'cos she kept it real secret. Aside from her brother, only me and Suzie and the crocs knew what she was up to, so far as I'm aware."

It made sense. Robert the pharmacist had said she was doing some private research on crocodile serum. He hadn't seemed to know what, in particular. Yumuru, on the other hand . . .

Georgia squinted to watch a large heron flying heavily across the river. Its flight was so ponderous that it reminded her of a bomber. Thinking for a bit, she then asked, "Do you know a Lee Denham?"

Dutch moved his head to watch a small crocodile drift past before it disappeared with a swirl of murky water. He shook his head.

"How did you collect wild crocodile blood?" she asked.

"With difficulty." He grinned, showing twin rows of white teeth that looked strong enough to bite through his shotgun without any trouble. "We'd use a harpoon, one designed to go through the thick scales on their backs, no further, then we'd play 'em till they tired out. Could take a while, depending on how big they were. Then we'd tie their snouts real well, tow them to shore, and Bob's your uncle."

He nudged the umbrella with a bare foot. "That's our secret weapon. When we're ready to release them, one of us strokes their eyes shut with the brolly—they won't move an inch with closed eyes—while the other releases the ropes. When we drop the brolly we both run like buggery."

Good God. Crocodile Dundee had nothing on Dutch, or Suzie for that matter.

They were silent for a while, then they had another beer. Dutch had made stacks of sausage-and-pickle sandwiches, and they ate them as they cruised back and forth, still searching for Nail-tooth. Eventually he turned the boat around and headed for Nail-tooth's slide.

"Reckon he's been watching our every move," he said. "Cunning sod." Dutch drifted the boat toward the bank. "Bet he's hiding in the mangroves . . . Shit! You see him? There he is!"

Georgia didn't see anything until Nail-tooth blinked. Suddenly a massive form sprang into view, just yards away, resting among the mangrove roots. His head was broad as a fridge, his eyes yellow with black vertical stripes, and his spine was ridged with scales the size of dinner plates. Although his mouth appeared to be closed, his teeth were visible. Thick, stubby blocks of stained ivory poked down his jaw and curved up toward his scaly snout. She realized Dutch would have to have been pretty close to give him his name—and nervously ran her eyes along the length of the beast and said, "Are you sure it isn't two crocodiles?"

"Nah. Just the one, and don't move. We're a bit too near for comfort. I'm going to back away real easy."

Infinitely slowly, Dutch switched the outboard into reverse and eased the tin boat back. He waited until they were well in the middle of the river before he spoke again.

"Sorry." He wiped his forehead of sweat. "Bit close there. Surprised he didn't have us, seeing as it's the silly season. The males get real aggressive in the wet. They'll attack anything going and a mate of mine had one bugger put its jaws around his outboard motor. They're not like the Nile croc, who won't do anything till you're in the water. The saltie will have you anytime, any place, quicker than you can say sausage sarnie."

She was still glancing behind them to check that Nail-tooth hadn't decided to follow and put his jaws around their outboard as they began to near the bank and Dutch's house. The water turned a murky brown-blue, and ibis and egrets waded through the mudflats, searching for shrimps and crabs.

"Aren't you scared of crocs, living so close to them?"

"Nah, not with Nail-tooth about," Dutch said. "He's mighty territorial and most other crocs keep well quiet. They hear me tramping around, assume it's him, and bugger off."

She glanced back downriver at the mangroves where Nail-tooth lay hidden. For sixty-five million years crocodiles had existed in a virtually unchanged form, and today they lay there as they always had, still and unmoving, crusted green-brown. To have survived so long, they'd have to be skilled not only in attack, but also in defense.

A quote from Daniel's two-thousand-year-old guru streamed through her mind: "It is important that form be concealed, and that movements be unexpected, so that preparedness against them be impossible."

Sun Tzu would have appreciated crocodiles, she thought. A crocodile has the art of invisibility. It doesn't become angered, or afraid, or join a battle of emotions simply to *win.*

It knows better, because it is a survivor.

TWENTY-THREE

Lee was propped against an Alexander palm, smoking a long, slender cigar and reading a yachting magazine when Georgia drove between the caravan park gates. He straightened as she approached and indicated for her to pull over.

She wished she'd seen him before he had seen her. Then she might have been able to call Jason Chen, tell him Lee was here, and he'd pick Lee up then release her mother. Wouldn't he?

Nerves jumping, she parked next to a silver Mitsubishi four-by-four with smoked glass windows, which she assumed was his since the driver's door was open and music was playing. She didn't climb out of her car, just looked at him through her open window. She didn't say hello or greet him in any way. She wasn't sure how she felt about seeing him standing there, relaxed and at ease, after her experience with the Chens and the way they'd interrogated her about him, smashed her mother's face.

Windsurfers Do It Standing Up.

The Chens wanted Lee, and she wanted her mother. What was Lee doing here?

He peeled himself from the palm and leaned against her car's bodywork. The Band-Aid had gone, and she could see a row of neat stitches along the jagged tear in his right ear. Another wound to wear along with the rest of his fighting-dog scars.

He looked at her bandaged hand on the steering wheel and said, "Did they do that? Chen Xiaoqiang and his gang?"

"Yes."

He looked away.

"I'd like to see them dead." Her tone was harsh.

"You're not the only one."

He took a slow pull on his cigar and inspected the glowing stub while he exhaled. "How've you been, anyway? Aside from the hand, I mean."

"Sweaty."

"Yeah. Stinking, isn't it?" He glanced over his shoulder at the park office, its whitewashed walls barely visible through the banana trees, then back. "Why'd they let you go?"

She decided to give him as little information as possible. "What happened to the rental car? The car you left in the creek?"

"I got rid of it."

"Why? They went mad. Ronnie Chen rented it and they were going crazy—"

"I rented the car. I just used Ronnie's name. His driver's license. His credit card."

"Why?"

"Smokescreen."

"Smokescreen?" she repeated blankly.

"Yeah." He took a pull of his cigar. "You know I worked with the RBG?"

She swallowed drily. "I might have heard something about it."

"From your mate Daniel, no doubt."

She didn't respond.

"Well, I kind of fell out with them. I'm now freelancing, you could say."

She was about to ask about the two guys from the Dragon Syndicate in Fuzhou, when he said, "What occurred with Chen Xiaoqiang and his mob?"

"What *occurred*?" An urge to hit him, to shake him out of his composure, swept over her. "Oh, nothing much. They just took a pair of pruning shears to me, shortened my finger an inch, grabbed a base-ball bat, and . . . and . . ."

It was on the tip of her tongue to tell him about her mother.

He was watching her unblinkingly. "And what?"

She looked away. "Nothing."

He took a studied drag on his cigar, looking to one side at a bunch of coconut palms. "They've got someone, haven't they?"

Georgia switched her gaze inside the car and at the speedometer, splintered with cracks.

"Who is it?" He suddenly sounded weary. "Tell me, Georgia. Who are they holding?"

The way the cracks ran from the dial made it look as though someone had slammed a screwdriver in its center. Vaguely she wondered if that's what had happened, and if not, how the dial came to be broken.

"Georgia." His voice was soft, insistent. "Tell me who they've got."

Her voice choked as she admitted, "My mother."

"Your *mother*?"

"They're keeping her hostage." She couldn't stop the tears welling. "They want me to find some disk. The one Suzie had in her fanny pack wasn't any good. They kept asking for 'the rest.'"

He looked down at his feet, rubbing the bridge of his nose. "And they want you to find me and turn me over to them. That's why they have your mother."

Her head jerked around to stare at him. He'd gotten it in one. No doubt being a criminal made it easy for him to see what the Chens were up to.

"You haven't called the police," he stated. "Any reason?"

"They said they have friends in the police . . ."

"Just the one."

"What?"

"One dirty cop."

Small pause while she took this in.

"Who is it?" she asked.

"They keep themselves anonymous and get paid through a numbered account in Panama. That's all I know."

A horrible thought crossed her mind. "It couldn't be Daniel, could it?"

Lee gave a choked laugh, almost a guffaw. "He'd like to see me strung up, sure, and he's capable of creating his own agenda when it suits . . . He tell you about Amy Robins?"

"Er . . . no."

"Whole town knows that story. You should hear it. It's a real eye-opener." The amusement left his face as he added, "One thing certain in this world is that Daniel Carter isn't Spider."

"Spider?"

"That's how dirty cops are known. They sit in their webs and pull the strings they want, stockpiling enough readies for a fat retirement."

"If I go to the police, will this Spider tell the Chens?"

"Oh yes. But they won't kill your mum . . . What's her name?"

"Linette."

"Well, Linette's more valuable to them alive than dead, as I'm sure you can appreciate. But having said that, should the cops get too close . . ."

She knew what he meant. The Chens wouldn't hesitate to kill her mother, dump her body, and get rid of any evidence of kidnapping.

"So what should I do?" she asked. "Can't the police help at all?"

He thought it over briefly. "Not with Spider sitting pretty. The cops make a move for you mum, they'll just shift her around. Make her even harder to find." He mulled a bit longer. "You tell anyone about Linette?"

"Just you."

"Best keep it that way. Not a word to anyone. Not even your pal Daniel, okay? Or Spider will hear."

She gave a nod.

"Good. Because the only hope we've got of getting your mum back is to do it on tiptoe. Ask a few quiet questions in the right places. Find out where they're holding her."

"How will you do that?"

Lee checked the tip of his cigar again. "I've ways and means."

Damp with sweat, she shifted a little, feeling the indentations from the plastic seat on the backs of her thighs. For the life of her she couldn't think why he would help her find her mother, and said so.

"You really want to know?"

"Yes, I do."

Steadily smoking his cigar, he told her he was born in a river town called Fuling, which was noisy, dirty, overcrowded, and the streets rose up the sides of the riverbank so steeply that they were like stairways and the residents had leg muscles thick and hard as rope.

He'd been eight years old when his grandmother Hairlip Jiang, a Taoist fortune-teller he shared a room with on one of the lower stairways of Fuling, told him that if you saved a person's life, you were responsible for them forever. When he'd asked why, she'd sighed and rolled her rheumy eyes.

"Ayieee! Young fireball, you know so little it makes me breathless! It is so simple that even an ignoramus like yourself can grasp it. When you save a person's life, you alter their destiny. If you intervene with destiny, you must be responsible for it."

He had argued with her about firemen, ambulance men, and earthquake rescue services, but she said it was their job, so it was okay for them not to be responsible.

"If you are walking along a river and you see a man drowning, think twice before you dive in and save him," Hairlip Jiang had insisted. "You might not only change his destiny, but your own."

When Lee fell silent, Georgia said, "But that doesn't make you responsible for my mother."

He looked at her like her boss would if she hadn't been listening at the sales meeting. Patiently, he said, "If I hadn't saved you, she wouldn't be where she is now." Tapping a length of ash from his cigar, Lee added, "Think of me as your own private hawk. Able to see far and wide and warn you of impending danger and, if necessary, to strike and kill in your defense."

She wasn't sure she found the thought of having Lee as her private hawk particularly reassuring, and remained silent.

"They give you a deadline?"

"Until Sunday. Then they're going to"—she took an unsteady breath—"kill her."

He nodded. "We've five days. Enough time to sort something."

Watching the way his lips closed around his cigar made something inside her shiver, and she felt a strange urge to touch him. It was relief, she thought, and gratitude. Relief that she had an ally who knew about her mother's danger, gratitude for an ally who was going to help get her back.

"You got a mobile?"

"Yes."

"Number?"

She watched him punch it into his own phone, cigar clamped between those lips that never smiled.

"I'll give you a buzz every day or so. See what's happening."

"Can I have your number?"

"I don't think so." He put his mobile back in his rear pocket. "You have any luck with Suzie's brother? Wang Mingjun? Know where he is?"

"Not really," she said, then frowned. "How did you know his first name?"

"Wang Ming Shu. Wang Ming Jun." He explained how Chinese names were different from their Western equivalents, in that their first name was their surname, their second generational, their third current. His was Denham Fong Lee. Hers would be Parish Davies Georgia.

"How come you want J—" she nearly said "Jon" by accident, and hastily amended, "Mingjun?"

"It's important I get in touch."

"What about?"

He shrugged. "This and that. You seen Carter lately?"

Her heart gave a bump. "Er . . . yesterday."

"Any news on finding who sabotaged our aircraft?"

He said it so matter-of-factly, like he had when they'd been sharing her deep-fried oysters on the beach, that she paused.

"Daniel did . . . um, mention it."

He brushed a speck of invisible dust from his arm. Studied his cigar some more. Then studied her. She found herself picking at her bandage, unable to meet his eyes. The moisture on her skin was like a layer of warm oil and she wiped her face, longing for a cold shower.

He said, "He thinks I've something to do with it?"

Startled, she looked up. "I didn't say that."

"He knows me. He knows I'm not suicidal."

She was on the verge of saying that Daniel thought Lee had fabricated the sabotage story when she was struck by a sudden sensation of being on a tightrope, balancing between two men with two different goals. One on the right side of the law, the other a fighting dog with his own rules. She had no way of knowing what to say between them, and mistrusted each in their war against the other. She was defending them both.

Lee said, "So where's the spoke in our wheel?"

"Insurance," she said, and told him that if the plane's sabotage was proved, the insurance company wouldn't pay out. "Becky will owe the bank something in the region of sixty grand and it'll cripple her."

Lee frowned. "You're right, but I'm amazed the insurers aren't crawling all over it. They've an interest, after all. You know who they are?"

She shook her head.

"My guess is someone doesn't want us looking too hard," he said, dropping his cigar and grinding it out with his boot. "Bet Spider's doing his worst."

She was about to ask him more about Spider when he put a hand in his front pocket and withdrew his beeper.

"Sorry," he said. "Got to go."

Immediately he spun on his heel and headed for his Mitsubishi.

"No, wait!" Georgia got out of the Suzuki and raced after him. "Do you know anything about Ronnie Chen's murder?"

He spoke over his shoulder. "Sure, I do."

"Who killed him?"

He was already in his car, and had started the engine.

"Lee!"

Snapping on his seat belt, he picked a gear and released the hand-brake. He glanced across at her as his foot pressed on the gas.

"You've guessed right. Don't push it."

Shocked into immobility, she watched the Mitsubishi barrel through the gates and swing right and away from the town. A hand-ful of crimson bougainvillea petals drifted through the dust kicked up by his car and settled on the road. They looked like drops of blood.

Twenty-four

On her way to meet Yumuru at the gun club the following morning, Georgia thought about what Lee had said about hiring the car in Ronnie Chen's name. *A smokescreen.* He had wanted to lay a false trail, she realized, tricking anyone following him into thinking Ronnie was alive, when he'd just murdered the man. Lee had obviously "stolen" Suzie, as the Chens thought, and it looked to her like it was a race between the Chens and Lee; whoever got Suzie's brother won the war.

Also, Lee appeared convinced that the Piper had been sabotaged, but she couldn't be sure he wasn't manipulating her to report this back to Daniel. Lee could tell her a barefaced lie and she'd never know it. The man's rocklike face was perfectly unreadable.

When she arrived at the gun club she saw Yumuru waiting for her in his Land Cruiser, and as she approached he opened the passenger door and indicated she get inside.

Settled in the passenger seat, she watched as he reached behind his seat and, grabbing a large foil-wrapped package, plonked it in her lap. It was still warm.

"You cooked breakfast?" she said, delighted.

He gave a grunt.

Georgia unwrapped the egg-and-bacon sandwiches, and passed Yumuru his before tucking into her own.

"I thought you'd be vegetarian," she remarked.

"I am," he said around a mouthful of bacon sandwich.

She gave a muffled laugh.

"Hey, don't come the high horse with me," he protested. "We always had a cooked breakfast in the services, and it's thanks to you I feel like I'm back in the army. You're the devil, aren't you?"

You little devil.

She was caught by a memory of her mother standing in the commune's clearing in the rainforest, face startled. Georgia was nine and had a ragged, very thin young dog at her side. She was out of breath, and so was the dog, whose tongue was lolling almost to the ground.

"Isn't that Jo Harris's dog?"

"She's mine," said Georgia. "I've called her Pickle."

"I think you'd better take her back, before Jo gets cross."

"No!" Georgia put a hand on the dog's skinny spine. "Jo was kicking her and Pickle was yelping but Jo wouldn't stop. Look." She showed her mother the bloody gash on the dog's rear leg, the fresh scabs on her muzzle and belly.

"You stole Jo's dog?"

Georgia concentrated on stroking the rough fur on Pickle's head. The dog looked up and gave a faint wag of its tail.

"You little devil." Her mother laughed.

The next day Linette went and bought the animal off Jo for fifty bucks. Georgia and Dawn ate nothing but eggs that week since their mother's grocery budget had been blown, but they didn't care. They had saved Pickle.

Around a mouthful of sandwich, Yumuru said, "How's the finger?"

"Better, thanks."

"It shouldn't hold you up much. I'll show you how to reload single-handed."

He ran her through a preparatory talk while they ate—how to respect a gun, and when handed a gun, not to point it at anything she didn't want to shoot and to always check and double-check it was unloaded. He ran her through safe "carry" procedures for a loaded gun, and when he'd finished his pep talk he passed her a pack of caramel Tim Tam cookies.

"Sugar hits before we begin," he said.

Her favorites. He was definitely a mind reader and was, as she'd hoped, a wonderfully patient teacher. He showed her how to use a 9mm Glock, a .38 revolver, a .22 rifle, then a .300 Winchester Magnum that had her ears ringing and her shoulders howling with pain because, Yumuru calmly told her, she hadn't been holding the weapon absolutely correct.

He showed her how to reload single-handed, and when they'd finished he went to the restroom, returning with his hair wet and water soaking his shirt front as though he'd tried to splash away the cloying smells of gun oil and burned cordite.

"The things I do . . ." he said with a wry smile, then his expression turned somber. "You're frightened, aren't you? Angry too, or you wouldn't have spent the past two hours firing at a silhouette like it was a real person."

He was right. Every time she'd aimed at the target, a black-and-white picture of an armed man racing toward her, she had pretended it was Jason Chen in his leather jacket.

"Can't you settle it without using guns?" he asked.

"I hope so," she said, but she could hear the doubt in her voice.

———————

Come midday, Georgia was approaching Evie's office, watching a cockatoo gliding past her, screeching away, and thinking how strange it was that such beautiful birds made such a terrible din, when she saw Jason Chen.

It was only a glimpse of him in the back of a black Mercedes sweeping past, windows open, but she knew it was him because he turned his head and looked at her, right into her eyes.

For a second, sheer terror drenched her, and then she was running after the car, yelling, "Where's my mother? Where is she, dammit? Wait!"

The car powered away, quickly vanishing behind a thick clump of banana trees. By the time Georgia reached the park gates, the black Merc was nowhere to be seen.

Knees like putty, she put a hand against a palm tree and tried to regain her breath. *He'd been waiting for her.*

After a few seconds Georgia pushed herself from the palm and walked fairly steadily back down the road, trying to ignore her finger's dull throbbing. The painkillers she'd taken at the shooting range had kicked in a while back, and she knew it had only started aching again because she'd been reminded of those white plastic shears with the little black button on the side.

Jason Chen had wanted to make sure she'd seen him, to keep her scared, and to let her know that he knew where she was staying. He saw her as he would a cockroach; insignificant and easily crushed.

A ball of rage lodged itself beneath her breastbone, and she felt an urge to scream. One day, she thought, I'll get the bastard. No matter what it takes.

———

Inside the office, Evie was eating her way through a packet of marshmallows and reading a newspaper, fleshy bare feet propped on a box of paper towels.

"You all right?" Evie asked. "You look a bit peaky."

"Have you seen a black Merc around this morning?"

"Nope. Friend of yours?"

"No." Georgia ran a hand over her cropped hair. "Just curious, that's all."

"Only thing of interest in my week was that copper Sergeant Carter turning up." Evie gave her a keen look. "He dropped off that mobile for you. Expensive prezzy, all up. You fancy him, then? He's a bit of all right, wouldn't blame you if you did."

Georgia decided not to go along the matchmaking route and said, "Evie, do you know the story about Daniel Carter and Amy Robins?"

"Sure, everyone knows that one."

"Not me."

"Oh, right then." She popped two marshmallows in her mouth

and spoke as she ate. "Your mate Carter brought Robins down. Oh, couple of years back now. She was part of some violent Triad gang in Brizzy and not over-enamored with being caught. She was facing more than fifteen years behind bars, leaving two kids behind . . . Rumor has it she swore she'd get him back for it, take his little girl and make her suffer . . . Tammy, isn't it?"

"Tabby."

"Yeah, right. Well, Robins knew where Daniel lived, where Tabby went to nursery school . . . She was going to get a mate to pick up the little girl and hold her till she got out on bail, but when Carter went and picked Robins up from jail to take her to court, funny thing, but Robins made a break for it and got shot in the head for her trouble."

Disbelieving, Georgia said, "Daniel killed her? An unarmed woman?"

"Officially she grabbed the other sergeant's gun. Riggs, I think it was, but unofficially, well, you've heard the story."

"Good grief." Her voice was slightly strangled.

It's a real eye-opener, Lee had said, and he was right. She could understand Daniel's terror for his daughter but even so . . . Threaten anyone this man loved and you certainly paid for it.

After a quick and deliciously cold shower, Georgia jumped into Evie's Suzuki and three hours later was on a dusty bare outback road and listening to Crowded House fade in and out on the car radio. Hot air was blasting through the open windows, and the freedom of being able to see clearly without great hanks of hair stinging her eyes was a revelation, as was the breeze against her neck. She would, she decided, keep her hair cropped short for a while yet; it was much cooler.

She felt much more positive, more confident than before, and knew it was because Lee was going to help her find her mother. Although on one level she found the idea of him as her own private hawk disturbing, she was also oddly comforted by his impassive pledge to protect her. She didn't suppose she could want for a better-qualified guardian, a man who killed others with no seeming regret.

A signpost pecked with bullet holes flashed past, and she hurriedly stuck her foot on the brakes and came to a sliding halt. Reversing through the cloud of dust settling behind her, she saw an ill-kempt single asphalt road to the right, and the signpost opposite read, "est ood."

Assuming it meant Restwood, she swung right and drove down the narrow road, passing the odd water tower, a couple of rotting homesteads, and a handful of bedraggled wallabies gorging on the sudden feast the storms had brought. Clumps of vivid green grass and wildflowers had sprung up after the rain, but she knew that in a couple of days they would have withered and died, dissolving into the baking dust.

She'd driven well over a hundred miles inland from Nulgarra, through the rainforested hills before dropping down into the red of the outback, when the Restwood Detention Camp loomed into view. An ugly sore of tin and fibro huts surrounded by tall metal fences, it was topped with rolls of razor wire and there were watchtowers on every corner. The sun was blazing between bunches of angry gray clouds, and the air was hot and moist and pulsing with the sounds of insects.

Remote, secluded, and far from prying eyes, the detention camp was set in a rain-soaked, dirt-dotted area with scraggly trees as far as you could see. The bleak vista would, Georgia thought grimly, give the inmates depression as well as deter escapees. Without a compass or GPS on hand, who'd want to break out to try their luck in this baking wasteland?

An armed guard in uniform slouched against a gate, smoking a cigarette. The huts were ranked in line, like an army camp, and their windows were thick with grime. As she approached, the guard dropped his cigarette and ground it out with his boot.

Georgia wound down her window and the guard bent to give her the once-over. "You're late," he said reprovingly. "We expected you half an hour ago."

"Sorry," she said.

"Any ID?"

She pulled her Visa card from her bag. "It's all I've got, I'm sorry."

"Can't let you in on that."

"But you were told I'd be coming!"

He didn't look as if he cared, just shrugged carelessly. "No authority, no can help."

Authority, authority . . . Georgia scrabbled in her handbag and pulled out her mobile. As she dialed Daniel's number, a cloud swallowed the sun and a handful of raindrops splashed onto the Suzuki's hood.

"Carter," he barked.

"It's me, I'm—"

"You know where Lee is?" His voice was sharp, eager.

"No, I'm at the gate. Can you talk to the guard? Confirm I'm legit?"

She passed the phone to the guard, who listened briefly as he looked at Georgia, nodding from time to time. "Yeah, yeah . . . Okay." He passed the phone back. "Park your vehicle there." He pointed at a handful of utes set on one side. "I'll wait here."

TWENTY-FIVE

It started to rain as another guard escorted Georgia around the periphery of the detention camp. She saw that one of the white fibro huts was streaked with black and that its roof had a great gaping hole in its middle.

"What happened there?" she asked the guard.

"Bunch of Afghanis burned it out." The guard hawked loudly and spat on the ground.

"They burned their own hut?"

"They do a lot more than that, believe me. If they're not given their visas the second they bloody turn up on our doorstep, they go nuts. We've three on hunger strike at the moment, had two burnouts, and a suicide attempt. And what about that lot in South Australia? Sewed their bloody lips together in a hunger strike. Jesus. What the fuck did we do to deserve them?"

Georgia glanced past the guard at the burned-out building, and said nothing. She followed him through a small gate at the far end of the complex and into a small muddy area wired off from the remainder of the camp and its rows of huts with their filthy windows. All she could hear was the rattle of rain on tin roofs.

"Where are the inmates?" she asked.

"Locked up."

"Is that usual? I mean it's midday, why—"

"Precaution."

"Because I'm here?"

The guard didn't reply, simply unlocked the door to the nearest hut and said, "This here's the visiting room."

The visiting room had bare boards, a white plastic table, and six chairs, four occupied by a Chinese man and woman, who were holding hands, a child of about six, and an ancient crone. Georgia hadn't expected to meet a whole family and stared at them. They stared back, motionless.

"I'll sit here till you're done," said the guard, grabbing a chair and taking it to the far end of the room, plonking it beneath a window dribbling with rain. There was a pile of old magazines and newspapers piled next to the door and he picked out a copy of *Deals on Wheels* and snapped it open.

Georgia ran a hand down her face. "Any chance of a coffee?"

"You think I look like a waiter?"

Biting back a sharp retort, she walked toward the family. As she approached, the man leaned across and kissed the little girl's hair, which made her giggle and him smile. Murmuring something to the woman, he rose and met her halfway, smiling warmly. His clothes were a size too big and stained with what could have been oil. He was older than her, she reckoned in his mid-thirties, and had a badly broken nose. His lips and face were covered with pale scars lying ridged and puckered on his skin like bacon rind. It looked as though someone had slammed a scalding-hot frying pan into his face.

"Paul Zhong," he said, hand outstretched. "Nice to meet you, Georgia."

Like his face, his hand was also badly scarred, and she gripped him cautiously, wary of hurting him, but he shook hands firmly, saying, "Doesn't bother me anymore, but thanks."

Georgia felt a huge relief that he spoke English and said so. He grinned, showing a full set of bright white false teeth. "I lived in L.A. for a while." He cocked an eye at her bandaged finger, and she told him she'd slammed it in a car door. Sucking in his breath, he said, "Must've hurt like hell."

"It certainly did."

"Come and meet my family." He ushered her across. "This is my wife, Julie."

Julie half rose from her chair to take Georgia's hand. Her features were angular but delicate, and her luminous paper-white skin brought out the dark rings around her eyes. When she moved, her plait danced in the small of her back, like a narrow, glossy snake. "Hi," she said with a shy smile.

"Hi," said Georgia.

Paul introduced his daughter, Vicki, who was six years old and obsessed with the color pink. Julie's mother, Fang Dongmei, a bent, twisted old woman with a sour expression was, on the other hand, clearly obsessed with the color black. She was also, for some reason, fascinated by Georgia. She spat a torrent of Cantonese at Julie while gesturing furiously at Georgia as though Georgia had done something terribly wrong.

"What's she saying?" Georgia asked.

Julie flushed. "Nothing."

"No, please. I'd like to know."

Julie shook her head, deeply embarrassed, and Paul spoke up. "She's worried about your wedding ring. With your bandage, it's hidden. She wants to know where you've put it, that's all."

"Oh. Well, tell her I'm not married. I have no ring."

Paul turned to Fang Dongmei and said something fast, shook his head. The old crone looked briefly alarmed then mumbled to herself, which made Paul laugh.

"I'm sorry. It's just that we have a different idea of marital status in China. If you're not married by twenty-one, you're an old maid, practically a social outcast."

"Tell her I like being single."

Paul reported back and Fang Dongmei did some wild eye-rolling and smacking of her long, giraffe-like lips. Chuckling to himself, Paul pulled out a chair for Georgia and gestured she sit.

"How long have you been here?" she asked.

He looked puzzled at her question, but said, "Two years."

"How did you get here?"

"Oh, the usual way. Paid sixty thousand bucks for a ride with another thirty desperate souls in a cramped, tiny boat we all thought might sink at any moment." He raised his eyebrows, tightening the scars on his forehead so they glowed white. "I take it you're from the immigration department?"

"No. Sorry."

He frowned. "You're not here about my appeal?"

"No."

"Jesus." He slumped back in his chair. His family were watching him closely, and despite his holding up a reassuring hand to them it didn't lessen the worry on their faces. "I was hoping . . ." His face spasmed and, to her horror, she thought he was going to weep.

"I'm sorry," Paul said, making an obvious effort to regain control. "I'm just a little . . . disappointed."

Vicki suddenly started chattering in Cantonese, and Fang Dongmei heaved the girl onto her lap and murmured into her ear. Vicki nodded, and the crone let down her bun of thick gray hair and let the girl begin to plait it.

"So," said Paul, rubbing the white plastic tabletop with his thumb, "why are you here?"

"I want to know how you know Suzie Wilson. And Lee Denham."

"What are you, some kind of cop?"

"No. Just someone in trouble, needing answers."

Silence.

"I need your help, please."

He sighed. "I don't suppose you can give us anything in return? Like get us out of here?"

Georgia wasn't sure what to say, and Paul seemed to realize it because he added drily, "Or perhaps some fresh-ground coffee? Haven't had a decent coffee for as long as I can remember. Colombian roast would be nice."

Georgia looked at Julie, the way Vicki was clumsily plaiting Fang Dongmei's hair, and said, "I could try to sponsor you."

He smiled. "That's kind of you, but it'll be too late."

"What do you mean, too late?"

Glancing at Vicki, he said calmly, "Not now. Later. When I see you out."

"Okay."

Small silence. All she could hear was the rain pattering on the roof, and smell the dead mustiness of an unused room.

"If I answer your questions," he said, "will you swear to help my family any way you can?"

"I don't understand, I thought you said it was too late."

"Too late for me." His voice was low. "Not for them."

With a vision of her mother sitting cross-legged on their cabin veranda, her Indian bangles tinkling as she shuffled a pack of tarot cards, Georgia pressed the palm of her right hand against her chest. "I swear."

Paul copied her gesture, then nodded. "Fire away, then."

"How do you know Suzie?"

"Through her brother, Mingjun. Jon Ming over here. Jon and I studied medicine together at uni. In Wuhan, China. He went on to become a research scientist. One of the best."

"Where can I find Jon?"

"In Brisbane."

"Talla-something, isn't it?"

"Tallagandra. Nice place, from the sound of it. He writes most weeks."

"What's his address?"

"I've only a post office box. That any good?"

It was better than nothing and, reaching into her handbag, she found a pen and scribbled it on the back of her receipt from Price's.

"No phone number?"

He shook his head.

"Why hasn't Jon sponsored you?"

"You'll have to ask him that. Sorry."

"What does Jon do in Brisbane?"

"He runs a laboratory with Suzie. Quantum Research. They're onto something exciting, but I don't know exactly what. All I know is that they've presented their latest findings to the Australian Medical Association and are waiting to hear the results."

A leap of excitement. He was talking about the antibiotic. Just as Dutch had said. And Paul didn't know Suzie was dead. Georgia wasn't sure if she wanted to break the news. It was bad enough coming here unable to help them, without chucking that in their faces. She decided to press on.

"How do you know Lee?"

"Oh, he's only the man who got us out of China and into this hellhole." He sighed. "Not that it was Lee's fault we got caught. His arrangements were impeccable. He reckoned it was a setup. That a cop on the payroll of the people smugglers let our one little boat be captured while the big one, with over three hundred illegals, slipped past."

He was talking about Spider, the dirty cop.

"You're in touch with Lee?"

"He writes from time to time."

"He *writes* to you?"

"When he has time. He's a busy man, our friend Lee."

Astounded, she managed to say, "Do you have his address?"

Paul grinned. "He doesn't have an address. He'll only be found if he wants to be."

———————

An hour later, Georgia had to make her voice loud over the sound of rain now pounding on the aluminum roof. "What forced you to leave your country?"

Paul said, "There was a warrant out for our arrest. We were to be publicly executed."

"Executed?"

"It's known as 'killing the chicken to scare the monkey.' Public executions are common and keep everybody terrified of stepping out of line. The judges like it, they say it stops crime. Which it does, I suppose, in that the executed cannot commit another offense."

She felt her jaw drop. "But why were you to be executed?"

"For freedom," he said on a sigh. "Freedom of speech, freedom to practice what religion we choose, freedom from propaganda."

Julie suddenly spoke up. "Freedom?" she said tartly. "You call where we are now freedom?"

Paul winked at Georgia before groaning theatrically at his wife. "Just because we currently live in a garden shed with our daughter and your mother is no reason to start complaining."

"We used to have this great big apartment," said Julie. "With sofas and rugs and computers and every kitchen appliance you could imagine." She looked wistful. "We had a DVD player, two cars, and a swimming pool."

Georgia asked Paul the question with raised eyebrows.

"Julie and I were wanted by the PSB. The Public Security Bureau." He paused, adding, "Because we're Falun Gong."

At her frown, he said, "Falun Gong is a kind of Buddhism, Taoism, and *qigong*-style deep breathing exercises. It promotes good living in a spiritual way. I used to advise my patients to take it up. When it got banned, I continued to prescribe it. Which got me into a whole lot of trouble."

"Why is it banned?"

Paul glanced over her shoulder, and she turned to see the guard pulling a packet of Winstons from his breast pocket and lighting up.

"When communism died as a belief system . . . I guess it comes down to the population needing to believe in something, and since nature hates a void, people started to turn to religion. Christianity, Falun Gong. Whatever turned them on."

He ran a hand over his head.

"The government has always quashed any large organizations, terrified they'll lose power to them, and when they saw how fast Falun Gong was growing, how popular it was, they started running scared. They banned it, and immediately started sending Falun Gong members to labor camps, or executing them."

Christ, she thought. Execution for calisthenics?

"Over fifty thousand of our members are in labor camps. Some fifteen hundred have died, the government say by suicide or heart attacks, but most under torture."

Appalled, she said quietly, "I'm sorry. I had no idea."

He gave her a wan smile. "Sadly, the Chinese government has taken the fact that they're hosting the Olympics as affirmation that the West agrees with what they are doing, and have redoubled their efforts."

Vicki had finished her plait and Fang Dongmei gave her a smacking kiss under her chin, which made the girl squirm and giggle.

Paul had a quick high-speed chat with them, and then Fang Dongmei turned to Julie and rapidly fired a bunch of questions at her. Suddenly the crone reached over and grabbed Georgia's forearm, and kept pinching it while she muttered furiously under her breath.

"Ow!" Georgia snatched her arm back.

"*Duibuqi*. Sorry." Julie looked embarrassed.

Fang Dongmei was waving her hands at Georgia as she continued her diatribe. Julie turned bright red.

"I don't mind, honestly," Georgia said. "What does she want to know?"

"Since you ask," Paul broke in with a grin, "she's confounded at the hair on your arms." He showed her his forearm. "Look, not a single hair."

Georgia studied Paul and Julie, then Vicki and her grandmother. He was right. None of them had any hair on their cheeks, hands, or arms. Not a single one. Compared to them she was hairy as a yak, or a yeti. No wonder the old hag was fascinated.

Paul started laughing as Julie's mother continued her arm-waving and finger-stabbing at Georgia.

He said, "Fang Dongmei says that's why you're not married. You're too hairy." He was cracking up, tears of laughter forming. "She wants to know why you don't shave."

"You tell her. She's your mother-in-law."

Twenty-six

Georgia spent the remainder of her visit chatting about general things. If she was going to help this family, she felt she ought to learn something about them. Like the fact that Julie was a doctor too, specializing in shiatsu and acupuncture, and that Vicki hadn't been to school since she'd been in the detention camp but they'd been giving her lessons and she could, if she wanted, speak English reasonably well. All Georgia gleaned about Fang Dongmei, however, was that she hated cereal and toast, thought marmalade the most execrable thing she'd ever tasted, and would give her right arm for a decent fish porridge breakfast.

Georgia wondered how the old hag would cope with Price's Supermarket. Probably extremely well, she decided, watching the way she was smacking and twisting her rubbery lips together. She looked as though she'd survive anything.

Eventually, she pushed her chair back and said her good-byes. When Julie kissed her cheek, Fang Dongmei looked astounded and pulled Vicki aside in case the girl might try to copy her mother. Georgia raised a hand in salute to Vicki, who saluted solemnly back, and smiled at Fang Dongmei, who pretended not to see, then let Paul walk her to the door.

The guard glanced up. "Been a bloody long time—"

"One minute, please," said Paul.

"No way, I'm bored to fucking tears here—"

"One minute," Georgia snapped.

The guard groaned and reached for another magazine.

Paul turned to her. He spoke fast. "You know how I got these scars? I got them in a *laogai*. Gulag."

"Gulag?" The word made her think of Stalinist Russia.

"Few people know of them. The Chinese government keeps *laogai* well hidden, but one day, the *laogaidui* system will be in the history books, alongside Dachau and Treblinka. They're labor reform camps. Same things as a gulag. Prisoners work in terrible conditions, making shoes, clothes, machines . . . mostly for export, like T-shirts."

He took a breath.

"I was sent to a chemical factory. At a reform camp they don't care about safety provisions for prisoners. The acid baths have no splash guards and we were always getting burned. I was forced to scoop out old acid with my hands. I didn't do it fast enough. Two men rubbed my face in it. They were laughing."

"Why were you sent to prison?" Her voice was very faint.

"For being Falun Gong," he said patiently. "I only got out of *laogai* because I signed a bunch of papers that said I would turn my back on Falun Gong. But I couldn't not help my patients. They love it. It helps them with their family, their relationships, their stress, and everything in between. So I'm on the PSB's death list. Because I've broken their rules."

Her brain was trying to catch up with all this horror when he said, "I'm going back to China next week."

"What?"

"It's the only way to stop the whole family being deported at the end of the month. Our application to stay has been rejected. The Chinese government doesn't often take back refugees, so the Australian authorities are leaping at the chance to get rid of us. Also, they've been assured Falon Gong followers aren't being persecuted, so the Aussies reckon our lives aren't threatened. They see no need for us to stay."

"But I thought you said if you go back . . . ?"

"I will be executed."

A clutch of panic in her belly. "You won't really, will you?"

He looked away. "I'd like to be proven wrong, then we can all return home, but if I die, then Julie and Vicki have a really strong case to stay. Fang Dongmei too."

She couldn't think of a word to say. Just gazed at him and his terrible scars.

"If I don't return to Australia, then at least I will know my family is safe here." He gave her a quick smile. "With you looking out for them."

───────────

Later that afternoon, Georgia was sitting on a sun-lounger on Kee Beach in the shade of the sturdy African oil palm, using Daniel's mobile to phone the immigration department. The Coral Sea spread to the horizon, sprinkling shards of sunlight into her eyes and making her squint. Soft clamshells were scattered across the beach, grayish white and translucent, and just beyond her lounger was a handsome, rounded seashell that appeared to have thin raw salmon glistening around its cone.

The shell was ridged but smooth and inviting to the touch, but she didn't pick it up, just in case. The last thing she needed was both hands bandaged.

The mobile was playing Tchaikovsky while she held. She'd already rung the wrong office, then got put through to the wrong department, and she'd been listening to *Swan Lake* for over ten minutes and wondered if she hung up and tried again whether she'd have to suffer the same process. Probably. Briefly she wondered how Tabitha's birthday party was going, and whether the clown had turned up on time.

Eight minutes later, a voice said, "'elp you?"

Georgia introduced herself, then said, "I'm ringing on behalf of some friends of mine, Julie and Paul Zhong. They applied for refugee status—"

"You've got the wrong section. I'll just transfer—"

"No! Wait!"

She was too late.

Another five minutes, then a woman's voice, "Hello?"

Georgia repeated what she'd said before.

"I'm sorry, we can't discuss individual cases over the phone."

"Oh. Okay, so let's make an appointment. How about tomorrow?"

"Oh no. We don't make appointments. We don't have meetings with relatives or friends of applicants."

"So how do I prevent my friends being returned to China to be executed?"

"You have to apply in writing—"

"But he's going to China next week! He'll probably be dead by the time you've opened my letter!"

"There's no need to take that tone, Miss Parish."

"But he's in terrible danger!"

"You'll have to exercise some patience. We're really very busy and don't have the time to—"

"Can't you at least tell me how to stop them being deported? Until I can sort out some sort of sponsorship? They can stay in my house until they find their feet, they won't need government benefits or anything, I'll look after them—"

"Oh no, if they've had their deportation notice, there's nothing you can do."

"There must be *something*. Like contact the prime minister—"

"Oh, we can't do that."

Georgia's tone turned hard. "What *can* you do?"

"I beg your pardon?"

The urge to shout at the woman was so overpowering that Georgia had to hang up. Then she had to have a beer. Then she grabbed a piece of paper and sketched out a childish cartoon of a man hanging from a noose while an immigration department clerk filed her nails.

Shit. Perhaps she ought to run an advertising campaign for Paul and Julie. *Something,* for God's sake. Tracking down the Zhongs' government representative was proving just as difficult. Three different people had promised to call her back, but her mobile had shown no missed calls over the past two hours. She had the sinking feeling that as soon as they'd hung up, they'd each chucked Paul and Julie's details in the bin and gone out for coffee.

Stamping into the van, she pulled out another beer. Drinking straight from the bottle, she choked when her mobile rang.

"Did you find out where Lee is?"

No hello, Georgia, how are you, how was your day? Which was probably a good thing since she had beer up her nose.

"No, Daniel, I didn't. Sorry."

"So what did you find out?"

"That he doesn't have an address, and he'll only be found if he wants to be found."

"Shit. Is that *all*?"

"Well, I learned he smuggled the Zhongs into Australia."

"Hang on." Then she heard him say, slightly muffled, "In a minute, sweetheart. Yup. No, Tabby, you can't play with my penknife, it's not a toy . . . Yes, okay, I'll read you a story in a minute . . . Georgia, sorry about that."

"How'd the birthday party go?"

"I'm more exhausted than if I'd arrested fifteen violent rugby fans single-handed. Gran's still clearing up. It's like a bomb site."

"Tabby like the Barbie cake?"

They talked a while longer about the party, then he began pressing her about Paul Zhong, so she told him pretty much everything she'd learned, but left out all references to Jon and Suzie's company, Quantum Research, in case he mentioned it to another cop and they mentioned it to the Chens. She wanted to discover Suzie's connection to the Chens without them knowing, find out why Lee wanted to get in touch with Suzie's brother, and maybe, in the process, discover an alternative route toward finding her mother.

"Poor bugger," Daniel said about Paul Zhong returning to China, to face certain execution in order to protect his family. "But I guess I can understand why he's doing it." She heard his sigh down the phone. "I'd do the same for Tabby without thinking twice."

Two fathers, two heroes, she thought. One a cop hell-bent on keeping illegal immigrants out of Australia, the other determined to keep his illegal family in Australia.

"Is there anything you can do to help Paul?" she asked. "I've been going mad talking to the immigration department. They can't help at all. They don't *want* to try." She could hear her own anger and frustration.

"If he's been given his deportation notice, no. But I'll give it a go. I can't promise anything, though."

"Thanks."

After they'd hung up, she dialed directory inquiries, got the number of Quantum Research in Brisbane, and the next minute she was talking to Suzie's brother, Jon Ming. Amazed that it had been so easy to find him, she wondered why the lab was publicly listed. Was it a legitimate business after all? She was glad she didn't have to break the news that his sister had died. Apparently a friend had told him, but he didn't say who. After condoling with him, she asked if she could fly down to see him.

"Is it really necessary?" He sounded extremely reluctant. "I'm grateful you were there for Suzie, but I'm terribly busy."

"Suzie gave me a disk to give to you. She told me to hand it to nobody else, and not to trust the mail." Which was stretching the truth, but since she needed some leverage . . .

"A disk? Really?" He brightened. "When were you thinking of coming?"

"Tomorrow morning?" She glanced at her watch. "Nine o'clock?"

"Nine o'clock would be fine."

"Your address?"

After she'd written it down and said good-bye, she immediately called Quantas and booked a return flight to Brisbane for the next morning. Easy. First flight barely half full. Excellent. Filled with energy, she flung open the fly screen and nearly crashed into India.

"Hey, where's the fire?" the reporter asked.

"No fire. Just fired up." Georgia smiled. "I don't suppose you've got a backpack I could borrow? Just for tonight? I haven't got anything to put my stuff in."

"Sure. Give me a sec."

India headed into her van and returned with a smart black, nylon-webbed pack and handed it over.

"Where are you going?"

"Brisbane."

"What's in Brizzy?"

Georgia shrugged.

"Sorry." India grinned. "Can't help myself sometimes. When are you leaving?"

"Now, actually. I want to get to Cairns tonight so I'm in time for the first flight out tomorrow. It leaves horribly early. Five forty-five."

"When are you flying back?"

"Four-forty the same day."

India regarded her thoughtfully. "I've got to be in Cairns tomorrow. I'm covering a fatal stabbing on some racecourse there. How about we travel down together, and you can keep me awake while I drive? We can check into a hotel, you can do your day trip, and I'll pick you up from the airport and we'll be back here in Nulgarra in time to barbecue a chicken and do serious damage on some wine."

Georgia looked down the beach and the sand littered with dozens of translucent bladders tinted with blue and pink: a shoal of jellyfish stranded by last night's northeasterly.

"I promise I will try not to ask you any questions." India grinned. "The accent on *try*, of course."

Georgia couldn't help grinning back. "So what are we waiting for?"

Twenty-seven

Sipping coffee in her upgraded seat at the front of the airplane the next morning, Georgia gazed through the double-skin window at the bright spears of lightning illuminating a massive, lone thundercloud at the same altitude. It could have been a mile away, or two, it was difficult to tell, and when the lightning stopped, everything fell gray for a handful of seconds, and she could see the sky was brightening into pink on the horizon.

She hadn't been as scared of flying as she thought. Yes, her heart had nearly leaped out of her chest when they'd charged along the runway, and when they'd lifted into the air her whole body was rigid, sweating, panic-stricken, but as soon as they reached cruising altitude and the seat-belt sign pinged off, amazingly, she managed to relax a little.

It may have been due to the fact that she'd crashed in a light aircraft, because she felt remarkably secure on the 737. Mind you, the half a bottle of Valium she had taken probably helped, along with a shot of brandy India had slugged into her coffee at the airport.

It had been India who had told the ground staff about her surviving an air disaster five days ago, and they had been wonderfully sympathetic, giving her an immediate upgrade and her own personal member of staff to swoop her on board and past all the lines. She was even introduced to the captain and copilot, who both smilingly reassured her the flight would be uneventful, and the second they'd reached cruising altitude, the flight attendants started clucking around her like mother hens. The flight service director asked if Miss Parish needed anything, perhaps another cup of coffee? Another newspaper?

Georgia accepted the newspaper and leaned back in her seat and watched the lone thundercloud slide past.

When the taxi dropped her outside a drab-looking building that looked more like a warehouse than a laboratory, she said to the driver, "Are you sure this is right?"

He pointed to a small fibro hut inside the gate and a piece of computer-printed A4 paper wrapped in plastic and thumbtacked to its wall: Quantum Research. Right. Some big-shot brother and high-powered lab. Paying the driver twenty-seven bucks, she took one of the taxi's cards, dropped it in the backpack India had lent her, and climbed outside. The taxi disappeared down the broad, almost empty street, and as it signaled to turn right at the traffic lights in the distance, Georgia looked around.

Acres of concrete yards. Dilapidated warehouses as far as the eye could see. One straggly, half-dead eucalyptus struggling to survive. A cool breeze picked up a polystyrene cup and blew it along the gutter with a little cloud of dust. Strangely, she felt more alone in this desolate city backwater than she ever had deep in the rainforest.

Turning to the gates, she saw twenty-odd trucks on the forecourt. They were an assorted variety, from vans and tray-tops to a couple of big semis. She saw an old prime mover with "Harry Hillyard" written on the side, and an ancient army jeep. A security guard had come out of the fibro hut and was standing there, watching her.

"Help you?"

"I've come to see Jon Ming."

"Give us a tick."

The guard punched some numbers on his mobile, announced her, then came across and unlocked a massive padlock. With a screech that set her teeth on edge, he opened the gate. He pointed past the prime mover and said, "That way," and disappeared back inside his hut.

Georgia was heading for the side of the warehouse when she heard barking. She paused as it grew louder, and the next instant an enormous, mottled gray dog with cropped ears and tail came tearing across the forecourt and straight for her. For a second, she nearly lost it and turned to flee, but then she heard her grandfather's voice:

You run from a guard dog, Tom said, *he's going to bite your ass. You stand your ground, he'll bail you up and make a din, but he shouldn't bite if you keep your cool. Remember, don't move a muscle.*

Heart pounding, she stood her ground, and the dog, which must have weighed a hundred pounds, came to a sliding halt just before her trembling knees and stood there barking madly.

"Sweetie," a man's voice called, and the dog paused briefly, glanced over its shoulders, then resumed its barking.

"Quieten down!"

A squat Chinese man was half walking, half trotting toward her, a thick roll of flesh bouncing and wobbling against the white shirt above his waistline. He was pink-faced and panting heavily when he arrived, his shirt dark with great rings of damp beneath the arms. He'd either just run a marathon, which Georgia doubted, or he must be awfully unfit.

As soon as he touched the dog's shoulders, it fell quiet.

"She is a giant schnauzer," he puffed proudly. "She guards me. She's called 'Binggan', which means Cookie."

"And a good job she does too," Georgia said. She was rewarded with a pleased smile from the man.

"Are you Georgia?" he said.

"Yes."

"Jon." He extended a hand and they shook. Soft grip, fleshy and damp. Just the sort she hated. It was like holding a bunch of sausages. She made to pat the dog, but it pulled back its lips and gave her a deep growl until Jon told it to shut up.

"You mustn't approach her. Let her take her own time and she will come to you the instant she decides you are a friend."

She looked at Cookie, and Cookie looked back, her whiskers trembling with what Georgia assumed was a massive effort to stop herself from baring her teeth.

Jon glanced at her bandage. "What happened to your hand?"

She had rehearsed what she was going to say on the airplane, and launched straight in.

"The Chen family chopped off my fingertip to get me to give them what they wanted. Because I didn't know what they were talking about at the time, I couldn't help them, so they have taken my mother hostage, and will kill her on Sunday if I don't deliver what they're after."

The blood left Jon's face so fast that she put out both hands, expecting him to fall in a dead faint at her feet, but snatched them away when Cookie gave a huge snarl. Luckily, Jon just swayed violently, bent double at the waist, and did some deep breathing.

"Are you okay?" she asked after what felt like five minutes of listening to his breath whistling in and out of his lungs.

Slowly, he straightened. He was pasty and sweating heavily and looked terrible, but he managed to straighten right up and look past her and at the street.

"You came alone?"

"Yes."

He studied the street some more. "You weren't followed?"

Georgia hadn't been looking, but since she couldn't remember any cars driving past them or parking when she arrived, she said, "No."

He looked relieved. "Let's go inside."

Cookie led the way, her short stump of tail cocked high and ticking from side to side, like a happy brick. They rounded the side of the warehouse and walked to the back, where a long white building sat at the end of another huge stretch of concrete. Seven cars, one white van, and two motorcycles were parked outside. Each vehicle was facing in, except the bikes, which had reversed into their spaces. For a quick exit at the end of the working day, she thought, faintly amused. If she took Maggie's promotion, perhaps she ought to get a bike so she could do the same.

"They used to be the offices for one of the big sugar companies," Jon explained, still sounding out of breath as they approached. "But we converted them."

Inside, it was how she imagined a laboratory to be. The hut at the entrance was a good camouflage, which she assumed was the intention. Smart reception, if small, with a pretty Chinese girl behind the desk. Blue carpet. Lots of white walls and pictures of seascapes. Neutral smell.

"Coffee, sweetie, please," Jon said to the girl, who immediately got to her feet and scurried off.

Cookie sauntered down a corridor, pushed open the second door on the right, and shouldered herself inside. Jon and Georgia followed. More blue carpet. Two chairs. Computers, printouts, and two walls of reference books, all neat and orderly, aside from a big crystal ashtray the size of a flying saucer and overflowing with cigarette butts.

Jon sat behind his desk while Georgia took the chair opposite. Cookie settled on what appeared to be a dead sheep to the right of Georgia's chair, between her and the door. Clearing his throat, Jon opened a folder, glanced inside, and closed it. Cleared his throat again.

"How did you find me?"

"Paul Zhong, and"—she couldn't for the life of her recall any part of Dutch's real name, so decided not to bother trying—"Dutch, Suzie's friend at Cape Archer National Park."

He nodded. "Nobody else?"

"No."

"Who else knows you are here?"

"No one."

Jon's shoulders slumped in obvious relief. "Good. That is good."

Cookie made a groaning sound, and toppled onto her side as though she'd been felled.

"You have Suzie's disk?"

"I'm sorry, but the Chens have it."

"Oh." He blinked several times. "It won't mean anything to them on its own. They were Suzie's latest results. What a shame we don't have them." His voice suddenly choked. "Forgive me. I still find it hard . . ."

He did some more deep breathing, then, voice steady once more, said, "You know what research we are doing?"

"With crocodiles," she said firmly.

He gave a long sigh, then pulled out a pack of Rothmans and offered the pack to Georgia. She shook her head and watched him light up. "So you know it all," he said. "Are you going to hand me over to the Chens?"

She didn't hesitate. "Absolutely not. I want to hear what the Chen family have to do with all this, then we can decide what we should do."

"It is all my fault. Your mother's kidnapping. Your poor finger. If they knew where I was . . ." He passed a podgy hand across his face. He wasn't anything like Suzie, Georgia thought. Suzie was petite and smelled of jasmine; her brother was fat and stank of cigarettes.

"What do you mean, it's all your fault?" she prompted.

"You see, it all started when Suzie came to Australia five years ago." He slid a look at Georgia. "You've heard of our father? Wang Pak Man?"

Georgia shook her head.

"He was known as Patrick Wang here. A very prominent scientist. Suzie used to send samples of crocodile serum for analysis to him in his lab in New South Wales, but then he had to move overseas. So she turned to me instead." He gave her a sad smile. "Suzie was convinced their blood held the answer to why crocodiles survive injuries that would be lethal to humans. She air-freighted batches of blood in liquid nitrogen to me. I was working in China at the time. In Wuhan. I'd separate the serum from the red blood cells.

"Crocodile blood is full of many components, and it took a long time to isolate each one. Eventually I had over a hundred elements, each with its own test tube. It didn't take me long to realize there was something incredible in test tube twenty-one. I took some simple bacteria and added the contents to test tube twenty-one and I nearly fell over. The bacteria died in their millions."

He sucked so hard on his cigarette that Georgia wondered the entire stick didn't turn into ash. Exhaling a cloud of smoke, he said, "Then I tested test tube twenty-one against bacteria that were dangerous to people, bacteria that were resistant to all known antibiotics, such as MRSA. I placed a few of these superbugs in a petri dish, and in the center of the dish was a single drop from test tube twenty-one. The next day, when I pulled the plate out of the incubator and had a look, the drop of crocodile blood was surrounded by colonies of this deadly bacteria. As soon as they touched the crocodile blood they were killed.

"My colleagues and I finally isolated the protein that kills these bacteria, and this protein forms the basis of our entirely new kind of antibiotic." He took a deep breath and swallowed, but Georgia could hear that his voice was rough with emotion. "I am sad my sister will not be here to see the results of her work."

Georgia was suddenly caught in a vision of walking along the Lotus Healing Center's corridor behind Joanie in her too-tight dress. *Yumuru can't cure cancer, but he's sure got a talent for croc bites.*

"Some days, I can't believe what we created," Jon added.

Both of them glanced around as coffee arrived. It came fresh with a plunger, cream, a plate of assorted doughnuts, and a pretty smile. Georgia looked at the doughnuts and wished she wasn't so wired. She hadn't been able to eat breakfast with the thought of flying looming, and she knew she needed fuel to keep her going, but she couldn't contemplate eating. Not right now. Later.

When the door had closed, Jon stubbed out his cigarette, lit another, picked up a chocolate doughnut and took a bite. He spoke while he ate.

"You see, I realized we had something so amazing, so incredible, that I could emigrate to Australia at last. Not that I could apply for emigration without my employers knowing, of course. So I decided to take a chance and I took all our research and fled the country two years ago."

He took another bite of doughnut and, while still chewing, took a drag of his cigarette.

"As you can imagine, my work colleagues were not impressed. I left nothing for them to work with. Nothing." He suddenly looked cheerful. "They will have to find their own crocodiles."

"So why are the Chens involved?"

"Oh, because the company I worked for in China want me and my research back. Suzie's work. They employed the Chens, the Red Bamboo Gang, to track me down. If they got hold of Suzie, they would have used her to blackmail me to return to China. If they got hold of me, they would have blackmailed Suzie."

He finished the last bite of his doughnut in thoughtful silence.

"However, it wouldn't surprise me if the gang found out just how valuable we are, and want to find us for themselves so they can hold us to auction." His face fell. "Hold me to auction, I mean."

"How did they find Suzie, and not you?"

Another drag of cigarette. Another industrial-sized cloud of smoke.

"If she hadn't wanted to help people, they would never have found her." He grimaced. "She left many friends behind when she left China, friends who wanted to follow her to Australia. She paid snake-heads to bring them over. The snakeheads are run by the gangs. Gang members know each other, they talk."

Georgia jumped six inches out of her chair when Cookie suddenly convulsed and gave a loud bark.

"She is dreaming. Don't worry about her."

The giant schnauzer's legs were jerking wildly, as though she was chasing a burglar, albeit horizontally.

Watching the dog galloping through its dream, Georgia ran over what she knew. Ronnie Chen and Lee had sailed up to Nulgarra to snatch Suzie for the RBG, but Lee had killed Ronnie Chen to keep Suzie for himself. A small spurt of doubt. Suzie hadn't acted like she'd been kidnapped, but like she'd been with Lee willingly.

"Do you know a Lee Denham?" she asked.

Jon blinked. "But of course. It is he who helped Suzie's friends."

Along with Paul and Julie Zhong, Vicki, and the old crone. Mr.

People Smuggler extraordinaire, who even wrote letters to them afterward. Weird, but it could explain Suzie's trust in Lee.

"Jon, do you have a visa yet? To allow you to stay here?"

"As soon as the Australian Medical Association passes our tests, the Australian government will give me one. They won't want me to return, with all my knowledge, to China. They will want to keep me."

"But if you've presented them with the antibiotic, don't they know you're here illegally?"

"I haven't received a deportation notice yet." He looked amused. "Besides, as the owner of Quantum Research, Suzie presented it and in total confidentiality until their decision. I am just one of the scientists listed, and as Jon Ming, not Wang Mingjun."

"How can she own it if she's an illegal immigrant?"

He reached into a drawer on his right and threw across an Australian passport. "Who says she is?"

Georgia opened it to see Suzie's name. The photograph was of a Chinese woman around Suzie's age. The resemblance was minimal.

"Is this forged?"

He shrugged. "It is her passport."

Yumuru had said he had paid Suzie cash every month. For the snakeheads, no doubt.

"How did you manage to set all this up?" She gestured around the room. "Must have cost a packet."

"We have a wealthy benefactor. He funds us, we do the work."

"Who is he?"

He flicked ash into the ashtray and said, "He is a sleeping partner only, and likes to be anonymous."

Georgia frowned. "Who owns Quantum Research now?"

"Our sleeping partner. I am merely an employee."

Perhaps this sleeping partner had sabotaged the airplane to own Quantum Research? It was another possibility.

"Jon, I'd really like to know his name."

He shook his head. "Sorry."

"Look, if you don't tell me, I'll only ring a cop friend of mine to help me out. You wouldn't want the police turning up on your doorstep, would you? Being an illegal immigrant?"

He was taken aback. "Are you threatening me?"

"One hundred percent."

Taut silence, then he said, "His name is Marc Wheeler."

The name rang a bell, but she couldn't think why. "Where can I reach him?"

"He used Suzie's address."

She suddenly remembered the letter from American Express lying with Suzie's unopened mail. It had been addressed to Marc Wheeler.

"Isn't there another way of contacting him?" she asked.

Without looking at her, he shook his head. "How are you going to get your mother back? Without using me?"

She thought, then said, "They went ballistic over Suzie's disk, so I'd say they'd only be too happy with the formula of the antibiotic."

He looked appalled.

"Is there any way you can fake a formula and put it on disk for me? So I can give them something they think is legitimate, but doesn't actually work?"

Slowly, a smile crept onto his face. "Oh yes. Very much. In fact, I can give you something even better. I suggest giving them an exciting taster of the antibiotic with one disk, which they can check out, then in exchange for the whole formula you will get your mother. And they will have a real formula, and will recognize it as such. One for the common cold, which should keep them busy for quite a while."

He stubbed out his cigarette with a flourish. "I shall go and do that now. It shouldn't take long. Everything is to hand. Then I can take Cookie for a pee."

Cookie looked as though she needed a pee as much as she needed a mortgage, and when Jon sprang to his feet and shot out of the room, his guard dog raised her head from the dead sheep, watched the door bang behind him, then turned and looked at Georgia.

Georgia said, "Hello, Cookie. Are we friends yet?"

The dog held her eyes a second, then slumped back into her supine position.

Georgia looked out of the window at the string of cars parked there. Two Nissans, three Mitsubishis, a Toyota, and a Suzuki. All Japanese. She studied the two motorcycles and saw that one was a Yamaha, the other a Ducati. The Ducati had sweeping red curves and huge, fat tires. A pair of massive exhausts thrust skyward. She bet it would go like a rocket.

She was gazing at the bike, mind drifting over what Jon had told her, when she saw a figure dart across the expanse of concrete forecourt. Then another. Both crouched low. Both had guns in their hands. Assault rifles.

She hadn't ever known a more terrible feeling. She felt as though a bomb had exploded inside her, as if her lungs were being ripped apart. She couldn't get her breath.

The Chens were here.

She'd led them to Jon.

TWENTY-EIGHT

Georgia leaped to her feet and lunged for the door. Cookie made it first. The dog was blocking her way, growling.

"Get out of the way!" she yelled. "Jon's in danger!"

Cookie peeled her lips back and showed her teeth, bunching her hindquarters as though about to spring.

Georgia dived for the phone. Dialed triple zero. The instant it was answered she shouted, "Robbery in progress! Quantum Research in Tallagandra, they're armed! They're going to kill me!" and dropped the phone, leaving the line open.

She had to get Jon and escape.

Cookie was still at the door, a growl rumbling deep in her throat.

Georgia glanced through the window. Saw three more figures scooting past, assault rifles at the ready. An army. They'd brought a goddamn army.

"Look, there's your bloody enemy! Not me!" She pointed at the window and, amazingly, Cookie darted past her and heaved her front paws onto the window sill.

Georgia grabbed her backpack and raced to the door, yanked it open, and charged outside. She sprinted down the corridor. Seconds later Cookie galloped past her, ears flat, legs pumping, alert to danger and racing for her master. Georgia picked up speed, trying to keep the dog in sight. She passed reception, yelling, "Call the police!" at the bewildered girl behind the desk, "Call triple zero, *now!*" and blasted through a swing door, down another corridor, where Cookie swung right at the end.

Jesus, the dog was going so fast, she was going to lose her.

Running flat out, Georgia hit the end of the corridor, bounced her left wrist agonizingly against the wall, and pounded after the dog.

She came to the end of the corridor and glanced right, then left. Cookie was butting her head against a door, looking at her. Georgia belted for the door, opened it. Cookie muscled her aside and started barking madly. Georgia fell inside a room filled with gleaming white and chrome equipment. People looked up from their work, expressions shocked. Jon was halfway down a long bench, pulling a disk from a computer, his face alarmed.

"They're here," she gasped. "The Chens. They're here."

Half a second's pause as he registered her words, then he leaped to his feet.

"Fire!" he shouted. "Everyone out! Fire!"

Grabbing a handful of disks, Jon tore down the room, Cookie cantering along with him, treading on his heels. He sprang for a fire alarm. Smashed the glass and pressed a big red button. The noise was deafening.

Everyone snatching things, shouting, running outside.

"Here." He shoved two disks at her. "For your mother."

Into her backpack, zipped up tight. Backpack shrugged on. Cookie barking fit to burst. Alarms shrieking. Jon running for the door, shouting, "Follow me!"

Rushing left, breath scalding her throat, racing for the fire door ahead. Knocking people aside, infecting them with panic, more shouts, a couple of screams.

Bursting outside, Jon swung left around the building, Cookie cruising easily beside him, tongue lolling. Left again and they were suddenly in the forecourt and Georgia slowed, frantically trying to see the men with their assault rifles . . .

A crack of gunshot, but Jon didn't react, duck for cover, or dive to the ground, just shouted, "Get on the bike!"

He was astride the Ducati, the engine bursting into life, roaring.

"Cookie, stay! Guard!" He swept his arm to the building. The dog paused a second, then spun away.

"Georgia, hurry! Get on!"

He was still shouting, and the second Georgia swung a leg over the saddle behind him, he accelerated full-throttle. Without thought, she threw her arms around his waist to avoid getting thrown off, clinging on to rolls of flesh as he pelted around the side of the warehouse.

Crack! Crack!

Still off balance, Georgia tried to wriggle into position and the bike suddenly jinked to one side. He shouted, "Wait! Keep still!"

Half on, half off the bike, Georgia clung on to Jon as he blasted past the parked trucks, heading for the gate. Georgia took a peek ahead, and saw the security guard slumped next to his hut, unconscious or maybe dead. The gate was wide open. Two men stood there, caught unawares. She saw their startled faces. They were yelling at each other and trying to get their rifles up. Jon accelerated straight for them. No hesitation. He was going to take them down.

At the last minute, they dived aside, faces stretched as they shouted, and the bike was through. Decelerating fast to turn into the street, he put the bike into a skidding turn, Georgia hanging on to him like grim death even though she reckoned they were going to tip over. She could feel the bike's rear wheel slipping out from under her and she thought, *This is it, it's all over,* but the bike was righting itself and as Jon aligned the machine she gave a huge lunge and settled on it straight.

One of the men loosed off a shot. She heard the *clank* as it hit metal, then Jon yelled, "Hang on!" and he opened the throttle. Both fists straight back. She'd bet Jon had never asked his bike to go at full speed, but it certainly rose to the occasion. Like the purebred it was, it dug its tires in briefly, then rocketed forward like a pellet released from a slingshot.

The noise as they screamed ahead was deafening, like the sound of a fighter jet taking off. Buildings streamed past in a blur, the engine's howl ricocheting off the brickwork, and Georgia was waiting for the boom when they broke the sound barrier, but the shriek of the engine was so loud she never heard it.

They charged straight through the red light at the end of the street, dodging a bus and a yellow sedan, veered right to pass a taxi, then swung left and accelerated to overtake a slow-moving truck, narrowly missing a scooter that wobbled violently in their wake, horn beeping in protest.

Then she heard a siren. Then another, and another. Three cop cars blasted past, hotly pursued by two fire engines. A police van brought up the rear. They were all heading to Quantum Research.

People leaped aside as Jon charged the bike across a junction with a pedestrian light flashing. Glimpses of shocked and angry faces flashed past.

They rode fast with blaring horn along a highway, veering around buses and shaving the odd cyclist by inches. Other horns blasted back, drivers making rude gestures and yelling at them. Another siren started up. The wail steadily increased and she realized the siren wasn't going to Quantum Research. It was coming after *them*.

They were approaching town and even more traffic, pedestrians, and bicycles. She saw tall gleaming buildings and rows of palm trees, people eating sandwiches and drinking from long glasses. A bunch of schoolgirls with blue pleated skirts and immaculate white socks crowded around an ice-cream vendor.

The bike slowed to a crawl at traffic jammed in front of a set of red lights. The siren pulsed closer. Jon swung his bike onto the sidewalk and started to force his way through pedestrians, crashing into a newspaper stall and sending magazines and papers flying into the air.

People were shouting, horns honking. With a lurch, Jon bounced the bike back onto the road past the traffic jam, and tore away.

Georgia turned on her seat to look behind. She couldn't see the cop car, but she could hear it, getting louder every second. So could Jon, who started to brake, slowing the bike to turn it into a long, dark alley, then immediately accelerating. They burst into bright light at the other end and kept going, straight across a main road.

Two cars swerved around them and coming fast on their right was a red Grace Bros truck, air horn bellowing. Jon didn't seem to have seen it. He kept the throttle wide open and charged for the other side, for another long, dark alley.

The Grace Bros truck was so close that all she could see was the massive radiator grill studded with insects. She opened her mouth to yell, her hands desperately clutching Jon's middle, when there was a hideous shriek of brakes and, air horn still bellowing, the truck swerved wildly sideways, four wheels locked, and with a screeching, tearing noise, scythed into a lane of parked vehicles.

Georgia saw a car's windshield shatter, its hood compress against the dead weight of the truck, crumpling like newspaper. Sparks wrenched. The air was a shrieking, screaming mayhem of metal until the truck finally slammed into a department store window, juddering briefly before it stilled.

Georgia's ears were buzzing from the noise as she turned her head to look over Jon's shoulder again, part of her exultant that they'd made it, another part horrified, realizing she'd nearly been killed. Had the truck driver been hurt? Anyone in the parked cars? And what about pedestrians? No time to think, just hang on and pray.

Diving the bike into the dark alley on the other side of the road, Jon immediately started to slow, down-changing gears, bouncing on the rough pavement, and then he jammed on the brakes, slewing the bike to the right and down another, broader alley.

They passed people delivering cartons of lettuce and tomatoes, men shouldering whole carcasses of beef and lamb from refrigerated trucks. She saw a woman with a tray of cheeses, another lugging two whole salmon. A hot dog stand on the sidewalk filled her mouth with the hot savory smell of sausages, and then the air was full of Thai spices: coriander, chili, garlic.

A left turn, and they were on a broad road heading north. She saw a sign for the airport, then another. Jon was riding more cautiously now, not wanting to draw attention. Approaching the airport, they passed an open-top Mazda, and the woman in the passenger seat glanced across and tapped her head furiously with her hand. Georgia thought she meant they were mad, then realized the woman was telling them they had no helmets. They were breaking the law.

Then they were slowing down, sweeping along the road to departures, pulling over gently, braking, and coming to a stop. Jon set the kickstand, ran a hand through his hair, and switched off the engine.

The silence seemed deafening. Georgia sat there, wondering if she could move. She felt shell-shocked and tottery as a newborn foal.

Jon craned his head around. "Best if you go first," he said.

She realized she was still clutching his middle and hurriedly released her grip. Scrambling off the bike, she found her legs were limp and she had to hold on to the rear of the bike frame until they steadied. Jon hopped off with seemingly no ill effects whatsoever. He stood with his hands on his hips and looked at his bike, then at her, and said, "What a rush!"

"You were amazing."

He grinned, and it was then that she saw Suzie in him, the same slanting almond eyes filled with humor, the same curve to his lips.

"And you're not a bad pillion. You done much riding before?"

"Er, no."

"I'd never have known it," he said enthusiastically. "You're a natural."

———

While Jon rang a work colleague from a public phone, Georgia bought them drinks; coffee for Jon, a double whiskey for her. She was still trembling, but after a few sips she felt her nerves steady. Talk about a close call. If Jon hadn't had that bike . . .

She watched him hang up and make another call. Then another. When he eventually joined her, she had finished her whiskey and his coffee was cold. Not that he seemed to notice, he just drank it down in four quick swallows.

"It looks like the Chen's didn't get much, if anything at all." He looked relieved. "They disappeared pretty fast when the police turned up. Brad got wounded, the security guard, before they blasted the padlock to pieces. I should have made better precautions."

He gazed dolefully at a no-smoking sign on the wall. "Cookie bit a policeman."

"Oh dear."

"She's gone to the pound, poor darling. Lizzie, that's our receptionist, is going to try to get her out. Lizzie says the police want to talk to us. Urgently, as you can imagine."

"I haven't time to talk to them," said Georgia. "It'll take hours, and with my mother . . ."

"I've no time either. I've got to get to Sydney and meet with the AMA. Get them to fast-track their approval of the antibiotic. Once it's approved and in production, maybe the Chens will leave me alone." He didn't appear too confident about this, but then his expression hardened. "I've a team of security guards turning up at the lab in the next hour. Fully armed. Twenty-four-hour protection. All a bit late, but never mind. I'm going to hide out in Sydney and hire myself a personal bodyguard. Or four. Then I'll go to the police."

He picked up his cup, realized it was empty, and put it down again. "You should go to the police as well."

"As soon as my mother's safe, I will."

———

Georgia took an earlier return flight, having text messaged India to let her know, and spent it trying to ignore the way her heart galloped every time the airplane's engine note changed. After the bike chase her nerves were shot and she was convinced they were going to crash any minute. She'd had two more shots of whiskey, but they hadn't helped.

"Nervous flier, eh?" her neighbor said when they'd roared down the runway.

She hadn't even been able to unclench her teeth to say yes, just gave a jerky nod.

"We'll be fine," he said confidently, and reached over to pat her sweat-slicked hand. "Built like brick shithouses, these things. You know they test aircraft to hell and back before they go into service? They even chuck frozen chickens at the engines to test against bird strikes. If they do that, you know they've tested for just about every-thing. No way can anything happen to us. Trust me."

Another pat, a warm smile.

She managed a tense smile back. The kindness of strangers. Her mother was like that, always kind, even to the bailiffs when they'd ap-peared in Glastonbury. She'd made them coffee and given them a plate of chocolate cookies, telling them it wasn't their fault they had to strip the house.

Then there was the time Dick Cooper had lost his wife, killed in a boating accident off Port Douglas. Her mother didn't just leave casseroles or home-baked cakes on the doorstep for Dick, his six-month-old baby, and four-year-old twins, she'd moved in.

"The poor man doesn't have anyone," she'd told Georgia and Dawn. "He nearly fainted with relief when I said I'd help out. Just for the week, until the funeral's over."

"But what about his brothers?" Georgia had protested. "He's got Pat and Jimmy."

"Darling, they're men." She hadn't cared that the town would go mad with gossip, and had firmly handed the sisters into Evie's care.

Her selfless, generous mother. It was all very well Lee saying he was going to try to find her, but surely she could find another route? Like trapping Lee into meeting the Chens, and freeing her that way? Could she really betray the man who had saved her from certain death? His face swam into her mind: his torn ear, the scar running up through his eyebrow, the wide mouth that never smiled. Her heart squeezed and she shifted in her seat, uncomfortable that she could picture him so easily. He saved your life, she reminded herself, it's no wonder he seems to be indelibly printed on your brain.

If she couldn't use Lee, she had to try something else. Mum . . . God, she hoped they were looking after her. And what about her head? They'd smashed it so hard, all that *blood.*

Her throat began to ache with suppressed tears and she fought against the urge to weep, desperately trying to calm herself. She knew she was reacting from the shock of the Chens turning up at Quantum Research, the bullets fired at her, being on an airplane, but if she didn't get control of herself she thought she might become hysterical.

Like a whimbrel searching for crabs in the mangroves, she scanned her mind for something else to think about, and gradually another memory emerged. She was ten years old and holding the tiny dead body of a puppy, the runt of Pickles's litter. She couldn't stop sobbing, and a voice was telling her to concentrate on breathing deeply. It was her mother, and she could have been beside her, her voice was so clear.

Concentrate on filling your lungs, darling, then feel your tummy fill with air and hold it . . . lovely. Now, release it slowly, let it dribble through your mouth, and do the same again. Keep your mind focused on breathing slowly and deeply and you'll feel much better. And yes, of course we can have a funeral. We'll bury him under the big black palm and you can pick some wildflowers to put on his grave.

Her mother once told her she could sense her and Dawn's distress through telepathic airwaves, but Georgia had never believed her. Oddly enough, though, whenever she was deeply upset, like when Charlie dumped her after his last proposal, the phone would invariably ring, and it would be her mother asking if everything was all right.

Soon, Georgia was calm. She looked out of the window at the blanket of altocumulus spreading across most of the sky, then at her fruit-decorated watch. Not long until she met with India again and headed back to Nulgarra for barbecued chicken and wine. She would, she decided, tell India about the antibiotic. She might even tell her about her mother. She liked the reporter a lot, and needed someone on her side whom she could trust.

Just under an hour later, they landed at Cairns.

Where the police were waiting for her.

TWENTY-NINE

The constable behind reception looked up as Georgia entered the police station, a uniformed cop on either side of her, India hustling behind.

"You can't just snatch her from the airport and drag her in here," the reporter was protesting. "What about a lawyer?"

"Like we said already, Miz Kane," one of the cops replied. "We just want to ask Miz Parish a couple of questions, that's all. Then we'll let her be on her way. You stay here and read a paper, why don't you? Sorry we don't have the *Sydney Morning Herald* for you to browse. Try *Fishing Weekly* instead, it might settle you."

The two cops marched Georgia past reception and through a door on the right. Lit with fluorescent strip lights, the corridor was icy cold with air-conditioning and smelled of french fries and takeout.

"I'll wait for you, Georgia!" India yelled after her. "I won't budge an inch! Promise!"

The cops halted outside a door, and one of them opened it and stuck his head inside. "Where's the chief? Got Georgia Parish for him."

"He'll be here soon. Riggs is down to deal with her."

"Riggs?" she repeated, dismayed.

Sergeant Riggs appeared in the doorway, and her stomach dropped into her shoes. For a second she had hoped there were two policemen called Riggs, but obviously there weren't. She'd been dragged from the airport to be faced with the same piggy-eyed cop who had questioned her at Mrs. Scutchings's house all those days ago.

"Why, hello again, Miz Parish," he said, grinning. His teeth were unnaturally small, almost like milk teeth, and when he licked his lips, his tongue was a shocking crimson against the pallor of his face. "What a pleasant surprise, seeing you all the way down here."

Turning briefly to the two cops, he said, "Thanks guys, I'll take it from here."

The two cops nodded and left.

Riggs glanced at her breasts, still smiling. "The chief told me to take care of you till he's ready."

Georgia crossed her arms.

"Come to my parlor, then." Riggs showed her through two more corridors to the squad room. He walked surprisingly fast for a man of his bulk, and she felt she was galloping to keep up.

The squad room was huge. High ceilings, enormous desks, and an inordinate amount of clutter. People were on phones and calling across the room, tapping on keyboards, their faces lit by computer screens. The smell of french fries intensified and she felt her mouth water. If anyone offered her a bag of fries right now, she'd devour the lot. She was *starving*.

Riggs offered her a chair, then leaned back in his own, his jacket falling open to reveal a popped button above his waistband and some red hairs poking through. He said, "How's life treating you, then?"

Georgia declined to respond. The last thing she felt like was making small talk with him.

"What about Danny boy? He's been seeing a bit of you, I gather?" His eyes latched back onto her breasts. "I can sure see why."

"What do you want with me?"

"The chief wants to ask you some questions. About that fracas in Brizzy. Sounds like you started a war down there. You want to tell me what happened?"

A mobile started ringing somewhere, and when nobody answered it she realized it was hers. Lunging for her backpack, she yanked the thing out.

"How's tricks?"

Her heart gave a leap, and she hurriedly turned away from Riggs, ducking her head and pressing the receiver hard against her ear.

"Er . . . I'm at the police station, actually. In Cairns."

"You going to be long?"

"No idea. Apparently the chief wants to ask me some questions."

Pause.

"What about?"

"Oh, something that happened earlier today."

"Must've been mighty big to catch the chief's eye. He's an important bloke, all up. You okay?"

She was surprised by the anxiety in his tone, and even more surprised by her reaction. A rush of tenderness for his concern, which she immediately put down to feeling vulnerable at the day's events.

"Fine."

Another pause.

"Listen up. I think I know where your mother is."

She bolted upright in her chair. *"What?"*

"Get yourself back up to Nulgarra quick smart, okay?"

"Yes, yes, but where is she, are you saying she's—"

"I'm going to do a recon tonight. Check the place out. If I can, I'll grab her. Okay with you?"

"God, absolutely, definitely, but be careful, won't you, please?"

"Cautious as a leopard, cunning as a snake."

Before she could give him a message for her mother, he hung up.

Trembling with excitement, she pushed her phone back into her backpack. Lee had found her mother! She and Mum could be flying out tomorrow, away from all this mayhem, away from the Chens!

"Good news?" Riggs asked.

"Oh, a friend's just had a baby." She smiled brilliantly at him.

His expression had turned peculiarly withdrawn.

"It's a little girl," she added firmly for good measure.

"My boy was a preemie. Nearly died." He opened a drawer and took out a photograph and showed it to her. A smiling, remarkably handsome woman in blue was holding a strapping toddler in her arms. "Looks just like me, eh? Bit podgy, but handsome as hell." He was beaming from ear to ear.

Startled by this sudden change from bullying cop to proud parent, she was about to say, "How lovely," or something along those lines, when he snatched the photo and shoved it back inside the drawer.

"Heard from our friend Lee lately?" he asked.

Her skin tightened but she kept her face bland.

"Why are you so interested in Lee?" she responded. "I mean, I know he's a people smuggler, but you all seem so hell-bent on finding him, I'm starting to wonder if there isn't something else."

"Danny boy hasn't told you?"

"Well, no, not really."

He flicked another look at her breasts. "Guess I can understand that."

She resisted the urge to grind her teeth and said again, "Why do you want Lee?"

"To tear his head off and stick it on a pole, that's why. If it wasn't for Lee, Sergeant Tatts would still be alive. Sodding Lee."

Heart thumping, she said, "He killed a cop?"

"Too bloody right. Greedy bastard, Lee. Do anything for a buck. He was brought up like a Chinese, you know, by some ancient old hag. Believe me, you can't trust him further than you can throw your average Chinaman."

He checked that the drawer with the photograph of his family was shut, as though protecting them against what he was about to say, before leaning forward in his chair.

"Years ago, the powers-that-be thought it was a brilliant idea to take this thug off the streets and make him a copper because he had a white father, some bigwig swanky lawyer in Hong Kong, and because he spoke fluent Cantonese and Mandarin. They regretted it big-time when he tipped the Red Bamboo Gang off about Tatts."

Georgia felt as though she'd been punched in the stomach. "Lee's a *policeman*?"

"*Was* a fucking policeman. A fucking joke, the whole thing. He'd been transferred from Hong Kong to work with our feds to plug the illegal immigrants and was working for the other side the whole fucking time. No wonder we never caught any bloody boats with him tipping the RBG off."

Her voice was faint as she said, "You said he killed a cop."

"Yeah. Not personally, but there's not a whole lot of difference. He may as well have pulled the trigger himself. Tatts had been working undercover on the biggest drug deal we'd seen in the past decade, pretending to be the broker between the RBG and a buyer. It was all set up. Tatts had the money. Jason Chen and his father the drugs. We were going to nail the two top honchos of the RBG, and then fucking Lee dobbed Tatts in."

Sucking on his small milk teeth briefly, he continued. "Tatts vanished four hours before the rendezvous. Jason Chen wanted to make a statement to us cops, to make sure none of us would go undercover against them again. So he chopped off all the sergeant's fingers and toes with pruning shears, you know, like for gardening? Then he dumped Tatts on a garbage dump just out of town . . . to bleed to death."

Appalled, Georgia sat there and stared at him.

"You know the worst thing?"

Numbly, she shook her head.

"Tatts was Lee's fucking partner."

He slammed his palm down onto the table, making everyone in the room pause and look up.

"What do you think of Lee Denham?" he roared into the room.

"Arsehole!" someone yelled, followed by, "Shoot the fucker!" and "Waste of fucking space!"

"He's not a popular man," added Riggs, looking gratified. "If we see Lee, we'll nail him to the wall and—"

"Riggs, put a sock in it," a man said wearily behind her. "You're like a stuck record."

The room fell quiet. Riggs's expression turned formal as he looked over Georgia's shoulder. "Chief."

"Miz Parish, sorry about that. If you'd like to join me."

Stunned, Georgia had to make an extreme effort to appear in control of her limbs as she got to her feet. *Lee was an ex-cop.* That explained the slightly military aura, his knowing who Riggs and his sidekick were when they'd questioned her about the intruder at Mrs. Scutchings's house. And he knew Daniel. Sweet Jesus. He was a cop who had betrayed a fellow policeman to suffer a terrible death. His *partner.*

"I'm Chief Inspector Harris."

She turned around to discover a tall man with a close-cut white beard. Very distinguished, almost patriarchal, with pink cheeks and a gentle smile. Aware that her palm was cold and sweaty, she surreptitiously wiped it on her trousers before shaking, but as she glanced up she saw he'd caught her doing it. The smile turned sympathetic.

"Not everything feels comfortable in police stations," he said kindly. "I've just a few questions, then I'll let you be on your way." A nod at Riggs, who nodded back, and then he ushered her into a room next door.

"My office. We might be able to hear ourselves think in here, not like next door. They seem to be under the mistaken impression that if they shout, things get done faster."

The chief's office had the same high ceiling but was tiny in comparison to the enormous squad room. Three walls were taken up with folders, books, and journals, and his desk was a clutter of paper. He sat behind the desk, Georgia took the battered armchair in front.

"I heard them slagging Lee off," he remarked casually, but she could see the tension at the corners of his mouth. "I should be used to it, but some days . . . I liked Lee a lot, and although he betrayed me and my men . . ." He ran a hand over his beard and glanced away. "We were all very . . . ah, close to Sergeant Tatts."

Lifting a pen from his desk, he rolled it between his fingers like a cigar. Sudden vision of Lee smoking. Lee who had told her he knew where her mother was. Her own personal hawk. A hawk every cop wanted to see shot from the skies with an Exocet missile.

"You want to tell me what happened in Brisbane?"

"Um . . ." She didn't know where to start, or rather, how to start lying. She had to in order to protect Jon and Lee, and keep her mother safe.

"My Brisbane colleagues were seriously unimpressed with your sudden exit from their city. Hence calling us to pick you up once they knew you were on a plane to Cairns." He gave her a wry smile. "You gave them a run for their money, I gather, but thankfully nobody got hurt, which is what counts."

She couldn't work out how the cops knew it was her at Quantum Research, nor the chain of events that had led the Chens to Jon. She frantically backtracked over the past twenty-four hours, trying to think who knew where she was going. As far as she could recall, only India knew about Brisbane, and then her brain jumped a little further back. Paul Zhong. Paul had told her about the lab in Brisbane. And who knew about Paul Zhong? Sergeant Daniel Carter, that's who. Who was also a cop.

We have friends in the police.

Spider.

Dear God, who had Daniel told about her seeing Paul Zhong?

"I was going to go back and talk to them," she offered weakly.

He gave a dry chuckle. "Sure you were."

"It's just that I was visiting a friend, you see. And then suddenly the fire alarm went off . . . and shots were fired. I didn't know what on earth was going on, I just wanted to get the hell out, to be honest."

"And your friend is Wang Mingjun. Jon Ming."

She dithered briefly, then admitted, "Yes."

"Where is he now?" He arched a pair of thick white eyebrows, pen poised above a yellow legal pad as though to take down Jon's address. "Well?"

"Why do you want him?"

"Several reasons. One, to fill in the gaps. We know he's considered a valuable commodity by the Red Bamboo Gang. We'd like to talk to him. See who he knows, maybe get a new trail into the RBG."

"You *know* about . . . what they're researching?"

"Oh yes."

Jon being questioned by the police wasn't an option. For all she knew, he'd end up in a detention center like Paul Zhong and his family, an illegal immigrant with no rights, so she said, "He dropped me off at the airport, then left. I don't know where he's gone."

The chief put down his pen, frowning. "His bike was found outside departures. He flew to Sydney, we've got that far, but we don't know where he's headed."

I won't tell you, she thought. I won't, not until Jon's met with the AMA and is a citizen of Australia, so help me God.

He sent her a look of compassion. "I understand you must feel a strong bond with Jon Ming, having been with his sister in the air crash, but we really need to find him. For his own good. We want to protect him. From what we can gather, the RBG want to haul him back to China. It's my guess he doesn't particularly want to return there. And we don't want him to either. He's extremely valuable to us. As I'm sure you can appreciate."

In the distance she heard a horn beep and the distinctive chatter of a parrot.

"We want to help Jon. He's in danger. After the morning's events, surely you can see that?"

She could, and she honestly wanted to help Jon too, but the thought of Spider . . . *They sit in their webs and pull the strings they want.*

"I'm sorry, I don't know where he is now." Which was true. He could be in a taxi, in a restaurant, in the AMA's offices, caught in a traffic jam on the Sydney Harbour Bridge.

Long pause while the chief spun his pen on his legal yellow pad.

"If we had Jon Ming, then we would have the RBG. We could set something up. Catch them unawares."

And use Jon as a hostage, like the Chens had her mother? she thought. You must be joking. He'd get doughnut withdrawal. He may be a fat bastard who reeks of nicotine, but at least he's a fat bastard who rides a motorcycle like a demon, even with a sack of potatoes on the back. Besides, Cookie needs him. Poor darling's in the pound.

Another lengthy pause. The chief dropped his pen, leaned back in his chair, and steepled his fingers on his beard. He looked at her hard.

"Sergeant Carter tells me he thinks you might be in touch with Lee."

The skin tightened all over her body at the realization that Daniel could obviously see through her like a pane of glass. What else had she given away? She hadn't thought she was *that* transparent.

"And I think he could be right. However, I'm also thinking things are a lot more complicated than you're letting on . . . But we're here to help *you*. And we can't do that unless you help us. Do you understand?"

"Yes. And . . . thank you."

"Do you know where Lee is?"

"No." Not exactly, anyway. Just that he's in Nulgarra somewhere and about to rescue my mother.

"Rumor has it he'll be sailing soon. On his yacht, *Songtao*." He shot her a look she couldn't quite read. Half curious, half wary. "Do you know how the boat got her name?"

She shook her head, wondering where this was leading.

"*Songtao* means 'waves of pines,' the sound the wind makes when it blows through a pine forest. Apparently there was such a forest where his grandmother used to take him when he was a child. In China, roots are incredibly important, so he named his boat *Songtao*, in memory of his grandmother, the person he grew up with."

"How on earth," she said faintly, "did you find that out?"

"*Guangxi*," he said, fiddling some more with his pen. "It's a debt of favors the Chinese use. Put it this way, Riggs was owed a favor. Got put in touch with a boat captain in Fuling who told him the story. We know a lot about Lee."

She wasn't sure why he'd repeated it to her, but thought he might be trying to gain her trust by showing her some police work and the trouble they were taking to get to Lee.

"If you hear from Lee," he said, "tell him I'd like to chat, would you?"

Get in line, she thought, but said, "Sure."

"And what about Jason Chen and his father? Seen them lately?"

"Who?" she said, injecting her tone with doubt.

She watched the chief exhale fractionally. He hadn't expected her to know the Chens, she realized, just chucked a baited line out in the faint hope she might bite.

"Oh, a couple of miscreants," said the chief. He scribbled something on his pad, but she wasn't much good at reading upside down and couldn't see what he'd written unless she craned really obviously.

"Just to reiterate," he said, putting down the pen and looking up, "my main priorities are to find Jon Ming, to protect him, and to find Lee."

No can do, she thought.

As if he had heard her thoughts, the chief suddenly leaned forward. "If I find you've been obstructing police business and withholding information . . ."

His tone was deceptively soft, but she got the message.

Georgia left the police station feeling in need of another stiff drink.

THIRTY

No wonder you're rattled. Talk about walking a bloody tightrope. I wish you'd let me in from the start."

Georgia wished she had too. India hadn't lunged for her phone since she'd confessed, or pulled out a microphone and shoved it in her face. After she'd met Georgia in police reception and bundled her into her ute outside, looking over her shoulder the entire time as though expecting the cop shop to erupt with armed police at any second, she'd simply started the car and shot away saying, "What the hell is going on? For God's sake spill the beans, will you? I promise I won't tell anyone. Not a soul, unless you want me to." Georgia had looked at her, and India had solemnly crossed her heart with a long brown finger. "Hope to die," she'd added.

So Georgia told her everything. Everything she could remember, that was. The cops and their hatred of Lee; Yumuru and Suzie and the antibiotic; Daniel, Tilly, and Dutch. Her mum. It was as if a dam had broken. God, what a relief to spill it all out.

They were halfway to Nulgarra when she stopped talking. Her mouth was dry, and India reached behind and into her rear seat pocket, pulling out a liter bottle of Evian. "Never travel without at least ten of these suckers," she said. "Never know when you're going to break down, and I don't ever want to go thirsty."

Georgia had a long drink, then recapped the bottle and laid it along her thighs.

"So Lee's going to break your mum out tonight?"

"I hope so."

India stepped on the gas when the road broadened, stretching between grasses the color of flax like a long black snake that had been flattened by a giant boot.

"What's this bloke's name again? The one on the bike from Quantum Research?"

"Jon Ming. Wang Mingjun. He's Suzie's brother, and—"

"That rings a bell. What's *her* name? Her Chinese name?"

"Wang Mingshu."

A Toyota Hilux pulled out from a side road ahead and India jammed her foot on the brakes.

"Hey, India, take it easy, will you?"

"Say her name again?"

"Wang Mingshu."

"Wang Mingshu?" India repeated. "You don't happen to know the name of their father?"

Georgia thought a bit. "Wang . . . Pak Man, I think. But Jon said he's known as Patrick Wang."

"Patrick Wang." India's voice was faint. "Holy fuck."

Georgia studied the side of the reporter's face. Her cheeks seemed to have lost color.

A horn sounded and Georgia jumped. They were practically in the middle of the road. The car coming from the opposite direction swept past, horn still blaring.

"Christ, India!"

India heaved her ute onto the dirt shoulder and switched off the engine. Her hands, Georgia saw with a little shock, were shaking.

"Georgia. You're saying Patrick Wang is Suzie Wilson's father? And that Suzie Wilson and Mingshu were the same person?"

Alarmed, unsure where this was going, Georgia decided on sticking to the truth. "Yes. I am."

India scrabbled in the well between them and shook a Marlboro from the pack, lit it from the car's lighter. She buzzed her window down and exhaled a stream of smoke outside. She said softly, "Jesus."

Warm air drifted over them, blanketing the air-conditioning and making Georgia start to sweat. "India, what is it?"

The reporter looked around. She was staring at Georgia but she wasn't connecting with her. She was staring at something beyond her and in her own mind.

"I know Mingshu," she said. Her tone was distant. "Well, not *know* her as such, we never met, but yes, I knew of her because of her father. I've been after Patrick Wang for the last eighteen months, and got hold of letters to him from his kids. Mingshu and Mingjun." She sent Georgia a sharp look. "Are you *sure* it's her? Was her?"

"Of course I am!"

India dragged deeply on her Marlboro.

"I don't get it." India was shaking her head in bewilderment. "Why did she want to see me? *Me,* of all people."

Confused, Georgia said, "I don't know. Sorry."

"Fuck it . . ." The reporter stubbed her half-smoked Marlboro out in the dashboard tray with sharp, jabbing motions until the filter was pulped. "Could you expand a bit on Jon, what he said, then maybe I can see where Suzie fits into it all?"

Georgia told India about how Suzie captured wild crocodiles and sent the serum to Jon in China in the hope of finding an extraordinary new antibiotic, how Jon realized the immensity of what they were creating and took all his research and fled to Australia, and the Chens' determination to get their hands on either one of them, Suzie or Jon, and get the research back to China and the company Jon used to work for, their clients.

India was on her third cigarette by the time Georgia finished.

"No wonder they're such hot property," the reporter said. "Not just because they're valuable scientists themselves, and the Chinese want them back, but their father was another scientist. Patrick Wang. He's been on the run from the Australian authorities ever since his killing spree. Remember those people who died in the Northern Territory two years back?"

Georgia could feel the shock on her face. Over seven hundred people had died from an incurable virus, and it had been India who had exposed the truth behind the murders.

"Their father did that?"

"Sure did. The total bastard . . ."

India was still talking and suddenly Dutch was in Georgia's mind, telling her about his bony-assed friend whose father had done something really bad, and Suzie had wanted to do something really good, to make amends.

"Now she's dead," India said, looking frustrated. "We'll probably never find her father now. Not unless Jon gives him up."

"Jon said he'd had to go overseas."

"Where?"

"He didn't say."

India's mobile chirped, and she stubbed out her cigarette as she answered it. "Hi. Yes, probably. Say I'll be with you at—" she looked at Georgia and said, "Can I drop you in town?"

Georgia nodded. She could always get a taxi to the caravan park, and besides, she needed a bandage for her finger, acetaminophen, and maybe some antiseptic cream. It was aching more than usual. God, she hoped it hadn't gotten infected.

India turned her wrist to look at her watch and said into her phone, "Six o'clock." Shoving her phone between her thighs, she turned the ignition and swung the ute back onto the road and accelerated hard, overtaking a four-wheel drive towing a horse box.

"So," said India, "do you have any ideas who sabotaged the plane?"

"Not really." Georgia sighed and turned her head to look outside. Baked red dirt speckled with low dry bushes and red anthills flashed past. You'd never think they were just forty minutes from tropical rainforests and beaches rimmed with aquamarine sea.

Georgia thought about the saboteur and who, aside from the entire police force of Australia, wanted Lee Denham dead. Or had they wanted to kill someone else? Not her, but what about Bri? No, that was impossible. And who in the world would want to kill Suzie, when she was so valuable?

Her mind made a giant leap.

Suzie, wanting to see India about exploitation at the healing center. Tilly, one minute dying, the next day healed. What if someone had wanted to kill Suzie, in order to maintain the illusion of an incredible healing gift *and* keep the money flooding in?

India had tuned the radio to Sea FM and was humming along to George Harrison's "My Sweet Lord," oblivious to Georgia's silence. She'd barreled through the little settlement of Mount Molloy, barely pausing at the forty-mile-an-hour speed limit, and was now cruising along the smooth, sweeping asphalt road at over eighty.

"India," Georgia ventured, "could you keep the fact about Suzie and the antibiotic quiet for a bit?"

"My lips are zipped, remember?" India flashed her a narrow look. "Why? You've made some connection?"

"Er . . ." Georgia wasn't sure she wanted to voice her newfound skepticism of Yumuru. What if she'd gotten it wrong? India could destroy him with a flick of her pen, not to mention all those patients currently in his care, and those he might cure in the future.

"Georgia!" India erupted. "Will you just trust me, goddammit! I'm on your side! Don't you get it? I won't tell anything to anyone you don't want me to, not my partner, not the cops, not Scotto." Her lips twitched mischievously. "He's my editor. He's gorgeous, by the way. And very single."

"Not right now, thanks," Georgia told the reporter drily.

"Later, then," said India. "What's on your mind about Suzie and the antibiotic?"

Georgia dithered briefly, then caved in. India listened without interrupting. Georgia ended by saying, "I've a plan."

"Spill it."

Obediently Georgia did so.

"Excellent," said India. "I'd say all systems go, no holds barred." She slowed behind a road train until the road was clear ahead, then passed. "You're okay still staying at Newview?"

Georgia hadn't given it much thought, but now she realized it wasn't the best place. Jason Chen would probably be waiting for her after the debacle in Brisbane, wanting to know where Jon was, his pruning shears at the ready.

"Probably not."

"How about the National in town?" India suggested without missing a beat. "Their rooms aren't great, but at least people will be around. And we can head round the corner to Mick's for something to eat tonight. I fancy some serious grease after today. Something deep-fried and battered to death."

It was just under 125 miles from Mount Molloy to Nulgarra but they made good time thanks to India's speeding. As India pulled up outside the National Hotel, she leaned across and hooked her arm around Georgia's neck, gave her a hug. Pressed a kiss against her cheek.

"Thanks for the trust in me," she said. "You did good."

Georgia put her hand against the reporter's and held it briefly. "Thanks for waiting for me at the cop shop."

"Anytime."

After she'd climbed outside, Georgia walked around the front of the ute, keeping a hand on the hot metal of the hood like she was soothing a restless steed in its stall. She bent to India's window. India buzzed it down, expression expectant.

Georgia said, "I know why Suzie wanted to see you."

India stared at her, surprise in her eyes.

"She would have made up the exploitation story to get you up here. Because her father did something terribly bad and you broke the story, she wanted to do something incredibly good and to tell you she was trying to redress the balance."

India's face closed. "She doesn't get any sympathy from me. Her sodding father played God, and people *died*."

She gunned the ute so hard that the tires spun a handful of gravel into Georgia's face.

THIRTY-ONE

Fresh bandage to hand, antiseptic tube on the sink, Georgia steeled herself as she unwrapped her old bandage. Her finger was throbbing unmercifully and she dreaded seeing what was beneath. Yumuru had said to change the bandage daily, but when she'd gotten to Cairns last night she had been too tired, and this morning too terrified of flying to contemplate it.

The last of the bandage stuck a little, and she gritted her teeth as she tugged until it was free. She still couldn't look.

Bandage now off. Bandage now in trash can.

Breathe, for goodness' sake, she told herself. Breathe into your lungs, right into your belly, and be calm. Be calm.

She looked down and saw a bulbous scab sitting on top of her stump like a leech. Bristles of stitches. No blood, no liquid seeping, no redness, no infection.

It was fine.

The sodding thing was fine. It barely looked as if it needed antiseptic cream, but she smeared a gob over it just in case, then quickly rebandaged it, trying to emulate Yumuru's neat wrapping but failing dismally. It looked as though a goblin had attempted to erect a tent over the bloody thing. Ah well, she'd do better next time, when she'd had some practice.

She was aware that she was forcing herself to be lighthearted, reasoning that if she concentrated on being normal, Lee would rescue her mother. Ridiculous logic, she knew, but she couldn't think what else to do, except go mad with worry. Her mother believed in the power of positive thought. When their ancient ute had finally packed up and they'd needed a new car, for instance, she hadn't panicked, just added an extra affirmation to her daily ritual: "Thank you, Great Creator, for this wonderful new car."

Two weeks later, Dick Cooper had driven his wife's battered old Moke into the commune and handed her the keys.

Recalling it, Georgia made her own affirmation: "Thank you, Great Creator, for my mother's freedom."

Going to the running bath, she turned off the taps and tested the water with her other hand. Undressing, she eased herself into the water, up to her neck, holding her goblin tent high. The bath was huge, and since she couldn't reach the other end with her feet, she felt she was swimming, which was not exactly relaxing.

Finally she pulled the plug and stood, dripping, wondering what to wear, as the majority of her stuff was at the caravan; the clothes from yesterday, which she'd worn sweating to the detention center and then to Cairns? Or the clothes from today, reeking with the sweat of fear of being shot at, of being caught by the Chens . . . No contest. Yesterday's clothes were today's. At least she had a clean pair of knickers and a toothbrush. As a child, when they'd flown to Australia, her mother had told her their baggage might go missing and to carry fresh undies in her hand luggage just in case.

Thanks, Mum, she thought as she pulled a spare pair from the bottom of her handbag. Have clean knickers, will kick ass. Talking of which, where was Lee? He hadn't rung. Had he rescued her mum yet? Was he on his way to her? They had only three days until the deadline on Sunday . . . Her mind started to gallop into panic, and she hurriedly checked her mobile. No missed calls, no messages.

Call me, dammit, she told him. Call me. Be like Mum and have a little telepathic sensitivity, will you? Tune in for a second. I want to know what's happening. *Call me.*

Nothing.

Must get him trained, she thought, shoving her mobile on top of her dirty clothes. Ringing me at the police station was not telepathically sensitive. Not sensitive at all.

Clearing the bathroom of her stuff—she shared it with the whole floor—she dumped everything in her room before making her way downstairs, looking forward to a meal, hoping India would be there already. She was so hungry that her stomach was groaning away like her throat had been cut. Deep-fried oysters, here I come, she thought, feeling proud that she was doing a reasonable job of keeping her thoughts upbeat. But she checked her mobile, just in case the power was running low. It wasn't.

Outside, the National looked pretty with its wrought-iron balcony, but inside it was a different story. Nobody seemed to have bothered with it since she'd last been in Nulgarra all those years ago. Paint was hanging in strips along the corridor, and the wood around the windows was pitted. In the bar, the carpet was thin with worn patches and the walls a yellow-brown. The aroma of cigarette smoke clung to the air. She was the only customer.

Above the bar was a sign saying, "Free bungee jumps for politicians—no strings attached," and normally she'd have smiled, but right now she had never felt less like smiling in her life.

The barman wore an oil-stained T-shirt that suggested he was a mechanic when he wasn't working at the pub, and she ordered a glass of wine and played with it for a while. Looked at her watch. Eight-fifteen. She ordered another wine. Played with that one another while. No India. No call from Lee. Maybe she'd have to ring the Chens herself and arrange to swap the disks Jon had given her for her mother. But would they really fall for a formula for the common cold? Tense as a bowstring, she was sipping her third wine when India appeared.

"Jesus, sorry I'm so late." She glanced at Georgia's drink, then at the barman. "Same for me, Rog, but make it two, would you? The first won't touch the sides."

Georgia watched the reporter light a cigarette, down her first glass of wine, then ease onto the stool beside her, fingers playing with the stem of her second wineglass.

"Filing a goddamn report should be easier," India grumbled. "I've been covering that murder I was telling you about, the stabbing, but felt like I was back at school. Scotto was giving me hell, demanding links in my story. There are no goddamn links. Just some poor bastard in the middle of a racecourse with his stomach slashed. No clues, no nothing. But your Sergeant Carter was muttering it could be a gang killing and connected to the murder of Ronnie Chen, the man found washed up on our beach."

She looked across at Georgia. "Anything to do with the Chens, do you think?"

Like India, she couldn't think what it meant and shook her head. "Could it be an inter-gang fight? You said the Dragon Syndicate were pretty pissed off with the RBG after Lee had stuffed them."

India looked thoughtful. "Maybe. But Carter didn't think so."

Glancing out the window, Georgia saw Joanie wobbling down the street, a dog tagging along beside her. "Are you still on for tomorrow?" she asked India.

"You bet." India took a slug of wine that drained half her glass and set it back on the counter. "I take it you haven't heard from Lee."

"No."

"Shit."

Long pause while India smoked her cigarette and Georgia checked her mobile. Nothing.

"Only thing for it," said India, "is to get a feed and some sleep, and face what tomorrow brings. Jesus, I hope Mick's isn't closed. Hick towns like this tend to shut up shop as soon as the sun sinks."

The reporter downed the remainder of her wine, and with her cigarette in one hand, ushered Georgia speedily outside and down the street.

"Thank God, he's still open." India flicked a quick glance at Georgia as they stepped inside the café. "You may not feel like eating, but eat you will, even if I have to force-feed you," she said. "What'll it be?"

"A dozen deep-fried oysters."

India's face cracked into a smile. "Well, bloody hell, if I haven't found my soul sister." She turned to Mick. "Three dozen of your best, thanks, mate."

Despite India's strength, her reassuring presence, Georgia found it hard to eat, and even more difficult to sleep. Lee should have her mother by now.

Why hadn't he called?

Next morning, brain fuddled and eyes gritty from lack of sleep, Georgia climbed out of the taxi and, when it had gone, slipped into the rainforest. All was quiet. No traffic, nobody to see the taxi dropping her off just outside the Lotus Healing Center. She didn't want to alert Yumuru to her presence, still less the reason for it. Mist curled around the trunks of the trees as she followed an animal track into the gloom of the forest. The sun was still low, the atmosphere moist and permeated with the smell of rotting vegetation. She heard nothing but the whine of mosquitoes, the sound of leaves brushing against her, the faint squelch of her shoes in mud. It was so still that she could almost hear the moisture oozing from the forest.

A rustle behind her. She spun around, heart thudding. Nobody. Just a lizard she'd disturbed, maybe a snake.

Georgia brushed her arms and face free of sweat and insects, longing for Dutch's Deet; she'd been bitten so many times she wondered the mozzies hadn't drained her of blood.

She passed the small waterfall on Lamb's Creek where the rocks were smooth and shiny from years of turbulent currents fed from the mountains, and the bark of trees was covered in moss. A huge cycad loomed skyward, a primitive, slow-growing fern barely changed in two hundred million years. It was astonishing to think how many plant relics had survived, by sheer fortune, for eons in this rainforest.

Gradually the sky, seemingly distant through the closely knitted canopy of leaves, brightened, and sunlight beamed like yellow flashlights through the trees. Georgia recognized an old fig tree bristling with birds' nests and basket ferns and knew she was nearing the healing center.

All was quiet when she came to the parking lot. The sun had cleared the treetops and the temperature had risen several degrees. Georgia hunkered behind a thick clump of silver tree ferns and willed herself not to scratch her bites. A week ago she wouldn't have done this, she realized. She would have believed in Yumuru and felt an urge to protect him. Back then, however, she hadn't known what was at stake.

The first car belonged to a uniformed nurse, the second to Florid-Face from the pharmacy. Both greeted the other—"Good morning," and "Isn't it hot already?"—and went inside.

By nine-fifteen the lot in front of the clinic was filling quickly, and people of every age and description were climbing out of vehicles, grabbing pads of paper and pens, slinging handbags over shoulders and gripping briefcases, heading for the seminar building.

Excellent, thought Georgia. It's Friday and obviously one of Yumuru's designated healing weekends. He should have finished his rounds by now and would be well out of the way.

Quietly, after the parking lot had emptied, Georgia headed to the pharmacy, rehearsing her speech as she went. She intended to convince Robert about what was going on, and work out a way he could get her a sample of Yumuru's vitamins. She was in the nursing wing and nearing the pharmacy when she heard footsteps ahead of her.

Coming around the corner, head down, was Yumuru.

Georgia lunged for the nearest door and quickly shut it behind her.

"Hey, Georgia!"

Hell. She was in Tilly's room.

Yumuru's footsteps approached. Georgia hurriedly positioned herself next to Tilly's beside table. Her breathing stopped when the footsteps slowed, the door opened, and Yumuru stepped inside.

Standing tall, she tried her best to look nonchalant.

"What the . . . Georgia!"

Yumuru was blinking behind his little gold glasses, looking surprised. He was wearing his white coat and held a little aluminum bowl and a syringe. Her gaze latched onto the syringe, then away. A sudden thought gripped her: What if she could snatch it?

He walked across and carefully put the bowl and syringe onto Tilly's bedside table. Then he came to her, his brown eyes warm. "How's the finger?"

Georgia concentrated on giving him a smile. "It's fine."

"You up for a therapy hug?"

She let him fold herself into his arms and tried to relax, but her body felt like a board.

"You are so tense!" he exclaimed, leaning back and peering into her face. "Are you sure your finger isn't bothering you?"

"It's fine, honestly. I've just had a rough couple of days, that's all."

His expression clouded. "Not anything to do with . . ." His voice lowered. "That training session we had at Helenvale, I hope."

"Oh, no. Nothing to do with that. Other stuff."

He raised a hand and brushed aside a stray strand of hair from her forehead. "If you need any help, I'm your friend. Call me anytime, day or night, I'll be there for you. Any capacity you choose. Doctor, car mechanic, ex-soldier. Okay?"

She could hardly bear the gentleness of his voice, or his tender gesture, and she smiled stiffly, her emotions at war, wanting to trust him, but unable to. "Okay."

He stepped back, face still troubled. "Something's wrong, isn't it?"

"I'm just a little tired, that's all. I was passing the gates and thought I'd pop in and say hi to Tilly."

"That's kind of you."

"It's amazing how well she is," Georgia added. "I can't believe she's the same person I saw last week."

She was smiling a bright false smile and was sure Yumuru could see right through her. She glanced at the aluminum bowl and syringe on the bedside table; she was unable to think how to grab the thing without him seeing.

"She's a strong patient," Yumuru said, watching her guardedly. "Determined too, which is a big asset in a case like hers."

The door opened, and Georgia's stomach gave a lurch as Yumuru swung his head to look at whoever was coming in. Before she could think twice, she had taken a step and snatched the syringe and thrust it behind her back at the same time as Joanie stepped inside.

"Hey, if it ain't Georgia Parish," said Joanie. "How's it going?"

Heart tripping, she said breezily, "Good, thanks."

Joanie said measuredly to nobody in particular, "Another shipload of immigrants slipped through the net."

"Not again," said Tilly.

"Yup. Definitely a tip-off. There's talk it's a cop."

"A *cop*?" Tilly was agog.

Georgia had the syringe at her side and was walking for the door.

"Yeah. Don't know who, yet," Joanie responded, "but my mate at the station says whoever it is gets twenty grand for each boat of illegals that makes it. Not just illegals either; apparently the bugger's tipping crims off about police business all over. When they catch him, they'll string him up for sure."

Tilly and Yumuru were riveted by Joanie, barely noticing Georgia as she murmured a vague excuse about needing the restroom, she'd be back in a sec . . .

Georgia hit the corridor and ran for the pharmacy. She held her breath as she banged on the door, exhaled when the lock clicked and the door was opened. She pushed inside.

Florid-Face reared to one side, face alarmed.

Robert was just ahead, measuring white pills shaped like bullets into a plastic bag. Georgia forced herself to slow. Robert looked up, startled.

She carefully raised the syringe, showed it to him. "I need to put this on ice. I've got to take it to the police. Do you have a container I can use? I know I'm out of context here, but I really need your help. It's to do with your colleague Suzie Wilson. Her plane was sabotaged. My plane. Someone wanted to kill Suzie and I think I might know who." She held the syringe high. "Put this on ice, and we might find an answer."

Robert blinked.

"Please, Robert! I've got to find out what's in this syringe. I don't think it's vitamins. I think Suzie created a new antibiotic and Yumuru's pretending his healing is curing patients."

"You're joking," he said, his tone pitched high with disbelief.

She leaped when a hand brushed her arm.

Florid-Face was extending a small blue polystyrene box toward her. "There's dry ice in here, but if it's what you say it is, you won't really need it. It'll last a couple of weeks, even in the heat."

"Really?"

"Yup. But for safety's sake, let's hedge our bets and protect that needle." He took the syringe from Georgia and tucked it neatly into the box, locked the lid, and passed it over.

Faintly she said, "Thanks."

Florid-Face said, "Go for it, but for God's sake don't tell Yumuru I helped you," and then she turned and was tearing across the pharmacy, box gripped tightly in her hand, and she was through the door and in the corridor, belting along and past reception and bursting into bright clean sunshine, into the parking lot.

Have to hide, she thought. Yumuru will be going mad looking for me, for his missing syringe.

Sprinting for the cover of the trees, Georgia hunched down behind the broad stubby trunk of a sago palm, box at her feet. She called a number on her mobile, and heard a monotone: "We have been unable to connect you, please try again." She tried again, to receive the same message. Third time lucky. She held her breath.

When it was answered she said, "It's me. I'm in the parking lot."

"On my way."

THIRTY-TWO

India was half eyeing the polystyrene box as she drove. They had exited the healing center's gates and were headed east into town.

"You really got it? A sample of his vitamins?"

"Sure did."

India was grinning. "You're definitely SAS material. Thought of applying?"

"As if. I don't want my life story spread over the tabloids."

India tapped the steering wheel with excitement. "It all makes sense, don't you think? Yumuru using Suzie's miracle cure to keep his healing center alive; Suzie being kidnapped by Lee Denham—"

"Hang on a minute, India! I never said Lee kidnapped Suzie!"

"No, but he had every reason. She's worth a *fortune.*"

"But Suzie was with him willingly!"

"Sure, and I live in a yurt when I'm at home." Turning a cynical look onto Georgia, she added, "You really think your pal Lee, people smuggler, cop killer, didn't snatch Suzie for himself? You think he feels an obligation to you, having saved your life, but why is he really still around? He's not stupid, he knows the cops are after him. Surely you can't believe he's sticking around just for you?"

Georgia turned her head to look through the window but didn't take in the scenery. India's cold logic was like a blast from Siberia. Lee had killed Ronnie Chen, she knew that. Lee was in a race to find Jon

Ming before the Chens, she knew that also. She had a problem with her loyalties, she realized. Lee was a bad guy, but she couldn't assimilate that fact with the man who'd saved her life, and who was trying to rescue her mother.

"I'd still like to give him the benefit of the doubt," she said stoutly.

"Your prerogative," India replied, her voice indicating Georgia was a fool, but she'd tolerate it. "So, I'll ship this down to Sydney, get it tested. Then what?"

Find her mother, that's what. Her heart and lungs began to implode. She felt a violent urge to punch out the windshield, to yell into the peerless blue sky. Mum, are you okay? I'm sorry I'm doing such a shit job of trying to find you, but I'm doing the best I can. And what about you, Lee? Where the hell are you?

"Georgia?"

She swallowed, said, "Could you drop me at the National?"

"What's the plan?"

She shook her head. "No plan. Aside from an Irish coffee, that is."

India grimaced, looking disappointed, and Georgia felt a surge of bright white anger, just like she used to against Bridie's endless enthusiasm, her boundless energy.

"Just drop me off, will you?" Her voice was tight.

"Keep your knickers on," the reporter snapped. "I only thought—"

"That I'm naive and stupid? That you could do a far better job in my place?"

Silence.

To Georgia's relief she saw the National come into view. Her hand was already opening the door before India's ute came to a full stop.

"Georgia, I'm sorry, I know I need brushing up on my communication skills, but please, don't—"

"Just test the contents of the syringe, okay? And call me when you get the results."

Slamming the door shut, Georgia marched into the hotel. Behind her she heard the click as India's ute engaged drive. Then the sound of the car pulling away, gently, as though driving on glass.

Georgia went to Price's and bought a hundred dollars' worth of phone cards, then spent the remainder of the afternoon using the National's public phone outside the gents' loo, her mobile on top of the box, where she could snatch it should Lee ring.

After what felt like her twentieth round of being put on hold and transferred, she finally tried a pressure group the immigration department had mentioned and got through to a man called Zed. Zed sounded horrified that Paul Zhong was returning to China to be executed, and promised he'd do something immediately. He even gave her his mobile number, and when they'd finished speaking he sounded out of breath, as though he was already running to Paul's rescue.

Highly relieved that at last someone was taking her seriously, Georgia was heading for the bar and a cup of coffee when a man behind her said, "Georgia?"

Daniel was in the corridor, tapping a newspaper against his thigh, and she couldn't help noticing him look her over; messy hair, sweat-stained T-shirt and shorts, bare legs.

"Looking good as usual." He grinned.

He was casually dressed in jeans and a faded blue shirt and looked handsome as hell, but she wasn't going to say it.

"Thought I'd come round and see if you fancy a drink. Maybe a glass of wine or something."

She wondered if it wasn't a bit early, but when she glanced through the open door and at the street outside she saw that the light had softened into evening. Amazingly, it was past six. She must have spent hours on the phone before she'd fallen on Zed.

"Or would you prefer a beer?" Daniel asked Georgia, walking her into the saloon, where the man behind the bar was emptying a dishwasher.

"A beer would be great."

The barman straightened up, and as soon as he saw Daniel he took a step back, expression wary.

"How's it going, Rog?" Daniel asked him. "Been behaving yourself?"

The barman nodded.

"Glad to hear it," Daniel said. "Make it two 4Xs, thanks, mate, and a couple of packs of nuts."

Daniel pulled out his wallet, and as he pushed a ten-dollar note to Rog the barman, a battered, slightly torn photograph fell onto the counter. The instant she took in the picture, her breath caught.

Daniel in the sunshine, with a little girl on his shoulders. A woman, with her arms around Daniel's waist, peeked past his ribs. Her skin was dark and her hair short, generously curly around her temples. All three were laughing, carefree, eyes creased, mouths wide and happy. The woman, Georgia realized, had to be Daniel's dead wife, Lucy.

Without missing a beat, Daniel picked up the photograph and tucked it back inside his wallet. Georgia found herself gazing where the photograph now lay, snug in warm leather, and thought it was no wonder he felt the pain of Lucy's death. She was beautiful.

They sat on barstools near windows streaked with salt from the last set of storms. Wearing shorts meant her thighs stuck to the plastic, but at least they were cooler than jeans. She pushed her handbag onto the counter and looked outside. A battered white ute, colored a vivid tangerine in the sunset, pulled up outside the Three Mile Store and its beer-bellied driver vanished inside.

"How did you know I was here?" she asked Daniel. The beer was ice-cold, the beer nuts salty, staple fodder for pubgoers in Australia.

"I asked around. You know what this place is like."

Holy heck. If Daniel had found her, then the Chens would too. Perhaps she'd better stay somewhere else tonight. Like inside a cell in the cop shop.

"I heard about the mayhem you caused in Brisbane. What are you, a magnet for trouble?"

She checked her mobile again. Put it on top of her handbag.

"I got caught up in events, that's all."

"With Suzie's brother." He held up a hand as she started to explain. "It's okay. I heard all about it from the chief. You're lucky he likes you or you could have been there days. Also lucky he straightened the Brizzy cops out over you, or they'd be raising hell. Good bloke, the chief. One hell of a good cop."

Daniel raised his glass and drank half his schooner of beer down slowly and steadily, obviously thirsty. She could see his chest muscles outlined beneath his shirt. Solid and broad. In her mind she caught him checking her out again. *Looking good as usual.* She found herself wondering what would have happened if she'd had dinner with him in Cairns. Would something now be going on with Daniel? Would they be dating? Would they have kissed? A little shock ran through her at the thought, and as she sat there she wondered if what she felt was the residue of her schoolgirl crush or if she wasn't half in love with him.

Putting his glass down, he licked his lips of foam, and said, "When are you going home?"

She shifted on her stool, realizing that something with Daniel was a daydream. A nice daydream to be sure, but just that.

"When I find out who sabotaged our plane."

Out of the corner of her eye she saw the barman turn his head, tuning in to what they were saying, but she didn't care if he overheard, spread the gossip around. Bri hadn't been at fault and she wanted the whole town to know.

Daniel's voice was tinged with disbelief when he said, "You really think it was?"

"I saw Becky. Bri told her he knew it was sabotaged. He *knew.*"

"Well, he would say that, wouldn't he?" Daniel's tone softened. "He wouldn't want Becky thinking he cocked up so badly. Nor his kids."

"Did you contact the AAI?"

"I thought we went into this outside Suzie's house."

"But Becky wants to know the truth. Please, Daniel, will you talk to them?"

He gave it some thought, then gave her one of those smiles she couldn't help but give herself over to. "How about we make a deal? I'll contact the AAI, then I'll take you to dinner and give you a full report. How about the Pier? I've heard it's pretty amazing."

She blinked a couple of times, a nervous tingling all over the surface of her skin. The Pier was only one of Sydney's best—overlooking the Harbour Bridge with a wine list two miles long—and to go with Daniel . . .

"It's a deal," she said

"Shall we make it Tuesday? I've a meeting in Sydney then, it would tie in nicely."

Instantly she felt pressured. Tuesday was only four days away and two days after the deadline. Would Lee have her mother by then?

"Um . . ." she said, and when his face clouded, decided not only to try to think positively, but act it too. "Tuesday would be great."

The cloud vanished as he smiled, and she crossed her fingers and prayed her mother would be free. Dinner with Daniel Carter was not something she wanted to cancel, thank you very much, and her mum would agree.

Emotions all over the place—delight at Daniel's invitation, despair at the continuing nightmare of her mother's situation—she drank some more beer, forced down a handful of nuts, and watched the street, the sun blushing cars and buildings a rich burnt orange. After a while, Daniel pushed his paper, a copy of the *Queensland Tribune,* in front of her.

"Seen this yet?"

She nearly choked at the headline.

GANG KILLING IN CAIRNS—VICTIM DISEMBOWELED
The man found disemboweled in Cairns two days ago has been confirmed as a member of the Red Bamboo Gang. Tan Zhang Dan, from Fuzhou, China, did not have official status in Australia. His body was found on the Cannon Park Racecourse.

Sergeant Daniel Carter, who works with PST, the People Smuggling Strike Team, and the National Crime Authority for South-East Asia organized crime intervention, said it was definitely a gang killing, and that the man found washed up on Kee Beach, Nulgarra, on Saturday, March 2, Ronnie Chen, could have been the victim of the same vendetta.

"Ronnie Chen was shot," Carter said. "We don't yet know why, but we do know that the murders are connected. We are talking about a brutal and ruthless killer."

The byline was India's. It was a story she'd reported last night, the reason she'd gone to Cairns.

"Your friend Lee has been hard at work," Daniel said.

"Lee?" she repeated blankly.

"Disemboweling his victims," he said. "It's his trademark. Who is he after? Do you know?"

"What do you mean?"

"This gang member had something Lee wanted. I'm thinking information."

Georgia started to tremble slightly and pushed her hands between her thighs before he could see.

"I've no doubt it's Lee," Daniel continued in a conversational tone. "He's well-known for it. Taking his victim somewhere quiet, lulling them into a false sense of security, then slashing his victim's stomach until the entrails show, telling the poor bastard he'll call an ambulance if he gives him the information he wants. It always works. They know they're going to die anyway, but take the chance he might actually make the call."

Lee's voice in her head.

Ask a few questions in the right places. Fine out where they're holding her . . . I've ways and means.

Had Lee really killed this man in order to gain information about her mother?

Think of me as your own private hawk . . . able to see far and wide . . . to strike and kill in your defense.

She felt a wave of nausea crash over her.

"Excuse me a minute," she murmured, and pushed herself upright. Clutching her mobile, she added, "Need the bathroom."

Rinsing her face with water again and again, Georgia tried to stop her shuddering. She may have been glad of an ally hell-bent on saving her mother, but sweet Jesus, disemboweling a man for information? Raising her head, she stared at her reflection in the mirror. She had big black rings around her eyes, and her cheeks had hollowed, making her jaw and nose look enormous. She'd lost weight, she suddenly realized. A huge amount of weight. Must eat more, she told herself. More toast, more Special K, but no fish porridge, thank you, Fang Dongmei.

Drying her face on a paper towel, she went back to her barstool and concentrated on playing with the condensation on her beer glass.

"Sorry I was so brutal," Daniel said quietly. "Forgot I was talking to a member of the public."

"It's okay." She forced a smile then added, as casually as possible, "Have you seen Paul Zhong?"

He blinked. "No. You did that."

"Um . . . did you tell anyone I was seeing him?"

"Sure, we do share information in the police, you know. And since everyone's out for Lee as much as I am . . ."

Which confirmed that Spider was a cop Daniel worked with and that Lee was right, she couldn't tell Daniel anything without it getting back to Spider.

She checked her mobile again. Twenty-four hours had passed since she'd last spoken to Lee. She closed her eyes briefly, praying he was all right, that he hadn't gotten shot . . . At this moment, he was still her only hope, her mother's only hope. Her stomach gave a lurch at the thought of him lying alone and wounded beneath some bushes somewhere, blood pouring . . . Stop it, she told herself, he's the one who does the wounding. God, it was so confusing.

"Georgia." Daniel was on the edge of his stool, leaning close. "What's wrong? Tell me. Please."

"I want to find Lee," she said.

"Well, we have something in common."

"Badly," she added, her tone turning desperate.

"Hmm." He was nodding thoughtfully. "One reason I'm in town is because I wanted to check *Songtao* out again."

"Lee's yacht?"

"Yes. We've heard the crew are back in Nulgarra and that the captain's on board, bringing in supplies. I reckon Lee's going to make a sharp exit anytime now. There's a rumor that he was seen this morning with some woman, but nothing's confirmed. I've a suspicion Lee started the rumor anyway, as a red herring. But I'd still like to do a recon and, if he's there, send in the troops. And if he's not, I'd like to check *Songtao*'s chart drawer. The captain would have got hold of the appropriate charts for their journey and destination, maybe Hawaii and the USA, maybe Indonesia, China . . ."

He was still talking, but she wasn't listening anymore. *Lee was seen this morning with some woman.* Was her mother already safe?

Mind whirling, she half watched a couple walk past Jack Mundy's bait shop, and the next vehicle that came into view was a black Mercedes.

She sat there in shock.

It was Jason Chen's car.

The Merc cruised along Ocean Road and disappeared from view, leaving her with sweat springing on her skin and a sick shivering inside. Sunday was the day after tomorrow. Thirty-six hours until the deadline.

Daniel pulled out his mobile and dialed. "Pete? Yeah, it's me . . . Oh. Right. Okay." He glanced at his watch. "I'll give it a try. Otherwise tomorrow. Owe you, mate. Thanks."

He pushed his phone back into his rear pocket. "Apparently the captain's still on board, but Pete says he usually goes ashore for a meal around six. He suggested I go down there and wait until the captain leaves." Daniel downed his beer in three long gulps. "I'll see you in an hour or so."

She glanced down the street where the black Merc had vanished. Were they also headed for *Songtao* and maybe Lee and her mother?

"I'm coming too."

"No."

Daniel's face was set hard and she could see that gleam of something dangerous and dark sliding at the back of his eyes.

"If you see Lee, you'll shoot him, won't you?"

"Given half the chance, yes, I will." Putting his glass on the bar, he said, "You wait here," and walked outside. She slung her handbag strap over her head and across her chest and tore after him.

On the street, he turned around, faced her. "Go away."

She stuck her jaw out at him. "No. You'll have to handcuff me to the bar, and since you don't seem to have any handcuffs, I'm coming too."

"Okay, I promise I won't shoot him. Just arrest him and stick him in jail for the rest of his life. Does that help?"

"No."

"Seriously, Georgia, it might be dangerous—"

"I can look after myself," she said defensively. "I know how to shoot a gun."

"So I heard." His tone was astringent.

Hell, she thought. Was nothing sacrosanct in this town?

"And since you mention it," he added, "I do have some cuffs. In the car. You really want me to cuff you?"

She wanted to be flippant and say, "Only if there are a couple of bedposts to hand and you're naked," but didn't dare. He didn't look as though he'd appreciate such a comment right now.

Sweeping a hand back at the National, he said, "Inside. And *stay*."

His gesture reminded her of Jon, and Cookie's immediate response to obey her master, but she wasn't Cookie, and Daniel certainly wasn't her master.

THIRTY-THREE

By the time Daniel came out of the harbormaster's office and padded down the southernmost pontoon, the moon was above the horizon, turning the fiberglass hulls silver. Georgia never had become used to how fast night fell out here. For the first part of her life in England she'd experienced long dusks that in summer stretched for three or four hours, but in Australia it was as though somebody switched off a light.

Treading carefully, she followed the dark shadow that was Daniel as he slipped from boat to boat. The air was warm and soft and smelled of leaves rotting in mud. She was jumpy and kept glancing around, looking for the Chens, but all was quiet and still. The black Mercedes was nowhere to be seen.

Nor, suddenly, was Daniel. Pausing, she looked hard down the pontoon but couldn't see any movement. Cautiously, she crept forward, past a handful of tin boats bobbing on the tide, scanning the area, anxious now, wondering if he'd seen something she hadn't, whether he—

A rush of cloth, and before she could turn a hand clamped over her mouth, a strong arm went around her waist, and she was being dragged to one side and she was wriggling and yelping with fright until she heard him hissing, "Shut up, Georgia. It's me. *Shut up.*"

Breathing hard, she felt him release his grip, step back.

"Christ," he whispered. "You nearly gave me a heart attack."

"Tell me about it."

"You're like a piece of chewing gum stuck to the bottom of my shoe!" He was running a hand through his hair despairingly. "Why won't you go *away*!"

He then gave her a lengthy lecture on letting the police do their job, followed by a string of clichés about how the cops know everything and the general public are a clueless bunch who should leave them alone, and by the time he'd finished, his breathing had leveled and he was calm.

"So you'll let me come with you," she said.

"Jesus. You are so *stubborn*!"

"I'll take that as a yes."

"No. I want you to turn around and go back to the hotel. Now."

"But what if someone sees me? Won't it jeopardize your recon?"

"I don't care. I don't want you around."

They were whispering furiously in the shadows of an elegant sloop called *Hopalong Too* and a riviera from Nelson, New Zealand, named *Micky's Dream. Songtao* was brightly lit but she couldn't see anyone moving inside. Nobody else appeared to be on their boats. It was eerily silent except for the odd mosquito whining past her ear.

"I won't let you shoot Lee," she said. "He saved my life."

"Sometimes," he said, sounding like he was gritting his teeth, "I wish he hadn't."

"How are you going to get on board?" she asked. "Won't the captain lock it up when he leaves? Doesn't it have an alarm?"

"I've a key and Pete gave me the code."

"How come Pete knows it?"

"What is this? Twenty questions? Will you please . . . Shit."

Daniel held up his hand, pointing at *Songtao*. All but two lights had gone out. Daniel took her hand and pulled her toward *Hopalong Too*.

"Get on," he whispered. "The captain's leaving."

She scrambled over the railings and dropped inside, ducking low behind the cockpit coaming. Daniel followed. He was peering through the railings and just as he whispered, "Here he comes," she heard the soft thud-thud of deck shoes on the pontoon. Daniel pulled his head back.

The footsteps faded, then disappeared.

Silence.

Daniel whispered that they should give the captain five minutes before they moved.

"Is the captain part of the RBG?" she asked.

"Not that I'm aware of. Lee hired him full-time a year or so back, to keep his boat ticking over when he's away. He turns the engines over, keeps the carpets vacuumed, and so on. Lee can turn up anytime he wants and the captain's ready to go."

"This captain sailed *Songtao* from Cairns?"

"Yup."

She wanted to ask Daniel what the captain had said about Ronnie Chen's murder, but decided not to go down that path since she might let something slip implicating Lee. No doubt the captain earned a bucketload of money to keep his mouth shut on behalf of his employer.

"What about crew?"

"The captain hires them."

He glanced at his watch, gave it a couple more minutes, then they clambered back onto the pontoon.

"Off you go," he told her, shooing her away. "And if I find you following me . . ."

Daniel suddenly bent over and slapped at a mosquito on his ankle and at the same time she heard a fish plop nearby. It sounded like a stone being dropped in the water. She paused at another *plop* and peered down into the sea.

Fish, she thought, and at the same time Daniel lunged for her and dragged her facedown onto the pontoon. She was yelping, but she wasn't making enough noise to prevent her hearing another plopping sound. Daniel was pressing her low, his voice urgent. "They're shooting at us. Get into the water."

"Why the—"

"Just do it," he snapped.

Georgia opened her mouth to say something but yelped when there was a *thunk* and a splinter sprang in front of Daniel's chin.

"You can swim, can't you?" he bit out, but she was already wriggling to the side of the pontoon and sliding over the edge, handbag still across her chest, and into the sea. She saw Daniel yank his mobile free and, holding it high, lunge after her, feet first, head and shoulders following.

Georgia's lungs contracted at the chill. Being in the tropics, she had expected the sea to be warm, but it wasn't. She kicked off her shoes and, hanging on to a wooden piling, held Daniel's phone while he pulled off his boots. Immediately she started punching numbers with her thumb. Dialed India's number.

Footfalls hammered on the wooden planking above. She kept looking upward, dreading seeing an assassin's face, a gun. She started to shiver and wondered if Daniel was doing the same.

"Hello?" said India.

"We're at the harbor, get help, quick"—but fell silent as Daniel held up his hand.

"Georgia?" India was whispering back. "You still there?"

A flash pierced the darkness, and she clutched the slimy, limpet-crusted wood, shuddering as the flashlight swept the water all around.

Daniel snatched the phone from her and punched in another number. Hissed something into the receiver. Reaching into her sodden handbag, she pulled out her own phone and pressed start but nothing happened. The thing was waterlogged.

She heard the low guttural sound of Cantonese, and then the beam came toward them, carefully scanning the surface of the water. Pinching his nostrils between two fingers, Daniel sent Georgia an urgent look and pointed downward with his other hand.

No, no! she thought, panicky, pointing at his phone. Daniel gestured his helplessness. The flashlight shifted position to light the water beneath the planks. It was coming directly for them.

He whispered, "Harbor, now," into the phone. They both looked desperately for somewhere to lodge it. Shit. She saw him shove it in his breast pocket and give her a nod. Both of them took a deep lungful of air and slowly sank underwater, forcing themselves down the length of the piling with their arms and legs. Georgia kept her eyes open, looking at the surface, ignoring the way they stung and throbbed against the salt water. Everything was murky and blurred, but the flashlight seemed bright as the sun. She realized her T-shirt was billowing vivid yellow around her and inched herself down farther. The flashlight slowly approached.

Her lungs began to protest as she watched the flashlight's beam. In tortuous slow motion, it scanned the water above their heads.

Come on, come on, she thought. We've gone the other way.

The flashlight continued methodically to search the surface. Lungs aching, she released a little air, and saw a twin tiny trail of bubbles rise from Daniel's lips. Desperate now, she concentrated on the flashlight and not the screaming in her chest.

Have to go up soon, she thought, or I'll explode to the surface and they won't miss that. She saw the flashlight move away and Daniel point upward. Thank God. They began to inch their way to the surface.

It took every effort to rise in slow motion, not to ruffle the water's surface as she rose. Her lungs were shrieking with the need to inhale. She cautiously released a little more air.

Abruptly, the flashlight changed direction and she forgot all about breathing as it skimmed over them once again. Then it changed direction, sweeping the water toward the shore.

Her head broke the surface and her mouth was open, her lungs heaving, pumping gallons of blissful oxygen through her body. Her heart pounded and her vision was distorted from salt water. Her body's emergency responses seemed so loud that she was amazed their would-be killers didn't hear them. They were gasping and heaving like a couple of sperm whales breaching.

Georgia pointed at his pocket but his phone had gone, sunk to the bottom of the harbor, dammit. Gradually she tuned in to the faint muttering of Cantonese, fading now. Daniel touched Georgia's shoulder, raised his eyebrows, mouthed, "Okay?"

She gave him a thumbs-up.

His voice was low as he said, "Swim to *Songtao*? They're expecting us to swim to the shore, not away from it. We can use the boat's sat phones to call for more help."

She gave him another thumbs-up.

"Stay under cover," he whispered, "and submerge if any more shooting starts."

She didn't reply, simply pushed herself gently from the piling and started swimming. By the time they made it to *Songtao*'s stern they were both breathing heavily. Daniel checked Georgia as she gripped the swim ladder and started to pull herself out of the water, and whispered, "Me first."

"You think there are more?" she whispered back, dismayed.

"I'll check."

She watched him ease silently onto the swim platform, up the vertical ladder, and over the transom.

She was damned if she was going to wallow here freezing cold, she thought, and scrambled onto the swim platform after him. Soundless, she congratulated herself, until she realized she was streaming with water, which in turn dripped loudly onto teak. Hastily she slipped up the ladder to the stern deck and the glass doors leading to the saloon, where she thought Daniel had gone.

Cautiously she tried the glass door and, finding it unlocked, started to open it and follow Daniel inside. She thought she heard someone call her name and turned to see Daniel racing down the starboard steps. He seemed to be mouthing, "No, no," and she felt a spurt of panic and tried to shut the door again but it was too late because the next second there was a distant, rhythmic beeping that made her heart clench. An alarm. Jesus. She'd tripped the sodding alarm. The code, what was the code? And where the hell was the keypad?

Daniel threw back the door and darted across the saloon for the bridge, legs pumping. Georgia surged after him.

Dear God, she prayed, please, *please* let him make it in time.

The beeping increased as she tore after Daniel. She saw him yanking open an innocent-looking cupboard opposite the galley, and she was slowing, seeing the bright green glare of the alarm system, and Daniel's fingers reaching to punch in the disarmament code, knowing he'd made it, that he'd disarm it in the next second . . .

The beeps suddenly turned into a deafening howl.

Daniel punched in the number and the sirens abruptly cut out, but it was too late.

"I'll cast off!" he shouted and pushed two keys at her before spinning for the stern. "You start the engines! Fast as you can!"

Georgia sprang for the bridge, thrust the keys into their ignitions, and turned. Nothing happened.

She stared at the array of dials before her. Took in the brass plaque stating the yacht was a Ferretti. An Italian boat. Shit. She was in the nautical equivalent of a Ferrari and hadn't a clue how to turn on the engines. She swung around, snapped open a glass door with two rows of switches inside, thanking God everything was marked in English. Flicked two down, marked "engines," then the next two labeled "blowers," and spun back and turned the two ignition keys again. A hideous shrieking alarm informed her she'd gotten it right so far. What else, something else . . .

God, the micro-commander. She hurriedly pressed the small square button marked "control" and punched the two huge red start buttons. There was a brief, thundering rumble, then the twin Caterpillars roared into life.

She looked outside. Daniel had freed the bow and midsection, and was racing down the pontoon to the stern. Two shadows were rushing for him. God, they were close, too close.

Georgia sprang across the bridge for the port window and yanked it open, yelling, "Look out!"

Daniel whirled, and she knew he'd seen the two gunmen, yards away, running hard and fast straight for him. Adrenaline must have given him wings, because one second he was on the pontoon and then he was sprawled on the stern deck and scrambling up and she immediately spun away and slammed open the twin throttles.

She wasn't prepared for the surge of power. *Songtao* sprang forward, her bow rearing, stern digging into the water, and Georgia lost her footing, regained it, and kept the throttles wide. There was a groaning, creaking sound, and *Songtao* dug in further, straining against her leash that was the marina, and Georgia spun the wheel to starboard, muttering, "Come on, girl, *come on.*"

As if she'd heard, the boat suddenly shivered, and there was a great tearing and splintering noise like a tree being felled as the yacht tore her berth from the marina and charged forward. Georgia shoved the inboard throttle to kick the stern sideways, narrowly missing the forty-foot racing yacht berthed opposite, but the stern was still swinging and she heard an almighty crash, which she took to be the port side hitting the neighboring yacht, *Micky's Dream.*

Songtao surged out of the harbor, for the horizon. She could feel that the boat was unbalanced, still dragging the marina's debris, but she didn't lessen the power. She was racing for the open sea, knowing they needed every second's advantage should the gunmen pursue them.

She allowed herself a quick look to check on Daniel, to make sure he wasn't hurt, or that one of the gunmen hadn't managed to fling himself on board, and saw him racing outside with what looked like a hacksaw, preparing to saw free the remaining marina planks, which were bounding and slamming in their wake. Wow, she thought. What a team we make. Me driver, he he-man.

Georgia returned to the helm. The sea was beautifully calm, and *Songtao* sliced through the water like a cheese wire through butter. Keeping the prow pointed at the horizon, she pulled out a slim drawer on her left and yanked out a handful of nautical charts. She checked the first blankly, not recognizing any part of it. She peered closer. *Fujian.* It was a chart of China's southeastern waters. Hurriedly she shuffled through the next few. The South China Sea, Vietnam, Indonesia. Ah, here it was, Queensland's northeastern coast. Pulling out the chart table, she spread the map across, quickly found Nulgarra, and checked the GPS. A few calculations, taking in their speed and time of departure, and since she reckoned they had less than twenty minutes before they reached the Great Barrier Reef and grounded, she swung north.

Setting the autopilot, she shrugged off her handbag and dumped it on the bridge. Her hands were trembling as she sank onto the pilot's chair. She took a deep breath, then another as she gazed at *Songtao*'s broad hooked beak swooping over the water. All the tanks are full, she told herself. We've water for weeks, fuel for hundreds of miles. We'll outrun them, no problem. We're safe now.

THIRTY-FOUR

When Daniel returned to the bridge he was breathing hard and he had blood on his hands.

"Are you okay?" she asked him.

"Rope burns. Not a problem." He pulled the chart around to look at it straight.

"We're about here," she said, sticking a finger firmly on a bit of blue just north of Nulgarra. "I think," she added.

"Well done," he said. "Very well done, in fact."

"I've set the autopilot," she told him, feeling obscurely proud of herself, "and we're headed for Cooktown at the moment."

He studied the chart some more before standing back and gazing through the huge windscreen and at the sea unfurling beneath the hull.

"They were shooting at me." His voice was steady. "To put me out of action, so they could grab you. The chief told me the Chens want you badly, especially since you appear to be the only person who might know where Jon Ming's gone."

She waited for him to ask where Jon was, but he didn't.

The boat gave a small shudder and while Daniel quickly checked the bridge, Georgia looked at the sea. It was more choppy now that they were in open water, with long, high swells that *Songtao* took easily. The boat quickly resumed her smooth ride. Just a patch of dirty water.

"Time to call the coast guard," said Daniel.

"A nerve-steadier would be nice," she said and, thinking of a brac-
ing shot of scotch, looked around for a drinks cabinet. No way would
a boat like this not have one stuffed to the brim. With thick cream
carpets and lacquered wood the color of honey, gleaming chrome fittings and cushions wrapped in milky Italian leather, she didn't doubt
that crystal glasses and ingredients for margaritas and whiskey sours
came as standard. Nothing like doing a runner in a floating gin palace
with bidets in every bathroom, if Bridie was to be believed.

Glancing across at the electronic weather chart, she groaned
aloud.

"What is it?"

She pointed at the storm unfurling in the southeast and moving
steadily north.

"Not nice," he agreed, and she watched him hurriedly adjust their
course to swing farther west before resetting the autopilot once again.
He glanced aside and said, "Ah."

Georgia said, "What is it?"

"I'm wondering where the sat phone is." He pointed at the empty
cradle.

"I'll get another," she said, and bolted for the galley.

Her breathing increased when she saw another empty cradle.
Telling herself not to panic, Georgia began to search the yacht. She
found two more empty cradles in the staterooms and another missing in the saloon. She tore back to Daniel, and although she tried to
look calm, she knew she didn't.

"All the phones are gone," she panted. "Every single one."

To her horror, she saw the blood drain from his cheeks.

"What is it?"

"The Chens," he said in a strangled tone. "We're on Lee's boat. I
should have thought . . . Jesus."

"The Chens have swiped the phones?"

"We've got to go back. Who knows what else they've done? They
would have heard he was planning to set sail . . . Christ. The nav
equipment might be sabotaged too."

Face pale and strained, he glanced at the wake behind, shining like ice-cream foam beneath the moon. She watched him check the GPS and compass. Easing the throttles back, he swung the wheel around.

Songtao spun lazily in a full circle, settled gently on her own turbulence, and nudged forward at half-throttle. Georgia tried to gauge how long they'd been going full blast. Ten minutes? Twenty? Time had stretched, become elastic, and she couldn't be sure. She saw that Daniel was doing the same. He was glancing at his watch, then staring at the compass and GPS.

"Can't rely on them," he said, and looked through the huge windscreen into the sky, as though checking the stars.

Georgia was impressed until he said, "What I know about stellar navigation I could write on my thumbnail, so let's drop anchor when we lose sight of our wake. People will be looking for us. The owner of *Micky's Dream,* in particular, since we pretty much wiped them—"

His words were lost in a resounding dull *whump.*

She looked at Daniel in horror, and he looked back, mouth dropping wide.

Before they could speak, WHUMP.

The yacht jumped violently forward, then listed to one side. Georgia was catapulted against Daniel and together they crashed to the deck.

WHUMP.

A wall of flame reared through a gaping hole that used to be the saloon. In a split second, she knew they had less than thirty seconds before the whole boat blew sky-high.

"Top deck!" she yelled and made to grab his wrist, but Daniel was already haring through the galley onto the portside deck. She pounded after him. He rounded left and charged up the steps. Smoke was in her lungs, and the roar of flames was deafening. As they burst onto the flybridge, she realized *Songtao* was already wallowing. Her stern already underwater and dipping, tilting hesitantly for the seabed.

Daniel yanked open a broad hatch and hauled the square white box of a life raft free. The brief feeling of cheer was instantly swamped by the stern lurching down sickeningly. Down, down. *Songtao* was beginning to drown.

Her mind was screaming at Daniel. *Hurry!* He scrambled to the edge of the boat and was twisting his torso to fling the box into the ocean, when water thundered over them as though they'd suddenly been thrown beneath Niagara Falls.

She was choking and shouting as sea washed around her thighs. "Hurry, for God's sake!" she yelled at Daniel. "Chuck it overboard! Inflate the bloody thing before it's too late!"

"It should have activated!" he shouted back. "Something's wrong . . ." He was yanking on the painter to trigger the raft's CO_2 canister.

The water rose to her chest. She lunged for a life belt attached to an aluminum rail and fumbled with the ropes, desperately trying to free it before they sank.

Behind her she heard a *swoosh* and glanced around to see that the life raft had inflated into an orange ball. Sea poured over the deck, and her hands fell from the life belt as she suddenly realized that she had to launch herself for the life raft before it was too late. No time to think. Just a desperate leap into the air, arms and legs reaching, fingers extended for the safety of the orange ball, and she never knew how, through a wave that left her choking and spluttering, but she was hauling herself over the orange rim and through the mouth of the canopy and inside the raft floating away from the boat, with Daniel clinging to it like a limpet.

Georgia had his wrists, was trying to heave him on board. His legs were paddling furiously, his fingers searching for a purchase. Georgia wished he was smaller and forty pounds lighter. Clamping her hands around his wrists, tight as she could, she heaved with all her strength.

BOOM!

A fourth explosion.

The rush of sea. She saw Daniel rise high, then fall. His wrists slipped from Georgia's grip.

"No!" she yelled.

"Georgia!" he yelled back.

"No!" she was shouting.

He was drifting fast away from her and the life raft. Sweet Jesus. Was there a rip current all the way out here?

She lunged inside the raft and yanked a life jacket free from its plastic tabs on the floor, scrambled to the opening, and flung it as hard as she could for him.

It fell way short, but she thought he might have seen it, because he was swimming strongly in the right direction. Then suddenly, she couldn't see the life jacket anymore. Nor could she see Daniel.

"Daniel!" she yelled.

Silence.

"Daniel!" she yelled again, searching for him, but all she could see was the sinking *Songtao*.

Flames and smoke poured into the air; would anybody see? The yacht's huge hawk's beak was just visible, and for a brief, desperate instant Georgia thought she might fight and remain afloat, but a second later a warning growl encompassed the air as her bow gave in to the ongoing pressure. In a single swift motion, she sank. There was no breaking up, no shattering of wood. A single low growl and that was it.

An eighty-foot mega-yacht, gone in less than two minutes. Christ.

"Daniel!" she yelled.

Still nothing.

Diving back inside the raft, she yanked at the bag strapped to the floor, pulled it open, and ripped the contents free, hands shaking, heart pounding. There was a tin inside, of what, she wasn't sure. A hard plastic square. A waterproof flashlight. She switched it on and her heart lifted.

Flares. Lots of flares.

Quick scan of the instructions, then Georgia hung through the entrance of the life raft and lit a mini-flare. It shot high and wide— 150 feet in the air, the packet read—and with a pop hung there before slowly arcing for the sea. It was impossible he wouldn't see it.

I'm here. *Swim for me. Swim.*

She grabbed the paddle from the bottom of the raft and sculled

furiously to where she thought she'd last seen him. When she reached
the crest of a wave she thought she saw a man's torso bobbing in the
water.

"Daniel!"

Paddling hard, she headed to the spot but saw nothing.

Have to find Daniel, she thought. Can't stop until I've found him.

She continued paddling. High on the next wave, she was convinced she saw a light winking to her left. The life jacket, she thought.
Did it have a self-igniting light? Putting her head down, she pelted
for the wink of light. Rising on the next crest, she looked vainly for
it, but saw nothing. She was shuddering and shaking and her hands
were numb. Was he hidden by another wave? Had he been swept
away by a current?

She lit another mini-flare, then another and another. In between,
she paddled like fury, determined to keep searching until she found
him.

I'm here, Daniel. Swim for me, dammit.

Gallons of water sloshed in the bottom of the raft. She ignored it
and kept paddling. It warmed her, but she knew she was tiring
rapidly.

Mustn't stop. He might be over the next wave.

She lit a night-and-day flare, which didn't fire into the air but was
designed to be handheld, smoke one end of the tube, a flare at the
other. Hanging out of the raft, she reached as high as she could. It
fizzed and spat and spewed green, and she gazed at the black of the
sea, lit as though it was day, and part of her couldn't quite believe
what was happening, but the other part, the selfish, self-survival part,
was telling her not to waste her last mini-flare. Just in case.

Georgia ignored the selfish voice and lit the last mini-flare. She
held her breath as hissing waves, black as ink, were lit all around,
rolling and curling. None of them bore Daniel or a winking light
from the life jacket.

Georgia paddled until the muscles in her shoulders and arms were
aching red-hot. Then she lit a night-and-day flare, rested a while,
paddled some more, lit another, rested, and paddled until she could

barely raise the oar. Finally, after she'd nearly lost the oar overboard, she gave in to her exhaustion and slumped back inside the raft.

She had two night-and-day flares left.

Oh God. Please let Daniel survive. Please, please.

THIRTY-FIVE

To stem the feeling of hysteria, Georgia concentrated on her raft, along with the conviction that Daniel had the life jacket. The inside diameter of her raft was about ten feet, and smelled nauseatingly of rubber and talcum powder. Maybe the powder was to prevent the rubber chafing, keep it pristine in its container. She didn't know, but she wished they'd used something else. It made her want to throw up.

The raft had a single tube, about eighteen inches high, around its circumference, and what she took to be several safety valves dotted along it. Attached to the tube was another, smaller tube that supported the canopy. Like a tent, it stretched over the raft. A quarter of it was loose, and hung open to provide the entrance.

Using the flashlight, she carefully inspected the basic survival equipment she'd spilled from the bag: a first aid kit, fishing lines and five fishing hooks in another small tin, two knives, five packs of seasickness pills, a signal mirror, a liter of water in a tin.

She stared at the tin of water. There should have been at least ten liters in a life raft this size. There couldn't be just one. Repressing the urge to panic, she meticulously checked the life raft and the contents from the survival bag.

One liter of water.

Don't think about it, she told herself. Think about what else will help you.

She peered at the hard plastic package she'd tossed aside earlier and saw it was a drogue, a type of sea anchor. It was a piece of fabric that would operate like a parachute and slow the raft down, keeping her in the area where *Songtao* had sunk. The next package contained sea dye, which would, it told her, create a green fluorescent slick and alert aircraft that she wasn't far away.

Georgia decided to use the dye when the sun came up, but in the meantime she'd set the drogue in place. She didn't know how far she'd already drifted, and the sooner she did it the better. Her fingers were stiff and cold, but she persevered, reading the instructions by flashlight and finally tying the anchor's rope to a cleat positioned just outside the entrance of the life raft, next to what looked like an antenna.

A surge of elation rocketed through her when she saw the antenna. You pathetic, panic-stricken idiot, she told herself, both you and Daniel will be rescued within the hour. It's a personal locator beacon! Activated the second it hit seawater, she knew it would already be transmitting her location on the international distress frequency. An airplane might hear it, and the police and coast guard certainly would.

Georgia settled back inside the raft. Help is on its way. Help is just around the corner. Thank you, God.

———————

Later. Maybe an hour or so, it was difficult to tell. She was shivering with cold, but through her numbed senses, she kept seeing Daniel's strained face, hearing his voice.

We're on Lee's boat. The Chens . . . They would have heard he was planning to set sail . . . Who knows what else they've done?

Huddled in her icy raft, arms wrapped around herself, she tried not to think where she was but instead about what had happened. She knew now for certain that the Chens wanted Lee dead, hence blowing up his boat. Had they tampered with the Piper's wire-lock as well? But she couldn't deny Jason Chen's surprise when she'd mentioned the airplane's sabotage. The Chens had destroyed *Songtao* in revenge for Lee killing Ronnie Chen, annihilating their plans to team up with the Dragon Syndicate, and "stealing" Suzie, but who had destroyed Bri's airplane?

It was the middle of the night, and Georgia's body was racked with shudders. Her clothes were sodden, her body slopping in the water on the floor of the life raft. She'd never been so cold. Crawling to the entrance, she peered outside. Where was the coast guard? They should be here by now. It was at least two hours since the PLB had been activated. Was it working?

She checked the antenna. It seemed all right, and although it wasn't exactly erect, pointing more dead ahead than into the sky, she didn't think it would prevent the thing from functioning. *What if it wasn't working?* No, don't think of that. There was no point in panicking. She had no control over it.

The wind started to rise and whistled through the entrance of the life raft's canopy, cold as a blast from the Arctic. She took in the froth whipping off the tops of the waves, the way the life raft was rising and rolling more violently, and thought, God, please blow the storm out, they'll never find me in a storm, let alone Daniel.

It didn't take long before a gale was sweeping in, and the life raft scudded up and down waves that were rapidly growing into mountains. A rush of water poured through the entrance and she yelped, scrambling to close the canopy. Gradually the waves and wind grew more fierce and the raft began swooping into troughs that grew steeper and steeper, until sometimes it stopped dead against a wall of water before rising high once again to fall into another endless valley.

She heard a low grumbling sound start to approach, and her lips were trembling, her whole body shaking, as the center of the storm approached, growing louder and louder, the seas higher and higher.

Thank God for the drogue, she thought. It would be acting as a stabilizer, preventing the raft from capsizing, being tipped over . . . Don't even contemplate the thought . . .

The raft was bending around her like plasticine against the somersaulting waves, and Georgia hunched there, too scared to do anything but sit tight and pray for the storm to pass quickly. A wave broke beneath the raft and gallons of water gushed inside. She grabbed the fishing tin and started to bail. The ocean battered and punched the raft, the wind a howling, shrieking creature that relentlessly rattled the entry-flap.

Throughout the night, Georgia alternately bailed and rested, bailed and rested, the sickening smell of talcum powder making her feel endlessly nauseous. The storm never lessened, raging and roaring against her and the life raft, lifting them high for a second before dropping them down a steep bank to be pounded wildly before lifting them high again.

The light inside the raft turned from black to gray, the only indication it was day. It was Saturday, the day before the deadline. She peeped outside to see waves as tall as houses towering high, the clouds a deep black and racing overhead, the sky dark.

Inside the raft, Georgia shivered in a sodden, waterlogged world that churned and boiled around her. She drifted into unconsciousness throughout the day, then woke with a terrified jerk when a larger wave slammed into the raft. The day felt as long as a year, the storm endless, until the waves started lessening, easing from their towering mountains into hills, and it was finally passing.

She wondered briefly where she was, but she knew there was no point thinking about it as she had no choice but to sit and let the life raft take her where it would. The drogue would only have stabilized her to an extent. She could be miles from *Songtao*'s wreck.

Her mouth was parched from salt water, and she took her first sip of fresh water and rolled it around her mouth before swallowing. Then she sank against the raft's tube, her thoughts returning to *Songtao*, the explosion, Daniel's final yells, the water pouring over the top deck. A rush of desolation. Where was Daniel now? Had he really caught the life jacket she'd thrown him? She hoped so much that he'd put it on, that it was one of those belts with a drogue, and that he'd been picked up before the storm hit and was now ashore, tucked up in a warm bed with a hot cup of his too-strong coffee.

She fell into an uneasy doze, and when she awoke it was night again, a second interminable night of sodden shuddering and shaking in a rising and rolling world of rubber.

Finally, dawn broke. Peeking over the horizon, the yellow crescent of sun turned the sky a pale cotton-wool blue. Not a cloud could be seen. A soft breeze had replaced the gale, and Georgia found herself filled with amazement that not only had she survived the storm, but that the drogue was still in place and her plastic Price's watch still working. The bright fruit face cheerfully informed her it was 6:20 AM.

It was the morning of the Chens' deadline. Today was Sunday. Desperately she turned her mind to Lee, what he'd said when he was standing outside the caravan park, smoking his long cigar.

Linette's more valuable to them alive than dead.

She had to cling on to that, and pray the Chens wouldn't jettison her mother just because she'd fled on the boat they'd blown up, and hang on to her as a precaution, in case Georgia survived.

Flash of Lee across her vision, the starbursts of scars on his knuckles, and her mind froze briefly in a shock of awful realization. She hadn't wanted to face it before, but she knew Lee was in trouble, had known it the instant he hadn't rung her when she arrived in Nulgarra. She'd been in denial.

Gazing across an ocean shimmering like blue mercury under the rising sun, she felt a stabbing pain of something that felt like guilt beneath her diaphragm, near her heart. She'd been so angry with him and only now could she see that his silence meant he couldn't ring her, was unable to, and she could almost see his face drawn white as he lay on the ground with a bullet lodged in his chest, bleeding into the dirt. For her. For her mother. Living out some debt his wizened granny had warned him against. Sweet Jesus. Lee and Daniel. One a criminal. The other a cop. Two men she cared for were in danger and there was nothing she could do for them.

Would they survive? Were they both already dead?

They were in fate's hands. So was she. And she was going to survive. She'd lived through the storm, hadn't she?

Despite her initial optimism, when she looked at the antenna

Georgia felt her spirits plummet. The PLB was obviously broken. Christ. Tears ballooned in her throat and she fought them down. She tried to pull the antenna erect, but it remained at its half-cocked angle. Bloody, bloody thing. My life depends on you and you're not bloody working, you piece of shit.

To distract herself, Georgia concentrated on the instructions for the dye, which she had saved, and soon there was a great slick of fluorescent green spreading across the waves. Excellent, she thought. Should a plane pass overhead right now, they wouldn't miss it, but the waves would eventually disperse the stuff. She hoped someone would fly over soon.

It was already hot, and as the sun rose it grew hotter, and she could feel her skin drying out, tightening, flaky with salt. She wanted to sit outside, away from the loathsome rubber smell, but she would burn badly without the canopy, so she stayed inside, forced to sit in water like a piece of chicken broiling in an oven.

She felt sweat trickle down her flanks. Loss of water. Loss of precious water. She couldn't think what she could do to prevent it, so she rummaged through the survival kit. No idea came to mind.

Already she was incredibly thirsty. She didn't know how much water it took in these sorts of conditions to stay alive, but reckoned on a liter taken in sips, slowly, throughout the day, which meant she had to eke out her single liter for as long as she could.

She took a small mouthful, rolling it around her teeth and gums before swallowing it in little gulps. The urge to upend the can's contents down her throat was so overwhelming that her hands were trembling. She had to force the tin immediately out of sight and in the bag.

Flopping back in the raft, she leaned against the tube and closed her eyes.

She awoke when something hit her. It came from beneath, and struck her full on her thighs. She catapulted to her knees in shock, her vision blurred. She tore the entrance open. White glare all around. Her heart was pounding in shock.

Blinking, scanning the emptiness of water, she saw a fin break the surface of the sea to the left of the raft. Georgia scrambled to the side, squinting hard. Please, not a shark, she prayed, not a shark.

Nothing. No fin, no shape in the water.

Still she scanned, terror sitting like a sack of stones in her stomach.

There! A slice of fin, cutting cleanly through blue. A rush of relief. It was a bonito. A fish.

Georgia sank back in the raft, suddenly exhausted. The sun was at its zenith and thumped down like a massive pile driver. Her tongue had thickened, and her lips were already sore and swollen. She took another sip of water. This time she couldn't resist it, and she found herself on her third blissful liquid roll-of-the-mouth before sanity kicked in.

They might not come. They might miss me. I might be way off course. I have to save water. This is just the second day. There might be more.

She pushed the water out of sight and lay in the sauna of raft and canopy. Drifted and dreamed. A vague awareness of heat lessening. Night drew in, and as she began to shiver she realized Sunday was over. Had the Chens killed her mother? Huddled on the floor of cold rubber, she tried not to think about Jason Chen's pruning shears, or Sergeant Tatts lying on a garbage dump bleeding to death.

She didn't want to cry. Not when she needed every drop of water to remain in her body. And she knew her mother would be exhorting her not to cry too, to hold tight until she was safe, but she couldn't help the tears trickling from her eyes. She scooped them carefully with her fingertips and licked them. The gesture steadied her. Her tears dried up.

Another endless night spent shivering with stars speckled above. The floor of the raft like chilled putty. Skin cold as marble. Shivering. Shaking in a little rubber cave on an ocean of nothing.

Day three, another dawn. Same dawn. Same soft cotton-wool blue melting into identical, relentless sun and heat. She decided there wasn't any point in using the remaining night-and-day flares unless she actually saw another craft.

Taking off her bandage, Georgia inspected her stump. In the heat it had puckered and was tight and dry and clean-looking. To avoid it sweating, she left it unbandaged. The wound in the pad of her palm from the air crash was a raised pink worm, and she wondered what a forensics department would say about her scarred and damaged hand should her body end up on a beach somewhere.

The sun rose, and she started to sweat. More water torment. She was violently hungry, but all she could think about was water. Water in Evian bottles. Water running from a tap. She'd stick her head down a toilet to drink the water, no problem. Cookie would do just that if she were as thirsty.

A day of remorseless discipline. She wondered where it came from. Why not drink every drop from the tin, then take whatever came as it may? Was her survival instinct so strong? Why? Why not just gorge for an instant, then let go?

She sank into a disturbed sleep, her hips and knees rubbed raw from the soaking salt-caress of rubber.

Midafternoon, Georgia struggled to survey the gleaming hard blue water. A haze hung in the distance and she concentrated on it, wondering if it heralded land, and as she stared, a tiny white dot appeared on the horizon. For a second she thought it might be a giant ray flipping out of the sea, showing its white underbelly like a big square handkerchief, but after she had blinked a couple of times, it hadn't dived back into the ocean. It was still there.

She squinted at it, waiting for it to vanish. When it didn't, she set off a night-and-day flare, holding it high so the smoke poured skyward. Heart pumping, she watched the little white dot, but it didn't seem to move.

With a small sputter, her flare died, but the white dot remained.

She knew it could be nothing, or a supertanker, perhaps, barreling past with its crew absorbed in watching videos down below, or a fishing boat heading in the opposite direction, nets full.

Georgia looked around at the expanse of hard white sky and endless eye-creasing ocean and decided to go for broke.

She lit her last flare.

The white dot remained on the horizon, and eventually her flare spluttered out and died.

She couldn't be sure, but she thought the white dot was growing. Slowly, tantalizingly, it was getting bigger. Georgia lay at the entrance of the raft and watched it gradually expand into a triangle that she realized was a mainsail. For a second, she couldn't believe her eyes. It was a yacht.

Rocketing to her feet, she nearly overbalanced into the sea when the rubber of the floor dipped violently. The yacht was heading straight for her! Whooping out loud, she jigged on the spot. She was saved!

Grabbing the tin of water, she took a huge gulp. She desperately wanted to drink the lot but didn't dare, not until she was absolutely *sure* she was rescued.

The yacht was closing fast, and she had taken another gulp of water and was grinning. The sores on her lips had cracked and she tasted blood in her mouth, but she couldn't stop grinning, hopping up and down and whooping like a madwoman, willing the yacht closer with every breath.

The yacht gave a blast of its horn.

This time she didn't hesitate. She upended the tin and swallowed the remaining water straight down, half spluttering and gasping in her haste as she watched the yacht creaming through the water. It was big, an oceangoing yacht, about ten yards and broad, with a blue stripe from bow to stern. One man stood on the bow, another at the helm. Both wore matching shorts and T-shirts. Just a hundred yards away now. She could hear the hiss of the sea against the hull. The helmsman was shouting. She stood up and waved her arms furiously above her head.

Both of them waved back, just as furiously.

She was crying in elation and joy and relief. *I can't believe it, I can't believe it! I'm going to live!*

THIRTY-SIX

The yacht was nearly upon Georgia when the man at the helm yelled and the man on the bow leaped into action. Sails snapping, ratchets grinding, the yacht slid effortlessly to rest beside the raft.

Two brawny, fit-looking men looked anxiously at her.

"Hello," she rasped.

"My God," said the man from the helm. He had a red baseball cap with "Fireball" stitched on it in yellow, and wraparound sunglasses.

Nobody moved for a few seconds, or said anything. Finally Mr. Fireball said, "You don't happen to be Georgia Parish, do you?"

"Yes! That's me. I'm her."

"Bugger me," he said, looking lost for words. "You wiped out *Micky's Dream,* then vanished. They've been going crazy looking for you. The coast guard, *Micky's* crew, and some reporter who's been doing her nut on the telly, radio, whatever, and here you are."

"Here I am," she agreed.

"Can we take you ashore?"

"Yes, oh, yes, please."

Mr. Fireball uncurled a length of rope and dropped it inside the raft. She grabbed the rope and wound it around her arm and let them gently pull and guide her to the yacht's stern. Gentle, careful hands lifted her inside. They looked appalled, and spoke in hushed tones as though a loud voice might shatter her.

"I'm okay, honestly," she said.

"Of course you are," Mr. Fireball said, trying not to stare at her stump.

"Thank you so much."

"Thank Stevo, he was the one who spotted you." He introduced her to a blond man with reddish stubble and freckles, adding, "I'm Des. Des Bailey."

Des and Stevo. Her saviors.

"I can't believe I'm here."

They grinned broadly at her. "We can't either," said Stevo. "It's not often we get to rescue shipwreck survivors."

"You bloody trouper," Des said, and shook his head admiringly. "Bloody good on yer."

"There's someone else out there," she said. "You've got to find him."

Des listened intently as she told him about Daniel. She could tell from the look on his face that he didn't think Daniel would have survived.

"Last we heard, he hadn't been picked up. That reporter woman grabbed a chopper and started looking for you straightaway, but the search didn't start officially till some of *Songtao*'s planking turned up on Kee Beach."

He looked at her raft. "You're nowhere near where everyone's been looking for you, though. The storm came from the southeast, and they reckoned you'd be swept along with it, back to Nulgarra, but you obviously hit a rip, maybe an ocean current or something, cos you're way south of where they've been searching. I'll radio in and get the score and organize another search for your friend round here, pronto."

She was so grateful she found it hard to speak. "Thank you."

As Des stepped across the cockpit and for the radio, she said, "Wait."

He turned and looked at her.

"You can't tell anyone I'm alive. Can you report you've found the raft, but not me?"

Des looked shocked, so she explained as much as she could about the Chens sabotaging *Songtao* and wanting to get hold of her, not to mention the dirty cop called Spider, who, the instant he heard she had survived, would send the Chens after her.

"You've got to tell the coast guard you found the life raft empty. *Find Daniel* but without telling anyone I'm alive."

Stevo rubbed the stubble on his chin. "Jeez. This is unreal. Like we're in a movie or something."

Small pause, then Des said, "I'm not sure . . ."

Georgia held his gaze, willing him to believe her, take her side.

"Okay," he relented. "I'll report the life raft and organize the search. I won't mention we've found you."

"Des, thanks," said Georgia, relieved. "You're wonderful."

Small pause.

"Let's get you something to eat," he said.

Within an hour she had showered, eaten one and a half beef-and-mustard sandwiches—she couldn't manage any more, as her stomach had shrunk to the size of a walnut after her recent abysmal diet, which had faded into zero in the life raft—and was wearing a pair of Stevo's shorts and a sweatshirt with "Fireball" across her chest. She sprawled facedown on the fore cabin's bed, feeling so drained that she wondered how she could still find the energy to breathe. She relished the dark cool that felt like satin on her skin. Four liters of mineral water stood on the carpeted deck beside her. She hadn't been able to settle with less. She was still looking at the bottles when she succumbed to exhaustion and closed her eyes.

She refused to think of Daniel still out there in the scorching, relentless ocean. If she did, she thought she might go mad with rage and grief and fear.

So she didn't think about him at all.

She simply took a breath, exhaled, buried her face in a clean, soft white pillow, and fell asleep.

———

"You've got to be checked out."

Des was looking worried, Stevo uncomfortable.

"All I need is a few hours of undisturbed sleep and I'll be fine, okay?"

"But what if you're in some sort of shock?"

"Do I look as though I'm in shock?" Georgia pressured them. "Thanks to you guys, I'm not shocked at all and I'm alive and I am *fine.*"

Neither of them appeared to believe her. They were at *Fireball's* helm and sailing past Pilgrim Sands Holiday Park, just north of Cape Tribulation and its rugged, jungle-covered mountains. They were about twenty-five miles south of Nulgarra, and Des was following the coastline as he headed from Cape Trib's ranger station, the life raft chugging on the wake behind them.

"Please, love," said Des. "We need to know you're all right."

Georgia reached across and squeezed his arm. "Des, what more do you need than me sitting here, grateful and glad and loving you for saving me?"

"I'd just feel happier, that's all, to hear you're okay."

She raised her left hand a little and immediately they both looked away.

The skin over her scalp tightened at their reaction. Bloody hell, she thought, looking at her stump for the first time in an age. I feel ugly as sin. Ugly, ugly, ugly.

Forcing her left hand high, she said, "They did this to me, the Chen family. They cut it off with a pair of pruning shears."

She ignored the way Stevo's skin blanched and continued. "Guys, *please.* I can't go to hospital because it'll be in the newspapers in two seconds and they'll be after me and I'll be killed before you can say, 'Two Fosters, please.' They want to chop off *all* my fingers and toes until I'm dead. *Dead.*"

Georgia leaned forward, her tone earnest.

"I don't need a hospital. I just need to get ashore, and so long as you keep quiet about finding me for a week or so, I'll have everything sorted. I promise."

Stevo rubbed his face as though his skin had numbed and he was trying to stimulate it into life. He kept looking at her stump then away. Eventually he said, "How about I drop you and Des off here, at Cape Trib, and get you run up to Nulgarra? The coast road's in pretty good shape at the moment, shouldn't take too long. I won't say we found you," he added, "not until you let us know when it's okay."

"Stevo, thanks," said Georgia, relieved. "You're brilliant."

"You need somewhere safe to stay in Nulgarra," Stevo continued, the color gradually returning to his face. "Des'll sort you, won't you, mate? You've somewhere where nobody'd think of looking, eh? She's a nurse, too, remember?"

Des groaned. "Please, tell me you don't mean Margey?"

"Safest place I can think of," Stevo insisted. "You know another?"

"She'll brain me."

"Take a crash helmet with you, then."

———————

Margaret wore specs and a voluminous dress the color of strawberries. Margaret hadn't spoken to Des since their divorce a year ago, after she'd found out about his affair with Price's Supermarket's big-bosomed manager, but she'd taken one look at Georgia tottering across her backyard and swept her inside.

Des had taken the precaution of parking at the rear of his ex-wife's house, and so far as Georgia could tell, nobody had seen them.

Margaret didn't say a word to Des, simply popped Georgia into a bath clouded with Dettol, rebandaged her finger, then put her to bed. Heaven, Georgia thought, is a bed of feathers and cotton swirling over skin like cold milk.

Hushed voices. Des sounded worried, Margaret irritable. Georgia drifted. She wanted to sleep for a week. Margaret made murmuring, soothing noises. It reminded her of the time she'd had chicken pox when she was six. Her mother had brought her into her own bed and sung her to sleep with her own soft version of Janis Joplin's "Mercedes Benz." So comforting, so loving. Georgia fell asleep praying to a God she didn't know that her mother was still alive.

Twenty-four hours later, she was half propped up in bed with a cup of Lipton's on her bedside table that she hadn't the strength to reach.

"I'm sorry. We haven't found your friend," Des said. He looked depressed. "We won't give up yet, but it doesn't look good."

She was so tired, her body so weak, it was a monumental effort just to talk, let alone feel much emotion.

"The coast guard's going to search for him until tonight and then, well, it'll have been four days . . ." Des trailed off and wouldn't look at Georgia, but she knew what he meant. After four days in an ocean of baking heat with no water, no food, and just one life jacket, he'd be dead. Des was telling her there was no hope, not really, but they wanted to do their bit. The newspapers were full of photographs of her empty life raft and coast guard boats and helicopters, and an old picture of herself with hair that hung between her shoulder blades, probably dug up from her housemate or the office. Were they grieving for her? They felt a lifetime away. Her booksellers, her surfing. She tried to drum up Maggie's face but could barely picture her boss, or her life in Sydney.

Her life had shrunk to a pinpoint of nothing but survival.

Everything else was superfluous.

She watched Des leave. She didn't say anything, didn't cry. She simply lay there, an aching hollowness inside.

———————

Five AM. Dawn was an hour away. Margaret's house was dark and silent.

Georgia padded for the phone on the hall side table and dialed.

"Yes?" the voice answered on a half-yawn.

"It's me. Georgia."

Silence.

Georgia fingered the little lace doily on the table and congratulated herself for probably being the first person in the universe to stupefy India Kane.

"Christ, what the *hell* . . ." India said in a choked tone. "Where *are* you? Are you okay?"

"Fine, India. I'm at a friend's. Miranda Street. In Nulgarra."

"*Nulgarra?* You're kidding me! You must have nine bloody lives! Jesus!"

"Can you collect me?"

"Can't. Sorry. I'm in Cairns, looking for you actually, but I'll send someone immediately, he'll be there—"

"No! Just you!"

"Trust me, okay?" There was a long pause and she heard a small beeping sound, then India's muffled tones, like she was talking on another phone. "He's in Nulgarra and on his way as we speak, okay? Sit tight, he'll be there soon as poss."

She was about to ask who when India said, "Shit, Georgia, you'd better know the syringe you nicked tested negative. As in negative for an antibiotic. They were just vitamins. Great idea, but no show."

Mind scrambling, Georgia managed to say, "Right. Okay. I'll wait at the end of the street. Next to a public phone, okay?"

"Hang fire, Georgia, he's on his way."

Tucked in the shadows behind a sago palm, the phone box a couple of yards away, Georgia waited for India's friend. The temperature was in the upper seventies, the air still and humid, and people would be sleeping without bedclothes, their fans whirring.

She'd left a note for Margaret, telling her not to worry and that she'd call her later. Signing the brief message, she had added a line of crosses along with a big circle, indicating a hug.

She hadn't had a decent hug in an age, she thought. Not since Yumuru's nearly a week ago, when he'd checked her finger. She couldn't believe Yumuru's vitamins really were just that. She'd honestly believed that Yumuru wanted Suzie dead so he could keep his miracle cures to himself. If it wasn't Yumuru, who else would have sabotaged the airplane? And for what? It had to be the Dragon Syndicate, enraged at Lee for botching their plans to join with the RBG. She couldn't think of anybody else.

The soft glow from a porch light across the road threw orange across a woodchip garden and the spread of asphalt between the houses, but otherwise it was dark and noiseless aside from the musical chirrup of insects. She found an enormous comfort knowing India was on her case, that she'd sent someone to collect her. No drawn-out questions about *Songtao*'s demise or how she'd survived, just, Are you okay? And, Someone's on the way.

As she sat there, mozzies droning around her wrists and ankles, Georgia wondered how India had found her vocation. Georgia wished she had a job she felt so strongly about. She didn't think she could return to being a book rep, not after what she'd been through this past week. She knew she would never be the same again, and that her life had changed irrevocably. She needed to do something completely different, that absorbed her. Like Daniel and the PST. He loved his job and, like India, was addicted to the chase. Her mind jumped. She should have been having dinner with him tonight. It was Tuesday today and she should have been looking forward to the Pier, to white-tableclothed luxury with Daniel . . . Oh God, what about Tabitha? What was going to happen to her now that her father was dead?

An emotion inside her belly, and her heart began to balloon into a great black ache.

No, can't think about Daniel or his daughter. Mustn't, can't, won't.

Resolutely she thought of India, and asked herself why, in her job, full of stress, the reporter didn't have a single gray hair. This kept her occupied for quite a while and eventually she glanced at her watch.

Even if India's friend was coming from the other side of town, he should be here any minute. Nulgarra wasn't that big.

She touched the soft glossy leaves of a large cycad, her bandage gleaming white in the dark and covering her repulsive stump, and turned her mind to consider the fact that these prehistoric plants grew a little less than an inch a year, meaning this specimen would be roughly twenty-five years old. Which meant the sixty-five-foot monster cycad at Lamb's Creek would be around a thousand. Not bad for a fern.

An engine started up a few streets away, and Georgia jumped to her feet. She listened to the engine note gradually fade as the car went through the gears. Someone off to work bright and early.

Three minutes later, a pale-colored Mitsubishi came barreling down the street. Lee, she thought, her heartbeat doubling. *I don't believe it. It's Lee.*

The Mitsubishi swung with a screech of rubber for the public phone. The passenger door was flung wide. A single blip of the horn.

Georgia erupted from behind the sago palm, flying for Lee's car and leaping inside. "Where the hell have you been?" she gasped without looking at the driver. The car immediately surged forward, and she slammed the door shut, pushing the lock in place as she spoke, "Christ, I've been so worried. You didn't ring me, dammit—"

"How on earth could I ring you when I didn't know where you were?"

Her stomach and heart and entrails swooped, as though she'd been thrown out of an airplane without a parachute.

"For God's sake, Georgia, I didn't even know you were *alive.*"

Slow motion. Tick-tick-tick, her head clicking around to the driver's seat. Not believing it. Unable to believe it.

The Mitsubishi was rocketing down the street, engine roaring.

His hands were steady on the wheel. Lean and strong and brown. He was looking dead ahead. His skin was clean and healthy. He was tanned and wearing a rumpled shirt and creased pair of shorts the color of charcoal.

She was sunburned and flaky-skinned and wearing Stevo's oversized shorts and sweatshirt.

She hit him full on the side of his face. The car slewed sideways. She hit him again, and again, and he was yelling, "Hell, Georgia, Christ, hang on a minute, just hang on a minute, will you?" and she was hitting him with all her strength and he was pulling the car to one side and she was still thumping him but he was out of the car and she leaped out and sprang for him, pummeling madly, out of control, and he was trying to soothe her—"It's okay, I'm sorry, okay, I'm sorry"—and she was sobbing and hitting him hard as she could, she was so angry and relieved. She could *kill him.*

"I'm sorry, Georgia, I got it all wrong, okay? I got a call from India saying to get here for you, and fast, and I couldn't use my car because I don't want anyone to know I'm around, okay? So I borrowed one from the guesthouse . . . I thought India told you how she requisitioned a chopper and got me winched out of the sea just before the storm hit."

She was standing with her arms hanging by her sides, crying.

"You shit, Daniel Carter," she said, her words muffled with tears. "You complete and utter *shit*."

Thirty-Seven

Two hours later they were breakfasting at Mick's and dawdling over their coffee. She asked him how the helicopter had spotted him in acres of ocean but failed to notice her bright orange raft, and he looked away.

"It was night, remember? Your raft could have been any color you chose and we still couldn't have seen you. Everything goes monochrome out there without light . . ."

She'd used all her flares almost immediately and then all she'd had was her little waterproof flashlight. Scrabbling around in the cold wet darkness inside the raft, trying to set the drogue. Not much of a light in the middle of an ocean.

"Waves look like anything you want them to," he added. "I saw the flares and then kept seeing your raft. I swam for it, but it was never there. You know what it's like."

She remembered rising on the crest of a wave, paddling furiously for his torso bobbing in the sea, and knew what he meant.

Taking a gulp of coffee, she put her mug down. Thought a while, then said, "But you were just a single person. I was—"

"Your light."

"What light?"

"My life jacket had a self-igniting light."

She didn't think she could feel much horror after what she'd been through, but her body gave a sudden chill.

Her voice trembled as she said, "The raft was sabotaged too."

"Yup." He nodded. "I discovered it was serviced last week. I'm betting the Chens took the opportunity to disable what they could. I'd say they left the one liter of water as a sick joke."

The Chens seemed to have thought of everything. Removing the sat phones. Blowing *Songtao* apart within minutes. But they hadn't tampered with Daniel's life jacket, thank God. They'd reckoned sabotaging the boat and the life raft would be enough to wipe Lee clean from their slate. And it would have been, had it not been for Des and Stevo. And India. *You must have nine bloody lives.*

"India and I searched for you in the helicopter as long as we could. The pilot wasn't too happy, we ran dangerously low on fuel, and by the time we'd returned to base, the storm was up. We couldn't fly for thirty-six hours, and by then you were way off the course we'd plotted."

They sat in silence a while, and she stroked a finger over her bandaged stump and wondered when she'd get the courage to discard the gauze. Given Des and Stevo's horrified reactions, probably never.

Finishing his coffee, Daniel asked her a bunch of general questions about her life in Sydney, trying to regain a sense of normality, she guessed, and she was glad for the change of subject. She told him a bit about her repping job and her surfing, her housemate Annie. As she spoke, she felt disconnected and peculiar, as though she was talking about someone else, a person who was dead, or a character in a movie she'd once seen.

They settled their bill with Mick and headed outside. The second her feet hit the pavement her pores opened and sweat streamed from her skin. She felt as though she was walking through a bubbling casserole of mangrove roots and was glad of the air-conditioning in Daniel's borrowed Mitsubishi.

They headed for Nulgarra's police station, where Chief Inspector Harris was waiting to talk to her. The chief had flown up especially for a chat, but the thought of the oncoming interrogation didn't make a dent in her sensation of well-being. Staring death in the face a couple of times certainly polished life's little marvels to a high sheen: being able to drink water whenever she wanted; feeling Daniel's hands on her shoulders, albeit extremely briefly, and when she was thumping him half to death; being alive.

"When the chief's done with you," Daniel said, "you'll leave town?"

Not until I know what's happened to Mum, she thought. She was alive, she had to be. "Any word on Lee?" she asked.

"Rumor is he's left the country."

"Not dead?"

He glanced across at her. "No, not dead. Unfortunately."

She felt a rush of horror that Lee might have abandoned her mother to the Chens and another illogical rush of emotion that Lee wasn't in a morgue somewhere. Which meant . . . God, she didn't know. Just that he was probably alive. But where was he? He wouldn't have left her, she just *knew,* like she was sure the sun rose in the west and set in the east. Was he hiding in a safe house somewhere? Was he all right?

She felt a petal of anxiety unfurl inside her, its color the deep purple of the heart of a pansy. She hurriedly took a handful of deep breaths, forced her apprehension away. Lee was a survivor. He'd be fine. No doubt he'd turn up one day, cigar clamped between his lips, like nothing had happened. So much for being her personal hawk, she sighed. Personal pain in the behind, more like.

They were cruising along Palm Road, appropriately named for the African oil palms lined on either side, when she thought of something.

"Daniel, why didn't you want anyone to know you'd survived the boat explosion?"

"For the same reason you did. I was with you, remember, and since they'll do anything to get hold of Jon Ming . . ."

As they crested a rise in the road, the sun hit the windshield, lighting the multicolored entrails of various insects, but he didn't activate the washer, presumably because they'd only smear the glass and make it impossible to see.

"I decided to lay low. I didn't want Tabby . . . involved."

She could understand that. The Chens wouldn't hesitate to snatch a little girl if they thought it would help them.

"How is she?"

"Apparently she whacked a wooden spoon over some kid's head at preschool for wanting to borrow her yellow crayon. She's going to have to smarten up and learn to share or we'll be in trouble. Poor old Gran, she's having a rough time of it. She's pushing eighty now, finding it harder and harder . . . God, if anything happened to me, Social Services would have a field day . . ." His face turned bleak. "They'd take Tabs away from me, stick her with strangers, some awful foster home—"

"Nothing's going to happen to you," she said firmly.

He shot her a look that told her she didn't understand, so she asked him where he thought Lee might have gone, sidetracking him nicely, and then he was pulling up outside Nulgarra's police station, a low-slung building with sun glinting off its tin roof.

As he set the handbrake and turned off the engine, a car passed them, slowly, as though it was looking for somewhere to park. It blipped its horn briefly, and as Daniel raised his head, it accelerated past.

Snapping his seat belt free, Daniel turned to open the door. She watched the car go, thinking nothing of it, until it flashed its hazard lights twice, then switched them off. She suddenly took in the make of the car. A silver Mitsubishi with smoked-glass windows. It was sitting on its brakes at the entrance to the street, signaling left, but not moving. A hand came out of the driver's window and flicked some ash from what looked like a long, slim cigar.

Lee? she thought. *Lee?*

She was scrambling out of the cop car, readying herself to run for the Mitsubishi, when the brake lights went blank and it swung left and out of sight. Another blip of the horn.

He's trying to lead me, without being seen.

"Hey, what's the rush?" Daniel was out of the car, watching her. He clearly hadn't clocked the Mitsubishi.

"I don't feel well," she said, which was true. Her heart was galloping loud as horse's hooves on gravel and she knew she was sweating.

"You want the ladies'? Some water?" Daniel was ushering her solicitously into the police station.

"Ladies'," she panted.

"This way. God, Georgia. All those days in that raft . . . Are you going to be okay?"

He led her inside and left, then right. Pushed open a door marked "Staff Only." "Shall I leave you, or would you like—"

"Leave me."

"I'll be right outside."

As soon as the door banged shut she spun around. Two stalls, a single sink. A small window set high in the wall. Rushing to the window, she reached up and pushed it open. Wide enough, but how to get up there? She scanned the room and saw a plastic bin in the corner, half-filled with used paper towels. She raced for it, turned it over by the window, got one foot on it, and was just hooking her elbows on the sill when she heard Daniel's knock.

"Georgia? Are you okay?"

"Yes, thanks! It's just that . . . it's that time of month. Give me five, okay?"

"God, sorry. Of course."

Kicking off the plastic bin, she heaved her torso up and over the sill, the aluminum digging into her breasts, then her ribs. Wriggling hard, she dragged her stomach through, then her hips. Hanging there, she looked up and down the building, saw nothing but scrubby bush and gravel, a handful of trash lying on the ground. She tried to turn around, wanting to grip the top of the window and swing her legs down, but there was no space. She'd have to fall headfirst.

Looking at the ground, she knew it wasn't far, maybe seven feet, and it didn't sound much, but right that minute it could have been seventy feet, and for the first time in her life she wished she'd taken a parachute course and knew how to break her fall, to avoid snapping her hands and wrists, or smashing her face.

She was hesitating, taking up valuable time. She'd better just do it.

Lunging forward, she felt her thighs slide agonizingly over the aluminum.

Her body was hanging, balanced so she could tumble either way if she wanted, and she was reaching for the brickwork below, searching for a handhold, but there wasn't one. In the distance she heard a car horn. Blasting long and clear.

Lee. *Calling to her.* Did he have her mother? Was she safe?

Covering her head with her arms, just as she had in the air crash, she gave a huge lunge to clear her knees. Gravity did the rest.

Searing pain along her shins. It felt as though they were being stripped. Then she was crashing to the ground, onto her right shoulder with a dull thud. The breath was knocked from her body, and for a moment she lay there, feeling the sting of gravel on her cheek, the smacking pain of her thighs and shins. But it wasn't as bad as having her finger chopped, and the thought gave her strength.

Georgia stumbled upright, took her bearings. She could see the flank of a cop car to her right and she trotted down the side of the building, ducking low past a window to avoid being seen, and paused when she came to the edge of the parking lot. No cover. Should she blast across it, come what may, or take the longer route and cut across the bush?

She decided to go for broke. After all, what could the cops do her for? Running across their forecourt without due care?

Taking a breath, she sprinted across the asphalt, and just as she hit the street she heard a shout.

"Hey, you!"

As she swung left she saw the Mitsubishi's white reversing lights glaring, wheels spinning for her. She raced for the passenger door, which was already opening, and flung it wide, jumping inside. With a screech of rubber on hot pavement, the car surged forward. Grabbing the door handle, she yanked the door shut.

"Took your time," Lee said.

Without taking his eyes off the road, he popped open the glove box and pulled out a pack of tissues, which he passed to her.

"You've got blood on your cheek."

She snatched the tissues from him. "Took my time? You're the one who's been taking time! Where's my mother? You said you'd ring me, but you didn't! Where is she?"

Expecting platitudes, maybe an apology, she was prepared to punch him for letting her down when she'd been relying on him *so much,* but he took the wind right out of her sails when he said calmly, "We're going there right now."

"She's alive?"

"Oh yes. Very much so. The Chens want to know if you're alive or dead before deciding what to do with her. She's been reciting quotations from the Dalai Lama. Chanting a lot. Or so I've heard."

Out of nowhere, her throat swelled and tears spilled down her cheeks. In the commune Linette Parish's chanting *"Om"* had been legendary. The Dalai Lama was her spiritual focus. *Her mother was alive.* She blew her nose and mopped her face.

"We're going to her?" she choked. "Now?"

"Couldn't do it before. They moved her. Twice. Then I had a bit of a run-in with a couple of their blokes and took a bit of damage. Had to lay up for a while. And your phone wasn't working."

That was true; it was at the bottom of the Coral Sea, along with *Songtao.*

It was only when the word "damage" sunk in that she saw the distinctive white of gauze bandage peeking from the neck of his shirt.

She felt the sudden poker-red heat of anxiety. She'd been right all along. "You're hurt?"

"Not anymore. Your friend Yumuru fixed me up."

She checked his bandage to see that it was clean, no blood seeping through. Then she scanned his arms, his hands, the cashew-colored cords standing out in his neck. Aside from the bandage, he looked fine. Ignoring the tidal wave of relief crashing over her, she said, "Mum?" Her tone turned pleading, frantic. "Where is she? My mother?"

"In the rear storeroom of a Chinese restaurant."

"And we're—"

"Driving there now."

Georgia turned the pack of tissues over in her hands. "Is she guarded?"

"Oh yes."

"Won't we need the police?"

"No."

She looked outside and saw they were sweeping along Ocean Street and past the Bendigo Bank, and then he swung left down Musgrave Street and left again onto Crown. They were a street away from Mrs. Scutchings's, she realized. She could see the cemetery.

"That one, there," Lee said, pointing at Timothy Wu's Chinese restaurant, the Mighty Chopstick.

"My mother's there? In a *storeroom*?"

"Yup."

He was cruising past and making no attempt to brake.

Alarmed, she said, "Aren't you going to stop?"

"No. We're going to come back tonight when it's dark. Just thought I'd show you, that's all."

She was craning her head around as he continued steadily down Crown Street for Harbour Road, gazing at the restaurant she'd had umpteen takeouts from as a kid. Timothy Wu, with his broad smile, had handed over spring rolls and buckets of sweet-and-sour chicken topped with sweet, thick rice.

"Is Timothy Wu *involved*?"

"Only so far as he's handed over the keys. He's down in Gympie for a christening."

"How did you find out she was there?"

He changed down into second, a smooth double-declutch, matching the engine note perfectly with the gears, and she suddenly noted that the Mitsubishi wasn't automatic, but stickshift. All the better for getting out of tricky situations, she thought to herself. Automatics were all very well, but you couldn't beat having complete control of your revs.

"Long story," he said. "Not one you really want to hear."

Since it probably involved slashing men's stomachs until their entrails showed, she decided against pressing him. Instead, she said, "How on earth did you know I was going to be at the police station?"

He had turned right into Harbour Road and was heading along Julian Street, for the western side of town.

"Because I'm a cop. And a cop always knows what's going on."

Startled, she looked at the side of his face. "You *were* a cop. You got chucked out, for . . . for . . ." She couldn't say the words. *Betraying your partner to bleed to death, fingers and toes chopped off, on a garbage dump.*

"I didn't do it."

"Didn't do what?"

"Give Tatts away."

She suddenly saw that his face was drawn and pale, the grooves around his mouth deep as canyons.

"Someone else did that. Not me." He turned his head for a second to look at her. "Why do you think I'm here? For the scenery?"

India's voice in her mind. *He's not stupid . . . Surely you can't believe he's sticking around just for you?*

"You want to find whoever killed your partner," she said breathlessly, and he nodded.

"Someone packed a ton of cash into my account an hour after Tatts was snatched. If I'd hung around, they'd have lynched me. The evidence was that tight. Even had a bunch of phone calls I never made on my mobile, to the RBG. No way would they look elsewhere. My coming from out of town . . . with a different way of thinking, made it easier for them to hate me."

She knew he meant because he'd come from Hong Kong, and was half-Chinese.

"Spider set me up," he continued in the same level tone. "Spider knows that I know what they did . . . but I still don't know who it is. The paper trail leads straight to Panama; two hours later it hops to Saint Lucia for barely ten minutes, and after that there's no trace. Not from want of looking. You've stirred things up nicely, though. I'm hoping to get a bead on them soon."

"You stopped the two gangs getting together," she said, recalling his wiping out two guys in the Dragon Syndicate.

"Yeah. My boss liked that."

"Who's your boss?"

"He's on the board of the People Smuggling Strike Team, the PST. The board is made up of senior representatives from the feds and DIMIA, the Department of Immigration and Multicultural and Indigenous Affairs. Daniel's boss is in the feds but mine is from DIMIA. He knew me in Hong Kong, was aware I'd been set up. When Tatts got wiped out, we decided to stick me undercover. See what we could get."

So he was legit. She was shocked. Could you be legit and still kill people, disembowel them? "Weren't the RBG suspicious?"

"They welcomed me with open arms. They thought I'd been their snitch for years, and I didn't disillusion them. After Tatts died, Spider stopped his dealings with them for six months or so, and when he started up again, with Jason Chen as his handler, the RBG assumed it was a new source."

"Doesn't Spider know you're undercover? Trying to find him?"

"Nope. With my background, I took to crime like a flea to a dog and let it be known I was grateful to Spider for showing me the light. Spider—and every other police officer here—thinks I'm a full-blown happy hood. All the same, he wouldn't mind if I met with an untimely end, considering I'm the only person who knows the true story behind Tatts."

He was barreling the car through the outskirts of town, and she could see the rainforest looming ahead, foliage thick and green, sturdy trunks of trees planted firmly into mossy soil.

"I still don't get how you found me at the cop shop."

He shot her one of his looks that told her she hadn't been listening properly. "My boss. We keep in touch."

"Oh. Of course."

They'd swept past the last house on the edge of Nulgarra and were heading northwest, as far as she knew, into the middle of nowhere.

"Where are we going?"

"To rest up at my place."

"You've a place?"

"What, you think I sleep in a tree?"

THIRTY-EIGHT

Lee's place was a rented timber cabin near Bountiful Point and up a steep winding forest track that looked as though it had been made by a wandering goat. The simplicity of the cabin suited Lee. Four walls, a sturdy veranda, and an aluminum roof. No frills.

He showed her a bedroom with a view of his car sitting in the clearing at the front of the cabin. "You want to sleep, put your head down."

"Maybe later." She didn't think she'd ever felt so wide awake. They'd be springing her mum tonight!

Lee made coffee for her, and green tea for him. She sat opposite him in the lounge with the sweet smell of gun oil at the back of her mouth, and watched him clean his firearms. Two Glocks, a .357 Magnum, and a Beretta. She asked if she could handle the Beretta, and he passed it over.

He raised an eyebrow when she checked the chamber, eased the slide back, and decocked it on an empty magazine.

"You do much shooting?"

"Just two hours on the range."

The Beretta had a fifteen-round magazine, and was relatively handy too, weighing in, Lee told her, at around two pounds fully loaded.

"Nice weapon," she said, and passed it back.

"I prefer the Magnum. But you can have a Glock, if you like. For tonight. You know about the safe action trigger system?"

"Yes."

Yumuru had taught her all about it. The Glock had a semi-cocked double action, which meant no fiddling about with external safety catches or cocking hammers before the gun was ready to fire. You just loaded it and pulled the trigger. Yumuru had reassured her she could drop the gun, kick it, or throw it over a cliff and it wouldn't go off. There were three automatic independently operating mechanical safeties, which were sequentially disengaged when the trigger was pulled, and which were automatically reengaged when the trigger was released.

Lee finished cleaning the Magnum, then started over again.

"You're supposed to clean them twice?"

"I find it helps settle the mind before a raid. Besides, as my grandmother would say over and over, you can never be too prepared." He gave a small smile. "She always said if I listened to her I'd grow up to be a wise man. Wish I'd paid more attention."

He dropped oil onto a yellow pipe cleaner, which made a soft snicking sound as he cleaned the barrel, but she wasn't looking at his hands, just at his face, enchanted with the echo of the smile she'd seen, the way it had softened his face, brought a sheen of wry amusement into his eyes.

"Something wrong?"

She looked away. "No. I was just wondering . . . when we've got my mother, where will we go?"

"We won't be using my yacht for a quick getaway, since you trashed it."

"I didn't trash it! It blew up!"

"Not of its own accord."

"I reckon it was a bomb," she said.

"Yeah. You reckon right."

She blinked. "You knew there was a bomb on your boat?"

"Yup."

"Lee!" God, getting information from him was like trying to squeeze orange juice from a lump of coral.

"I instructed the captain to prep the boat and let it be known around town I was about to set sail. The RBG fell for it. I saw the thing they'd planted the day you took your ride." He shot her a look of admonishment. "If I'd known you were a Ferretti joyrider, I'd have dismantled it."

"There was talk of you with a woman . . ."

"Yeah. I spread the rumor. To unsettle the Chens a fraction."

"Do the RBG know I'm alive?"

"I'd say so."

"Expand, would you?"

"If I heard you were around, then Spider would too. And I did pick you up outside a police station. Word'll be out."

She mulled it over, how the Chens were still holding her mother despite *Songtao*'s demise, and a sick horror flooded through her at her next thought. "Are you *sure* Daniel's not Spider?"

He looked up, and she saw with astonishment that she'd shocked him. "Jeez, you've got an even worse opinion of the world than I have. And there was I thinking you liked the bloke."

"I do!"

"Well, then. Trust your instincts."

———

Lee spent the remainder of the day repetitively checking his guns, then his car. Fluid levels, filters, tires, even the windows got a wash. Then he ran through his plan. Made her repeat it back. After she'd gotten it word perfect three times running, he disappeared for a nap, suggesting she did too, but she was too hyped up to lie still enough to relax, let alone fall asleep. She wondered what Daniel thought of her disappearing from the cop shop, and whether he was worried. She tried to read a paperback, and by the time she'd gotten to the second chapter and realized she hadn't taken in a word, Lee returned and started preparing supper.

Honey duck and crackling with fresh green beans and steamed

rice. Lots of preparation. Garlic to be finely chopped, fresh ginger grated, shallots stripped, sesame seeds roasted.

"Do you always cook like this?"

"Nope. But I find it helps settle the mind—"

"Before a raid."

It felt weird, helping him in the kitchen. Like she was playing sous-chef to Darth Vader, or Superman. She wasn't quite sure whether he was a superhero or a supervillian, and decided he was both.

"You've one hell of an appetite on you," he said when they were finally on their way. "Must have been all that sea air."

"You're one hell of a cook," she said. "Are you married?"

"What, in my job? You're kidding?"

They fell silent as they headed into Nulgarra, Lee cruising cautiously, constantly checking his rearview mirror, his side mirrors. It was eleven-thirty when he doused the lights, shut off the engine, and silently rolled to a halt a hundred yards from the Mighty Chopstick.

Her breathing was shallow and she was trembling. She dreaded to think what she'd be like come 2 AM. A basket case, probably.

Buzzing down their windows, Lee lit a cigar and exhaled steadily outside. "One thing I haven't told you," he said.

From the way he studied the tip of his cigar, she guessed she wasn't going to like it.

"My boss has put out a rumor I've discovered who Spider is, but haven't given him a name. Spider will do anything to wipe me out, now he thinks I know who he is. And he's up for a bonus if the RBG get hold of Mingjun—Jon Ming—for their Chinese clients. Eighty grand or thereabouts, I've been told. One hell of a bonus, wouldn't you say? Worth killing for."

Flicking some imaginary ash from his shirt, he continued. "The RBG have told Spider I'm after your mum. But Spider doesn't want us to get Linette. He still thinks it's the only way to keep you in line and tell the RBG where Jon is, thus guaranteeing his bonus. He's been blocking me all the way. He got Jason Chen to move Linette when he heard I was getting close. He even suggested the restaurant. Immediately after we have Linette on board, my boss is going to tell the force what I'm doing, but not where. Spider will come here like a shot, and try to take me down."

His hands clenched and unclenched.

"And I'll be waiting."

Anxious, she said, "He won't jeopardize Mum?"

"Nope. You'll both be far away by then. No problem."

Waiting was torture. Her natural instinct was to get stuck in and make things happen. Patience never had been one of her stronger points. She tried to strike up a conversation with Lee, but since it was like chatting with a retarded mollusk, she gave up after a while. She studied the street a thousandth time. There were rows of fig and palm trees and streetlights, with weatherboard houses on the right and closed-up shops on the left. Milk bar, small grocery store, fishing and dive shop, and newsagent were all flanked by the Mighty Chopstick at one end and the All Italia Pizza at the other.

Occasionally a vehicle drove past, but they hardly saw anyone on foot. One man walked his dog. Another popped from one house to the next, and back again five minutes later, a pack of cigarettes in his hand. Through the open car window she could hear the background noise she usually never noticed, a steady faint hum that was the sound of a town falling asleep; the mutter of TVs, people chatting, stereos playing, phones ringing.

As the clock ticked to 1 AM, the hum had all but gone, and the insects had taken over, clicking and chirruping. She could even hear a bunch of frogs croaking.

Lee suddenly stiffened. A side door to the Mighty Chopstick cracked open and light spilled out. Lee slid down in his seat and Georgia followed suit, eyes latched to the figure emerging. It was a slender Chinese man dressed in cotton trousers and baggy shirt, shiny black shoes, and a big black belt with silver studs.

"One less to worry about," said Lee.

"How many are in there guarding my mother?"

"Just the two now."

"How do you know for sure?"

He gave her a sideways look. "I do this for a living."

Oh, God. She kept forgetting his trademark. Disemboweling his victims for information. Did his DIMIA boss know he did that sort of stuff? Surely not—the Aussie government wouldn't sanction such torture.

Lee forced her to wait until 2:45 AM before leaning over and raising his trouser leg. He had a holster next to his skin. She watched him withdraw a knife. Wickedly curved, its steel was matte black, for night work she guessed, and had a blood gutter. A flashback to the air crash. He'd hacked her hair free with that same knife.

He passed her a mobile phone and said, "Let's run through it one more time."

Tucking the mobile in her front shorts pocket, she repeated what he'd told her earlier in the day. She was to wait in the driver's seat of the car until he came out with Linette and make sure they were alone before driving forward to pick them up. If anyone remotely suspicious arrived at the restaurant, she was to ring him and let his mobile ring just twice. No more, no less. His would be set to vibrate. Hers too. If anything went wrong, she was to drive away immediately. Should he and Linette not appear within twenty minutes, same story.

He gave a nod to tell her she'd gotten it right, then he took his Beretta and gently racked the slide to chamber a round. Did the same with the Magnum. He gestured to her, and she primed the two Glocks, stuffing one in the small of her back, in her waistband, the second in the well between the seats. Another nod, then he quietly opened his car door and slid outside. She did the same, crept around to the driver's seat and snicked the door shut, watching him move soundlessly down the road.

Slipping down the side of the restaurant, he vanished from sight. It was only then that she realized she'd been holding her breath, and let it out in a little rush.

One minute. Two minutes. Three. How long would it take to pick a couple of locks, disable two men, and release a hostage? Four. Five. She was getting mesmerized by the car's digital clock and hurriedly started scanning the street. God, some lookout. Must concentrate. Keep alert.

Quick flick to the clock. Six minutes.

All was still and silent, aside from the insects and frogs.

She didn't know when she first noticed. A flash at the end of the street, then a pair of headlights turning into Crown Street.

Ducking low in her seat, she prayed. Please, just be going home after dinner with friends. Just be going home.

In the next ten seconds she saw the car sweep to its right and slow as it approached the Chinese restaurant.

It was a black Mercedes.

THIRTY-NINE

Fingers unsteady, she called Lee's number and let it ring twice. She pushed her phone back into her pocket and picked up the Glock from the seat well. Her hands were sweaty, but the grip was ribbed and didn't slip.

She didn't take her eyes off the Merc. Three men climbed out. Two from the front, one from the back. The driver she didn't recognize, but the man from the passenger seat wore jeans and a leather jacket, even in the heat . . . Jason Chen turned to his father and said something. They were too far away for her to make out their features or see their lips move, but she could tell they were talking by their body language: little gestures, head movements, posturing.

They looked relaxed. No guns that she could see, although she didn't doubt they were armed. And they hadn't looked her way or checked the street.

The three men walked steadily for the side of the restaurant, still talking. She debated whether to call Lee again, and decided not to distract him. One warning would be enough.

She watched the men, terrified she'd see a head turn, look straight at her. Her hands were shaking, and she double-checked that her finger was off the Glock's trigger. She didn't want to loose off a shot by accident.

When they vanished from sight, she stared after them.

I don't believe this is happening.

Could she just sit there and wait for them to kill her personal hawk and drag her mother somewhere else?

The next second she clicked open the car door and slid outside, leaving the keys in the ignition. Glock in her right hand, she forced herself around the hood of the Mitsubishi, trying to tread quietly, flinching at the tiny scrunches of grit against her shoes. She took four more steps and was on the pavement, walking as fast and soundlessly as she could. She bent low and headed for the side of the restaurant.

What she was going to do when she got there, she hadn't a clue. Cautiously she peered down the narrow alley between the newsagent and the restaurant. And jerked like she'd been shot when her mobile vibrated.

"Yes," she whispered.

"How many?"

"Three."

She was opening her mouth to ask if he had her mother but he'd disconnected. Hell. She'd wished he'd given her an order, like go to the front of the restaurant and shoot the door down. But then, he assumed she was waiting in the car.

Glock tight in her hand, she headed down the alley, moving step by nerve-racking step, trying to see where her feet trod, making sure there wasn't a tin can in the way, a rustling paper bag. She reached the end of the alley and peered right to the rear of the restaurant. The back door was ajar, spilling light across two industrial-sized garbage cans, four white plastic chairs, and a load of bindweed growing up the surrounding fence.

She still had no idea what to do. If she opened the door, she might alert the Chens that she was there and blow whatever plan Lee had. All she could think was that she couldn't stand there and do nothing.

Tiptoeing to the door, she peered through the crack. All she could see was a wall. Whitewashed. No pictures. No flaking paint. Tucking her forefinger around the door, she pulled it, infinitesimally slowly, open an inch.

Crack!

She jerked back, a scream forming in her throat.

A gunshot from inside the restaurant.

Crack! Crack!

The sound of shouting, feet thundering. More shots. Men hollering in Cantonese. A crash as something hit the floor. It sounded big, like a piece of furniture, not a person.

Crack!

Another crash. A smashing sound, like china. Lots of yelling.

She found herself cowering, making herself small against the bedlam.

Boom!

Lee's Magnum.

Boom! Boom!

Crack!

Sudden silence. Her ears were ringing from the shots and she could hear nothing aside from a dog's mad nonstop barking nearby. She had no doubt the entire neighborhood was currently dialing triple zero from under their beds.

"Aiyee!" An exclamation of what sounded like relief.

A long stream of Cantonese. Small silence.

Oh, Jesus, sweet Lord. Is Lee all right? Mum?

More chattering. Excited and relieved all at once. A couple of clicks that sounded like gun chambers being emptied, or loaded.

She stood there trembling, flinching with each sound, sweat pouring, her grip on the Glock spasmodically tight.

A roll of Cantonese. Slightly slurred. Deeper than the rest.

Lee. Lee's voice. Had he been shot? What about her mother? She couldn't hear a woman's voice.

The rustle of cloth. A small thud. Lee's groan.

They'd kicked him.

Strangely, it was this realization that prompted her into action. Not that they'd shot him, which they probably had, but that they'd kicked him, like Jason Chen had kicked her, to make themselves feel big.

She was only a foot from the door leaking its light. Frozen into place, she'd barely moved since the shots had started.

Another thud. Another long, agonized groan.

Lots of chattering. A laugh. The Chens releasing their tension.

Georgia took a step and curled her fingers around the door and tugged it gently open, praying it wouldn't squeak. Amazingly, it didn't, and she pulled it wider, seeing whitewashed wall, more wall, then a boot. Two boots. One was Lee's. The other she didn't recognize. As she inched the door open she realized Lee was sprawled next to the inert body of the driver of the Merc. She saw the bodies of the two guards at the far end of the room. If Lee had been correct about the number of guards, the only enemies left in the room were Jason Chen and his father. She couldn't see her mother. God, please let Mum be safe.

She saw that Lee's black shirt was wet and glistening with what could have been dark paint. Blood. He was covered in blood. And he wasn't moving.

Although she'd guessed he'd been shot, she hadn't reckoned on her reaction to seeing him like that. It was as though her heart had been torn from her chest and sliced in half. She couldn't breathe, and the pain in her heart grew and grew until she thought she was having a heart attack. She had to see if he was alive. If he was alive, she knew the pain would stop.

She was dimly aware of the chatter of Cantonese, the smell of cigarette smoke, but she put the danger aside in her all-consuming desire to open the door a bit farther . . . just to see Lee's face . . .

Gap-tooth Chen's shoulder came into view, a cloud of cigarette smoke drifting around it.

She pushed the door a little wider, craning to catch a glimpse of Lee . . . she saw his shirt collar, his cashew-smooth throat, then the angle of his jaw, the scar running behind his ear, his mouth, straight and unmoving, that narrow nose . . .

Black eyes staring straight back.

A sensation of roaches scurrying over her skin. He'd been aware of her all along. He was alive.

Black eyes flicking to Gap-tooth then back to her. His lips moving. *Shoot him.*

Georgia began to raise her Glock and curled her finger around the trigger. Next step, she knew, was to feel the resistance of the trigger against the pad of her finger and shoot.

I can't believe I'm doing this.

At that moment the door was flung open wide.

She flinched and jumped backwards, then yanked her finger on the trigger, but nothing happened. Her hesitation had activated the safety system. Her wrist was grabbed and she was flung inside, sprawling almost on top of Lee. She was swinging around, trying to bring her Glock up when she saw a boot aiming for her kidneys. Rolling, still holding the gun, she let the boot smash into her ribs like a stab of white lightning, and Lee was rolling too, toward her, and she felt his hand in the small of her back, pulling the second Glock free.

Crack!

Her eardrums contracted from the blast.

She saw Gap-tooth's chest erupt in a spray of blood and his body drop like a stone. Lee was surging left but Jason Chen was swinging around, aiming his gun at Lee. Lee was yelling something but she couldn't hear.

Her world was small and silent now. She was on her feet. Had the first Glock in both hands.

Lee diving for the floor. Jason Chen's gun following him. Lee's face a howl of pain as his shoulder slammed onto the floorboards. Lee trying to bring up his Glock, unable to, lips bared in agony. His blood was smeared across the floor like a paintbrush stroke.

Jason Chen taking his time, aiming for Lee's head.

Her arms were straight. She felt the cool metal of the trigger travel from her fingers into her hands and through her arms into her lungs, her heart. She closed her left eye, trained her right to the end of the barrel, to the foresight, and aligned it with the rear notch, aiming right between Jason Chen's shoulder blades, and gently, oh so gently, holding her breath, she increased the pressure and the trigger gave way.

Crack!

The pistol jolted, the slide cycling back and forward.

Jason Chen faltered, one foot raised. Georgia felt her finger squeezing the trigger again, and again.

Crack! Crack!

She was still firing, her mind yelling. Go down, you bastard, go down, you bastard, go down!

"Enough! Georgia, enough!"

Her wrist was smacked high and her fourth shot hit the ceiling. Little pieces of plasterboard floated down, like snow, and Lee had foiled her final shot, but she didn't care anymore, because Jason Chen was falling, not hard and fast like his father had, but falling all the same as he tried to turn and walk for her. His feet were dragging, his arms dangling at his sides, his head swinging. His gun lay on the floor where he had dropped it.

He stood swaying in front of Georgia and said, surprised, "You."

She felt a tingle in her wedding ring finger, her hideous stump, and raised her eyes to his. "Yes," she said. "Me."

Then suddenly she was lifted off her feet and bundled out of there, into the rear courtyard and left along the narrow alley. Lee hustled her along at a rate of knots, and as her senses began to clear, she could hear him groaning with each breath, and beyond his grunts of pain she heard sirens. Not as many as in Brisbane, but then they were in Nulgarra. Maybe two cop cars at most.

"Mum," she gasped.

"Car." Another groan and he staggered, fell to his knees. "Your mum . . . in the car. Waiting . . . for you."

Part of her wanted to burst into a run for his Mitsubishi and her mother, but the other part couldn't bear to leave him. She grabbed his hand, tried to pull him upright. "It's not far! Come on!"

He seemed to gather his strength, and for a moment she thought he really would get to his feet, run with her to the car, but he suddenly slumped and his body went limp, sprawled in the alley. His eyes were closed and his head lolled to one side.

Desperately, she grabbed his wrist. Putting all her weight behind her, she tried to drag him down the alley. She could have been trying to drag a sack of bricks—he barely moved.

"Wake up, Lee! For God's sake, please!"

One siren was still way off, but the other was closing fast.

"Lee!"

She was tugging and pulling at him, half sobbing, half yelling, but he didn't move, couldn't hear her pleas. Then she took in the flood of blood pouring from his chest and suddenly realized he wouldn't be getting up, not for a long time, if at all.

FORTY

Siren screaming down the street. Chirp of rubber. Blue beam of light pulsing over Lee's unconscious form.

The bulky form of a man raced for her, gun drawn, then he stopped.

"Put down your weapon!" he yelled.

She'd forgotten she was still holding the Glock.

"Put it down or I'll fire!"

Georgia bent forward and was about to place her gun on the ground by Lee, when he yelled, "Throw it toward me! Now! Do it!"

She chucked it his way and was standing there with raised hands, palms spread, when he yelled, "On your knees!"

She did as he said. Her bare thigh brushed Lee's arm and she could feel the heat of his skin against hers.

"Hands behind your head!"

Hurriedly, she complied.

The policeman stepped forward, gun extended, his body tense.

"Move away from him."

She wanted to obey, but she couldn't. Obscurely she felt that if she moved away, Lee's life force would move with her, and he'd die.

"Move away!"

Hands behind her head, she stared at the Glock gleaming dully a yard away. She didn't want to shoot a policeman. Besides, even if she got her hands on it, she'd be dead before she fired the thing.

"I'm giving you a final warning! Move away!"

Click.

The policeman stiffened. Georgia stiffened. And if Lee had been conscious, he'd have stiffened too.

Because someone had just primed their gun.

But none of them knew who. Or where. Just that it was close. Really close.

"Sergeant," a man said. "Drop the gun."

"Hey, wait up a minute—"

"Drop it."

The policeman slowly extended his arm and loosened his grip so his gun hung from his fingertips.

"*Now.* Not next week."

The policeman let his gun drop to the ground with a small thud and stood there with his hands hanging slightly from his sides, palms spread like a cowboy readying himself for a duel.

"Georgia. Leave Lee where he is. Walk to me."

She wanted to tear herself away from the heat of Lee's skin, run for her mother and for safety, but she felt unable to move. Like she'd been glued into place.

"Georgia, do it!"

Her senses had refined the heat between her and Lee. It wasn't just heat but the way the delicate hairs of her thigh could feel each hair on his arm. Like little electrodes, they were connected, sparking off one another.

"I think she might be wounded," the sergeant offered, but the other man didn't seem to hear. He started walking down the alley, gun in hand, and as he stepped past the sergeant he looked like he was going to clap the man on the shoulder, but instead he pressed the barrel beneath the policeman's chin and pulled the trigger. Head blown away, the sergeant toppled to the ground, and the man didn't pause a beat, just kept walking purposefully for her and Lee, gun raised, and she knew he'd killed the sergeant so he couldn't be a witness, that he was going to kill her and Lee too.

Spider had shown himself at last.

She didn't have a hope of protecting Lee, but she moved so her body was crouched over his, like an eagle protecting its prey. Legs bunched, ready to spring the instant Spider got close enough.

Blue flashing lights from a window reflected the glitter in his eyes. She felt a shock of recognition.

Chief Inspector Harris said, "Where's Jon Ming?"

Fear pumping, adrenaline rocketing through her, her voice was unsteady when she said, "In Sydney. He went to the AMA. I don't know where he is now, I swear it."

"Lee doesn't look too well." He sounded amused.

"I think he might be dead."

"I'd like to make sure of it."

"Please, let me go. I won't tell anyone I've seen you—"

"You're right about that."

Chief Inspector Harris pointed his gun straight at her.

His bullet would go straight through her and into Lee.

She took a breath and although she knew he was too far away, launched herself at him, a scream erupting from her throat.

Crack!

Georgia was a yard from the chief, still screaming, going for his gun.

Crack!

The chief toppled sideways and crashed against the wall, slid down it, and slumped facedown on the ground.

As he fell, she saw the slender silhouette of her mother against the blue, throbbing light, her hair wild, like a mad-spun halo of hay, running down the alley for her. And then she was skidding to her knees in front of Georgia, her hands cupping Georgia's face, pressing a kiss on the side of her mouth.

"Sweetness," she gasped, "whatever have you been up to, getting us into this mess?"

"Mum, you shot . . . the chief?"

"Not me, sweet. That nice policeman over there did it, but let's not worry about that now. Let's see to your friend, shall we?"

The nice policeman was Daniel. He was standing over the chief, head hanging, gun unsteady and wavering in the strobing blue light. She watched him fumble his pistol into its holster and go to kneel beside the dead sergeant. He put a hand on his chest. His shoulders were shaking. It looked at though he was weeping.

"Daniel," she called across to him, "who is it?"

"Riggs." His voice was choked. "My mate Riggs."

Despite her dislike for the sergeant, Georgia felt a rush of sadness. His poor handsome wife and bouncing baby boy.

Linette began to pull Lee's shirt free, and Georgia bent to Lee's ear. "We got Spider, the man who killed your partner."

———————

It didn't take the ambulance long to get there, maybe ten minutes, and during that time the entire police force of Nulgarra rocked up, all four of them, along with a small crowd of bare-chested men in jeans, their hair in tufts, and women in dressing gowns, all curious to know what had happened.

While the paramedics worked fast on Lee, Linette and Georgia hovering, trying to see what they were doing without getting in their way, Daniel hung back. He hadn't come to her, or asked if she was all right. He appeared to be in some sort of shock, which wasn't too surprising since he'd just killed a senior policeman and lost his friend Riggs. He looked shrunken, miserably pale and defeated.

As Lee was lifted onto a stretcher, Georgia raced across to Daniel. "Are you okay?"

"Lee was . . ." He cleared his throat, expression dazed. "Under-cover."

"He wanted to know who killed his partner."

Daniel swayed slightly and she put out a hand, but he waved her away.

"I thought he'd done it." His voice was very faint.

"You and everyone else." She tried to comfort him. "The only person who knew he hadn't betrayed Sergeant Tatts was Lee himself. And his boss on the PST, from DIMIA."

"I can't get my head around it . . ." He looked sick.

One of the rear ambulance doors started to close, and the same pain she'd felt in her heart when she first saw Lee covered in blood returned. Could she leave Daniel like this? But what about Lee?

"Daniel . . ." The door had shut and the pain was ballooning, almost out of control, her heart being ripped right down the middle. She didn't know what to do.

The second door of the ambulance was closing.

"Daniel, will you be okay? I'm sorry, but I . . ."

He turned a blank face on her, flicked a look at the ambulance, its blue light twirling, then back. He gave her a bitter smile.

"He did save your life, Georgia."

No hesitation. No second thoughts. Georgia belted for the ambulance, leaped for the door, not quite shut, and yanked it open.

"Can I come?" she panted.

The medic glanced over the crowd at Daniel, who gave a nod.

"In you hop, then."

The instant she held Lee's hand warm in hers, stroking the scars over his knuckles, the pain in her heart went away. But not Daniel's face, lit by blue lights from cop cars and the ambulance, his skin white and dry as chalk and his brilliant eyes haunted.

———

The next twenty-four hours were a flurried haze. Georgia and her mother were shuffled from office to office, to and from the hospital to check on Lee, and wherever she went, Linette went with her, and wherever her mum went, Georgia followed. They kept touching each other as though making sure they were alive. And smiling, hugging a lot. Linette looked pretty good considering she'd been a hostage for eleven days. She'd lost weight, but nothing serious. Not unless you raised the thick curly hair on the right side of her head and saw the mass of fresh pink scar tissue and faint traces of old blood clinging behind her ear.

"I did a lot of meditating," she told Georgia when she asked how she'd managed. "And praying for you. Sending you little messages. Did you get any?"

Georgia remembered the sense of her mother calming her near-hysteria on the plane from Brisbane and said, "Yes. They helped a lot, thanks."

Her mum looked pleased.

Now they were sitting in the cop shop, having explained everything to Daniel and his boss from the PST, a tall, reedlike man from Canberra called Patrick. Although Daniel seemed to have recovered his composure and was outwardly calm and businesslike, the shadows beneath his eyes indicated that he'd had little sleep, if any.

She wished she could have been there for him last night, talked him through the whole story one-on-one and without his boss, but her mother had briskly pointed out that Lee was their first concern. Lee had two bullets in him, whereas Daniel . . . He may have not taken any bullets, but he was hurting, she could see. It would, she thought, take him some time to adjust to the fact that the man he'd obviously loathed, been trying to bring down for years, had been one of the good guys all along.

Satisfied with their reports, Patrick and Daniel were winding up, and Georgia and Linette got to their feet, preparing to leave.

"Is Jon okay?" Georgia asked. "Will the gang still try to get him?"

Patrick gave a dry chuckle. "Not much of a gang now Jason Chen and his father are dead. We had intelligence the rest have split. The whole mob has dispersed. Some are heading south, others back to Fuzhou."

"Great," she said. "That is great news." She took a breath. "And what about the Piper's sabotage? Are you sure you can't do anything?"

Daniel looked intensely weary, while Patrick gave an audible sigh. She knew they were getting exasperated. She had asked the same question twice so far.

"The vitamins were vitamins," Patrick said yet again. "Also, Yumuru's got a cast-iron alibi. We've checked and double-checked. Bri Hutchison prepped the aircraft just after one and flew out at two. That leaves a fifty-minute window, during which Yumuru was with

Tilly at the healing center. Unless he had wings and flew himself, there's no way he could have been there."

"Tilly owes him her life," Georgia remarked. "She could be covering for him."

Patrick all but rolled his eyes at her. "But what was Yumuru's *motive*?"

Daniel spoke up, voice tinged with exhaustion. "Georgia, you didn't see anything. You admit it yourself. Are you *sure* it was sabotaged?"

"Yes. Yes!"

"Even Becky admitted—albeit under huge pressure—that Bri flew close to the edge fuel-wise a couple of times—"

"But Lee *saw* it."

"He could have been mistaken, what with everything going on at the time. The plane was up in smoke, wasn't it?"

Patrick started to fidget. "We've interviewed the staff at the aerodrome until they're sick of the sight of us. Jeez, what else can we . . ." Patrick trailed off as he turned to Daniel. "You go and see Lee. Get a statement or something. And make an apology for the department stringing the poor bugger up."

Daniel looked as if he'd swallowed a handful of razor blades, but managed to say, "Yes, Boss."

Patrick then turned to Georgia, hands spread wide. "Best we can do."

Frustrated, Georgia let it drop. They all shook hands, and then she and Linette went outside to Lee's car and headed for the hospital. When they arrived, Georgia expected her mother to come too, but she waved her aside, making her bangles tinkle. "You go on your own this time, darling. You don't want me cluttering up the place. I'll wait here for you."

There was a cop outside Lee's room when she arrived. He was sitting on a hard plastic chair with his arms crossed, long stick-insect legs splayed across the linoleum in front of him, and he was staring at the wall opposite. His expression was one of interminable boredom.

"Hi," she said.

The cop bolted upright, then leaped to his feet. He was incredibly tall and the width of a bamboo pole. Georgia reckoned if she stuck a finger in his chest and pushed, he'd fall over.

"I'm here to visit Lee Denham," she said.

"And you are?"

When she told him, he checked his notebook, then stepped back respectfully and let her go inside.

Lee was asleep. The last time she'd seen him, yesterday evening, he had been lying on his side, drawn and gray. Today, however, she found herself looking at a man with full color in his cheeks sleeping faceup between crisp white sheets. She paused, amazed.

What does it take, she wondered, to bring this guy down? He's been shot and looks as though he's having a snooze. He would, she thought, probably be up within twenty-four hours and jogging across the Atherton Tableland with a bunch of camping gear and two months of supplies on his back.

"Georgia?"

She went to his bedside and looked down at him. "Hey, how are you?"

His eyes were clear and bright. "Better after sleep."

She was grinning insanely.

"You?" he said.

"Busy."

"I can imagine."

She said, "They tell me you're going to be okay."

"Yup."

"Oh, I brought your mobile back." She was about to bring it out of her handbag when he held up a hand.

"I've got another. Keep it."

She was going to ask how she could pay the bill, but the look on his face reminded her of Evie and she hurriedly said, "Okay.

Thanks." Small pause, then she said, "How come there's a policeman outside your room?"

"Precaution."

"But haven't the Chens gone?"

"My boss wanted a safeguard."

"Oh. Right." She glanced at a pile of well-thumbed magazines on his bedside table, then back. "So what are you going to do when you get out of here?"

"Retire."

She blinked. "Did you win the lottery or something?"

"Got paid pretty well for risking my life for so long. Plus, my boss is grateful. Luckily for me, the Aussie government is showing its appreciation in cash terms."

"Won't you miss working for the police?"

He shuffled his torso up the pillow. His chest was encased in heavy white bandages and he had a deep gash on his forehead running into his thick hair. Aside from two bullets, most of his injuries were bruises, which were turning a spectacular black-purple.

"Nope."

"What will you do?"

"I was thinking of sailing around the world. Starting in the Caribbean. I've never been there before and quite fancy a break in the sun."

"You sail?" She was surprised.

"Only had the motor yacht for the image. Chinese gangsters don't respect a sailboat." He shuffled farther upright. "Any news on the sabotage?"

She told him of the police's remorseless skepticism, and that Daniel would be coming to get a statement from him.

"Tell him not to bother. He won't feel comfortable seeing me, and I sure won't either. You still want to get the lowlife that tampered with our plane?"

Through the window she could see a single ambulance and a man in white overalls smoking a cigarette. "Yes, I want them. Daniel said he'd talk to the AAI, but then the boat blew up. I doubt if he'll follow it through now. He's as dubious as the rest of them. Besides, there might be a problem with the insurance, I want to check with Becky—"

"Becky wants them too," he interrupted. "She came in earlier. Nice lady, all up." he gave a frown that made the scar through his eyebrow pucker. "You've a pen? Piece of paper?"

Digging in her bag, she handed him a pen and Mick's cash register receipt from breakfast, watched him scribble down a number. "Ring this number. Chris Cheung. He'll get the AAI investigating on your say-so, no problem. Tell him I reckon the wire-lock was taken off. He's like a pit bull, Chris. He's never let me down yet. If he can't find anything, then I'm an Eskimo."

The man seemed to have fingers in every pie imaginable. Curious, she asked, "How do you know him?"

"*Guangxi,*" he said. "It's a form of debt, of favors loaned."

A prickle of recognition ran over her skin. *Guangxi.* Chief Superintendent Harris had used the word when telling her how *Songtao* had been named. Riggs speaking to a boat captain in Fuling who knew about the sound of wind in a pine forest, then telling the chief, Spider, everything he knew, that Daniel knew.

"Chris Cheung owes you?"

"Big-time. China runs on *guangxi,* you know. Can't move without it. The favor can also be conveyed to a friend or colleague, even inherited."

He went on to explain that some families kept ledgers of *guangxi* so that a grandchild years hence could one day look at that ledger and recall their grandfather's *guangxi* of fifty years ago. Favors. That's all it was, Georgia realized, but it could go on for *generations.*

"So if I have kids," she said, "they'll owe you *guangxi* for saving my life."

"Yup."

She glanced at the receipt before she put it into her bag. Like him, his writing was bold and precise. "What *guangxi* do you have with Chris Cheung?"

"That's between me and him."

Fair enough. Nobody said *guangxi* had to be made public.

"You going back to Sydney?"

"Yes."

"I'll send you a postcard from Barbados, then."

"Lee . . ." She didn't know how to broach the subject that had been bothering her.

"Spill it."

"Those guys you, er . . . talked to when you were trying to find my mother. I heard something about . . . a man being . . . slashed. His stomach . . ." She fixed her gaze on the pile of magazines.

She heard him sigh. "Look, it's a myth. A nasty one, I admit. It started when I was in China. I stumbled on a Dragon Syndicate member who, despite the fact his stomach was in ribbons, had just managed to shoot the RBG man who'd done it. I was trying to help him when the Chens arrived. They thought I'd been torturing him for information, and, in my undercover role as an RBG member, I didn't deny it. I even exaggerated the story, and from then on, all I had to do was show my knife and I got all the answers I wanted.

"Needless to say, guys I interrogated didn't talk about it. They feared retribution, not just from me, but from their colleagues, who wouldn't have appreciated them giving me information without much of a fight."

"What about the guy in Cairns?"

"He got caught in the middle." His expression sobered, became withdrawn. "We used to get on okay, and because of that one fact, the RBG reckoned he was unreliable. So they killed him in a way that set me up for his murder."

Georgia turned when she heard someone come inside. It was Jill Hodges in her pristine uniform, ready to change Lee's bandages.

She told Lee that she'd be back that afternoon, and he said, "Come here, Georgia." He held out a hand.

She put her hand in his, totally unprepared for what he did next. He brought her hand to his mouth. Pressed a kiss in her palm. Closed her fingers around it.

She was quivering all over. No gesture had ever ignited the passion that now seared through her with such power.

He let go of her hand, said, "See you around, then."

She didn't want to go, but Jill Hodges was already beside the bed, asking how her patient was, if he thought he needed something for the pain, so she walked away on legs like jelly, her palm still tingling from his kiss, and just as she stepped through the door and into the corridor, he called out, "Car's all yours, okay?"

FORTY-ONE

It took her a little while to settle down after that. She kept glancing at her palm, wondering how someone's lips could have such an explosive effect on her body and emotions. Her nerves were still in a tense state of alert, her heart bumping every time she thought of him.

Her mother chattered away as Georgia drove them back into town. Gradually she felt her composure return and the tingling in her veins lessen. After she'd dropped her mum at the National she reckoned she'd recovered nicely from the shock of Lee's kiss and headed for her caravan on Kee Beach. She tried Chris Cheung on Lee's mobile, but apparently he was out and wouldn't be back until the following day. She didn't leave a message, just said she'd call back the next morning.

Thinking of making a coffee, she went to the kitchenette, and next to the kettle she saw the piece of paper she'd angrily scrawled on after speaking with the immigration department, a childlike sketch of a man hanging from a noose. God, how could she have forgotten . . .

Immediately she yanked out Lee's mobile and dialed. Zed answered on the second ring.

"Hi, it's Georgia here. We spoke about the Zhong family."

Huge silence.

"Zed?"

"I've been trying to reach you for ages," he said, almost gasping.

"Your phone isn't working or something, it's been driving me mad. Where have you been? It's been over a *week*."

"Sorry. I lost it. Look, did you have any luck keeping Paul in Australia?"

Another silence. Sound of heavy breathing.

"I'm sorry, I've some bad news. Really bad news."

Georgia rested her head on the plastic hood over the stove. *Please, no more.*

"I couldn't stop Paul's deportation. I'm sorry. He left at the weekend. But there's more." Zed's voice gave a tremor. "I've friends in Beijing. I got a call from them this morning. Apparently Paul was arrested at the airport, when he arrived. He didn't have a trial. My friends say he was"—Zed swallowed audibly—"executed two days ago. Shot."

She didn't feel any sensation of shock, just a weird feeling of numbness steeped in the anguish of grief. Just as she'd felt when she'd heard Tom had died. She closed her eyes against the rising tide of tears. Paul had died while she was in bed at Margaret's. While she was relishing those cool, clean sheets, caring murmurs lulling her to sleep, Paul had been executed. Without his wife on the same soil to comfort him, or his daughter, he had died for wanting to be free.

She could feel the warmth of Paul's handshake, hear his laughter, see his scarred face, his lopsided smile, the way he'd held his wife's hand, kissed his daughter's hair.

"Sorry to be the bearer of bad news." Zed cleared his throat. "His family will be able to stay, though. I've sorted it."

———

Georgia cried a long time, and by the time she'd finished mopping up her tears, her mouth and eyes were swollen to twice their normal size.

A knock on the caravan door.

"Georgia? You there?"

Georgia opened the door. India took one look at her puffy face and said, "What is it?"

Georgia told her. India immediately pulled her into her arms. She hadn't thought of India being a huggy person, too aloof and self-controlled for all that, but she gave a damn good hug. Shoulder to shoulder, hip to hip, no holds barred.

"I'm so sorry." India pulled back and peered in her face. "I'd break open a bottle of beer with you but I'm meant to be driving."

Wiping her eyes, Georgia said, "You're going back to Sydney?"

"Yeah. Flying out with SunAir"—she glanced at her watch—"in forty minutes." Her expression turned anxious. "Will you be okay? Would you like me to stay?"

"I'd love you to, but there's no need. I'll be fine."

"I don't have to fly out today."

Georgia managed a wobbly smile, gripped India's wrist and gave it a little shake. "I'm fine, honestly."

"If you're sure . . . I'd better get a hoof on. You'll come see me? Give me a big profile to do for the color supplement? You'll be famous, you know, unable to show your face on the street."

"I'll cope."

India grinned. "When are you going back?"

Georgia thought of Tilly and the piece of paper in her pocket with Chris Cheung's number. Just a few more loose ends. "In a couple of days."

"What about Daniel Carter?" India's expression was mischievous. "You seeing him?"

"I'm meeting him for lunch."

"Now, there's a hot date. Talk about gorgeous."

"It's not a hot date!"

"Sure, and I'm not a reporter about to go and file the second-best story of her life."

———

Georgia drove Lee's Mitsubishi to Mick's Café to find Daniel sitting on a stool in the café window, reading a newspaper.

As she approached, he folded the paper and got to his feet. He's lost weight, she realized. His jeans were loose on his hips and his face had hollowed. She felt an urge to take him to her caravan overlook-

ing Kee Beach and settle him on a sun-lounger with a bottle of wine
while she barbecued a fat sirloin steak, handfuls of sliced onions, and
hot garlic bread.

He looked so *gaunt.*

"Is something wrong?" he said, frowning.

She tried not to look at the way he'd had to tighten his belt,
bunching his jeans into thick denim creases, and said, "I just heard
Paul Zhong got executed."

"Who's Paul Zhong?" Georgia turned to see Mick in his blue overalls looking at her with raised eyebrows.

"Nobody from round here," she replied.

Shrugging, Mick went back to scrubbing a big metal pot with a
bunch of steel wool.

"He was executed?" Daniel said. "Jesus . . . what happened?"

She ran through what Zed had told her.

"That's terrible. His poor wife . . ."

Suddenly distracted, he slid off his stool and put a hand on his
front pocket and withdrew his mobile, studied the readout. "Won't be
a tick."

Turning away, he said, "Hi, sweetheart . . . Yes, I miss you too, but
look, I'm in a meeting right now . . . Yes, love you too. Yes, I'll be
back soon. Promise I'll read it to you, cover to cover, and then some
more."

Mobile back in his pocket, he turned back to her. "Sorry about
that."

"Is Tabby okay?"

"Nothing that a dose of Beatrix Potter won't fix." Glancing at the
laminated menu behind Mick, who was still scrubbing his pot, he
added, "Do you feel like something to eat?"

With Paul's execution hanging over her, she didn't feel like eating,
but she said, "I think we should." She gave him a wry smile. "My
shorts feel like they're going to fall off any minute, and your jeans . . .
well, I've seen them fit better."

He grinned, and as usual, her stomach lurched. She heard his
voice from the night before—*He did save your life, Georgia*—and saw

herself flying to Lee, his old enemy who wasn't anymore, her heart torn down the center.

"Burgers are good for weight gain," he said. "I'm planning on the cheese special. Lots of fat and mayo." He went to the counter, unfolding his wallet. "Double cheeseburger for me and . . ."

"The all-day brekky, sausage, beans, eggs, bacon, and fries."

While Mick prepped their food, Daniel came back with a couple of cans of cola, popped his tab, took a long drink. Then he said, "So what are you up to for the rest of the day? Heading back home?"

"Not yet. I'm going to Dutch's. I want to tell him everything that's happened. He's going to bush-roast a barramundi, but he did warn me he'd have to catch it first."

They talked about Dutch briefly, discussed their favorite ways of cooking fish, grilled or fried, with garlic or without, and when their meal arrived, Georgia took one look at her eggs, sunny side up, the crispy fries and bacon, and her appetite kicked in. They didn't speak much as they ate, which she reckoned was a good thing as she could concentrate on her fantastic, greasy, full-on breakfast without interruption.

She was wiping her plate clean with a fry when he said, "I ought to see Lee this afternoon. I know we owe him an apology, but . . ." He trailed off and picked at a stray thread hanging from his shirt.

"He said not to bother. He knew it would make you uncomfortable. He seems fine with it."

"Oh. Right." Pulling his penknife from his pocket, he clicked open a small blade and cut the thread free, rolled it between his fingers. "So when do you leave for Sydney?"

"I'm not leaving. Not until I find the saboteur."

His face smoothed into neutral, just like when they'd first met in Mrs. Scutchings's kitchen a fortnight ago. His cop face. "Georgia, didn't you hear what Patrick said? There's no *evidence*."

She leaned forward, her tone fierce. "Bri and Suzie died. I want whoever did it, no matter what."

"You're like a dog with a bone once you get started." He was leaning back, half smiling, but the neutral cop expression was still there. "I kind of admire your doggedness. You'd make a great police officer."

She gave a startled laugh. "No thanks!"

"Seriously, Georgia." His expression turned from neutral cop to concerned friend. "Don't you think enough is enough? I mean, it's not as if the insurance company isn't paying out."

"That's not the point!"

"But nobody's in the frame. If Yumuru's vitamins had turned out to be an antibiotic, then it would be a different story, but as it is . . ."

"What if he planned it? Made sure I took nothing but a sample of vitamins to absolve him?"

Daniel scrunched up his paper napkin, tossed it to one side. "You're saying that Yumuru knew you were going to come into his healing center one day, could be any day of the week, any day of the month, to trot into Tilly's room and grab the syringe?"

"Well, not exactly . . ." She hadn't thought it through.

He rolled his shoulders and gave a heavy sigh. "It's really bugging you, isn't it?"

"Yes."

She was about to tell him about Chris Cheung when he suddenly seemed to come to a decision and put his elbows on the counter, steepled his fingers in front of his face.

"Okay." He dropped his hands, looked at her direct. "So long as I get Becky's permission, I'll start an investigation."

"Oh, Daniel, thank you."

"But for God's sake, don't tell anyone. Least of all Patrick. If he thinks I'm wasting time . . ."

"I won't say a word."

"Meantime, I think you should go home. Take a break."

"No."

"Jesus, Georgia." He leaned forward, expression earnest. "Will you just take a look at yourself? You're obviously at the end of your rope. Your clothes are hanging off you, you look as though you haven't slept in weeks . . . You've been under enormous strain lately.

Don't you think you need a change of scenery to get your health into gear?"

"My health is just fine, thank you very much."

She thanked him for lunch, then grabbed her handbag and stalked out of Mick's Café without looking back.

—————

Half an hour later Georgia walked toward Lee's room, and despite her relief that at last Daniel was going to help, she was still angry. So she was at the end of her rope, was she? Well, talk about the pot calling the kettle black considering his newly haggard and wasted form. He should try a change of scenery for his own health, dammit.

Giving a brief wave to Dr. Ophir, who'd stitched the palm of her hand after the crash, she strode down the hospital corridor, wondering where the stringy policeman guarding Lee's room had gone. No chair. No interminably bored expression. She knocked on Lee's door, and entered on a woman's bright "Come in."

Georgia pushed open the door, and stopped dead.

The bed was being made and Lee wasn't there, nor was the pile of well-thumbed magazines. The nurse making the bed was Jill Hodges, who greeted Georgia with a sympathetic grimace.

"I know. We're all a bit gobsmacked too. One minute he's here, the next he's gone. He left a couple of hours ago. He didn't say anything about where he was going."

"But what about his wounds?" Georgia protested. "Surely he ought to be in hospital?"

"Not according to him."

Grabbing her mobile, she checked that Lee's number was still stored on her phone from the night he'd rescued her mother, and dialed. A woman's monotone answered: "Sorry, this number is unavailable. Please check the number and try again." She suddenly remembered him saying, "Car's all yours," and felt a clutch of panic beneath her breastbone. He'd already had a plan . . . he'd been telling her the Mitsubishi really *was* all hers. He knew he'd be leaving.

"Did he go by taxi?" She was almost gasping. "Did someone pick him up? Did you see?"

If Jill Hodges found her questions odd, she didn't show it. "A black Mercedes. One of those with tinted windows. Big bugger of a car, I have to say."

Not one of the Chen gang, surely? she thought. They'd all dispersed south or fled to Fuzhou. Maybe one of Lee's dodgy mates collected him. Or he'd rented a flashy car. Perhaps it had something to do with *guangxi*, some bloke in the area owing Lee a long-term debt of favors.

Confused, bereft, she looked around the sterile hospital room looking for any clue where he might have gone.

She said, pleading, "I didn't even say good-bye."

Jill Hodges dug in her pocket. "He left something for you."

She dropped something heavy and metallic in Georgia's palm.

It was his Tag Heuer watch.

FORTY-TWO

Emotions jammed down, watch shoved halfway up her arm—the steel-brushed bracelet would have to be altered by a jeweler—Georgia splashed Lee's Mitsubishi across Cassowary Creek. No raging torrent to combat this time, just a trickle of clear water over soft mud and rocks. Almost two weeks had passed since she had driven from Tom's funeral to SunAir. Two weeks during which she had learned that when someone is shot they don't fly backwards like in the movies, they simply crumple to the ground, that when a bullet flies past you there's no whistling sound but a crack like a bullwhip.

She'd learned to lie, to fire a gun, to kill a man, and how far she would go to honor her loyalty.

I went a long way for loyalty, she thought, accelerating down the graded road. I lied through my teeth to protect my mother and Lee. And I'd do the same all over again if I had to.

She was nearing the aerodrome when Lee's mobile rang, and she nearly drove off the road in her haste to answer it.

"Lee?" she said, almost breathless.

"Sweet, it's me."

Shocked at the strength of her disappointment, she said, "Oh. Hi, Mum."

"Is everything all right?"

Jinking right to avoid a pothole, she said, "Everything's fine."

"So why do you sound sad?"

"I'm not sad! It's just . . . um . . ." She couldn't put it into words, her intense feeling of loss. Perhaps she'd always feel like that about the man who'd hacked her free from a burning plane, taken it upon himself to find her mother, got shot for his trouble, then kissed the palm of her hand before walking out of the hospital without saying good-bye.

There was a small tapping noise, which Georgia took to be her mother's earrings swinging against the receiver. "Are you still going to Dutch's tonight?"

"Yup. I'll be back tomorrow. Say late afternoon. I fancy trying my hand at some fishing myself. Maybe I'll come back with a barra-mundi for you."

"Sweet, that would be lovely! I haven't had barra for ages."

They arranged to meet at the National the following evening and catch up on news then, maybe decide when they would head south.

Hanging up, Georgia swung the car down SunAir's drive and parked, then climbed outside. After the sterile air-conditioning of Lee's car the air felt thick and hot as burning lava, and for a second she doubted there was any oxygen to breathe. Pausing for a moment, she rested her hand on the scalding flank of the car, concentrating on the smells of aviation fuel and cut grass. Christ, it was *so hot*.

Straightening up, she made her way across the parking lot for the SunAir offices. She could see a neat row of light aircraft parked on the near side of the runway. A pilot was leaning inside the cockpit of a Piper, studying a map spread on the seat. Another Piper was preparing to take off, and when the engine note rose and the plane began its lurching, bounding gait along the runway, she had a violent sensation of déjà vu and her bowels abruptly turned to water. She rushed to the ladies', catching a brief sight of Becky's alarmed face watching her through the office window, and when she came out, Becky was on the steps.

"You all right, darl'?"

Becky didn't look much better than when she'd last seen her, and her blue overalls hung from her like an elephant's baggy skin.

"Fine, thanks," Georgia replied. What was a sudden attack of diarrhea compared to losing your husband?

"You flying anywhere?"

Georgia climbed the steps. "I just wanted to check something, about the day of the crash, that's all."

Becky led the way inside. "Check what?"

"Records of the day. Who was flying when and where."

Becky paused halfway across the office. A beam of sunlight hit the side of her face, making the shadows beneath her eyes deeper, even more hollowed. She said, "You still looking for the bugger who killed my Bri?"

"You bet."

"How can I help?"

"Um . . . did you tell the insurance company you thought it was sabotage?"

Becky looked away, "Darl', I'm sorry."

Georgia sighed. No wonder the insurance company hadn't been poking about the wreckage. They *didn't know* about the sabotage theory. They'd have taken the initial police report of pilot error at face value.

"I just thought . . ." Becky was twisting her hands. "That if you came up with something, well, then I'd know Bri was in the right, and we could tell the kids together . . ."

And still get the insurance money, Georgia thought. She couldn't blame Becky, not really, for wanting both: Bri unofficially absolved for her and her kids, *and* a new airplane.

"It's okay, Becky. I understand."

Becky gave her a mixed look of shame and relief.

"But should I find the saboteur and they're arrested . . ."

"You do it, love. I shouldn't have tried to play both sides."

"Okay. I'd like to see the records for the second of March. The day of the crash."

"Sure thing," Becky replied. The phone started to ring, and before she answered it Becky pointed at the old booking-out sheets stacked neatly on the bench beneath the window.

Georgia flipped through the sheets to Saturday.

VH CAT Piper PA28. Pilot: Matt Hayes. Passengers: Ronnie Chen, Suzie Wilson, Lee Denham. Estimated departure: 2 PM for Cairns. Returning date, March 3, estimated time, 3 PM.

VH DAM Cheetah. Pilot: Sergeant Daniel Carter. Passengers: Sergeant Riggs, Constable Cassell. Estimated arrival: 12:30 PM.

Becky was taking what sounded like a complicated itinerary from someone in Mackay when Georgia flipped to the previous page.

VH DAM Cessna 150. Pilot: Peter York. Passengers: Christina and John Palmer, Marc Wheeler. Estimated arrival: 1 PM from Brisbane. Intended landings: Townsville, Rockhampton.

Georgia went cold inside. Her scalp felt tight, her breathing unsteady. Marc Wheeler. The man who now owned Quantum Research and who used Suzie's address.

On the right-hand side of the page were the pilot's initials and Becky's, confirming the paperwork and the Cessna's arrival time of 12:50 PM. Marc Wheeler had flown into the Nulgarra Aerodrome an hour before Bri had flown out.

She waited until Becky finished her call and said, "Who's Marc Wheeler?"

Becky stopped making a note in a big diary in front of her and looked up. "Marc who?"

"Marc Wheeler. He's a passenger who flew in that day, with"—she checked the pilot's name—"Peter York."

Becky frowned. "I know Pete, but not Marc Wheeler. Probably some tourist."

"But it's not the tourist season . . . Did the police check up on Marc Wheeler at all, do you know?"

"No idea." Becky was still frowning. "First time I've taken the bloke's name in, to be honest. You think he had something to do with Bri's plane?"

Georgia walked across to Becky, leaned her palms on her desk. "Yes, I do. Please, can you remember anything about that particular flight?"

Becky squinted at the ceiling, thinking hard. Then she shook her head. "I'm sorry, darl'. All I know is that the Cessna came in pretty much when it was supposed to. Why don't you try Pete? He might know something?"

Becky flipped through a Rolodex, and Georgia pulled out Lee's mobile. As Becky read out Pete's number, Georgia dialed, to be met with the usual woman's monotone. "The mobile you have tried may be switched off. Please try again later."

"Is there anyone else who might have seen Pete land? What about Matt? The guy who was supposed to fly our plane. Is he around?"

"Sure, he's in the hangar." Becky gave her a tired smile. "Go for it."

———————

Inside, the hanger smelled of engine oil and coffee. There was a Cessna with an engine cowling raised and various tools spread on a greasy mat below. Two men in their early thirties were sitting on a couple of deck chairs set to one side, drinking from a Thermos. One wore a red shirt hanging over his shorts, the other a pair of overalls.

As she approached, she realized she had seen the man dressed in overalls before. It was Rog, the barman at the National.

"Hi," she said.

Rog gave a nod but didn't meet her eyes.

"We'd offer you some, but we're all out of cups," Red Shirt said, looking regretful.

"That's okay. I just want to ask you a couple of questions. About the day the plane crashed."

Both men's faces immediately became guarded.

"I'm Georgia Parish. I was—"

"Hey," said Red Shirt. "You was on the plane, wasn't you? With Bri."

"Yes."

"We didn't have anything to do with it," said Rog, suddenly looking aggressive. "We didn't do nothing."

"I know you didn't," Georgia said soothingly. "I just wanted to ask why the pilot on the booking-out sheet didn't fly that day. Why Matt Hayes was on the flight plan but Bri wasn't."

Red Shirt bit his lip. "Look, I was going to fly to Cairns but Bri decided he wanted to instead. He's the boss, I let him. Simple."

"You're Matt?"

"Yeah."

"Did you see anyone that morning? Anyone—"

"It was just us here," Matt said. "We didn't see nobody."

"Surely you would have seen Becks and Bri that morning?"

"Course we saw fucking Becks and Bri. I meant nobody *else*."

Georgia wanted to turn around and walk away, but she mentally gritted her teeth and persisted. "Maybe you saw someone who didn't appear out of place? A delivery guy, perhaps, dropping off an engine part or something? A passenger in the wrong place?"

Rog got to his feet, went and picked up a wrench off the floor by the Cessna. "We didn't see nobody, okay? If you don't mind, we've work to do."

Matt glanced at his watch, surprised, and Georgia realized Rog had just cut short their coffee break.

"Jesus, when's the baby due, Rog?" said Matt, but Rog already had his head under the engine cowling.

"Matt. Give me a hand, would you, mate?"

Ignoring Rog, Matt poured himself another coffee, grumbling about workaholics under his breath while Georgia walked over to Rog and stood close.

"Are you hiding something from me?"

Rog was tightening a screw on a pipe that looked to her as if it didn't need tightening. He didn't look up.

Steadily, she said, "Bri's Piper was sabotaged."

"Load of old cobblers," muttered Rog. "Bri's well-known for flying close to the edge, time to time. It's Becky, ain't it, putting you up to this?"

"No. It was the copilot. He saw the fuel pipe had been loosened. *Deliberately* loosened."

Rog twisted around, dropped the wrench to the ground, and picked up another, smaller wrench. Went to work on another bolt.

"You saw something, didn't you?" she insisted. "What was it? Someone fiddling with our Piper before we took off? Did you see them? Who was it?"

Rog spun around, wrench clenched in his hand. For the first time, he looked at her straight. Something was crawling at the back of his eyes. Fear, she thought with a little shock. Despite his aggressive stance, the mechanic was scared stiff.

"Just bugger off, would you?"

"Marc Wheeler," she said. "Has he threatened you? Threatened you not to tell anyone what you saw?"

He licked his lips. "If you don't fuck off right now, I'm going to call the . . ." She thought he was going to say cops, but he amended it to, "harassment board. For stopping me doing my job. So get out of my face, and don't come back."

"You heard the man." Matt was behind her. "Time you moved your pretty ass out of here."

Georgia walked away from Rog and Matt, then paused, turned around. "You'd better get yourselves ready, guys. Because this is just the start. I'm going to be getting the Air Accident Investigators in tomorrow, and nothing's going to stop them bringing you in and interrogating you until you crack. If you continue lying, you'll get sent to jail for obstructing a murder inquiry."

As she stepped outside she heard the clang of metal against concrete, then Rog say wearily, "Oh, fuck."

FORTY-THREE

Georgia left the aerodrome jittery with excitement. She couldn't wait to speak to Chris Cheung, get him to question Rog, find out what he saw. Marc Wheeler maybe, tampering with the Piper.

Bri's voice in her head. *Find 'em for me. Swear it.*

Becky. *Go catch the bloody bugger.*

Suzie. *I don't want to die. Not yet.*

With one hand on the steering wheel, she pressed redial on her mobile. This time a message machine kicked in. "Please leave a message," said a man's voice. "I'll call you back."

Georgia left her name and number for the pilot, Peter York, then tucked the mobile under her left thigh and downshifted into third for the approaching bend, accelerating just after the apex. The breeze was hot and moist on her skin, the heavy smell of rotting leaves all-pervasive. She'd left the Mitsubishi's windows open for the return trip, wanting to avoid the numbing dead weight of heat that had almost poleaxed her when she'd arrived at the aerodrome. It was all very well having air-conditioning, but when the body suddenly has to adjust to a thirty-degree hike, it saps the energy.

Cruising for the northwest side of Nulgarra, she reached across and pressed on the radio, expecting a hail of modern rock or news, only to be met with a small click, then the smooth husky tones of a woman singing a cross of jazz and country and pop. Melodious, warm as honey, the woman's voice sounded like the rainforest might sing. Sultry, melting, full of darkness and seductive promise.

It was a CD, she realized. Lee's. Hot air tugging her hair, she didn't pop the CD to see who was singing. She simply drove his car, leather hugging her body, and listened to the words.

> *Feeling tired*
> *In the sunset*
> *The long day is over . . .*
> *But you'll be on my mind*
> *Forever.*

Jesus. Had he left the CD ready to play on purpose? Was this his way of saying good-bye?

If it was, it sucked.

Midafternoon and she was pulling Lee's Mitsubishi into the Lotus Healing Center's parking lot and looking around, praying she wouldn't bump into Yumuru. She felt ashamed for stealing his syringe, and even more ashamed that she was still checking up on him.

Trotting quickly up the steps, she peered cautiously into reception. No Yumuru. Great.

"Is Tilly still around?" she asked the receptionist.

"She goes home tomorrow, but right now she's in the communal living room. She'll be glad to see you. It'll give her a break."

Georgia walked along the corridor with its tatami mats to find Tilly right where the receptionist said she'd be, tapping on a keyboard in front of a laptop computer. When she entered, Tilly glanced over her shoulder and said, "Hi, Georgia."

"Hi."

"What's another word for pain?" she asked, turning back to her gleaming blue screen. "I've already used agony, torment, suffering, and ache."

"Um . . . torture?"

"Ooh, yes. That'll do nicely."

"What are you doing?"

"Writing an article about my experience. I'm getting five hundred bucks." She sounded proud.

"Well done, you."

"Take a pew." Tilly waved a hand at the sofa beneath a tall window, which overlooked the fig tree being strangled by a vine, tapped seven letters on the keyboard, and swung around.

In fourteen days, Tilly was a changed woman. From an exhausted skeleton reeking of dead flesh, she had full color in her skin and her hair was freshly washed, luxuriant and flowing around her shoulders. Energy sparkled in her eyes.

"I'm going home tomorrow," she said.

"That is seriously great."

"The kids are holding a party. Big banner and all. Seafood barbie, lots of beer and cake. Even my in-laws are going to be there, all the way from Dismal Creek. Can't wait, but."

"I'm glad for you." Georgia's tone was sincere. "Really I am."

"So what're you doing here? Checking up on my progress?"

"Yes. I guess so."

Tilly was grinning, almost wriggling in her chair, like a kid who couldn't suppress a secret. She said, "You swiped 'Muru's syringe, didn't you?"

Pause. Beat.

"Yes," Georgia admitted.

"What'd you find?" She was almost bubbling with glee.

"Vitamins."

"Yeah. Vitamins." Tilly looked smug.

"But he has been using an antibiotic on you," Georgia said.

The smug look vanished. "You saying he didn't heal me?"

"That's right."

"Well, you're wrong." Her jaw was stuck out aggressively.

Georgia had just decided to tackle her head-on, when her mobile rang. "Sorry," she said.

Tilly shrugged, turning back to her computer like a sulky child. "Hello?"

"Pete here. Pete York. Returning your call."

"Thanks. Thanks a lot." Georgia got to her feet and walked to the far end of the living area, looked through the window at a vista with no laundry strung between the palms, no chicken sheds or flowering plants, no guitars strumming out of key or people chattering. Just five-star pristine rainforest all the way. "Look, it's about the day Bri Hutchison's plane crashed." She quickly filled the pilot in that she'd been on the aircraft, and was looking to find the saboteur.

"Yeah. I've heard the rumors. Poor old Becks has been doing her nut. It's bloody awful. Anything I can do to help?"

"I just wanted to know about a passenger on your flight. A Marc Wheeler. Whether you knew him or not."

"Nope. Didn't know none of them."

"Um . . . I'm sorry if this sounds like a strange question, but what did Marc Wheeler look like?"

"God. Don't know about that. I take people all over, all the time."

She gave him a few seconds, then said, "Bri crashed that day. Surely you must recall—"

"Suit. He had a suit on. I remember it seemed odd, given his hair. Ponytail and a suit. Seemed odd to me."

Small jump of her nerves.

"Did he wear glasses?"

"Couldn't say."

"What about his hands? It may sound weird, but hands are amazingly identifiable—"

"Hey, you're right." Pete sounded surprised. "He had glasses. Wanted to wear a headset and was fiddling about, trying to make them comfortable. Complained it wasn't like it used to be in the army or something. Like we fly crap in comparison."

"Was he white?" she asked.

"What?"

"Was he *white*?"

"Er . . . Well, sort of. Bit of mixture, I'd say. Not that I've anything against mixtures, if you know what I mean. I love my Thai takeout as much as the next bloke."

Mixed-race. Ponytail. Glasses. Ex-army.

Yumuru.

Trembling a little, she finished the call. Tilly, she saw, had abandoned all pretense of working at her computer and was watching her closely.

"What the hell was all that about?" Tilly asked.

Pushing her mobile into her pocket, Georgia walked across the room, stood over Tilly, and looked down.

"That was a man who gave me definitive evidence that Yumuru flew into the aerodrome just before Suzie, Bri, Lee, and I flew out. Yumuru's also known as Marc Wheeler. And funnily enough, Suzie used to own a successful company called Quantum Research, but now that she's dead, Marc Wheeler does. My bet is Yumuru killed Suzie to keep the antibiotic to himself."

Tilly's jaw dropped. "You *what*?"

"And you're his alibi for the second of March, when we crashed. But Yumuru wasn't here at all, was he? He was at the aerodrome, sabotaging my aircraft."

"No way! He was here! I swear!" Tilly exclaimed, but Georgia could see the tiny pearls of sweat forming on her forehead.

"Not according to an employee at the aerodrome who *saw* him." Patting her bag, she added, "And when Chris Cheung from Canberra gets here, he'll be organizing some arrests. Chris is like a pit bull. He won't even hesitate."

"Chris Cheung?" Tilly was shifting in her seat, squirming in distress. "Who the hell's he?"

Ignoring her question, Georgia said, "You'd better do some serious thinking, Tilly. About what'll happen if you lie in court, and get found out. Which you will. You really want to be taken to jail and away from your kids?"

Georgia walked to the door, leaving Tilly sitting there aghast, her mouth open.

"I'll be back tomorrow," Georgia said, tone hard, "to see if you change your story."

———————

Georgia swung out of the healing center parking lot, foot hard on the gas. Yumuru. It was Yumuru. It had to be. Peter York had all but told her he'd seen Yumuru with his head beneath the Piper's engine cowling with a bolt cutter, slicing the wire-lock to let the Piper's fuel jettison silently into the rainforest below.

She was barreling down the drive so fast that she had to jam on the brakes when a car swept from the opposite direction. There was a band of blue lights across its roof, the number twenty-two sprayed on its hood. Shit, a cop car was just what she didn't need to meet as she sped along a private driveway.

Heaving the Mitsubishi aside, she heard the clatter of branches against the car's flank, felt it judder as the tires bounced over edges of tree roots, and as the police car drove past, she looked around, hand raised to apologize, but it was already gone, just a small cloud of dust trailing in the sun to tell where it had been. Men with a mission, cops. Unless they were bored, that is. Then they'd give you hell for even thinking about running a red light, even if it was three o'clock in the morning with no traffic about.

Pushing the cop car out of her mind, she pressed on, turning left out of the healing center's gates and powering north. She had a lot to think and talk about, and she was heading to the right place for both—the Cape Archer National Park.

FORTY-FOUR

I'd never have thought it of him. He was Suzie's mate. Her *mate.*" Dutch was shaking his big battered head, baffled. "You don't do that stuff to a mate."

She took a long pull of her ice-cold beer. "Well, he did. He was at the airfield. And he owns Quantum Research now Suzie's dead. He'll make a packet out of the antibiotic."

Dutch swung his head to the river. Looked past his aluminum boat swaying in the shallows and at the shroud of rainforest rasping with insects beneath the late-afternoon sky. "Bloody money," he said. "It always gets to folks in the end."

Heaving himself upright, he tipped his head back and swallowed the remainder of his beer. He gave a small belch, then muttered, "Sorry."

Georgia gave an acknowledging nod. She knew all too well how fizzy the beer was, especially when cold and emptied into a warm, empty stomach.

"You're up for barra?" he asked, plopping his empty beer bottle on the veranda.

"You bet."

"Give me an hour. I'll have a whopper by then. Guaranteed."

She raised her beer in a salute as he went, broad legs bowed, shoulders sloping sharply from his neck like a boxer, big bare feet making hardly any sound as he walked for his boat. He pushed the boat out and hopped aboard, then pulled the engine cord. The angry choking cut through the silence, nothing like *Songtao*'s deep, powerful, smooth roar. It was like comparing a knat with a speeding falcon.

A sudden image of a hawk in the sky, looking out for her . . . No hawk here, she told herself, trying to ignore the feeling of regret. It's long gone now, heading for warmer, more welcome winds.

Dutch sped the boat west and upriver, sitting in the stern, legs spread, hand sure on the tiller, his fishing gear stowed by his feet, along with his shotgun and his umbrella for stroking crocs' eyes shut. He'd told her he fished for barramundi with a fly, but she wasn't sure she believed him. She could imagine him simply chucking a hand grenade in the river and grabbing whatever came to the surface. But what the hell, if he returned with a fresh barramundi, she wasn't going to be picky. Her lunch with Daniel felt like days ago. What she needed was a pile of vegetables. The last time she'd eaten anything green was . . . Her mind jumped back in time to the small pile of salad on the edge of her paper plate at Tom's wake. She hadn't felt like eating then. She remembered shoveling her meal into the garbage can out the back, looking over her shoulder in case anyone noticed.

No veggies for fourteen days. No wonder she felt tired. A mozzie droned past her ear and she suddenly saw a monster one on her ankle, almost swelling as it sucked hard on her blood. The one square inch of skin she hadn't drenched in Deet and the bastard had found it. She bent forward to slap the mozzie dead against her skin and at the same time—

Crack!

She didn't even hesitate. One second she was sitting on the steps of Dutch's veranda, the next she was sprawled in dirt, clawing her way beneath the house, between the pilings, scrambling for cover. She'd been shot at! Jesus! Not again.

Crack!

A thunk of wood behind her. Near her feet. She burrowed deeper, heading for the center of the house, using her elbows and knees, desperate for cover. The taste of earth was in her mouth, stale mulchy air

in her lungs, and her breath was loud in her ears as she scrabbled, trying to get away, waiting for the next crack of gunfire.

Eventually she became aware of the silence and paused to listen.
Couldn't hear anything above the beating of her heart, her ragged
gasps. She took a deep breath into her belly and let it go. Took another breath, concentrating on filling her belly, let that one go. Felt
her breathing steady, her heartbeat slow.

She crouched under the house, unmoving, alert.

No sound reached her. Nothing.

Her mind raced over the past few hours. Who knew she'd be here
with Dutch? What she'd said to India, Daniel, Becky, and Tilly. Yumuru, she thought. Yumuru's talked to Tilly. He knows I'm onto him.
He wants to silence me before I get Chris Cheung up here. He's taking one hell of a chance that I haven't already rung.

A small sound behind her. Low down. At her level. Like a mole,
unable to see but aware of danger, she began to shuffle away from the
sound. Then she heard the tiniest of clicks. A wet, metallic click she
knew all too well.

Georgia bolted for the other side of the house. Head down,
mouth in gravel, knees and legs swimming, pumping for the other
side, waiting for the bullet in her thighs, her shins, her back, her
spine . . .

CRACK!

Her whole body jerked at the sound, loud in the confined space—
he hasn't hit me, he hasn't hit me—and she was still swarming under
Dutch's house, elbows and feet digging hard and propelling her forward, and the next instant she was bursting outside, warm fresh air
against her face, the darkness of the rainforest beckoning. Sweet darkness, a blanket to hide behind. No thought of snakes or spiders or
crocs, just belting for the forest and away from a white-hot bullet that
would blow her apart.

Tearing across the small expanse of clearing surrounding Dutch's
house, she raced into the forest. Crashing and stumbling against a
tree, swinging around it, grazing her palm, uncaring. Branches scouring her face, grabbing her clothes. Creepers curling around her feet

and she's trying not to yelp—they feel like human hands pulling her down—and she's yanking herself free and trying to run through the rainforest, but it's like running through a dense hedge of gorse, thorns pulling at her, holding her back, but she keeps running, forcing her way through a dark maze of forest and she can't hear anything but the sound of leaves and branches crackling and breaking around her, and her breathing . . . panting desperately like a deer on the run . . .

Georgia paused in the gloom of the rainforest, trying to steady herself, hear if anything was behind her.

Silence.

Cautiously she crept forward to a mangrove tree with a solid girth, at least two yards in diameter. Walking around the tree, she studied its branches. There was one angling her way, a big, heavy slab of wood, and, looking up, she saw another sturdy branch, higher, where no one would look. She hoped.

Easy, she thought. I'll just climb up there, be out of the way and safe until Dutch returns. No problem.

Ten minutes later—she knew how long it took thanks to Lee's swanky Tag Heuer—she was still struggling to get up the tree. Easy to look at a couple of branches and think you can climb the thing, she thought, but in real life, it just wasn't the same, dammit.

She was barely two yards from the ground, hands clutching bark, her knees clamped to the tree trunk, when she heard the small snap of a twig breaking nearby. Instantly, she stilled.

Rustle of what sounded like a soft leather belt being dragged against leaves.

She reckoned it was a goanna, a big lizard tracking through the forest, but couldn't be sure, so she waited. Listened to insects humming, frogs croaking. The sound of leather on leaves stopping and starting.

Definitely a lizard, she thought, and gripped the upper branch in both hands and half swung, half heaved herself up there, throwing her right leg over pitted wood, feeling the bare skin of her inner thigh catch against the rough bark and trying to stifle her whimpers and groans as she rescraped her thigh and opened its grazes from piling out of the cop shop after Lee.

Another heave and she was nearly there, but not quite. In the balance, so to speak, she was hanging from one knee and one arm, just as she was when Jon rocketed through the gate of Quantum Research on his superbike.

The faint buzz of an engine reached her.

She paused, listening.

The buzz grew louder, and she recognized the angry clatter of Dutch's outboard motor approaching.

Crack! Crack!

Georgia bolted upright, her body catapulting straight onto the branch. Next second she was balancing on top of it, arms reaching up for the next branch, and she was scrambling onto the next, hauling herself arm over leg up the tree, with no thought of how she'd get down. She had no urge but to climb, to get out of sight.

Huddled high in the tree, knees clamping each side of a branch, she leaned back against the trunk, sweating, her heart knocking. No sound of an outboard motor. No more shots. Just a rainforest shocked into silence.

What had happened?

Must keep absolutely still, she told herself. For as long as it takes. Think tree. Think branch. You are a leaf. You are part of the rainforest. Part of nature. You don't breathe. You don't think. You are a part of this tree. He'll never see you.

FORTY-FIVE

After a few minutes she had calmed and became aware that the sounds of the rainforest had returned. Insects resumed their humming and birds were calling as they flew from branch to branch.

Through the trees she could just make out the gleam of the river sliding east. She thought she'd run dead straight into the forest but she'd obviously made a loop because she was remarkably near the water.

Oh God. Her mind suddenly kicked into action. The shots fired had been from a pistol, not Dutch's shotgun. Had Yumuru shot Dutch? Yumuru wouldn't want any witnesses. Nobody knew what she'd found out today, except Tilly, who was on Yumuru's side. Sweet Jesus. Without herself or Dutch, who would now call Chris Cheung? She'd have to pray that if she vanished into thin air, Daniel would push aside his doubts about the aircraft's sabotage and continue the investigation.

She could see the headline already: BOATING ACCIDENT KILLS TWO. BODIES FOUND DISMEMBERED BY CROCODILES.

Leaning her head against the trunk of the tree, she gazed at a wispy beard of lichen on the branch above. She knew Yumuru wouldn't leave until she was dead.

———

Georgia knew she was in trouble when the sun began to sink. Aside from an awkward moment when she'd had to pee—first time for everything, she told herself—she had been on her branch for two hours and she was aching and itchy and stinking with sweat and Deet, and nothing, absolutely nothing since she'd heard the pistol shots had distracted her, aside from a turquoise butterfly the size of a saucer fluttering past.

Brilliant, just brilliant. Running into the rainforest seemed like a great idea, and it was, for a complete idiot. It would be night in under an hour, and it would be so black she wouldn't be able to see her hand in front of her face, not unless there was a full moon, which there wasn't; it had been waning when she blasted out of Nulgarra on *Songtao*. So now what? Was she going to sit in this horrendously uncomfortable tree all night? She'd fall asleep and then fall out of the damn thing, and straight into the jaws of a goddamn crocodile . . .

What else, then? Climb down now at dusk, just the time of day when the crocs come alive, when their blood has been warmed by the day's heat and they're in hunting mode? And what about Yumuru? Where was he? Army-trained, special jungle forces for all she knew, he could be tracking her panic-stricken route through the forest. Waiting for her anywhere.

Georgia shuffled her lower back against the trunk of the tree. I shall stay where I am, she decided, until dawn. I have no intention of getting eaten by a croc at prime time. I'll wait until daybreak, when a croc's blood is cold and they're reluctant to move, then I'll slip through the forest to Lee's car, and drive until I get to Sydney. There I'll be safe and I can ring Chris Cheung and he'll sort everything out, and then I can forget all about this nightmare. It'll take some time, but eventually it'll fade, like the intensity of a riveting film. And as it fades, I'll be getting on with my life.

Excellent, she thought, straightening her spine and hearing it click. The day after tomorrow I'll take Annie to the Sydney café overlooking the Opera House and Circular Quay, and order a bottle of their most expensive champagne.

She felt better having made a decision, and she picked at the black fungi trailing like veins up the tree trunk, trying to distract herself from her discomfort. Impossible. Trees were incredibly uncomfortable. She had to keep shifting to prevent each limb from going numb, and she seemed to have pins and needles in some part of her body all the time. It was excruciating.

She wished she had Lee's mobile with her. Then she could phone for help. But since it was in her handbag on Dutch's veranda it may as well have been in Mozambique. She watched the sun slip to the edge of her world, and then the night creatures burst into life. There was a massive exodus of flying foxes from their camps, heading toward their nocturnal feeding grounds. The noise they made was incredible. You'd think bats would be silent, but not these guys. Their continual high-pitched screeching set her teeth on edge until the last one had vanished upriver.

Small bats, no bigger than her hand, flicked along the riverbank and across the sky. Mosquitoes whined. Crickets chirruped. She could hear a cacophony of other sounds, cackles and whirrings and clickings, but she didn't know what creatures made them. A frog of some sort was making a deep-throated *gullop gullop* and another was responding with a *cahboom cahboom.*

My God, it was dark. She could make out the river, a smudged gray ribbon, but not much else. Black stretched all around.

She closed her eyes before she could panic. You're just in a tree, is all. You're in a tree, and you're nice and high so old Nail-tooth can't reach you should he mooch on by and see you up there and make a lunge for a fancy snack so cling on here—

A branch snapped.

Georgia jerked upright, eyes wide, hoping they'd see something, anything that wasn't black . . .

The faintest rustle from below. To her right, she reckoned, but she couldn't be certain.

She tilted her head, angling her ear to where she thought the sound had been, concentrated every effort on identifying it. A croc? A possum?

Leaning forward, she clamped her arms and legs around the

branch of the tree and stared down, but all she could see was black . . .

Another rustle.

"I can smell you, Georgia," said a man's voice. "I can smell your Deet."

FORTY-SIX

Her blood froze.

"You should have gone home, Georgia. Gone back to Sydney. You're so *stubborn*."

Tiny crackle of leaves being crunched underfoot.

"You shouldn't be here. You should be with your booksellers. Not meddling like some private investigator."

She hugged the tree, her arms and legs wrapped tight around her branch, brain jammed in shock.

"I didn't *know* you were on board the plane, okay? I thought I was doing the world a favor, getting rid of Ronnie Chen and Lee and a woman I thought was a female hood. I'd heard Lee was in the area somewhere, and there he was at the aerodrome, being offered to me on a plate."

She pressed her cheek against unforgiving bark, filled with a sense of horror. Disbelief.

Daniel.

"I didn't know Lee was undercover. I thought he'd killed Lucy, can you understand? Killed his own partner. *My wife*."

Sweet Jesus. Sergeant Tatts was Daniel's wife, Lucy? Sergeant Lucy Tatts, dark-skinned, dark-haired, a police sergeant off-duty and laughing carefree in the sun with her daughter on her husband's shoulders, her arms around his waist. Sergeant Lucy Tatts.

"How was I supposed to know it was the chief who'd betrayed

Lucy when Lee went down for it? Jesus, Georgia, can't you see it was all a terrible mistake?"

No, no, she thought. What about an innocent man? You were so obsessed with plunging your avenging Scorpio tail deep into your prey that *you didn't think about Bri.*

"I saw Tilly this afternoon. She told me everything. That you're getting Chris Cheung to start an investigation. Good job he was out of the office when you rang. He doesn't even know you exist, thank God."

Sound of brushing leaves. His voice coming nearer.

"Christ. Chris bloody Cheung, of all people. He'll have me behind bars within *seconds.*"

She hugged the tree, loving the tree, filled with sick dread. It was like she'd been wearing a blindfold all this time and it had suddenly been whipped away.

Would you like a lift to Cairns? We could have dinner . . .

I'll contact the AAI, then I'll take you to dinner and give you a full report. How about the Pier?

When are you going home?

When do you leave for Sydney?

I think you should go home. Take a break.

Daniel had been trying to get her away from Nulgarra from the start. He'd seen straight through her all along, her attraction for him, and he'd tried to bribe her with free rides, dinner, concern for her health. She wondered if he'd purposely misdirected the search for her life raft. A scattering of images streamed across her vision. Her reaching for him when *Songtao* exploded, but he was already ahead of her and racing for the portside deck. Her standing in front of him, arms hanging as she wept after he'd picked her up from Margaret's. He'd never touched her, she realized. She doubted he'd ever had any feelings for her. He was still in love with his wife.

"You know I can't go to jail." His tone was reasonable, calm. "I can't leave Tabby to the Social Services, shoved from foster home to foster home, living with strangers. You can understand that, can't you?"

It was then that she comprehended the danger she was in. Tabby.

He'd already killed for his daughter when Amy Robins got shot in the head on the way to court. There was no way Daniel would let her live. Not when Lee was on the other side of the world, gone for good, and she was the only person left with the guts to testify.

"Look, all I want is for us to come to some agreement."

What, she thought, like poor old Rog? Living every day in fear of being murdered should he say a word?

"Just come out and swear you won't tell a soul, or call Chris Cheung. Go back to Sydney and forget all this."

Fat chance, she thought. You know I'm like a dog with a bone. You don't trust me an inch, and you know it.

"Dutch has agreed not to say anything. He's waiting for you at the house. He caught that barramundi he promised you."

You're lying. You've shot him. You've killed Dutch.

"Please, Georgia." Another rustling sound. "I won't hurt you. I swear."

He was so *close*!

"Ah, there you are. I can see you hiding there. You must be exhausted. Come on out and I'll drive you back. I've been worried sick about you."

Can't see me, impossible, too dark, too dark, black black black.

"Come on, Georgia. Let's go home."

Tree, my friend, hard bark against my cheek like stubble, and you're my friend, my tree.

"Georgia. You're scared, but there's no need to be."

Rough bark absorbing tears. Tears of fright. Of death.

"I don't *want* you to be scared. Please, trust me on this."

Another rustle and the dry snap of a twig.

"Why would I hurt you, of all people?" His voice had moved. It had moved *away*.

She felt a rush of adrenaline. *He hadn't seen her.* He'd smelled the Deet, that was all. He didn't know if she was in a tree, on the ground, or behind a bush, or he'd have come for her. He could have switched on a flashlight and found her in seconds, but he knew her well and wasn't going to risk exposing himself to her in case she was armed.

"You thought you were safe hiding here, didn't you, Georgia?" His voice had lost its cajoling tone and turned hard as he moved nearer again. She kept her eyes tight shut in case he saw them glisten in the dark.

"You're thinking invincibility is a matter of defense, but you're wrong. You may have read Sun Tzu but you're not a master warrior, never will be. You've put yourself in an extremely vulnerable position, don't you realize?"

You're more vulnerable than me because I'm up a tree and you're on-the-ground croc food.

"Haven't you had enough?" Back to cajoling. "Don't you fancy a nice big glass of wine and having a laugh over tonight?"

Georgia hugged the tree and longed for a croc to come along and eat him. Come on, Nail-tooth, she prayed. Nice juicy supper here for you.

Small sound of leaves crinkling.

"Come on, Georgia. Let's go home."

There was a rustle of a bush to her left.

"That you, Georgia? Good girl. Just come on out, you're safe, I swear it, just step out from where you are . . ."

Another rustle, larger this time, and, unable to help herself, she glanced down, wondering what was down there, but it was all *black* . . .

"Keep coming now, Georgia, take it gently, carefully, you're quite safe . . ."

An almighty crashing and tearing of branches made her open her mouth and inhale sharply, but she didn't yell.

Scrabbling sounds, another branch cracking, then a man's grunt.

Silence.

Her heart was pounding and she felt dizzy as she craned her neck around and around, searching for what had happened.

OhmyGod. Did a croc get him? OhmyGod.

A long rustle like something being dragged.

She was gripping the tree, trembling, sweating, breathing hard.

Silence.

"Georgia? You there? You okay?"

Her breath caught in her throat.

"I whacked him. He's out cold. Some master warrior. Master wanker, more like."

"Dutch?" she said. Her voice came out as a hoarse croak.

"Yeah. You really think I'd leave you to face this plonker alone? I heard shots and hared back . . . He took a couple of potshots at the boat, but I'm not daft. I wasn't anywhere near it. I tracked you, waited up for him to track you too. Been watching you all the time. You did real good, you know."

She heard him clear his throat.

"Didn't watch you when, you know . . . I didn't look, okay?"

When she'd peed. Oh, bless him, bless him.

"He's not going nowhere, okay? You're safe, it's just me here, no crocs, no nothing, just me. You wanna come down now?"

Oh yes, yes, yes. And she was wriggling in her tree, easing her legs to clamp them around the trunk, her hands reaching for branches to lower herself.

"Here, I'm just below. I'll catch you if you take a tumble. Oh, wait, Georgia, love, hang on . . ."

He clicked on a flashlight and shone it for her. Even with the flashlight's beam it seemed to take an age to clamber down. Her limbs were stiff and aching, her bottom and thighs numb. As she inched down the mangrove tree, her blood began to course, and pins and needles prickled and sang through her veins.

When her legs touched the forest floor they crumpled, but Dutch caught her, held her upright. She flung her arms around him.

"You amazing, wonderful person." She was half crying, half laughing, and she knew it was relief. "Dutch! I could kiss you to death!"

"Hey, steady on," he said, but he was grinning.

"I thought you were a croc!"

"Now that's a real compliment. Loyal to their offspring, patient, stealthy, and cunning as hell." He shone the torch at Daniel's slumped form. "Not like that wanker. Arrogant little shit thinking he could get one over us."

Georgia gazed at the rumpled dark blond hair, the handsome face lit white in the hard light of Dutch's flashlight. Slumped on the forest floor, Daniel Carter looked peaceful and calm.

It is important that form be concealed . . . so that preparedness against them be impossible.

Daniel's form had been so well concealed that she'd never once contemplated his involvement. Now it seemed obvious. He'd been on a flaming warpath to avenge his wife.

Without Dutch and his bush-lore, she knew she'd be dead. Daniel wouldn't have feared the jail sentence as much as being taken from his daughter. She gave a violent shudder. She owed Dutch as much she owed Lee and Des and Stevo.

She felt the weight of *guangxi* pressed on her shoulders, but she didn't care. She could see *guangxi* for what it was. Debts for her life that one day she would repay. She and her following generation owed four men big-time, because without them she'd be dead and her children wouldn't exist.

After a long while she said, "What are we going to do with him?"

"Truss him up, then take him to the cop shop. How does that sound?"

"Perfect."

Dutch shone the flashlight at Daniel's Glock by his feet and picked it up. "Meantime, we're not moving till it's light. Coming out here earlier I saw some croc tracks. Real big ones. I reckon Nail-tooth's displaced a big bull and he's about, and not in a very good mood."

"Jesus."

Dutch patted her on the shoulder. "We sit tight until light, okay? Then I'll scoot along and get the boat, and we'll be having a cooked brekky before you can say gidday."

She gave him a grateful smile.

"Right, let's hog-tie this fuckwit—I'll have to improvise, use some vines—and while we wait for daylight, I'm going to light a fire to keep that bull croc at arm's length."

FORTY-SEVEN

It was one of the longest nights of Georgia's life. Despite Dutch snoring like a truck engine—the first time she'd ever found that particular noise a comfort—every dark minute seemed interminable. She was propped against the trunk of another mangrove tree, hungry and thirsty, and she'd almost fallen asleep several times, but on each occasion she pulled herself from the brink with a little start, blinking rapidly in the pitch, terrified Daniel had escaped and was about to kill her.

The first sign that dawn was approaching was a bird twittering in its roost before falling quiet again. A couple more twittered, and her heart nearly jumped out of her chest when a flying fox crashed into a branch above her head.

Dutch gave a long, loud yawn, murmured, "All right, love?" and stretched. She heard a bone pop and his satisfied groan, then he busied himself building up the fire.

Georgia squinted through the trees and could just see the faintest dusting of light on the horizon past the river. Gradually the light thickened into a broad pale stroke of dawn, and more flying foxes flapped and crashed through the branches.

After Dutch's efforts, the fire was crackling nicely, and she could just make out the silhouettes of bushes and trees, and the dark shape of Daniel's slumped form on the rainforest floor. Daniel hadn't appeared to have moved during the night, and was in the same position

Dutch had left him after he'd bound his hands and feet. The vines looked frayed around his feet, but since vines usually looked frayed, she thought nothing of it because his eyes were closed, his chest seemingly motionless.

"Is he okay?" she asked Dutch.

Dutch didn't bother looking. "You care?"

"Well, not really, but—"

"And if he wakes and starts talking," Dutch added, "don't you even think of untying him, even if he says he's having an epileptic fit or heart attack or something. He'll have you so fast, you won't know it. Get it?"

He gave her a glare.

"Got it," she said meekly.

Passing her the Glock, Dutch got to his feet. "See you in a bit," he said. And with that, he disappeared.

Georgia glanced at Daniel—still motionless—and went to find a place to pee. Just out of sight, but not too far, in case she met the big croc Dutch had warned her about, she put the Glock on the ground and squatted behind an almost impenetrable root system of mangroves.

A leaf rustled to her right and her nerves fizzed. Jesus, it was just a skink scooting past, a bronze-colored lizard the length of her little finger, and it had nearly given her heart failure.

God, she hoped Dutch wouldn't be long. It was creepy being out here alone. She glanced at the Glock to one side, then saw that her urine had drowned an ant. Tough luck, she told it, it's survival of the fittest out here.

She was still crouched, just about to finish, when she heard a whisper of leaves behind her. She didn't even pause. With her mind screaming, *Crocodile,* Georgia launched herself forward at the same time as something grabbed her shirt from behind.

Yelling and screaming, she lashed backwards, heard a grunt, and then she was free, scrambling and yanking up her knickers and shorts and she was galloping past a clump of tassel ferns, pulling her shorts over her hips, fastening the top button—

Bang!

A great flurry of wings and startled cries from flying foxes and birds, she didn't see exactly what, her legs were already pumping her, driving for cover.

Two more shots.

Daniel had the Glock! How the hell had he untied himself?

Head down, she blasted through a barrier of dense bushes that slashed and cut her arms, and then she was clear and running so fast that she collided with a tree fern and sprawled to the ground. She could hear Daniel behind her, and she scrambled up and raced across a little glade of herringbone ferns, wanting to scoop around and head for Dutch's house, but he was heading her off and forcing her west and deeper into the rainforest, deeper into the mangroves.

Crocs love mangroves.

Georgia swung out, racing for the river again, the muscles in her back tight, waiting for a bullet to smash into her. Legs pounding, she hurdled fallen branches, leaves snapping against her face.

How could she outrun Daniel? How could she stop him in his tracks? Her hand-to-hand combat skills were zero. She could try to hide again . . .

Crack!

The blast from his pistol was close. He was closing in. Daniel was moving faster than her, much faster.

Got to stop him. Got to stop him before he kills me.

Dutch's voice in her head.

The males get real aggressive in the wet . . . The saltie will have you anytime, any place, quicker than you can say sausage sarnie.

Nail-tooth, she thought. Nail-tooth, wake up, boy, nice brekky coming for you.

The sound of a bullwhip next to her ear, a bullet just missing her, and Georgia dived left again, saw the glistening of wet mud ahead, and she burst onto the riverbank and immediately swung left.

The sky was turning blue, the forest lightening. The tide was out and the soft mud revealed crocodile tracks crisscrossing the riverbank.

Small tracks. She wanted big tracks. *Huge* tracks. She wanted Nail-tooth.

Up ahead a pint-size croc galloped down the muddy bank and exploded into the water. Her breath was hot and raw in her throat, and she knew she was beginning to tire. Daniel would catch up with her soon.

She was sobbing, almost chanting as she ran. Nail-tooth, Nail-tooth, Nail-tooth.

Georgia gave an involuntary yelp as she recognized the outcrop of elephant grass dead ahead, the swathe of flattened grasses beside it. Nail-tooth's highway to the river. Oh shit. She was here. She was in Nail-tooth's territory. Her legs suddenly weakened, and she had to scream at herself to keep running, *keep running.*

She hurdled a broken fan palm and ran straight down Nail-tooth's highway. She could hear vegetation snapping as Daniel raced behind her. He shouted something, she didn't hear what, because she had seen a warning shiver of grasses ahead.

Suddenly the grass parted, and he was there.

Rounded shoulders above an immense, armored head. Jaws as wide as the hood of a car, filled with teeth the size of her forearm. The crocodile faced her, ominously still, motionless.

She was screaming and yelling as they locked eyes.

The huge reptile slowly raised its plated body.

Then he charged.

The sound of grass hissing. His head snaking from side to side. His massive tail thrashing as it propelled him forward at a tremendous rate.

Her grandfather's words in her ears: *Look at where you want to go.* Her eyes fixed on an Alexander palm to her left and her body leaped for it, hands outstretched, knowing he would crush it in an instant, pulverize her as fast, but reaching all the same.

Her hands brushed the bark of the palm just as Nail-tooth hit her legs, and she went flying straight over his head and shoulders, crashing onto his spine hard as pavement before she was flung sideways and onto her left hip into the grasses.

Winded, Georgia struggled frantically to get up, her lungs shrieking for air, her legs not working properly . . .

Daniel's scream.

She swung her head and it took her a second to take in what she saw.

A man spread-eagled in midair alongside the enormous serrated form of a crocodile. Daniel and Nail-tooth flying over the riverbank and hitting the river with an almighty crash of spray. Daniel surfacing, choking, striking for the shore. Georgia took a huge gulp of air and was running for him when Nail-tooth surfaced. She saw the nostrils, eyes, and scaled back protruding through the water. Daniel suddenly puny and small and helpless against a giant reptile cruising through the water toward him.

She was on the edge of the riverbank, Daniel yelling just a few yards away, and could see the bow wave from the croc's snout, the water rippling around its tail as it powered forward.

Everything slowed to half-speed.

Eyes wild, Daniel was splashing frantically for the riverbank, his voice cracking from the force of his shouts. The crocodile was coming fast for him. Then it submerged.

Georgia yelled at him to swim, *swim faster, goddammit.*

Abruptly, Daniel vanished.

FORTY-EIGHT

"Oh God," she said. Her voice sounded unnaturally loud. The rainforest had fallen absolutely silent.

Daniel and Nail-tooth had gone.

She'd seen the water boil briefly, as though the river had given an almighty belch, but now it was still and smooth.

In the distance she thought she could hear an outboard motor, but put it down to the sudden silence buzzing in her ears. Her limbs felt shaky and fragile and she forced herself to walk to the water's edge.

She took in the yellow-flowered cottonwood tree and the mangrove lilies on the opposite bank. The color of the water was a dirty brown, but her mind was as blank as the water was calm, its ripples the ebbing tide heading for the Coral Sea.

Slowly, Georgia folded onto the riverbank and gazed numbly at the huge muddy slide where Nail-tooth had charged into the water. She could see a perfect cast of one of the reptile's feet, the size of a cauldron. The claw marks were the length of meat cleavers.

She thought of the ant drowning in her urine.

Tough luck, she thought dimly. *It's survival of the fittest out here.*

The buzzing in her ears became louder, and as she glanced downriver a little aluminum boat surged around the corner, bow high, huge wake creaming behind.

Dutch was on his feet, scanning the river, and the instant he saw her he swung the boat around. Seconds later, he came to a churning stop in front of her. He sprang onto the riverbank, bow rope in hand, sweat pouring from his face.

"I heard shots," he said. He was breathing hard and fast but paused when he took in the freshly churned mud of Nail-tooth's slide. "What the fuck—"

"Nail-tooth got Daniel."

His eyes widened. "You're kidding me."

She shook her head.

"Jesus."

Georgia gave him a garbled account of what had happened.

"I can't . . ." She glanced over her shoulder at the broken Alexander palm. "How come Nail-tooth . . . He charged straight for me."

"You face him head-on?"

"Yes."

"There you are then. Crocs strike to the left or right, see."

"But what about Daniel?"

"From what you said, Nail-tooth wasn't striking as much as running hell-for-leather for the river. I reckon he knocked Daniel into the water with him, and when they were there . . . well, that really is his territory."

She looked over the slow-moving river and the blinding glare of early-morning sun on its surface. A great-billed heron flapped slowly into view, heading downstream. The sounds of the bush had returned, and she could hear the deep bubbly call of a wompoo fruit-dove and the screech of a sulphur-crested cockatoo.

"Is there"—she cleared her throat—"any chance he'll survive?"

Dutch gazed at the slide a second before gesturing at the broad, slow-moving river full of crocodiles, then the mangroves full of crocodiles, and the dense rainforest all around. "You believe in miracles?"

She didn't say anything.

"Georgia, love, he's got no chance. A croc's jaws can exert a pressure of up to five tons. Think about it. And even if he did survive, how is he going to get out of here alive?"

"We should wait. Just in case."

Small pause while he studied her face. "Okay," he said. "Hop aboard. We'll go have a look around."

Settled on the central strut in the boat, she saw that her shorts zipper was still undone, leaned back a little, did it up. While Dutch cruised the area she searched the river and its banks for any sign of Daniel or Nail-tooth. Flying foxes continued flapping back to their roosts. Tiny birds the size of matchboxes fluttered through the trees. The rainforest was starting its day as usual, unchanged.

"How'd the bastard escape, anyway?" Dutch asked her. "I tied him up real good."

"Penknife. He always carried one."

"Shit. Thought he just had the gun. Didn't think to search the bugger for a knife. Sorry."

They fell quiet and kept cruising. An hour later, they hadn't seen anything; there was no sign of the giant crocodile, or its prey. The air was heating up as the sun rose, and she had started to sweat. She was incredibly dehydrated and longing for a drink, but her thirst was easily bearable when she thought of her sojourn in the life raft.

"I'd say Nail-tooth's wedged him underwater," said Dutch, "and gone to hide up till we've left."

They eased past Nail-tooth's slide, and when she saw the flattened grasses of his highway, the Alexander palm splintered practically in half from the crocodile's charge, she knew it was over.

"Let's go," she said.

He turned his sun-creased face to her. "What say you and I leave him here? Say nothing of it? Becky'd be glad of the insurance money."

Georgia thought it over, and shook her head. "No. Too complicated. They'll think we planned it or something."

"Okay, we'll go to the cop shop together, then." Checking the fuel mix, he added, "Bet Suzie's grinning from ear to ear. Talk about justice done, getting munched by Nail-tooth. Bastard deserved everything he got."

Georgia said nothing as Dutch opened the throttle. She didn't feel any elation or triumph, not even a sense of achievement in finding the saboteur. Just a lowering sensation of ineffable sadness for the person who would suffer most from all this.

Little Tabby.

FORTY-NINE

Seriously, deliciously amazing." Georgia licked her fingers and contemplated the stripped carcass in front of her. Could she squeeze in another mouthful?

"Yes, you can," said her mother, mind reader, and pushed across a pair of tongs for her to help herself. "You're still too thin, sweet. Eat every morsel at every meal until you feel like you're going to pop, and you'll fill out in no time."

Two little girls hurtled past, shrieking. A little boy pursued them, struggling to hold a giant fish head in both hands. They tumbled down the wooden steps, then raced through the tall grasses, bare feet flying.

"Little buggers, boys," Tilly said from the end of the table. "Always out to scare the girls."

They were sitting around a long trestle table on one of the Lotus Healing Center's rear terraces, and the table looked as though a bomb had hit it. Toys were jumbled between streamers and salad bowls, bottles of wine and a month-old copy of the *Sydney Morning Herald* carrying Georgia and Dutch's first story, by India Kane.

Photographs of Georgia and Dutch grinning, and another of a huge crocodile, jaws agape.

It had taken Yumuru days of phone calls to arrange for everyone to meet here for a weekend. Finally he'd managed it, and here they all were. Groaning with food and wine at their first celebratory lunch beneath the veranda's straw roof, overhead fans stirring the humid air, the hum and chirrup of the rainforest all around.

Becky poured them some more wine, repeating the toast she'd made earlier.

"To Chris Cheung."

Chris and the Air Accident Investigators had found the fuel pipe and the electric pump and sent them to forensics, but even after scouring the area for days, they never found the wire-lock. The court seriously doubted that Daniel, an upstanding police officer with no record of previous violence or vindictiveness, had sabotaged the Piper, but when forensics produced evidence that the pipe had been loosened deliberately, and then Rog testified that he saw Daniel working beneath the Piper's PA28's cowling half an hour before it flew, they changed their minds.

Georgia chinked her glass with Becky's. No wonder Becky was looking so much better. The insurance company might not be paying out, but Bri's exoneration had eased her grief immeasurably.

"We've a clean record," said Becky, "and the whole world knows it. They're saying Bri's a hero, getting you down where he did. And talk about great publicity for SunAir! We're swamped with next season's bookings already. Never known it so busy. The bank reckons it won't be long before we're square, maybe three years or so, then we can get another plane."

Georgia was reaching across her mother for a plump slab of barramundi when she felt a pair of arms wrap themselves around her neck and a child's shout. "Auntie Georgie! Auntie!"

She turned to look into Vicki's beaming face and found herself beaming back. "Hi, spratlet," she said.

"Spatett!" Vicki yelled, delighted.

"Georgia, so sorry!" Julie Zhong approached at a gallop and swept Vicki into her arms, where her daughter continued to shout "Spatett" at the top of her voice. Julie shushed Vicki and pointed at Tilly's kids, told her to go and play with them. Vicki shot off, screeching with delight.

"How's it going?" Georgia asked Julie, who smiled.

"I love it here. I wish Paul . . ." Her smile crumpled.

"I'm sorry," said Georgia, and reached out a hand and gripped Julie's forearm. "I didn't mean to remind you."

"No. It's all right." The smile returned, slightly wobbly, but it was still a smile. "He was such a brave man. He will be with us always. And I do love it here. Being able to practice my therapies again . . . I have three regular clients already!"

"Two," said a voice from behind them. "You've just lost one. There's no way that green runny stuff stops you smoking. Thank Christ for Nicorette or God knows what else you'd have me drinking."

It was India, looking disgruntled.

"For it to work," said Julie, drawing her small figure tall, "you must drink it three times a day."

"It's disgusting."

"But Jon is taking it, he says it is helping," Julie said, and Jon hurriedly hid his cigarette beneath the table, face turning pink.

Despite the fact that the AMA hadn't yet approved the antibiotic—there were countless more tests and trials to be run—Jon was filled with a boundless optimism, especially since he'd been given a work permit and an invitation to apply for Australian residency.

Georgia saw a drift of cigarette smoke rise from Jon's lap, as though his napkin was on fire, and laughed.

"Stop looking so happy," India grumbled, taking a seat and filling up her wineglass. "Don't know what's got into you lately."

Georgia glanced at her handbag by her left foot, the tip of a photograph protruding of a sleek yacht in blazing tropical sunshine. Although it looked new, the yacht was obviously well lived in, with washing hanging neatly in a row along the boom, a towel and pair of swimsuits draped across the stern railings, a cup of coffee and a pile of newspapers on deck.

The picture had arrived in a blank envelope with a first-class air ticket to Barbados, and on the back he'd written in his neat, precise script, "What have you got to lose?"

No signature, not even a postage stamp. Hand-delivered by a man in a suit, knocking on her front door. How he'd arranged it all was a mystery. A mystery she could ask him herself, if she chose. And though she knew he was a killer, she was a killer too. She'd shot Jason Chen dead and she hadn't lost a single minute's sleep over it. She doubted he had either.

"So when do you start the grind of nine-to-five?" India asked Georgia.

"Zed said whenever I liked. He suggested I take a break first before getting stuck in. He's hopping up and down with excitement."

"Yeah, I know," India said drily. "He rang wanting me to do a piece on the plight of illegals here. He's going to milk your celebrity status for everything it's worth."

Georgia didn't mind. At last she had a job she cared about, had something to fight for, and Zed had even suggested she take a trip to China, so she could see the place firsthand, meet his friends, to give her an understanding of their culture as well as their problems.

She picked up a plump piece of white flesh from the barramundi and popped it into her mouth. Food of the gods, she thought. Raising her glass, she said, "To Dutch. Hunter-gatherer."

He raised his bottle of beer with a grin. "Big bugger, eh?"

Big bugger the fish certainly was, weighing in at sixty pounds. They had enough food for weeks.

"So help me, God, that woman is driving me to drink."

Yumuru was suddenly there, his glasses all steamed up. His hands were wiping the tea towel tucked into his trousers and he was looking harassed.

"She's a brilliant cook," Georgia said.

"Brilliant she may be, but it's like being ordered about by a drill sergeant. When I wasn't quick enough chopping up the garlic, she rapped my fingers with her aluminum spoon!"

"Poor Yumuru," she commiserated, grinning.

"Sometimes, like right now, I wish I was in a nice cozy police cell where she couldn't get me."

He poured himself a glass of wine and downed it like a man dying of thirst in the desert. She was so glad he'd forgiven her, for her suspicions, for pinching his syringe. They had sat down the day after Daniel's death and talked everything through. How Yumuru had kept his birth name under wraps, terrified for Jon and Suzie, in case the Chens connected his name to them, and Quantum Research. How he'd used the antibiotic only three times, and only in desperation and when his patients would have died without it.

"The patients signed a consent form," Yumuru said. "They were fully aware the antibiotic wasn't approved, but they were willing to try anything."

Tilly and the other two patients had sworn secrecy, to protect Yumuru and Suzie for using an unapproved drug. It was a small price to pay for their lives.

Yumuru had asked Tilly to be his alibi for the day of the crash, as soon as he realized Georgia was on the trail of Suzie's antibiotic.

"I could see how it looked," he'd said. "How the finger would point to me. I know I shouldn't have put Tilly in that position, but I couldn't think of what else to do. The police believed Tilly, but I hadn't bargained on you."

Nor had Daniel. *You are so stubborn.*

Now Yumuru's hand paused in midair. "Oh God. Here she comes."

Dressed in black from head to toe, Julie's mother, Fang Dongmei, marched down the veranda and pushed a gaudily wrapped box at Georgia along with a stream of Cantonese.

Julie said, "She's saying thank you. She wants you to unwrap it."

Georgia freed the small box from the gold-and-red paper and opened it. Fang Dongmei was chatting at high speed to Julie and pinching the blonde hair on her forearm, and for the first time since she had known her, Georgia saw Julie collapse with laughter.

Inside was an electric razor.